The City of Spirits

Also by Paul Bajoria

THE PRINTER'S DEVIL
THE GOD OF MISCHIEF

The City of Spirits

PAUL BAJORIA

SIMON AND SCHUSTER

For Jacqui, with all the love in the world

First published in Great Britain in 2007 by Simon and Schuster UK Ltd
A CBS COMPANY

This paperback edition published in 2008

Simon & Schuster UK Ltd
Africa House
64–78 Kingsway
London WC2B 6AH

A CIP catalogue record for this book is available from the British Library.

ISBN: 978-1-41691-707-6

1 3 5 7 9 10 8 6 4 2

Typeset by Rowland Phototypesetting Ltd, Bury St Edmunds, Suffolk
Printed and bound in Great Britain by Cox & Wyman, Reading, Berkshire

www.simonsays.co.uk

CONTENTS

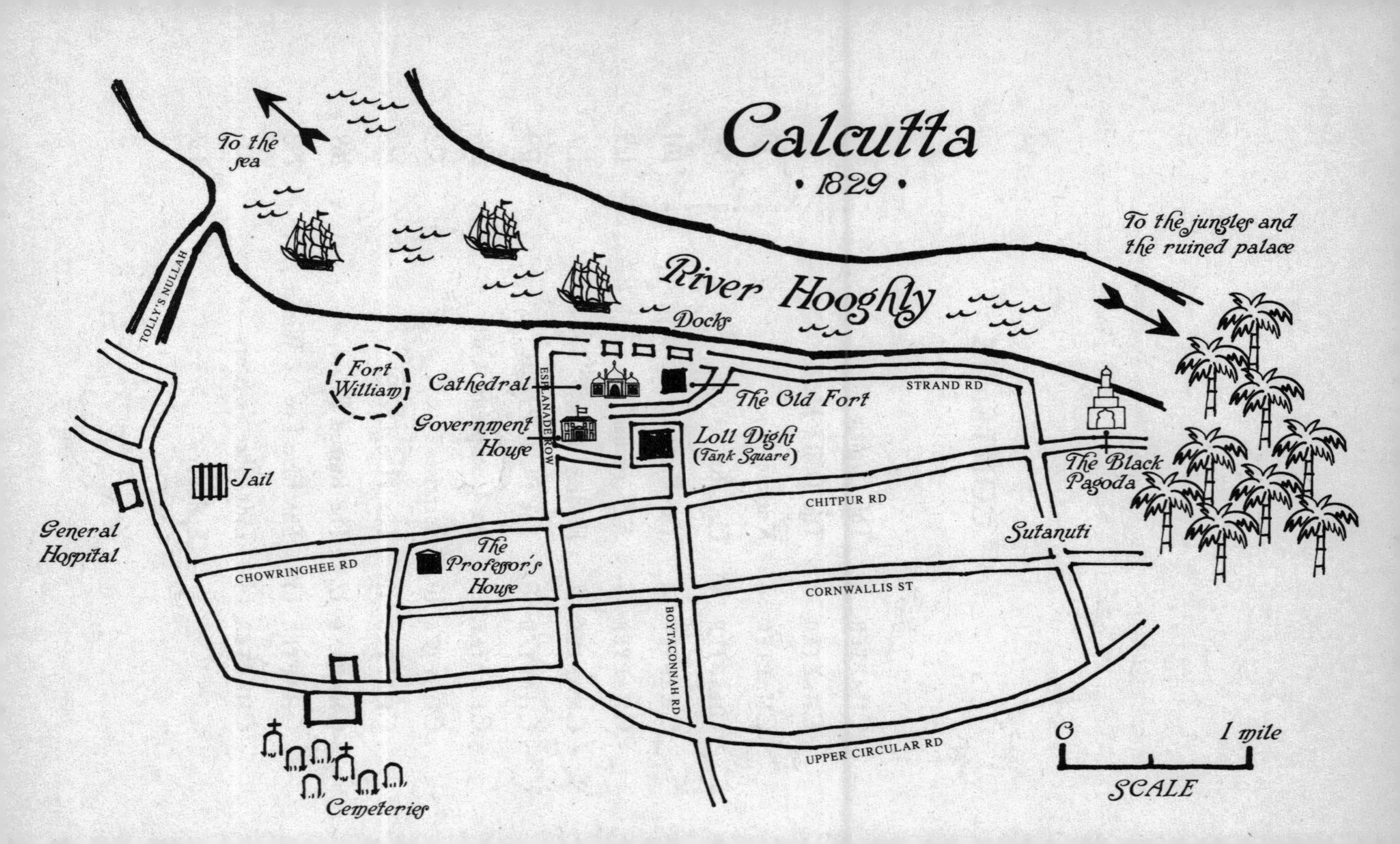
Calcutta
• 1829 •
To the sea
To the jungles and
the ruined palace
River Hooghly
Docks
TOLLY'S NULLAH
Fort William
Cathedral
The Old Fort
STRAND RD
Government House
ESPLANADE ROW
Loll Dighi
(Tank Square)
The Black Pagoda
Jail
CHITPUR RD
General Hospital
The Professor's House
Sutanuti
CHOWRINGHEE RD
CORNWALLIS ST
BOYTACONNAH RD
UPPER CIRCULAR RD
Cemeteries
0
1 mile
SCALE

The Map

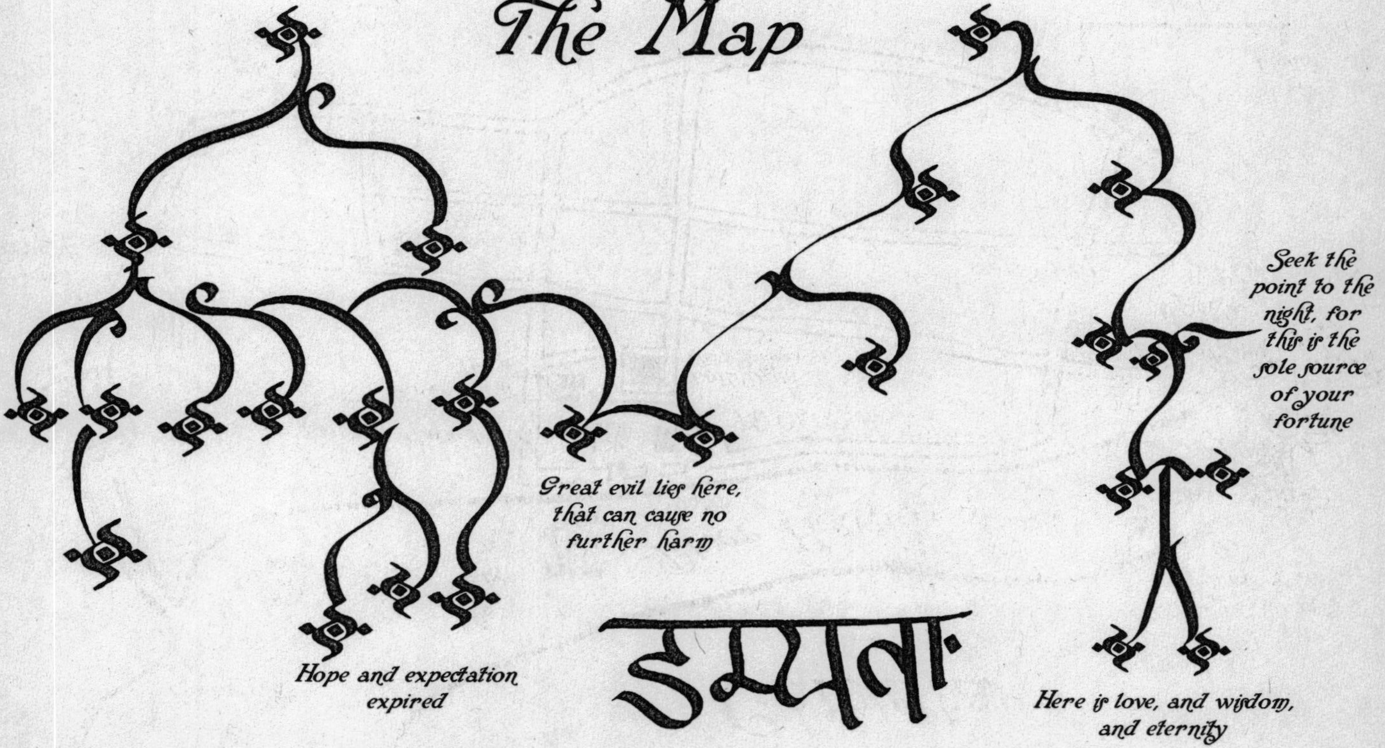

Seek the
point to the
night, for
this is the
sole source
of your
fortune

Great evil lies here,
that can cause no
further harm

Hope and expectation
expired

Here is love, and wisdom,
and eternity

CHAPTER 1
THE CAPTAIN

The first time I ever saw the Captain was the moment he stumped awkwardly out of the shadows, swinging himself on his makeshift crutches, coughing consumptively and cursing as the fog filled his sore lungs. I jumped. In the near-darkness he moved like a huge crustacean, his wooden crutches splayed out at his sides, a felt three-cornered hat on his head. I had no idea who he was. I shivered, pulled my dog's lead tight, and pressed myself back against the damp wall; but the man came so close I could feel the stinking vapour of his cough against the side of my face as he passed by.

Click ... *click* ... *click* ... The brass tips of his crutches made an irregular, inhuman sound on the cobbles, audible long after the sight of him had melted into the fog.

I was looking for Nick. He knew his way round these narrow walkways between the high brick walls of the Thames warehouses, where the icy water lapped against the boxes and barrels stacked high in the flooded cellars, and oozed its foul stench up through the gaps and gangways of the dock.

He'd spent a lifetime running along the wet wooden boards, ducking under the iron stairwells, hiding among the ropes and chains, listening for low voices amid the wheezing of canvas and the groaning of timbers. I had no such intimate knowledge of the layout of this part of London, and I'd realised a long time ago that I was lost.

Now, though, I could see the lower portion of a ship's rigging picked out in the middle distance by the orange light of a brazier on the dockside. I breathed a sigh of relief. If I could get to the water's edge, and away from these noxious lanes and the shadowy human figures which inhabited them, I might be able to get my bearings. I reached down to ruffle the wiry fur around Lash's ears, by way of reassurance – for myself as much as for him.

As I emerged into the light of the waterfront, a burst of raucous, drunken laughter met my ears, and I could see a group of about eight sailors staggering along the slippery dockside, some of them arm in arm, a couple of others swaying alone on the fringes. Silhouetted against the firelight from the nearest brazier, one of them raised the neck of a bottle to his lips and took a long swig, laughing as he did so, supported by his mates. A gruff song, carried first by one voice and then added to by one or two others, emerged from the group.

"*O my lovely blue eye*
Blue eye that twinkle and shine
If it takes till the day I die
I shall make your blue eye mine."

I moved back into the shadow of a brick archway as the

men staggered closer, and with a sudden start I felt the grip of a hand around my upper arm, pulling me deeper into the dark space. I almost cried out, until a low voice said: "It's me. Just shut up till they've gone." And my head sank back against the filthy wall in sheer relief as my brother peered around the corner of the arch, keeping a lookout as the staggering, singing figures approached, and pressing me protectively against the bricks with an outstretched hand as they passed by.

No wonder Lash hadn't barked. He had known it was Nick all along. I stayed in the shadows, breathless, Lash's lead held taut, to keep his flank close against my leg as we waited. The sailors' voices receded into the fog.

"Who were they?" I whispered after a minute or so.

"I'll tell you about them later," came the reply, through gritted teeth.

"Were they after you?"

"Just keep quiet!"

I stood still for what seemed like ages, getting colder and colder, waiting for him to relax. In the silence we could hear the haunted creaking of the ships' timbers, and the slow groans of the taut ropes, as the layers of damp within them turned to ice in the gathering night.

"*Surely* the coast's clear now," I said after a while.

"Shh!" Nick was still taking no chances. We stayed squeezed against the wall in our heavy coats for at least another thirty seconds, before the sudden sound of more footsteps made me freeze, and a boy, probably no older than us, passed within inches of us as he stumbled along the cobbles into the darkness, in pursuit of the others.

"How did you know there was another one?" I whispered, incredulous.

"I can count," said Nick quietly. "Now – stay quiet, and follow me. I'll tell you all about them when we're somewhere safe."

We seemed to walk through the fog for miles, staying in the shadows near the walls as we went, always looking this way and that at every corner. Nick didn't say a word as he led the way. These were perfect conditions for cutpurses, and cut-throats, who could have stepped out of the fog and quietly taken our money, or our lives, before melting back into oblivion, unseen by anyone. Once upon a time I wouldn't have worried about this, because anyone accosting me would have realised I was just a ragged child. Things were different, now that we were a little older and had inherited a fortune; and I felt a shudder of fear every time a human shape loomed before us like a ghost. Most of the horse-drawn traffic had simply stopped, because it was impossible to see where you were going. But at least one foolish driver must have attempted to steer his carriage through the fog-bound streets, because there was suddenly a lot of angry shouting, and we found ourselves on the fringe of a crowd which had gathered around someone lying in the road, having been trampled by the horse coming out of nowhere as they crossed. The horse, apparently none the worse for the accident, was standing blowing steam from its nostrils, still harnessed to the carriage, while a group of men berated the driver.

I had no idea where we were now. Lash and I were just following Nick, assuming he knew where he was taking us. I lost count of the number of times we changed direction, as though he was deliberately trying to shake someone off our trail; and I was quite sure we'd passed the same lane-end three or four times from different directions.

"Nick, *stop*," I complained, eventually, "this is driving me mad. Stop somewhere, for heaven's sake, and tell me what's going *on*."

"Keep quiet," he said again, shortly; but less than half a minute later, as we turned another corner, he took a good hard look around in every direction, and suddenly ducked out of sight to his left. The fog was so thick that it took me a while to realise where he'd gone, even though he was only a few feet away. He was standing in the doorway of a dark, narrow shop front, with grimy etched glass windows; and I suddenly knew where we were.

The occupant had been on the point of locking up and going to bed, when Nick knocked as discreetly as he could. Not having expected anyone at this hour, he peered very tentatively indeed round the door as he opened it to the freezing night. Our dark, heavy-coated shapes, faces indistinguishable in the shadows as we stood there, brought no flicker of recognition onto his childlike face. It was only when he saw Lash that he realised who his visitors were; and gasped, and flung the front door wide for us to enter.

Mr Spintwice, jeweller and silversmith, was certainly one of the smallest adults in London: so small that even quite young children had to look down into his face as they spoke to him; and now that we'd grown even taller since we last saw him, we seemed to tower almost twice his height. He had a round, earnest face which wore an almost permanent expression of enchantment or surprise; so his genuine enchantment and surprise at our unannounced arrival meant that his face tonight positively bulged with both. But he sensed Nick's urgency and the need for silence, and he showed us through to the passage without saying a word, stretching to secure the bolts on the front door again.

If I hadn't been here before, I'd have thought I was dreaming. Stepping into Mr Spintwice's house was like stepping into another world entirely. As he motioned us through the hallway towards his sitting room, we were enfolded by the sound of ticking: everywhere we looked, there were clocks, from tall grandfather clocks against the walls and under the stairwell, to fob-watches piled in shallow wooden boxes on the sideboard, like big clams on a fishmonger's stall. And, apart from the room at the front in which he served his customers, Mr Spintwice's house was all arranged to suit his own size rather than that of other people. The shelves, the doors, even the furniture, all were a great deal smaller than usual: too large for a doll's house, but really far too small to be of any practical use to a person of normal proportions.

"I hope it's not too late to drop in like this," Nick said to him.

"Nick and Mog, and Lash," said Mr Spintwice, "no time

would be too late to open the door to such welcome visitors. I didn't know you were in London, or I would have sent you an invitation to visit me the moment you arrived. Come in, come *in*, and get warm."

He motioned us towards the armchairs, as he scratched affectionately at the whiskers on either side of Lash's face, which was more or less on a level with his own. Lash responded by licking Mr Spintwice's face with his long slobbery tongue. "Sit down," the little man said, laughing: and at first I wasn't sure whether he was talking to Lash, or to us. "I'll put some water on," he continued. "Tea's the thing, on a night like this."

It was a relief to be here, out of the cold: but I was determined that Nick was going to explain himself. "Now maybe you can tell me what's going on," I hissed at him, as soon as Mr Spintwice had gone through to the parlour at the back. "What are we doing? Why all this lurking about in the fog? Who are we hiding from?"

"Wait!" was all Nick said. "I'll tell you the whole thing when Mr Spintwice is here. I think we might need him to help us."

Mr Spintwice had set a big kettle on the stove, and came back into the sitting room to talk to us while we waited for it to boil.

"The fire!" he exclaimed. "I must make you warmer." He scuttled over to the fire, making the late-evening embers flare with a few jabs of the poker, and suddenly a welcoming flame sprang up at the back, sending an orange glow around the room. He stood up again, and gazed from one to the other of us. "That's better. Now, tell me what brings the three of you here at this hour."

"Nick had better explain," I said, pointedly, "because I for one have no idea."

Spintwice's hospitality and the familiar surroundings had made Nick relax instantly. All the furtiveness with which he'd been behaving for the last hour had suddenly melted away. "Mr Spintwice," he said warmly, "I do declare you've *shrunk*."

Mr Spintwice's armchairs somehow seemed even smaller than we remembered them. For the first time, even after taking off our big coats, we felt cumbersome as we sat in the little chairs. The childlike scale of everything, and the music of the hundreds of clocks whose ticking and chiming meshed into the most complex and hypnotic of rhythms, made London and the fog seem a world away; and I found myself quickly forgetting my irritation with Nick, too.

"You looked as if you were in trouble," said Mr Spintwice. "When you came in. You looked as if you were trying to avoid someone."

"It feels very strange, coming back," said Nick after a pause. "It's always been home – but now suddenly we feel out of place."

Spintwice looked around. "But it's all just the same," he said, "I've kept it as it always was, haven't I?" Then it dawned on him what Nick meant. "But things have changed for *you*," he said.

"That's what I mean," explained Nick, slowly. "I don't

mean this house. I mean, London. We – we don't *belong* here any more, Mr Spintwice. People are talking about us."

And, as Lash flopped by the fire in a spot he'd made quite his own a year and a half ago, my brother gathered his thoughts, his face flushed and his eyes bright now in the firelight. We were all watching him, in anticipation.

"They're gossiping about us," he said. "The whole of London's gossiping about us. All the sailors. I've been listening to them. I've heard five or six different stories about us tonight, all different. The two scruffy little kids from round here who turned out to be worth a fortune. That's us."

That was, indeed, us. Nick and I had both spent our childhood among these streets: but, whilst Nick had mostly grown up in the company of sailors, I'd worked as a printer's devil, a few streets away in Clerkenwell, running errands and doing simple printing tasks for my boss, Mr Cramplock. Not until we were twelve did we ever meet, completely by accident; and even then it was a while before we worked out that we were not just brother and sister, but twins.

And that was just the start of the surprises. They'd all take much too long to tell, just now, but we'd also discovered, at about this time last year, that we were the only living heirs to a huge country estate nearly a hundred miles away; and we'd left London and gone to live there. Our ancient relative, Sir Septimus Cloy, hadn't exactly welcomed us with open arms: and we'd learned, over time, that he had been trying for many years to stop us from acquiring our rightful inheritance. But, just a few months ago, he had gone mad and died; and despite having hardly known him, we had inherited the whole estate; so, after many adventures, it all seemed to have worked out in our favour at last.

Now master and mistress of Kniveacres Hall in the county of Warwickshire, we'd returned to London because we missed it, and because our friends were here, and because, even without Sir Septimus to make our lives a misery, Kniveacres was a sombre, cold, rather scary place in the dead of winter.

And I should have realised, I suppose, that we wouldn't just be able to slip back in amongst these familiar streets unnoticed, and see our friends and run about without anyone giving us a second glance as we had before. We looked different: instead of grubby urchins' clothes we wore fine wool, and velveteen, and leather coats. (And why wouldn't we? It was cold, and for the first time in our lives we could afford to dress warmly.) We had our own carriage, and servants, and a coachman lodging tonight behind Gray's Inn, at our beck and call, just waiting until we instructed him to drive us home again into the country. Both of us had grown fast in the year we'd been gone: in just a few months we'd be fourteen, and I'd grown my hair so I no longer passed quite so easily for a boy, which everyone believed I was, for years. But, inside, despite all the visible changes, I didn't *feel* like the mistress of Kniveacres Hall, I felt like the same child I'd always been. And anyone who knew us back then, and looked closely enough now, would see that we were still recognisably Mog and Nick; though the loveable hairy golden-coloured dog who followed us everywhere was probably the real giveaway.

Nick had understood this much better than I had. People were going to want to make a fuss of us, to find out what our lives were like, and ask us questions, and tell us they'd always known we were destined for greatness, even when we were barely visible under a permanent coating of dirt, being told to shove off from shop doorways and being given regular clips round the ear by grown-ups. And, having heard of our good fortune, other people were going to want to get some of it for themselves.

"I'm not really sure where to start," Nick said. "It's going round and round in my head and I'm still trying to work it all out. I've heard some stories which just sound – incredible."

"Like what?" I asked.

"Mog and I heard some sailors singing, this evening," Nick explained to Mr Spintwice. "Do you remember what they were singing, Mog? About the blue eye?"

"*Blue eye that twinkle and shine*," I remembered, looking into the flickering fire. "It was just a sailor's song about someone – well, about someone with blue eyes."

"Yes. Well there's plenty more to it than that, by the sound of things." Nick leaned forward in his armchair. "Have either of you ever heard the words 'the blue eye of winter'?"

I looked at Mr Spintwice, who was staring very intently at Nick as he spoke; but who said nothing.

"No, I don't think so," I said. "Is it from a poem?"

"It's a jewel, Mog. There's a jewel – a famous diamond or something – called the Blue Eye of Winter. And do you know why it's called that?"

"Because it's blue?" I was being deliberately flippant, but I actually couldn't think of any better reason.

"Yes, and?"

"Because . . . I don't know – it looks like an eye?"

"Yes. And?"

I shook my head blankly. "I don't know what I'm supposed to say."

"The other bit. The last bit."

"Winter? Well, I suppose because it's got something to do with . . . no, I've no idea, Nick."

"It's got something to do with *us*," he said, in a half-whisper. "The Blue Eye of *Winter* – because it belongs to our family."

It would never have occurred to me, however long I'd thought about it. Winter was our surname, but to most people it was simply a season of the year, not a name at all. And the idea of anyone naming anything after me, or anyone associated with me, seemed so far-fetched as to be just silly.

"What do you mean?"

Nick looked at Mr Spintwice, who was gazing at him in silent fascination, and then back at me. He took a deep breath. "Let me start from the beginning," he said.

Nick hadn't been able to resist going down to the docks this afternoon, for the first time in more than a year, to explore the damp smelly maze of gangplanks, coiled ropes, tar barrels, warehouses, sluice-gates and dirty old yards in which he'd always been so much at home. He often told himself he'd left it all behind, and that he didn't miss it; but nevertheless he'd been drawn to it, and as soon as he'd caught the odour of the Thames water in his nostrils, and heard the creak of the halyards high above, and the squeal of the gulls who'd followed the ships upstream, he'd realised how much of his life was down here. Few of the sailors paid him any attention: a wiry, good-looking youth in a calf-length coat, healthy and brown-skinned, almost certainly from out of town, and bearing virtually no resemblance to the unkempt bosun's boy some of them might have remembered scuttling and cowering between decks a few years ago. He'd been pleasantly surprised to find he could stroll around more or less wherever he liked on the icy waterfront now.

Late in the afternoon he'd spotted a sailor he recognised, a man who used to crew the same ships as the cruel bosun Nick used to live with when he was younger. When he saw him going into the Jolly Lighterman, a notorious waterside inn, Nick had followed him, suddenly intrigued at the idea of listening in on conversations, picking up news, hearing gossip about names he used to know. And, there in the warmth, almost completely hidden in a high-backed wooden settle, he'd observed and eavesdropped.

The Captain – the man I'd seen stumping away from the dockside on crutches – had been sitting in the inn, holding court. A florid man with a short, bristly grey beard fringing his face, he'd spoken loudly and laughed often, in a way that suggested malice rather than amusement to Nick. As he'd laughed, the Captain had let the ends of his crutches rise into the air, like extra limbs he couldn't quite control. A rowdy and growing group of sailors had gathered around him to listen to his stories. They'd laughed about shipwrecks off the Maldives, adventures with pirates near St Kitts, encounters with the women of Santo Domingo. The names the Captain spoke of were exotic, the events he described stomach-turning. He described dead human bodies which had spent weeks in salty water; tortures invented by pirates in baking sunshine to force people to reveal where they had hidden things; attacks by sharks at sea and by crocodiles on land. Nick had spent long enough on sea voyages to know that there was a core of revolting truth in all of this, though the stories were being embellished for maximum grisly effect, in the manner so beloved of sailors.

The stories, and the ale, flowed on, as darkness fell and the fog curled around the inn. He'd been wondering if, at some stage, he might hear some stories about the bosun – the man under whose guardianship he'd spent his early childhood, and whom he used to call Pa when I'd first known him. The bosun had been killed a year and a half ago; but there were plenty of people who remembered him, by no means all of them with affection. But it wasn't his guardian's name that had made Nick sit up suddenly.

It was his own.

"If I'd had half a notion," the Captain was saying, "that that half-blooded little powder-monkey, that *Dominic*, would turn out to be worth all that – well, maybe I'd have kept 'im close. Nurtured 'im, ye might say. Like a father figure."

There had been a swell of guttural laughter from the others then, like a collective burp.

"Him," the Captain had continued, "and that other skin-and-bone creature, the printer's devil he hung around with. Nothing to look at, either of 'em. Pair of ratty little brown weaklings. Only a matter of someone's lily-livered charity they weren't drowned at birth. And now look at 'em. Inheritors of estates. Country squires, wouldn't ye believe? Elevated out from among us, lads. Where's the justice, eh? Why *them*?"

The murmur swelled again. There was a long pause while the Captain took a draught of beer, and gasped his enjoyment as he set the tankard down on the wooden board before him.

"Way I see it, lads," he continued, wiping his beard, "those what's elevated can be brought down again. Bide your time an' the old wheel of fate does the job for ye. But I reckon the wheel can be spun a bit faster, by those with some wits. Are ye with me?"

There had been a general banging of tankards. The men were getting gradually drunk.

"Now," said the Captain, lowering his voice so Nick had to slide right back into the corner of the settle to hear the words. "What if I was to tell ye, *all* of ye, that there's something that family's missing, and missing bad? Missing *treasure*." He paused for effect. "What if I was to tell ye the talk I've heard, what's led me into investigations, and what I've found to be the truth? That there's untold wealth what's been lost to that family for years, and that I knows where it is. Would ye believe me? Would ye trust me?"

Their drunken murmurs spurred him on. They were hanging on his every word. He had them spellbound, like a puppet-master.

"The Blue Eye of Winter," he hissed, lowering his voice further still. "Ever heard of that? Eh? Know what it is?" Another long pause, while he lapped up their excitement. "A precious stone, lads," he had continued, dramatically. "The family diamond, lost since scandal overtook 'em long years ago. A stone so enormous, so magnificent, it makes the Crown Jewels look like baubles. A stone so precious that anyone what owns it could nigh on buy the earth. By foul means it came to be theirs, and ain't it only right that by foul means it might be ours. The Blue . . . Eye . . . of Winter." He sat back with a creak, having impressed his audience into virtual silence.

Eventually, one of the other sailors had found the wit to ask a question. Nick couldn't hear what he said; but he heard the Captain's reply.

"Too right I knows where it is," he purred, overjoyed. "Too right I does, my lad, and it's the next place I'm going to. But I needs a crew." He looked around him at the intent, slightly-swaying faces in the firelight. "I needs a trustworthy crew, what can keep their mouths shut when needs be. Are ye with me?"

Someone else said something, from the other side of the table.

"Oh, I'll pay," the Captain said. "Albacore plays fair, they all says that, don't they? Well, don't they? And if we finds what we're lookin' for, you mark my words, I'll pay more than

I'll wager ye've ever seen. The Blue Eye, lads, remember? The ultimate prize."

There was a rush of excitement, as if the place had caught fire; but the Captain's fat calloused hands and battered crutches, raised in caution, quelled the hubbub for a few more moments.

"Now I ain't so foolish, lads," he said in his softest voice, "as to sign anyone up here and now, in the foul dark air of the Jolly Lighterman, and all of ye in yer cups. But if ye comes to see me, tomorrow, on board the *Lady Miranda*, and I still likes the look of ye, who knows? Who knows what riches? All of us country squires, lads, think about that. No need to worry for the rest of our days. The wheel of fate, come back round again."

Appreciative laughter: and the overexcited words of a sailor foolish enough to ask an obvious question. "Where we headed then?" his coarse voice piped up.

A hush fell, instantly. The Captain watched them all. Nick, hidden in his high-backed seat, went stiff.

The silence lasted about twenty seconds, and then the Captain began to laugh. It sounded more like coughing: a consumptive rattle from deep within his enormous barrel of a chest. He tried to speak, amid the spasms of laughter.

"Where . . ." he barked, "where . . . oh, dear oh dear." His laughter turned slowly to a sneer, and silence fell again. "You sticks with Albacore," he said, "and you proves your loyalty, and then, when we're nearly there, *then* maybe you finds out where. But I ain't going to tell any of ye, sittin' 'ere. If ye thinks I'm fool enough for that, ye haven't a fraction of the respect for a Captain's common sense as I'm lookin' for in a crewman. Are ye with me, sailor?"

He had mesmerised them. They exploded into drunken excitement, like monkeys, while he marshalled his limbs and his wooden crutches and heaved himself off the bench. And he didn't turn around, not even to glance at the brown-skinned boy in the shadows in the corner of the settle, who'd been listening to his every word, as he stumped off across the flagstones towards the door of the inn, and out into the fog.

Click . . . click . . . click . . .

My eyes must have grown wider and wider as Nick told his story, because by the time he'd finished my face was hurting. Now at least I could understand why he'd been so nervous about saying anything until he could be sure we were in a place of safety. The drunken song of the sailors rang in my ears . . . *I shall make your blue eye mine.* And all that about helping the wheel of fate to spin a bit more quickly made my blood curdle. This man meant us harm: and it was all because of greed and jealousy.

Mr Spintwice's expression had also grown more and more astonished as the story proceeded, and quite early on his mouth fell open, so that, after about five minutes, he looked for all the world like someone who'd just met a talking horse. Now, the story over, he was mouthing silent words to himself; repeating "The Blue Eye of Winter" over and over again. And I understood why Nick had brought us here: not just because

Spintwice was a friend, but because he was a jeweller. Of all the people in London who might be able to shed some light on the Captain's story, surely it was him.

"Have you heard of it, Mr Spintwice?" asked Nick quietly. "Can he have been telling the truth?"

"Could it be true, Mr Spintwice?" I asked. "A fabulous diamond, belonging to our family, lost at the time of a scandal? Have you ever heard of it?"

"The Blue Eye of Winter," Spintwice repeated, aloud this time. "You know, the more I think about it, the more I think it *does* sound familiar. If I'm not mistaken, there was a great deal of excitement about it, a lot of years ago now: but I'd completely forgotten about it. Of course it must be far more valuable than anything which has ever crossed *my* path. And I'd never made the connection with the name Winter before."

"If it belongs to our family," I said, "why should the Captain be allowed to go and get it for himself? Surely we must stop him?"

"*Untold wealth that's been lost to the family for years,*" quoted Nick. "That's what he said."

"Of course you must stop him," said Mr Spintwice, indignantly. "It's rightfully yours. And if it's come to light, it's only right that you should have it."

"Maybe you could do some investigation," suggested Nick. "Discreetly, I mean. Find out where it might be and how the Captain might have come to know so much about it?"

"I can try," said Spintwice, thinking hard. "If it ever did

exist, there must be documentation – authentication – and so on. Yes, yes. It will involve some hunting around, but – I'll find out what I can!"

"Well, we haven't got much time," said Nick, soberly. "The Captain talks as though he means business. If he really *does* know where it is, we've got some catching up to do."

"And we'll have to be careful we're not being watched," added Mr Spintwice. "A determined man like the Captain will have his spies everywhere." A thought seemed to strike him. "You know, there may be family records," he said. "If I were researching such a jewel, the first thing I'd do would be to seek out information among the documents in the family's possession. The best place to look might be in the library at Kniveacres."

Left to our own devices for weeks on end in the huge draughty house, the library was the place where Nick and I had taken refuge most often: and we both knew that looking for something specific among the hundreds of densely-packed yards of bookshelves would be like looking for a single grain of sand on a beach. I laughed, shortly.

"Have you *seen* the library at Kniveacres?" I said. "There must be about – seventeen hundred million books in there. Where would you start?"

"Well – you never know what you might find until you start looking," said Mr Spintwice optimistically. "Now, in the meantime, did anyone see you coming here tonight?"

"We were as careful as we could be," said Nick, looking at me. I allowed him a small smile of apology.

"In that case, stay," said Mr Spintwice. "The less moving around you do the better, especially in the dark. You can sleep in the room upstairs, just as you used to. It's right above this one, and it's always warm from the fire."

To tell the truth, the little bedroom wasn't anywhere near as warm, at first, as Mr Spintwice made out: but the bulk of Lash at the foot of the bed, and the sound of his breathing, were soothing. A few years ago, my feet didn't use to reach all the way down, and there had been plenty of room for a dog to sleep there: but these days, going to bed involved a lot of wriggling and negotiation of my legs either side of Lash, until I ended up splayed out like a wishbone.

Although Nick and I were exhausted, it took us both a long time to fall asleep. We lay in the dark, eyes open, our minds turning the day's revelations over and over.

"The family diamond," I said quietly. "It sounds incredible, doesn't it?"

"It sounds very strange," said Nick from the other side of the room. "Like the 'family estate'. That sounded pretty incredible this time last year, didn't it?"

"Not very long ago, even the word 'family' sounded strange," I added. "Neither of us knew we even belonged to one, did we?"

"We still hardly know the first thing about them," mused Nick, in the dark. "What our mother was like. Who Damyata really was, or is. What old Sir Septimus had to do with it all. Sometimes I think we're never really going to find out."

"The Captain said the diamond was lost at the time of a family scandal," I remembered. "Do you think the family scandal might have been – us being born?"

We didn't know much about our family, but we did know this much: our mother, Imogen, had spent a lot of her short life in India, where her father and other relatives had careers in the East India Company, trading on behalf of the British government. They were a rich and respectable family, but our mother had brought shame on them all by falling in love with a native – a man called Damyata – and had to be sent home to England by sea when it became clear she was pregnant. On the voyage home she gave birth to us; but she fell ill, and died soon after we arrived in London. Her nearest relative here, Sir Septimus Cloy, who might have taken us in and helped us, in fact had no intention of looking after us, and abandoned us to be brought up as orphans, in poverty, by other people – even going so far as to pretend to the family that *we* had died too, in order to conceal what he had done. We'd only discovered all this wickedness when, at long last, we'd been sent to live with Sir Septimus at Kniveacres Hall last year.

Meanwhile, most exciting and mysterious of all, we'd also discovered that Damyata – our father – was still alive, and had come to look for us. For a long time he had frightened us, with disguises, and with what we could only describe as magic; and there seemed to be an uncomfortable connection between his presence and the strange and horrible deaths of several of our worst enemies. A few months ago, after Sir Septimus's death, he had at last revealed himself: but just when we thought we might get to know him for the first time in our lives, he disappeared as quickly as he had materialised, back to India where he believed he belonged. Although we were fascinated by him, and felt drawn to him, we couldn't say with any certainty whether we had really even met him at all, or whether he'd been a kind of dream or apparition.

In fact, the whole story still seemed so peculiar and remote, as we had gradually uncovered its details, that it might have been someone else's family history we were learning about, or something out of a storybook. And so many strange things had happened to us in the past couple of years that we might have been forgiven for thinking there couldn't possibly be any more, and that the rest of our lives were destined to be completely ordinary and unsurprising. Sometimes it was quite reassuring to believe they might be.

"I wonder how the Captain managed to find out where the diamond is . . ." I said.

"I don't know," Nick sighed. "If he really *has* found out."

"Why would he make something like that up?" I asked.

Nick gave a short laugh. "Believe me, Mog, sailors make all sorts of things up," he said. "There's no kind of person better than a sailor, in the whole world, at making things up. But he's certainly up to *something* – and it's all to do with us. There can't be any doubt about that."

"I feel as though we shouldn't let him out of our sight," I said.

"I know," said Nick quietly. "But we can't afford to be

seen hanging around the docks. And, in any case, we haven't got long."

We had promised Melibee, Sir Septimus's blind old manservant who had continued to look after the house after his master had died, that we would be back the day after tomorrow. He had been anxious at the idea of our coming here at all, and we'd persuaded him we'd keep our visit brief this time. We also knew he wanted to discuss some business affairs with us when we got home, though he hadn't been very specific.

"I think there are some people we should try and have a word with, before we go," said Nick. "If the Captain can have his spies looking out for us, well so can we, in return. I know the very person who can keep an eye on things for us."

"Who's that, then?" I asked.

"A lad they call Water Jim," he said. "I knew him when he used to do some spying for the bosun. He lives down there somewhere, by the water, and spends all his time running around on decks, and working little tricks and schemes with the sailors. He's not all that bright, but he knows enough not to get caught – and he wouldn't arouse suspicion. If we can find him, I'm sure he'd do what we asked him to. For a price, of course."

I felt a deep sense of unease. Growing up in these streets, life had been hard, but not complicated. I'd generally always known what I was supposed to do, and for whom, and how to keep my nose clean, and where my next meal was likely to come from. People used to threaten to tan my hide when

I made a mistake with the printing of something, or when I didn't deliver a message or run some errand to their satisfaction. But, until I'd met Nick, and we'd found out who we really were, I'd never had the sense that someone meant me real harm. I'd possessed nothing of which anyone could be jealous. I was just a street-child, an apprentice, with no life story to speak of, nothing in which anyone else could possibly claim an interest.

Now, all of that had changed: and here we were, hiding in a dark upstairs room in a jeweller's shop, as clammy January fog curled its grey fingers around the city we'd always called home; not running recklessly through the familiar streets as we used to, but nervous of being seen, suspicious of every footfall. While forces we didn't understand seemed suddenly to be stirring, like shadowy monsters on the sea-bed, preparing to drag us down.

Chapter 2
THE DOLL'S HEAD

The next day the fog was still sitting over the city like a great frozen slab, going nowhere. It penetrated your bones and your lungs, seeping between layers of clothing, hunting out flesh and marrow. The bodies of passers-by were clenched, whether ragged or well-dressed, rich or poor; and they turned their grey, pinched faces away as we passed. The fog stank of coal-smoke and dirt, and, when the pale January light fell on it in a certain way, it appeared a sulphurous yellow-brown. London was often like this in the winter; but it was only since we'd lived in the countryside, where the air was so clean and clear, that we'd come to notice it at all.

I was leading the way, confident that I knew these streets far too well to get lost; but it was only when a huge diagonal object loomed out of the fog next to my head, so suddenly that I almost bumped into it, that I knew for certain where we were.

"It really hasn't changed," I said, in a low voice, venturing inside and peering around the door. "It's really exactly the same."

"I don't suppose it's changed very much for two hundred years," observed Nick. "A few months is hardly going to make a difference. Who's in?"

"Just two men, and the boy, as far as I can see. We'll be all right."

The Doll's Head Inn. No more than a stone's throw from where I'd worked for most of my childhood, it was the place I'd come almost every day to drink, and unwind, and hear the gossip, and be made a fuss of. In fact, it was hard to believe it was any more than a day or two since we'd last been here.

Nick and I strode in, unbuttoning our heavy coats. We'd slept well at Spintwice's, but since we'd woken up we hadn't stopped speculating about the diamond and the Captain's mission; and, now that we'd come outside, we couldn't escape from the shock of feeling threatened, and watched by jealous eyes, on the very streets we'd always called home. Nick was especially silent and nervous as we headed for the lunchtime assignation he'd arranged with Water Jim.

Still, there weren't many places in London where I felt more at home than here: a shabby little public room, with walls of dark, warped wooden planks, all at crazy angles to one another. The room was barely large enough to hold more than ten or twelve people, but a reassuring fire burned in a small grate in the far wall, reflected in the row of gleaming brass taps. I let go of Lash's lead and he went to stand by the bar, looking up expectantly, his tail wagging, just as he had done countless times before.

Now we could see there were three other people in the

room, two of whom I recognised immediately. A slaughterman I knew as Bill Goosefeather was at the bar, in conversation with an unfamiliar man in a shabby black coat so enormous he might comfortably have hidden several of his children inside it. And a wizened old gaoler by the name of Jessop, evidently on his day off, sat against the wall in the far corner, bent over what looked like a bowl of soup.

There was someone else too. A curious waxwork effigy of a child stood at one end of the bar, almost life-size, dressed in faded powder-blue clothes with pale gold braiding, like a drummer-boy. He didn't look as though he'd been very well looked after. Part of his nose was missing, and, if the moulded curls of hair on his head had ever had any colour to them, it had long since been rubbed off, and they were now as white as the rest of the pallid, serene face. The regulars treated him like a fellow drinker, and often tipped their hats to him as they entered; and he was such a trusty companion to the landlady that she used to talk to him when there was no one else there. "Just me and the boy," she'd say cheerfully when you asked her how trade had been today. Or, "Five in, if you include the boy." No one knew precisely how long he had been a feature here, but the story went that the body and the head had arrived at different times, the body much later than the head – which accounted for the fact that the two weren't really the right size for one another, if you looked closely, and also for the ancient and curious name, The Doll's Head Inn.

A well-fed woman with a generous expression appeared at

the bar; then stopped dead, her eyes almost popping out of her head, as she saw the two of us standing there .

"Maaster Mog!" she squealed. "And Maaster Nick! Well I—!"

I couldn't stop beaming as she bustled round the bar to come and greet us and make a fuss of Lash, pleasure shining in her rosy face. She'd been a bit like a mother to me, in years gone by – though, thinking I was a boy, she hadn't treated me with much in the way of sentimentality.

"Fancy you two coming to visit Tassie," she laughed, "and Lash too! And haven't the pair of you *growed*! You look like the finest, 'andsomest young gentlemen as ever lived. I swear it. And don't never a day go by when Tassie don't say to 'erself, those two young rascals, what must they be up to now? And what must they look like and how grand must they be, and I wonder when they'll come back to visit? You mark my words, you've never 'ardly been off my mind for a minute."

Lash was overjoyed to see her, and was licking her pudgy fingers all the time she spoke; and I was beaming at her, and trying to prompt her to keep her voice down in her excitement.

"But you, young Maaster Mog," she continued, peering at me delightedly, "I do declare you're letting that hair of yours grow, for the first time. You's starting to look like a proper young lady. 'Cept I can't say as I can get used to thinking of you as such, what with you having always been my young Maaster Mog, long as I can remember. Won't be long before people will be telling you you're a beauty," she said with a confidential wink. "Go on – you'll be telling me they says so already. And I for one would believe it."

That was Tassie: for all her eccentricity, you could always rely on her for a compliment. I beamed even more broadly.

Nick was silent through all this; and Tassie's flow of excited compliments suddenly stopped in mid-stream. "But you're in trouble," she said, looking at his face. "You look like you're trying to avoid someone. Do you want me to hide you? I won't give the game away, you know Tassie."

I *did* know Tassie, and I couldn't suppress a smile, for anyone more addicted to gossip, and less capable of keeping a secret, it would have been hard to encounter in the whole of London. But Nick was still looking solemn.

"Tassie," I said hastily, "could you find it in your heart to get us some ale? And water for Lash? Please? We can pay." After she'd scuttled back behind the bar I hissed at Nick: "What's got into you? Can't you even look pleased to see her?"

"It was a mistake coming in here," he said in a low voice. "She can't keep quiet to save her life."

"Well, then don't tell her anything," I whispered, furiously. "But don't be so *mean-spirited.*"

I'm sure Tassie could tell we were having an argument because her voice sailed blithely over the bar at that moment, with the sing-song tone of someone trying to bring cheer to an awkward situation.

"You all warm yourselves up, on this chilly old day, and I'll have these ales in front of you in no time at all," she cooed.

"I'll bring them over," said Nick. As Tassie was pouring the ale, the slaughterman and his friend in the huge coat, who'd been conversing at the bar, drained their glasses and left, bidding Tassie a monosyllabic goodbye as they went. Now there was only us and the silent gaoler by the wall.

"Not too fond of this kind of weather, Mr Jessop," I said, by way of polite conversation, as Lash and I settled ourselves at a table by the fire.

"What's that?" he returned, cupping a hand against one ear. "Can't hear as well as I used to."

"I said this cold weather's not to my liking," I repeated, loudly.

His expression didn't change. "Cold or 'ot, it's all the same to me these days," he said matter-of-factly. "Can't feel the cold, not like I used to be able to." He lifted his spoon clear of the bowl in front of him, which we could now see was full of a thick, cloudy stew. "You want to get some o' these vittles in you. Soon warm you up."

Nick came and sat down beside me, bringing the two pewter mugs of peaty-orange beer which spilled slightly as he put them down.

"Mr Jessop here says the stew's good," I told him.

He gazed across at the man's bowl, sceptically. "From what I remember of Tassie's stew, it's usually best avoided," he said, "but – don't let me stop you. Maybe she's turned over a new leaf."

Moments later, Tassie came out with a dish of water, which she placed on the floor in front of Lash.

"Mr Jessop recommends the stew," I said to her. "You don't think you could bring me some, Tassie, do you?"

I thought her eyes betrayed just a flicker of panic, before she smiled brightly and stood up. "Only the very best for friends such as you, Maaster Mog," she gushed.

When Tassie had gone into the back room to get the food, I leaned over and murmured into Nick's ear. "Relax. Jessop over there is as deaf as a post."

"I'd still rather not take any chances," he said in a whisper.

"Where's this character of yours then?" I wondered.

But I didn't have to wonder for very long. After we'd taken another few sips of ale, a sharp, snout-like face appeared around the tap-room door, and in came a grey-faced, shabbily-dressed boy a year or so younger than us. He peered from side to side, looking for all the world as though he were sniffing the air. He saw us, and loped over. As he sat down he wrinkled his nose and briefly lifted his top lip, exposing two large yellow front teeth. It was a kind of tic: but, along with his little darting eyes and greasy straggles of hair, it made him seem uncannily like an overgrown rat.

I'd never met him before, and I was immediately convinced he was completely untrustworthy. He barely even looked at me, preferring to address all of his brief, diffident comments to Nick.

"Keep your voice down," Nick warned him, before he'd even said anything. "Thanks for coming, Jim. This is Mog. We need you to make a promise."

The boy sniffed, lifting his top lip again. "Water Jim's

cokum. Ain't no flat. Granny you, and granny 'im. Wotcher got?"

There were only two or three words among all this that I was sure I understood; but Nick was evidently having no trouble following his slang.

"Captain Albacore," said Nick in a low voice. "Know him?"

"Could say," the boy grunted. His eyes darted around the room, never still. "Not toppin' 'im though. That's not Jim's poke. Flummat poke, that one."

"I just want you to watch him," Nick said, leaning over the table to speak even more quietly. "He's getting sailors together for a voyage. Watch him for me. Find out who he gets, where he's going, when his ship leaves. Do you understand?"

"Cokum," Jim repeated. "You know Water Jim."

Nick grimaced. "Yes," he said. "Will you do it?"

Water Jim sniffed and showed his ratty incisors again. "Nose for a good pogue," he observed. "Got hikey."

Nick took out a purse, and half opened it under the table to show Jim some coins. Jim made a sneering face.

"Got hikey," he said again. "Thicker. Or I slam."

Nick reached into his pocket and slowly took out a banknote. It was in Water Jim's pocket before I'd even noticed him passing it. The boy made a face that looked, for a moment, like a smile.

"Good though," he said. "Know where to bait me." He stood up. His ratty nose came close in to the table, and he looked briefly from one to the other of us. "Water Jim's cokum," he said again; and, with a single lurching motion, he was gone.

Nick exhaled with relief.

"Well, that seemed to go all right," I said, baffled. "I'm glad *you* understood what he was talking about. What a creepy little chap."

"I think we can trust him," said Nick.

"If you say so," I said sceptically.

"Look, Mog," said Nick, a bit impatiently, "he's going to attract far less attention down in those docks than someone *you* might choose to trust."

"Okay, okay," I said. "I'm sure you're right."

Almost as soon as Water Jim had slipped out of the door, Tassie returned with my bowl of stew. "You ain't changed your mind about the stew, then, Maaster Mog?" she inquired, casually.

"No, I'm starving," I said enthusiastically.

"I'll, ah – leave it here on the side to cool. Don't want you burning your tongue," she said, bending down to ruffle Lash's soft ears.

"Thanks, Tassie," I said, as the steam reached my nostrils.

"You must tell Tassie about your new life," she said. "Lookin' at you both now, it don't seem five minutes since you was in 'ere, thick as thieves in that corner, hatchin' your plots and layin' your plans. But I can see a lot's changed. So tell me about what's been 'appening. Fine, grand house in the countryside, by all accounts? Servants and gardens and plenty o' rabbits for Lash to chase? And the adventures you must be havin', what with that poor governess, what a dreadful business, and your wicked uncle gettin' killed, and heaven knows what trouble and turmoil."

"Well, that about sums it all up," said Nick.

I laughed. "I can see you haven't exactly been starved of news about us," I said.

"Well," Tassie replied, with mock indignation, "what's a body to do? Someone calls with news, I'm not one to turn 'em away without they has the pleasure of sharin' it."

"We've had some *very* strange adventures, Tassie," I said. "One day I promise we'll tell you about it all. From start to finish."

"I'd be glad if you would," she said warmly. "Now, I'll leave you to get on and eat. But what a truly happy day it is to see you back in 'ere, the pair of you. Like old times." And, as she moved back towards the bar, wiping her tall brass taps with a cloth as she passed them, she permitted herself a few bars of tuneless "la-la-las" that passed for singing.

"Here goes then," I said, digging my spoon into the stew and blowing gently. Nick was watching me with an expression of slight amusement, waiting.

I lifted the spoon to my lips. At first it was too hot to taste, and it took a while for the full flavour to seep across my tongue and palate. But as soon as I'd swallowed the first mouthful, I was overcome with the sheer horribleness of it. It tasted utterly rancid, as though it had been made with meat that had lain festering for weeks; added to which it was greasy in texture, and the chunks of potato mealy and brown. I should have listened to Nick; but it was too long since I'd been in here, and my hunger had got the better of my judgement. Tassie had never been renowned for her skills in the kitchen, but even by her standards this was disgusting.

"Graaaaagh!" I coughed, gripping the edge of the table as a wave of nausea washed over me. "That's *revolting*."

Nick didn't speak, but just looked at me with his head on one side, as if to say: What did I tell you?

"Yeeuch," I winced, pulling a handkerchief out of my pocket and wiping my tongue. "I don't think I'll be giving any of *this* to Lash." I looked across at Mr Jessop, who was still sitting impassively by the wall, having shown no sign of overhearing our conversation with Water Jim, or even properly registered his presence.

"Can't say I share your opinion of the stew," I said to him.

He cupped his hand to his ear. "Say again?" he shouted.

"The stew," I said, enunciating extra clearly. "It's *very bad*."

He shrugged. "Good or bad, it's much the same to me, at my time of life," he said. "Lost my sense of taste years ago. Makes no difference to me. Can't taste a thing, these days, not like I used to be able to."

The sludge and filth of Smithfield market had turned solid in the icy weather, and narrow streets of dark, rotting old wooden houses curved up the hill, out of the hard mud, towards Clerkenwell.

Lash trotted ahead, completely at home, his nose to the

ground as though picking up the same scents he had left there a year ago. As we came close to the street corner, a stone's throw from the priory gate, where I had worked as a printer's devil for so many years, we stopped. A large town house with an enclosed garden, surrounded on three sides by a high wall, frowned down at us, its brick facade more discoloured than ever by the grime and smuts of the city. A grubby plate mounted on the railings read *CHARNOCK HOUSE*: and, but for some haphazard piles of wooden planks and the smell of fresh putty, the place appeared as ramshackle and burned-out as it had been for the greater part of my childhood. Its enormous blackened windows and charred brickwork had always resembled the haunted features of a tragic, tortured face; and I had often felt a shiver of fear when running past it, on Mr Cramplock's daily errands.

But this was the old London home of the Cloy family, our relations by marriage: and, since Sir Septimus's death, rightly ours. After long autumn nights of discussion by the grand fireplace at Kniveacres, we'd decided we were going to come back and live here, with Kniveacres as no more than an occasional country retreat. Our advisors had told us that Charnock House could be made entirely habitable with some restoration: and how wonderful it would be to swap the chilly, echoey stone corridors of Kniveacres for a big, lively house in London, so near to the people and places we'd grown up with.

And so we had engaged workmen, to put in new floors, to clean the brickwork, to repair the roof, to restore the grand windows, to re-plaster and create wide new hallways and reception rooms, with cornices and architraves, and stained-glass lights, and panelling, and turned bannisters.

"It's very quiet," said Nick. "I thought there'd be people all over it, at this time of day."

Nick was right: there was no sign of any work going on inside at all – though the planks and the putty were at least indications that work had begun to restore it to the grandeur and comfort of the distant past. There was a rope tied across the steps leading up to the front door, with a large chalked sign hanging from it, reading *KEEP OUT* in huge, uneven letters; and, in slightly smaller letters beneath, the mis-spelled afterthought, *BEWEAR OF THE DOG.*

"I can't *see* a dog," I said, peering in through the gate. "Shall we have a look?

"Do you think we should?" asked Nick. "What if someone comes?"

I laughed. "Nick, it *belongs* to us!"

But, as I climbed under the rope, Lash started growling, his eyes fixed on something behind the fence a few yards away; and now I could see that, on the ground not far from the front steps, there *was* a dog – a huge one, lying asleep, with its back to us. It didn't stir; but Lash was keeping his distance, and still growling continuously, not taking his eyes off it.

"Well, it takes more than a chalk sign to keep the thieves out round here, I suppose," said Nick.

He ventured slightly closer to the animal than I had, and peered down at it as it slept. It was a huge creature with a long bushy tail, a grizzled, silvery back, and a sharp powerful muzzle like a wolf. It would have been a brave thief who chose to argue with it when it was awake.

But then Nick noticed something else. "Hey, Mog, come here and look."

The dog wasn't asleep. Its eyes and mouth were open and, though we looked hard, there was no rise and fall of its ribcage, no ripple of fur.

"It's dead," I said, dismayed.

Nick bent down, tentatively, and put a hand out to touch the dog's thick coat.

"He hasn't been dead long," he said quietly. "He's still warm, poor thing – there's not a mark on him. Do you think he's been poisoned?"

I held tight to Lash's lead, not wanting him to go anywhere near, in case there was poisoned meat lying around somewhere.

"Nick, someone's been in here," I said.

Nick stood up and went ahead of me, up the stairs to the front door. It opened without resistance.

"Careful, Nick," I said, anxiously. "They might still be inside."

We stood just inside the door for a few seconds, listening. There wasn't a sound. Nick tiptoed further in, and beckoned.

In the gloom, we could see and smell the evidence of new carpentry. It was just as though the workmen had lain down their tools and gone off for lunch, or to sleep, and not yet returned. In the nearest room we could see several trestles, with planks laid over them to be sawn to the correct length for laying the almost-completed timber floor. There were rags and sheets and rough offcuts of wood strewn haphazardly across the floorboards; but the place was in a much better state of repair than the last time we had been in here – when there were no floors at all, and no ceilings, just charred and blackened remains of beams, patches of spreading water all up the plaster walls, and the corpses and droppings of rats everywhere.

"I think it's all right," murmured Nick, venturing further into the entrance hallway and listening cautiously. "Whoever was here must have gone." Lash strained at the leash, trying to sniff into the corners: but I was still too nervous to let him go.

Nick put a finger up to his lips, to warn me to be quiet. As I hovered in the doorway, he crept through the ground-floor rooms, watching and listening as he went – wincing when his weight squeezed a creak or groan out of the newly-laid floorboards. It was a full two minutes before he came back to the front door to beckon me in, satisfied that the house was empty.

"It's hard to imagine, isn't it?" he said quietly. "These bare rooms . . . but just think what it's going to be like, Mog, when we've got rugs, and lamps, and furniture, and fires burning."

I shivered, and went over to the huge fireplace. I couldn't resist bending to peer up inside it. We had both hidden in this chimney-breast, once, when our lives depended on it.

"Did you hear something just then?" I asked.

Nick shook his head. "You're still imagining things. I've

been all round. There's nobody here but us." He turned around and around in the middle of the big empty room. Lash was tugging so hard on the leash now that, reluctantly, I let him go and sniff among the sawdust in the corners.

"It will be *so* much better, living here," said Nick, his voice reverberating off the bare walls. "To leave that cold, horrible castle where we never see anybody. To be able to have visits from Mr Spintwice and Mr Cramplock, and receive callers and tradesmen. Not like when we used to live round here, when there was never enough to eat and we used to get clobbered all the time – imagine, being able to live here in style, at last! I can't wait. Can you?"

We had certainly talked about it for long enough: turning this place into a proper home, bringing with us the few serving staff who remained in employment at Kniveacres, and living like the well-to-do people we used to watch and envy. But, attractive as the idea was, I was finding it harder than Nick to envisage this sawdust-smelling shell of a house transformed into the kind of cosy home he described.

I went out into the hallway, and listened. A new wooden staircase had been constructed, and, as I stood at the bottom and gazed up, I realised two things. Firstly, that I really didn't fancy going up there; and secondly, that my feet had already started walking up the stairs, almost of their own accord, making a hollow echo around the bare walls. I felt very strange: as though I was suddenly no longer in control of where I was going. As though something else, some other force, was drawing me silently upwards.

At the top of the stairs I found myself on a big landing, with doorways leading off it, none of which had yet had their doors fitted. I was suddenly slightly dizzy. It felt as though the floor wasn't quite level, and the doors were leaning at angles. None of the straight lines – the floorboard joints, the planes of the walls, the door-frames – seemed properly aligned, as though I were in some kind of optical illusion, where it was impossible to tell if things were larger, or smaller, or nearer, or further away, than they appeared.

Ahead of me, another flight of stairs rose towards the next storey – and stopped in mid-air, incomplete. Through one of the door-frames to my right I could see new timber panelling, still in the process of being fitted to the walls. Suddenly I felt my flesh creep. There was something – or *someone* – in here. In spite of Nick's assurances, I could feel it. A presence, a darkness – something inexplicable. I wanted to go back downstairs, very badly. All I could hear was my own breathing, but it sounded unnaturally loud, and made me panic. I had to get off this landing as quickly as I possibly could: and yet I was gripped by terror at the thought of turning my back on the empty rooms, the half-constructed floors.

"Nick!" I heard myself calling. "Nick! He's here!"

But suddenly I couldn't be sure whether Nick was still downstairs or not. I was no longer sure what day it was, even how old I was. I really felt as though I were in a dream.

Nick came out into the hallway as I got to the foot of the stairs, and so did Lash.

"He's here," I said again, looking at them blankly.

"Who is? What are you talking about?"

Nick's voice made me snap out of my trance. It was like being jolted awake. I bent and greeted Lash with sudden relief, as though I hadn't seen him for days.

"*Who's* here?" Nick repeated.

"I don't know," I said, laughing in confusion. "I don't – that is, I . . ."

The spell was broken. I felt silly for panicking.

Nick cast a brief glance around, and said, "Come on, then. There's not as much to see as I thought."

The front door cast very little light into the entrance hall as he opened it and the fog seemed to billow in from outside. As he walked out onto the front doorstep, he more or less disappeared altogether, as though he were passing into another world.

"Nick!" I called. "Nick, wait for me!"

I darted to catch up with him, and Lash's claws skittered on the bare boards as he followed.

"You've gone very quiet," Nick observed, as we reached the bottom of the steps. Neither of us could resist another glance at the poor dead dog; and I shivered, and pulled the lapels of my coat more tightly around my neck.

"It gives me the creeps, a bit," I confessed.

"It's just because it's empty," Nick said. "It won't when it's finished."

There was no traffic in the street. The railings melted into the fog to our left and right; the buildings on the opposite side of the street now no more than lumpy grey outlines. All the daily sounds of London – even the shouts of children, the street-cries of people selling things, and the sound of church bells – seemed to have been silenced today, as though they had to struggle so hard to penetrate the deadening fog that they had given up altogether.

"It's this way, isn't it?" said Nick, as we came around the side of the house towards the overhanging trees which bordered the back lane.

Lash and I had run up this lane hundreds of times, often when we were late returning from some errand and feared the sharp edge of Mr Cramplock's tongue. The houses on this row had small, shady back gardens, with foliage spilling out over the wall at intervals: but they can't have been very pleasant to be in, because of the stench from the nearby Fleet Ditch – a tar-black stream of sluggish sewage, which sent up its rancour into every house during the warm summer months, and at this time of the year occasionally overflowed, its egress into the Thames blocked by ice, so that it flooded the cellars and even the ground-floor rooms of the ancient buildings which backed onto it.

"Hang on," I said.

This was where Mr Cramplock's printing shop had stood, for years, leaning against the wall of the big house like a shabby but loyal old pet. Now he had vacated it, and the low building which had once glowed with light and clanked with the constant sound of the presses was just a tumbledown shell, as the workmen prepared to pull it down altogether as part of the process of restoring Charnock House to its old grandeur.

We had helped Mr Cramplock to find new premises, not far away: and they were larger and better. But, as I gazed at the sad, empty old brick shop which had been my home and workplace for years, I felt a twinge of regret, just as I knew he did whenever he passed.

Lash was pawing at the familiar old door, which he and I had run in and out of, countless times.

"Wait a minute, Nick," I said, "I can't leave without having one more look."

The lock had been smashed off, and, although someone had obviously tried to make the door secure by nailing planks repeatedly across it, the planks had all been torn off too. One of them was hanging, bent and splintered, by one nail.

"Someone's been in here too," I said, suddenly scared again.

"Just local thieves," said Nick dismissively, "trying to see what there is to take."

But, as we pushed the door open and ventured into the dim, dirty interior, I could see to my surprise that one of Mr Cramplock's printing presses was still here, in the same place it had always stood. And, as we got closer, I caught the distinct, familiar smell of fresh ink.

It *can't* be, I told myself: I must be imagining it, just because that's the way the place has always smelled.

But, as Lash trotted from corner to corner to reacquaint himself with his favourite old smells, I went up to the big black press, and it became obvious that it had been used very recently indeed. There was just enough daylight coming through the big dirty windows to see that someone had made up a page in a neatly-assembled forme: a kind of poster or design, with what looked like an engraved border, all still glistening with wet ink. The roller was wet too; and there was still a roll of paper, along with a few cut sheets, on a nearby shelf. Someone had been here printing something, no more than a few minutes ago. I looked around, nervously, but could see no one. Then I looked back at the press.

"Nick, come and see this!" I said, astonished.

Nick was intrigued. "Maybe Mr Cramplock's been back," he said. "Maybe, secretly, he still prefers working here. What does it say?"

"It looks like a very neat job," I said, craning my neck. After so many years working in a printing shop, I wasn't bad at reading reverse type laid out on a press, however tiny and ink-laden: but there was still a much easier way to find out.

"Pass me one of those sheets of paper," I said.

As Nick handed me one of the cut sheets, I slipped it over the type and pulled the handle that brought the platen down hard against it. Squeezing it to its tightest, as I'd been taught to do, I then let go of the handle; and peeled the paper off the blocks, as carefully as I could.

"Here we are," I said, holding it up towards Nick.

As he took it in, his eyes grew wider; and after a few seconds he gasped.

"Surely not!" he cried.

I turned it around so that I could look at it myself. The page had come out clean and perfect. The ink really *had* been fresh. I had printed something quite beautiful to look at, a page with an engraved pattern on it which at first seemed to be an abstract design of intertwining lines and flourishes, but which, as we inspected it more closely, looked more likely to be some sort of map. There were occasional words, not place-names as such, but instructions, dotted around at various points. To the left-hand side of the drawing there was a long, sinuous line – probably intended to indicate a road, or path – which branched, at one point, into seven byways. Beneath the last of these was written:

Great evil lies here, that can cause no further harm.

The roads gradually merged, and seemed to acquire a kind of upward momentum towards the top of the map, where they all converged on two distinct points, one to the left and one to the right. Leading away from the right-hand point were more sweeping and crisscrossing paths, tumbling down the other side of the page. Just below the middle, a boldly-curving line petered out as it approached the paper's edge. Beneath it were the words:

Seek the point to the right, for this is the sole source of your fortune.

And, at the very bottom of that right-hand line, a fork like the tongue of a snake.

Here is love, and wisdom, and eternity.

But what really made us stare was what was written at the very bottom of the page, beneath the map. Like a kind of signature, partly enveloped by the lower flourishes of the design, there was a neatly-printed line of characters like no type that had ever been kept anywhere in Mr Cramplock's chests and boxes.

डम्यता

I stared at Nick. We had seen this many times before: although it had been meaningless to us for a long time, we had later learned what it meant. It was the way the word "Damyata" was written in India. It was our father's name.

"I can't believe I'm seeing this," I said. "It's a joke, isn't it? Someone's playing a trick on us."

"Well, either that, or – he's back again," said Nick, his voice reedy with shock.

I stood rooted to the spot for a few seconds, thinking. Then I practically threw the sheet of paper at Nick.

"Keep this," I said. "Hang on to it. This ink's so fresh, whoever's just been here hasn't had time to get far." I held my arm out to summon Lash, and pulled him towards the door by his collar. "We *must* be able to catch up with them," I said. "Come with me."

We left the printing-shop door swinging open on its ancient hinges, and plunged back into the freezing fog. When we got to the corner near the back lanes of the houses, we hovered, listening.

"I can't hear anything," said Nick.

"Just a minute," I said abruptly.

We fell silent again: Lash's ears were erect and his head completely still, as he latched on first to the sound neither Nick nor I had yet picked up.

And now, in the disorienting silence of the fog, there came the sudden clatter of a gate from somewhere down the lane; and a horribly familiar footfall.

"There it is," I said quietly.

Receding, faster than I'd heard it yesterday, the echoing ring of an unmistakeable gait on the cold cobbles, as though someone had been disturbed and was now trying to get away down the back lane as quickly as possible.

Click . . . click . . . click . . .

CHAPTER 3

KNIVEACRES

"The situation, Master Winter, is far from satisfactory," said the tall man, as he closed the big black book. The skin of his face and on the back of his hands had the texture of dry, dead leaves. "My firm has now spent several months looking into every aspect of the estate and its finances. The harder we look, I regret to say, the more difficulties we find."

He leaned over the green felt of the desk, pipe in hand, and eyed us over his half-spectacles – with a serious, but not unkind, expression.

"Solutions are hard to come by. Difficulties are abundant."

We were gathered in Sir Septimus's old study, high in the chilly central tower of the castle. Almost no one had been in here since the old man's death, and the room smelled of leather and fusty old paper, to which the sour stench of the accountant's tobacco pipe had now been added. Sir Septimus had kept matters of money and business very close to his hollow old chest, and it had taken Mr Parchmold, of the London accountants Parchmold and Coot, every day of the three or four months since the old man's death to work through the books and draw any conclusions about what he had been up to. Now, finally, he had come to Kniveacres to give us his findings. Nick and I sat on the opposite side of the desk, in high-backed chairs; and between us sat Melibee, our blind old manservant, who had also been Sir Septimus's faithful servant for more years than even he could calculate, and almost certainly had more knowledge of the affairs of the estate than anyone else left alive. Opposite the gaunt, imposing accountant, he cut a shabby figure: dressed in the old-fashioned black frock-coat he always wore, with its dusting of fluff picked up from the ill-kept servants' rooms he frequented. He looked tired and stooped – and, just now, visibly nervous. He couldn't see the man opposite him, of course, but he couldn't fail to be aware of his sheer presence and air of authority. He kept clearing his throat, as though preparing to answer a question at any moment: but the accountant asked him none.

Mr Parchmold spoke slowly and deliberately, perhaps to ensure that there were no misunderstandings; and his measured, unexcited voice was curiously soporific. The winter sunshine was filtering weakly in through the big windows and picking up the slow swirls of pipe-smoke, and I kept feeling an overwhelming urge to close my eyes as the black-coated man smoothed out the big gilt-edged pages, and coughed occasionally.

"Dear, dear," Melibee murmured faintly, as much to break the silence as anything else.

The accountant took a single sheet of paper out from beneath a heavy pile of documents, and arranged it squarely in front of him. "I have here a summary," he said, "which omits many necessary complications, but which I fancy sets out the position clearly enough that a lay person may get the measure of it." He slid it the short distance across the desk to us, fell silent, and sat back, clamping his pipe between his teeth and watching us.

I leaned over to look at it: a dense, neat grid of numbers, precisely written in dark ink, with three particularly bold figures underlined in red ink at the very foot of the page. But there was no way I could make sense of the meticulous columns. Totting up three or four items on a customer's bill as he stood waiting at the counter of the printing shop had been as much involvement as I had ever had with accounts when I was growing up; and I could see from Nick's expression that he was even more at sea than I was.

"Er – thank you, Mr Parchmold, that all seems very clear; but perhaps you'd like to summarise the basics for Mr Melibee's benefit," I suggested. I tried not to catch Nick's eye, because he was trying very hard not to laugh.

For the first time, Parchmold was caught off-guard. "Of course . . . of course. I was forgetting," he stuttered. "Forgive me, Mr Melibee, if you please. The position is broadly this. Sir Septimus has incurred long years of debt to various parties, for reasons which are not entirely clear from the current documentation, but which plainly represent incremental settlements going back into the last century. These alone have ensured that the estate has probably never been as solvent as might have been assumed. Add to this his more recent business dealings, many of which appear to have entailed high degrees of risk invested with rather, ah – *unreliable* parties . . . desperate measures, one might surmise. Debts have been called in long ago, which the estate simply would not permit him to service. In short, gentlemen, debt has been piled upon debt. Kniveacres has been sustained on borrowed money for decades, at heavy interest. I say again, it is *far* from satisfactory."

Melibee had gone whiter than usual while this damning verdict was being delivered. He was opening and closing his lips, as though trying to stop his mouth from drying out.

"I had only the sketchiest idea of Sir Septimus's affairs," he croaked. "I swear, he did not take me sufficiently into his confidence – it sounds, Mr Parchmold, most uncomfortable. May one know the implications, as you estimate them?"

"The *implications*," replied Mr Parchmold, "as I see them, Mr Melibee, are these. That the estate generates far less income than it expends, and that this has been the case for years. There is no obvious prospect of a change in this pattern. The Hall, its contents and its grounds must be sold, and with luck that may recoup most of what is needed to clear the debt . . . and, of course, the small matter of my firm's fees. Unless anyone here knows of substantial assets to which we have not been made party, I can suggest no other course."

Melibee opened and closed his mouth a few more times, like a lizard impassively chewing a large insect. "I see," he said at length.

"So – let me understand you correctly," Nick said, quietly. "We don't *really* own Kniveacres at all."

"It's yours to sell," he explained, trying to sound soothing. "But the proceeds will almost certainly not be yours to spend. One could, of course, suggest paying off the debt piecemeal, by selling the more valuable assets a few at a time. Giving you time to live here until such time as other arrangements might be made. Unfortunately . . . your relative, Sir Septimus, appears to have begun to make use of that ploy some time ago, and our records suggest that most of the family possessions of any real value are long since disposed of."

"But the house in London," Nick pressed him, "that must be worth something. It's being restored. We went to look round, last week. It will soon be finished."

The accountant sighed. "And at *considerable* expense, Master Winter," he said condescendingly. "I am bound to tell you that our calculations of the family assets have taken Charnock House into account. Stripped of all its furnishings, and in the ruined state in which it has found itself for so many years, its value barely compensates for any attempt at renovation. Indeed, you will doubtless have observed, when you were there, that no work was progressing. The fact is, our instructions to the builders are that on no account must they undertake even the smallest further task in that house until we give permission."

I fought to grasp the reality of the situation. "And our inheritance," I said, "that is, Nick's and mine . . ."

"Amounts to almost nothing," said Mr Parchmold, almost

soothingly. "Indeed, it is still conceivable you may turn out to have inherited a burden of debt greater than you can repay."

"So we aren't wealthy after all," I said, crestfallen.

He beamed at me, relieved to see that I had finally understood. "In what I believe is the popular phrase, Miss Winter," he said gently, "you haven't a bean."

It was barely the middle of the afternoon, and yet the sky was darkening over the weather-beaten chimneys and crenellations of Kniveacres Hall. There was a biting wind, whose Arctic purpose the bare trees did almost nothing to interrupt. The fields beyond the woods still had narrow lines of snow clinging to their southern edges, and the brown beech leaves did a cold, agitated dance on their tangled branches. We were kicking our way through slimy leaf-piles in the further reaches of the sprawling gardens, unable to bear the shadows and clammy stone of the house while there was daylight outside. It had always seemed an inhospitable place: but now that we knew what a financial burden it was, and what a lot of worry and debt we'd inherited with it, it was suddenly impossible to see any redeeming features in it at all.

When we'd arrived here, a year or so ago, bewildered at the open space and the silence, we'd spent a long time exploring every inch of the grounds. It had taken us a long time to realise that there was as much to observe, and wonder at, and be excited by – in the changing colours and seasons, the behaviour of animals, the intricacies of the forest landscape – as there was in London. Tramping the estate, we'd always been animated by some novelty and excitement, whether it was climbing a particular tree for the first time to get a view from a new angle, or discovering some overgrown out-building we'd never found before, or watching deer in the spring dusk. We'd been full of discoveries, and plans, and chatter. But, after this morning, there seemed little point in any of these: and we'd barely said a word to one another since the accountant had climbed into his carriage and driven away. We sat, aimlessly flinging twigs into the stream that fed the big ornamental lake.

"To be honest," I sighed, "I'm not sure I'd ever really allowed myself to believe it. That we were rich, I mean – that Kniveacres was really ours. It's just been like a dream."

"Which we've just woken up from," grunted Nick.

Lash was somewhere in the undergrowth, too busy sniffing out the lairs of intriguing woodland creatures to share our troubles.

"We'd better go back," I said. "It's going to be dark soon. Come on, Lash. Here, boy! Time to go."

We could see the lake from here, its edges frilled with ice under which lily leaves crowded in the dark water, bent and trapped. The lake had been created many years ago on the orders of Sir Septimus's late wife, Harriet Cloy, upon whose kindness our mother Imogen had hoped to prevail after we were born, in order to give us a safe and comfortable up-bringing. It hadn't quite worked out that way. Sir Septimus had intervened, not willing to have Imogen's children living in his house and inconveniencing him. He had ruthlessly pretended that we were dead, secretly consigning both of us to orphanages and a largely joyless, underfed childhood in the streets of London. Now, having at last earned our right to live here, it seemed we had been thwarted by Sir Septimus yet again. He had spent all his money, *our* money, and more besides.

"It's not that I really *like* this place," Nick said, as we began walking slowly back towards the forbidding roofline of the house. We could already see the icicles which had been growing from the lintels for the past three weeks, some of them as long as I was from head to toe. Some of the windows at the back of the house had three or four thick icicles hanging almost to the sill, making them look like silvery bars on the windows of a prison. "I mean, look at it," Nick continued. "It's hard to believe anything happy ever went on here. And we don't *need* grand things. We can go back and make our way in London, just as we always have. No . . . it's the people we're letting down, *that's* what's unfair. What's going to happen to Melibeem?" he said, using the nickname for Melibee he always used, an imitation of the murmuring way Sir Septimus used to pronounce his name. "And the others?"

Something else Mr Parchmold, the accountant, had made abundantly clear this morning was that we could no longer afford to keep up our generosity towards the people who had helped us all our lives, and whom we'd at last believed we were able to repay. Mr Cramplock, for one, was living in handsome premises which we were paying for. We had also pledged our help to people in the village a mile from Kniveacres, who had been the best of friends to us since we came to live here – especially the nervous widow, Mrs Nisbet, and her disfigured teenage son. And, as Nick pointed out, what about Melibee? Old and blind as he was, if the estate were sold off, with no money to give him any kind of pension, he'd be doomed.

"I don't know what we're going to say to them," I said. "Melibee must realise already. He was there. He knows exactly what's going on. But how are we ever going to look Fanny Nisbet in the eye and confess we've lost Kniveacres and can't pay her another penny, and furthermore that she's probably lost her tied cottage? Or tell Mr Cramplock we've made a terrible mistake? After all he's done for us?"

A cacophony of rooks in the trees fringeing the driveway ahead of us, and the distant sound of horses' hooves, told us we had another visitor. Lash, scampering ahead of us, stood still in the middle of the path with his ears pricked up, and began barking at the horses, still out of sight beyond the trees.

"Now who can *this* be?" groaned Nick. "Another lawyer, or vulture, to tell us even more things we don't want to know?"

But, as we emerged onto the edge of the lawn, and saw a neat carriage pulled up before the front entrance of the house, and Melibee already standing there fussing over the driver and occupant, we realised it was someone we were very pleased to see.

"Mr Spintwice!" exclaimed Nick. And we took off and ran excitedly across the gravel towards him.

By the time we got to the carriage he'd handed his small

black case to Melibee, but hadn't yet jumped down: and, for the first time, his eye level was above ours as we greeted him. "I just *had* to come," he said. He looked tired, but there was excitement in his eyes, and relief at having reached the end of his two-day journey from London. Lash scampered breathlessly around him, and we helped him jump down onto the gravel, all of us talking at once. Melibee was explaining to the driver how to reach the courtyard at the back of the house, where he could water the horse, park the carriage under cover, and find a welcome meal for himself.

"I've got some news for you," said Mr Spintwice. "I couldn't wait to tell you. I think you'll find it rather exciting. I thought of sending some sort of message, but then I thought, I could be here myself almost as quickly as any message, and then you wouldn't have to go to the trouble of coming to see me."

"It's really good of you to come, Mr Spintwice," said Nick. "But you've had a long journey. Let's go in and talk somewhere warm and comfortable."

"What's the news you've brought, Mr Spintwice?" I asked eagerly. "Have you found something out about the diamond?"

But Nick was clutching my arm, and when I mentioned the word "diamond" his grip tightened so hard he actually hurt me.

"Ow!" I complained, wresting back my arm. "What's the matter with you?"

"Keep your voice down," Nick hissed.

"What on earth for?" I hissed back. "Who can hear us?

Only *Melibee.*" I stared at him. "You're not seriously suggesting . . . ?"

"Hush," said Nick again, shortly.

We followed Melibee into the house, at a slight distance. Lash trotted beside me as I nursed my bruised arm, glaring at Nick. Melibee had been keeping a low, nervous profile since the meeting this morning, as though he was afraid we might blame *him* for not realising what Sir Septimus had been up to for all those years, and for not doing more to prevent the frittering away of the estate. But I couldn't believe Nick was still suspicious of him, after the way he'd helped us while Sir Septimus was alive, and all these months since, when he'd been nothing but loyal and diligent. He stayed several paces ahead, showing no sign of having heard any of our argument; and once we were inside he disappeared silently up the stairs with Mr Spintwice's case, leaving us to entertain our friend in the huge ancient hall.

The hall was cold. The enormous expanses of blank grey stone seemed to suck any warmth out of the air inside; and the windows, high in the walls, had a film of ice clinging to their stained-glass decorations. There was a low, dying fire in the enormous grate, with a little three-sided square made by a long sofa and a couple of armchairs gathered around it. Apart from this, the cavernous room was dark and empty: there was no other furniture, just a few of Sir Septimus's collected statues and stuffed animals watching us from the corners, some curtain hangings against the far walls and a few dusty gilt-framed pictures high on the walls. We hardly noticed them any longer, but Mr Spintwice was spinning around, gazing up at the high ceiling and the ancient portraits as we walked in, even though he'd been here before.

Nick wrenched apart the two halves of a log that the axe had just failed to split cleanly, and rolled them onto the fire with a clatter.

"Might as well keep warm," he said. The fire flared as the logs caught, and an orange glow flickered up the stone walls. Lash settled himself into a long low mound on the rug, his chin on one of his front paws.

"I'm so excited about this news," beamed Mr Spintwice, "I can hardly speak. But – if you don't mind, Nick and Mog – I've been on the road for rather a long time and I need to, ah – that is, would you be able to remind me where I can, ah . . . ?"

"Of course," said Nick, and led the little man by the arm back through the heavy oak door.

"What was *that* all about?" I asked him when he came back, rubbing my arm a lot more obviously than I needed to.

"He's been in a one-horse carriage since yesterday morning," Nick said quietly. "Surely you can give him time to get inside the house before you start quizzing him."

"It was Melibee, wasn't it?" I accused him. "You didn't want me to ask him questions in front of Melibee."

Nick was silent for a few seconds. "You know what Melibeem's like," he said. "What he can't see, he makes up for with his hearing. He could hear a cat washing its whiskers three rooms away."

"And why not?" I hissed. "What have we got to hide

from him? *Let* him hear. Why *shouldn't* he know about the diamond?"

"Mog," he said gently, "we've no idea whether—"

But I was in no mood to be pacified. "We've *every* idea," I retorted. "He's our friend, Nick. Well, isn't he? He's been pretty much our *only* friend, ever since we got here. But you've never trusted him, have you?"

"I just think we have to be a bit cautious," said Nick. "We've no idea what Melibeem's past is like. Yes, he's been nice enough to us since Sir Septimus died, but we've only known him a year. Sir Septimus isn't here any longer to confirm or deny it, but Melibeem could well have been up to his neck in the whole business all along – and you know it."

"You never trust anybody," I told him. "You're the most suspicious person I've ever met. What harm could it do, talking to Mr Spintwice within earshot of a blind old man?"

"Hasn't it ever occurred to you that that might be exactly what he *wants* you to think?" said Nick. "Look at what he's been like today. He was a nervous wreck in the study this morning, and he's been hiding from us ever since. He's completely *shifty*. He can't stay in the same room with us for two seconds."

"I expect he's upset," I said.

"I'm sure he is," said Nick. "We all are. Look, Mog, I'm not saying he's definitely up to no good, I just don't think we know him well enough to be sure. It doesn't hurt to be careful."

"You're a fine one to talk about what hurts and doesn't

hurt," I complained, nursing my arm conspicuously again. "Sometimes you get *so*—"

But I had to stop because Mr Spintwice came back into the hall, his footsteps echoing on the big flagstones, and it was impossible to remain cross when I saw his happy, open face coming towards the fireside.

"Goodness," he said, "what an enormous place this is. I'm sure I'll never get used to it. All those stairs . . ."

"Come and sit down," said Nick. "Tell us what you've been finding out."

Mr Spintwice sat on the edge of the armchair, his feet not quite touching the floor. He was so small that, if he had attempted to sit right back into it, he'd have been swallowed up almost completely. The fire shone in his eyes, and I felt a surge of excitement as he leaned even further forward to speak.

"I've been thinking about nothing else. I've spent nearly every *minute* since you came to London, trying to track it down," he said – and I was sure he wasn't exaggerating. "For days I found nothing," said Mr Spintwice, his voice falling to little more than a whisper. "Shelf after shelf I searched, with no result, and I was on the point of giving up. But it was your friend, Mr Cramplock, who put me onto it, Mog. I suddenly remembered that his father used to know the Cloy family, and that they sometimes employed him to print documents for them. So I went to call on him. And sure enough, Mr Cramplock suggested I try a lawyer's office where some of the family's old records are stored. I had to invent an excuse for going through their files, of course, and I'm afraid I might have looked at a few books and boxes I'd, ah – been told not to touch. But among them I found – this."

He reached inside his coat, and with a triumphant little smile he brought out a little black notebook. It was extremely old and battered and, as he passed it across to us, I could see it had been torn in half down the spine so that only the front half of the binding, and the first forty or fifty pages of the original book, remained. Nick took it from him and opened it gingerly. The pages were fragile and crispy, many of them stuck together, and most of the handwriting inside was very badly smudged from water damage. Enough of it was decipherable, though, to see that many of the pages had begun with a date.

"It's a diary," he said.

"It's *part* of a diary," said Mr Spintwice. "It's been torn in two, and I'm afraid the rest is missing. It was with documents which must have been brought from India when Sir Septimus returned to England for the last time, so it would appear it's been damaged on a sea voyage, or possibly stored in a damp place since then. But look at the back – the very last page!"

Nick turned it over. Ink had run all over the page, creating a swirling pattern like layers of cloud spreading down from the top left-hand corner; but, lower down, some words emerged intact from the general smudginess, and the last few lines were perfectly legible. Nick gave a gasp.

"Can you see, Mog?" He held it out so I could look at it too.

The handwriting was neat, in ink which had faded to a pale turquoise. As I looked at the page, I couldn't help feeling I'd seen writing very much like it, somewhere before. The only section we could read, right at the bottom, began and ended in mid-sentence.

> ... bear it any longer. I should think she simply wishes she were dead. In any case, among all this uproar about the Eye of Winter, there is one advantage she has over the Cloys which they don't even realise, thank God: it is that she knows where it is. She has sworn me to secrecy, but I can hardly contain ...

And that was where it stopped, the next page completely torn off, along with the whole of the rest of the diary.

"How *annoying*!" cried Nick, dismayed. He turned the book over and over in his hands a few times.

"Well – yes," said Mr Spintwice. "It obviously stops in mid-stream. It is a little frustrating. But, what do you think of that line? This uproar about the Eye of Winter? And that reference to the Cloys! There's your proof, isn't there?"

"Well," said Nick, "it looks as if the Captain wasn't making it up, at least. But fancy it stopping there! If we even had the next *page*, it would tell us where the diamond is."

"Well," laughed Spintwice, uncertainly, "that may be so, of course – although it's unlikely to have stayed in the same place for all these years. But – how exciting to find the stone mentioned! Isn't it, Mog?" he said. "Mog?"

It was obvious we weren't as thrilled as he'd expected us

to be, and he seemed a bit crestfallen. I think he wanted us to thank him for finding it: but any excitement we felt at the mention of the diamond was outweighed by the disappointment at the crucial sections being missing altogether.

"Pass it here," I said.

I had had a sudden very strange thought; and as I gazed at the ragged little book, and reread the words on the final page, the more peculiar I felt. I *knew* what this was, and what it was about. I even felt a mounting certainty that I knew who had written it.

The first few leaves were stuck to the shabby board cover, but by slipping a finger around the inside I managed to prise the cover free and pull the book gently open, with a slight tearing sound, at the first page. The water which had stuck the pages together had done its predictable damage to the writing here, too. Only the odd few words were legible. But my heart leaped as I saw that they included the very first few words the owner had written when it was new. A name, a date, and the opening lines of a new year's reflections.

– Justina Thynne –

3rd January, 1814.
No going back: the strange old year is out, and
any thought that the new one may prove less
strange already appears . . .

At that point the cloudy patterns created by the invading, erasing water took over. But those few words were more than significant enough to make me and Nick stare at one another in wonder; and to make me impossibly curious about what the rest of the little book contained.

It had been written by our mother's closest friend, when they were together in Calcutta, and these opening lines were from the year before we were born: almost exactly fifteen years ago.

"Miss Thynne," I said quietly. I couldn't quite believe it.

"Is it someone you know?" asked Mr Spintwice.

"She was our governess," I said, finding a sudden unexpected lump in my throat. "She died – here – a few months back. But she'd been a friend of our mother's, years and years ago. This is her diary from *exactly* the time when they must have been together in India. If only we could read it, it might tell us so much about her. About what happened to her."

And yet, as I leafed through it, only the occasional intact lines stood out among the smeary pages.

> I dearly wish that what I had to relate were fitter for the eyes of posterity ...

began one entry.

> ... before taking his leave, had the temerity to argue that I must be sanguine and look upon it as an educational experience. It was a very long time indeed before ...

read the only decipherable lines on a slightly later page. I flicked through further still.

> *. . . bear the smell of that terrible place, let alone bear the gaze of all those eyes, and all that talk of spirits . . .*

It was terribly frustrating. No clear picture of any event could possibly emerge: the three or four lines on the final page about the Eye of Winter constituted possibly the longest legible passage in the entire book.

"What a shame," I said. "It's so badly damaged it's not really any use to anyone."

"It's a wonder anyone thought it was worth shipping home," said Nick. "Half a diary, with the most interesting parts torn off, and the rest so spoiled you can't even read them."

"I expect it was just packed away along with a whole load of other papers, and no one inspected it too closely," said Mr Spintwice. "In any case, perhaps it was complete when it came here. It may have been damaged in some accident since it was stored away."

"Or," I said with a horrible sense of foreboding, "maybe it was no accident. Maybe somebody *stole* the rest of it. What if someone else found it first, and tore off the part that matters, and took it away with them?" I looked at Nick. "You're sure no one else had been snooping around the lawyer's office where you found this, are you, Mr Spintwice?"

Mr Spintwice looked uncomfortable.

"Well – they didn't *say* they'd seen anyone else," he said. "But I, ah – didn't really ask, as such."

Nick leaned forward. Something had occurred to him. "Mr Spintwice," he said, "you know you said the best source of information may be right here, in the family library? Well, we haven't had any luck finding it since we got back. Perhaps you could help us look? If we show you the collection, you never know what you might be able to find."

Sure enough, this brought the smile back to Mr Spintwice's round face.

"I should like that very much. When might we start? First thing in the morning?"

Nick looked across at me. He opened his mouth to say something, but I got in first.

"Are you too tired to start straight away?" I asked.

The library, if possible, was even colder than the hall: and, once we'd lit some of the lamps around the big room, we could see our breath as we took Mr Spintwice from shelf to shelf. We'd only ever looked at a tiny fraction of the thousands of books, but we knew the arrangement well enough to give him some idea, at least, of where to start. For a long time we helped him, pulling out the heavy books, moving the library ladder around to help us lift down books which were stored way up near the ceiling. Mr Spintwice was so short he had to use the ladder for shelves which were well within most people's reach.

We'd been hunting for half an hour or so, without getting very far, when there was a polite cough. We looked up, and Melibee was standing there with a tray.

"This may, ah – warm you up during your search," he said. There was steam coming off a tall silver jug of warm, weak punch: something Melibee often served on winter evenings, and for which we had developed quite a taste.

Nick jumped off the ladder.

"Thank you very much, Melibee," he said. "Just leave it there on the desk, and I'll pour it for everyone."

Melibee stood with his head slightly tilted up into the air, as he often did, like an animal catching a scent. Of course he couldn't see what books we had open on the desk, but it was as though he were trying to identify them using all of his other senses: the smell of their foxed old pages, the location of our footsteps as we came away from the shelves to share out the drink.

"It may be presumptuous of me to give you advice," he said, quietly. "But I fancy you may find something of use to you in the large book with the buckram binding, two shelves up above your head, Miss Imogen, in that cabinet beside the mongoose."

Nick stared at him as he bowed shortly and retired, closing the library door softly behind him and leaving us in silence with the steaming punch.

"How on earth . . . ?" he began. He stared at the closed door through which Melibee had just gone. "He's been listening at the door. That's the only explanation."

But I had rushed over to the bookshelves nearest to the stuffed mongoose that stood, like many other family trophies and mementoes of India, peering out from a shelf amid the spines.

"What are we waiting for?" I muttered. "Let's have a look." I pulled the library steps over to where I needed them, and climbed up to reach for the biggest cloth-bound book on the shelf. "This must be the one," I said, pulling it down with a struggle.

I brought it over to the desk, and opened it for the others to look at.

"Well I never," said Spintwice, suddenly thrilled. "**Treasures of Bengal. A survey of documented precious objects in the possession of the East India Company and Others.** This could be very promising indeed." He began leafing through the big pages while we watched. There were detailed descriptions and drawings of hundreds of items of jewellery, sculptures, paintings, ceremonial weapons, elaborate clothing, even jewelled horse-tackle. After a few minutes of searching, Mr Spintwice gave a cry.

"Aha!"

He'd found it. The open page showed a drawing of a diamond, and beneath it the words: **Sasanka-ki-aankh.**

I craned my neck. "Is that the right one?"

"Yes, yes," said Spintwice excitedly. "Look!"

"Read what it says, then," I said.

Nick had the best vantage point.

"**The Sasanka-ki-aankh,**" he read, "**also referred to in more** recent times as the Winter Diamond because of its association with, and possession by, the Winter family. A Golconda stone reputedly weighing some nine mishkals, or as much as 192 carats, it is by common assent the most valuable diamond still extant in India, perhaps exceeding the Koh-i-Noor of Punjab. Prominent in the folklore of the region since the fifteenth century at the latest, the Sasanka-ki-aankh was gifted to the Company by the Princes of Bengal, stolen back, and seized again in 1757 as part of the settlement following the Battle of Plassey. It carries a powerful legend of a curse by which the natives set great store, and many refuse to enter its presence. It has changed hands too many times to document, and there have been long periods in its history when its whereabouts was uncertain. Some have romanticised its fate as embodying the fortunes of Bengal, even the state of the whole of India herself. Thought to have passed into the possession of the Cloy dynasty following a marriage alliance, and kept for many years at their home in Calcutta, it has not been recently documented, and according to some reports it is again lately lost or stolen. It derives its name from a characteristic slight blue tint in certain light: early theories that this coloration resulted from mineral impurities have been cast into doubt by the observation that the colour does not appear when the weather is overcast."

"Well," said Mr Spintwice, with a sigh, "now we know what the fuss is about."

Nick was thinking hard. "What if," he said, "that map we found in the printing shop was intended to show where the diamond is now? That would explain why the Captain was looking for it, wouldn't it?"

"Perhaps it's a map of Calcutta?" sugggested Mr Spintwice.

I flashed a glance at Nick. "Go and find Melibee," I said. "He knew *all* about this. Exactly where to find it, and everything."

Melibee turned out not to be far away, though he denied, politely, that he'd been hovering.

"Melibee, we *have* to know about this diamond," I said to him solemnly when he was back in the room. "Is this all true?"

"The book says all there is to say," said Melibee.

"How long have you known about this?" I demanded.

"I have been in the service of the Cloy family for more than sixty years, Miss Imogen," he said carefully.

I looked at Nick again. He was tight-lipped; but he gave a barely-perceptible nod. "Melibee, we may need your help," I went on. "We have heard rumours that a person in London knows the whereabouts of the diamond, and is planning an expedition to find it."

Melibee's gnarled, blind old face betrayed alarm.

"May one know which person in London?" he asked, hoarsely.

"A sea captain," said Nick in a quiet voice. "Someone whose motives aren't honest. He certainly isn't hunting it for *our* benefit."

"The fact is, Melibee," I said, "if the diamond does exist, it's rightfully ours. Isn't it?"

Melibee's thoughts were catching up with ours: but he spoke cautiously.

"I – would strongly advise *against* building up hopes that

the jewel might furnish us with an end to our difficulties," he said. "I fear the book is right in all particulars. The diamond has been a cause of more misfortune than happiness, for many long years."

"He has to be stopped," I said. "He's doing it out of spite."

"In which case, Miss Imogen, it may spite *him*," said Melibee. "And what would you propose? That we somehow arrange for him to be disposed of? Such a thought would be unworthy of both of you. And, in any case, that was more in Bonefinger's line."

I caught Nick's eye, and he raised his eyebrows. That was the most barbed remark we had ever heard Melibee utter about his late colleague, or about anyone.

"I don't believe we had that kind of thing in mind," Nick put in.

A bell rang from downstairs, and Melibee bowed. "If you will excuse me again," he said, and took his leave, backwards.

"That sounds like a visitor," I said, puzzled. "At this time of night?"

Nick shrugged. "It's not so late," he said. "Could be someone making a delivery. Or a message from one of the servants who's too ill to come tomorrow. Could be anything."

Mr Spintwice was still leafing through the big book to see if he could find any more useful information; but there must have been a thousand pages, and without knowing what we were looking for we might search for days.

"Well, your instinct was right, Mr Spintwice," said Nick. "Look in the family library, that's what you said, wasn't it?"

My mind was racing. "If *only* we knew where it was," I said. "The Captain *mustn't* find it first. We've got to stop him. I don't care what Melibee says."

"Mog, you've no idea what we'd be letting ourselves in for," said Nick. "Maybe Melibeem's right. A few minutes ago you were all for believing every word he said, until he told you something you didn't like."

"That's not fair," I argued, "just because—"

"And how exactly are you proposing we stop the Captain?" Nick interrupted. "He's not going to give in without a fight."

"Nick, we can't sit here and do nothing," I said, heatedly, "knowing that he's on a voyage to find the diamond. It would drive me mad. I'll go on my own, and find out where he's sailing to, and follow him. I'll take Lash. I'll be all right."

"Don't be ridiculous, Mog," said Nick.

At that moment, the door opened and Melibee came back in. He was holding a letter, folded and sealed.

"A post has come with a message for Master Dominic," he said. And he handed the letter to Nick, who took it in surprise, and had ripped it open before Melibee could politely proffer a knife.

His eyes darted across the page.

"It's from Water Jim," he said. "At least, it's from someone who's written down what he told them. Listen." His eyes widened. "Albacore setting sail for Calcutta, Thursday. *Lady Miranda*, with thirty-two hands. Old rogues and halfwit boys. Bounty promised. Cadiz, then the Cape. They are already plotting. Water Jim's cokum." He guffawed. "That's all it says."

"But that's what we need to know," I said, my excitement mounting. "Calcutta! It's still out there, Nick. The diamond is still there, and the Captain's tracked it down somehow. We have to go too. We *have* to!"

Nick turned to Melibee. "Has the post gone?" he asked.

"Awaiting reply, Master Dominic," said Melibee.

Nick thought for a moment. "There's none," he said. "I've paid Jim enough already. Tell the post he can stable his horse and go back in the morning."

"Indeed," said Melibee.

"And in the morning, perhaps," he said, looking at me with a slight smile, "we can also start making arrangements for a voyage."

My dreams were full of Bengal princes and humourless accountants, along with Melibee, and several of the villagers, and Nick, and myself, all fighting over a diamond as slippery as soap. Each time one of us picked it up, it would leap out of our grasp as if it had a mind of its own, and skid along the ground, pursued by the rest; and there would be a mad scrabble as it got lost under the furniture. After we had chased it around for a long time, the stone finally slid, with a clunk, up against a solid object, which turned out to be the wooden leg of a stranger who had been standing silently watching the confusion. From our crawling position we all gazed up, cowed, into the eyes of Captain Albacore – who roared with villainous laughter, and leaned forward on his crutch, as if to menace any of us who might dare try and pick it up from beneath him.

When I woke up, and cleared a circle with my sleeve in the misted window-pane to look out onto the icy courtyard, the stablehands were already hard at work grooming and saddling horses for Mr Spintwice's journey back to London. Their breath as they worked, and that of the horses, made clouds of steam in the dawn air.

Mr Spintwice took his leave after breakfast, with fulsome entreaties that we must call in to see him in London before setting off on our long journey.

"I can't *tell* you how excited I am," he said, as he shook our hands. "What an adventure!"

"You've been a great help, as always, Mr Spintwice," said Nick. "When we know our arrangements, we'll send word. It might take a little while to sort it out."

"Of course," he said. "And please don't worry about the fare for your passage. It's the least I can do."

"It's a *loan*, Mr Spintwice," said Nick. "We'll pay it back to you. As soon as we've found what we're looking for. I promise."

We helped him up into the carriage.

"Have a safe journey," I told him.

"I will," said Mr Spintwice, leaning out of the window. "Good luck, both of you."

We watched Mr Spintwice's carriage as it followed the curve of the drive, and disappeared among the trees on its way to the gatehouse and the main road. We could still hear the horses' hooves for a long time after the carriage had disappeared from view, and we stood outside the house until the sound had faded away completely.

"Good luck," echoed Nick, pensively. "Bless his soul. By the sound of things, that's one thing we're certainly going to need."

I wanted Nick to be as excited as I was; but in my heart, of course, I knew he was right. Who knew what dangers and adventures lay in store for us? As we turned to walk back in, I gazed up into the icy sky: at the turrets and chimneys of the Hall poking up like rotten teeth against the winter clouds; at the crows whirling in a jagged, laughing throng; and I shivered.

CHAPTER 4
CALCUTTA

The squealing of the birds that had followed us up the river was intensified, the nearer we got to the docks, by the swarming and divebombing of jackdaws and kites, and the cacophony from the parrots and jays in the trees along the waterline. They made so much noise it was hard even to hear the constant jabbering of the dock-hands, sepoys, bearers, traders and onlookers who thronged the dockside: more people in one place than I had ever seen before in my life. The river here was cluttered with ships, rows of brigantines, clippers and frigates lying at anchor, their masts bristling against the profound blue sky. We were moving very slowly, our ship's prow nosing gingerly between the other hulls and chains.

It was impossibly hot. Nick and I had been hanging over the rail since the morning, watching the steaming green and yellow vegetation passing by along the riverbank, and the chocolatey mud of the river flowing endlessly past the ship. But, as we approached the town, everyone else on board had crowded in behind us, waiting to disembark, and the pressing of impatient bodies, which blocked out the breeze of the ship's movement, made me feel sick and faint.

We had been on board for several months. We'd almost forgotten what it was like to stand on firm ground, or to eat decent food, or to see much else but vast expanses of water whenever we looked towards the horizon. Although, as paying passengers, we'd had a much more comfortable time of it than Nick used to when he accompanied his guardian, the bosun, on sea voyages, we still couldn't wait to get off. Nothing, not cool fountains of iced water poured by angels and mermaids, could have induced us to stay on board that ship for a single moment longer.

And yet, as the small boats and punts glided and jostled around in the water below, waiting to take us ashore, with a huge amount of shouting and gesticulating, and as I surveyed the waiting crowd spilling down the waterside steps, I suddenly felt scared. What were we getting ourselves into? I had allowed myself not to worry about it during the journey: but now, here we were five thousand miles from home, in Calcutta, with grinning faces and outstretched hands everywhere beneath me, and a constant hum of voices talking and shouting and imploring, in a language I couldn't understand. Momentarily, I felt a shiver of familiarity, as though I had experienced this before; then I realised this was almost exactly what I'd imagined my mother must have been feeling, when she came to Calcutta as a girl, decades ago. I'd thought about her voyage out here, and the tragic one she later made in the opposite direction, several times while we'd been at sea. I grasped the rail tightly, and froze.

"We've made a mistake," I said to Nick. "We've made the most enormous mistake."

"Don't worry," Nick said, "there'll be someone here for us. Melibeem said there would be. Just move."

I didn't have a choice, as it happened, because even before the ladder was properly secured, the press of bodies behind me pushed me over the edge. I found myself sliding down the wooden steps, almost vertically, into the nearest boat, no more than a couple of feet wide, which teetered alarmingly on its keel as I stood up. The old boatman, dressed only in a cotton garment wrapped loosely around his pelvis, held out a scrawny arm to steady me. Above us, Lash hesitated, whimpering, his front paws scrabbling on the edge of the plank; and I turned and bellowed at him to follow me, terrified that he'd be left behind, even drowned in the filthy river-water as the oblivious crowds pushed their way forward. After a few seconds he took a single great leap and skidded down the ladder after me, his long legs flailing. Nick jumped down after him. There really wasn't room for any more than the three of us in the boat, but we were followed by seven, eight, nine others, until the boatman called out to signal that we were fully laden.

Somehow the little boat made it to the bank without sinking; and we jumped ashore onto the green, slippery riverside steps.

Brown skin and white clothes all around me now, nothing

else in sight. An impenetrable wall of noise; people shouting in my ear, looming in my face. The smell of hot leaves and rank water, sweet rotting mangoes, sweat and bad teeth. Nick's hand gripped my upper arm and moved me forward, guiding me through the crowd to find somewhere we could breathe, and where there might be a bit of open space to see where we were. Soldiers with batons and fearsome black moustaches appeared now, holding people back, creating a gangway for the disembarking passengers, occasionally dealing a blow to an overenthusiastic hawker or driver clamouring for custom.

And suddenly there was a voice calling my name, and an anxious-looking brown face bobbed into view, and broke into a smile of relief when he saw the pair of us coming through the crowd and immediately concluded who we must be.

"Master Dominic? Miss Imogen?" he beamed, hopefully. "Wery good. *Wery*-wery good."

"Have you been sent to meet us?" I asked him, having to shout to make myself heard above the noise of the crowd.

"Yes," he shouted back. "From the Professor. *Wery*-wery good to see you. Just the tickety! Please to coming with me. Too many people here."

He waited until Nick had caught up, and held out an arm to guide us further out of the crowd.

"*Chaliye*," he said. "Please, come this way." And he kept his arm held out as we walked with him, as though he were trying to hold back the crowd.

"What about our things?" I asked anxiously, fearing that, among all these hundreds of people, there was almost no chance of our luggage ever finding us after it was unloaded.

"It will be collected," said our guide, with a sideways nodding motion of his head that was designed to reassure.

The further we got from the pressing crowd on the docks, the more trees there were, their broad leaves exuding humidity into the air, the foliage rolling into the distance with the shining spires and white rooftops of the city peeping above. Our guide showed us into an open-topped carriage drawn by a single grey and rickety-looking horse.

"Please to making yourselves comfortable," he said, brushing imaginary specks of dirt from the seats before we sat down. "And welcome to Calcutta, aaaah?"

Lash bounded up to sit between us; the guide jumped onto the narrow running-board on the side of the carriage; and we were off, down roads fringed with wide lawns, past cattle plodging and grazing in the waterlogged grass. His tongue hanging out, Lash sat up in the cart, alert, relishing the breeze the movement created. We quickly left the docks behind, and entered the dusty but imperiously broad streets of the city of Calcutta.

Melibee had set about the task of arranging for us to travel to India with the same uncomplaining, undaunted air of duty as he would have brought to bear if we'd asked him to make us a pot of tea. He had sent word ahead to an old Calcutta friend of the Cloy family, a Professor Shugborough, that we would be arriving: but there was no time to wait for a reply before we left, so he had booked us a passage leaving London just a few days after the letter. It was something of a miracle, now that we were here, to find that, not only were we expected, but we appeared to be welcome. As we jogged along in the tonga between the grand buildings, our guide took the trouble to introduce himself properly, calling himself by the intriguing name of Mystery: he was the senior household servant, and it was evident that he took his duties as seriously as a manservant or butler in the most prestigious of English houses. His cheerful expression never slipped, even when he was berating the driver, which he did often.

Many of the buildings we were passing were like the grandest of London's palaces, painted white, gleaming so much in the hot sunlight it was hard to look at them, and set comfortably back from the road in wide gardens fringed with lush trees. It was so hot that the air seemed to be shimmering, and figures materialised suddenly out of the heat-haze, and disappeared into it, as if in a dream. Immaculately-dressed but hot-looking soldiers were exercising handsome horses, and sitting watching them by the roadside were people in ragged clothes, women with water pots on their head, and small children with no clothes on at all. We passed churches too, and colonnades, and imposing arches and statues, and a great open space with a kind of giant square pond in it, full of black water and surrounded by stone steps, on which throngs of people were gathering, and gossiping, and buying and selling, and cooling themselves in the roasting afternoon. Mystery said something as we passed that sounded like, "This is loll diggy" – and I nodded politely, not having understood him at all. It wasn't long before we turned into a road lined with big white houses set behind a high wall, over which breathtakingly-beautiful tropical trees spilled their foliage and flowers. Mystery was telling us, "This is chow ringy," or something, and we nodded again.

On the corner, we passed close by a young man in a fashionably-cut frock-coat, who stopped and gazed after us. There was something about him that was oddly, indefinably familiar.

I turned my head to look at him. "Did you see that?" I asked Nick, as we rolled along.

"What?"

"That man. I thought I recognised him."

"Didn't see anyone," he said.

But here we were, at our destination. Almost immediately we turned in through the wide gates of one of the houses, and a sprawling colonial villa met our eyes, surrounded by lawns fringed with trees and dotted with huge, unflappable, slowly-striding birds. Monkeys ran across the lawns at the sound of our approach, and leaped up the tree-trunks to sit in the branches and watch us – including mothers with tiny babies clinging rather desperately beneath them as they ran.

"Look at that!" exclaimed Nick as we drove in. And, beneath the shade of one of the trees, though at first I didn't believe what I was seeing, was an elephant, standing calm and sedate, the expression in its great brown eyes a mixture of fatigue and blissful lack of worry.

"Ah," said Mystery, seeing our curiosity, "this is Punch. Punch you meeting later. Punch is older than the house.

Nearly as old as the Professor." And, still grinning, he barked at the driver, "*Bas! Bas! Bas!*" When the tonga-cart had ground to a halt in the yellow dust, Mystery jumped down, and stood to attention by the carriage as we climbed down after him.

"Please to coming inside, and welcome," he said. "I will show you where you are to staying, and introduce you. This way please. This side." And he went ahead of us up the few wide, white-painted wooden steps that led up to the front door of the house. Marching into the entrance hall, he barked orders at a couple of craven-looking servants who promptly disappeared. As we stood, looking around in relief at being in the shade of the big cool hallway, Lash stiffened and stared over at one of the doors.

Slinking lazily out into the hallway, skinny and almost impossibly long as it stretched out and shook its hind legs, was a cat. But it was the most enormous cat we had ever seen: standing taller than Lash on thin elegant legs, its pelt the colour of pale gold, and mottled with black spots which seemed to shift and blur as the flesh rolled over its sharp bones. It didn't cast so much as a glance in our direction, but strode with slow self-possession towards a large wicker basket, into which it stepped, and then sank and curled up with its back to us.

"What's that?" I asked, incredulous.

Mystery laughed. "Have no fear," he said, "she will not harming. That is Majara. She is totally tame. Raised in the house all her life. Not wild."

"But – I've never seen a cat as big as that," I squeaked.

"No ordinary cat," explained Mystery with another sideways

nod of his head. "A cheetah. *Wery* proud. But she will not harming you."

"Is she a pet?" Nick asked.

"She was given as a gift," Mystery explained. "There were two cubs, brother and sister. The maharajas use them for hunting. They bring down black buck. Wery-wery good hunters, wery-wery quick. But the Professor wished to having them in the household, and they grew up tame. The brother has died. Now Majara is left, and quite old now. But she is no pet. We are all *her* pets."

"I don't think you'll think much of that, will you?" Nick said to Lash.

I put my hand on Lash's head. "He doesn't chase cats," I said.

Mystery roared with laughter. "Let him try!" he teased. "Let him try! That would be a sight!"

There was a clatter, and through a doorway behind the stairs, from a room at the back of the house, a white man appeared. I couldn't help staring at him, because he looked so peculiar. He was stockily built, with a large head and quite strikingly enormous ears. The skin of his face was very wrinkled – although, to judge from the vigour of his movements, he didn't seem to be an old man. His forehead was broad, with lines and ridges in it, and he was bald apart from some silvery, whiskery hair above his ears. The other remarkable feature about him was his nose, which was very long indeed, with the two points of an untidy, wiry white moustache splayed out to either side of it – like tusks, I thought suddenly. In fact, as he turned to look at us, seeming rather confused, it struck me that he looked about as much like an elephant as a person reasonably can. Mystery stood to attention.

"May I presenting the visitors from London, Professor sahib," he said. "Miss Imogen and Master Dominic. And Lash. They have arrived safely. Just the tickety!"

He had a little difficulty with the pronunications of our names, and they both seemed to come out missing a syllable, as "Im'gen and Dom'nic".

But the Professor bumbled over, his eyes crinkling in good-natured surprise, and held out a hand.

"Welcome," he said, coughing. "Ah, welcome, Imogen and Dominic, most welcome. Undoubtedly. Forgive the lack of, ah – ceremony. Funny sort of day." He looked around, and clapped his hands together twice.

"I'm sorry if we weren't expected—" began Nick, but the Professor cut him short.

"Good heavens, what nonsense," he said. "Funny sort of day, that's all . . . Tea," he said to a boy of about our age, who had appeared at his summons. "*Chai.* For the visitors, *jaldi.* And fruit. Something to eat. *Jaldi!*"

"I have given instructions already, Professor sahib," Mystery reassured him.

"Very good," said the Professor. "Quite. Undoubtedly. Well." He stood there, surveying us, for a few moments; and I was quite sure I knew what he was going to say next. "Imogen, and Dominic," he said. "Ah – goodness, forgive me."

"I'm Imogen," I said, helpfully. I'd cut my hair very short on the voyage, because the constant heat and salt on board ship made having long hair a misery, and the lice were impossible to avoid. But it meant, I realised, that Nick and I were almost impossible to tell apart.

"Of course you are!" he exclaimed, relieved. "Undoubtedly! Well, you are very alike, aren't you?"

"It's more difficult when Mog's hair is short," said Nick.

"Quite," said the Professor. "I can see I shall have trouble. Well, you've met Mistry, and he's sorted you out. You must be in need of a wash and a change of clothes after your journey. It's so intolerably hot, you poor things, you're not used to it. If only this dashed monsoon would break. Have you been shown, ah, your quarters?"

"I think we were just on our way there," I said.

"Quite. Well, I hope everything will be to your liking. You're very welcome. And when you've settled in, come and eat. You must be in need of something." His little eyes crinkled again in a smile. "Well! Funny sort of day."

Mystery led us up the stairs and along a long, shady veranda, to rooms at the far end with doors and shutters made of rattan. We had a room each, side by side: and they were enormous and cool, with fans made of what looked like woven palm leaves hanging from the ceiling, moving back and forth.

"How do they do that?" I wondered.

"There are two men sitting outside pulling ropes," said Nick. "Downstairs. I saw them as we came in."

There wasn't much furniture in the rooms, but there were big beds, with fine milk-white mosquito nets draped over them; a wash-stand, a desk, and some long low cupboards. In one corner of my room there was an enormous old leather armchair, its seat saggy and worn from years of use: and Lash jumped up into it and curled up almost the moment he laid eyes on it. Long months ago on our sea voyage, he'd decided tropical weather was ideal for only one kind of activity, and that was sleeping. I bent to tease his panting, grinning face, but I could tell nothing was going to persuade him to move from here for some hours now.

On the far side of the rooms, doors opened onto another veranda, this one private, from which we could look out over the Professor's garden, and over the wall towards the trees and protruding rooftops of the city. I stepped out and, the moment I left the shade and gently-moving air of the room, the huge, static heat of outside hit me again like a brick. The humid rising air was making the view from the veranda shimmer, like a mirage. We were surrounded by plants, but almost none of them were the same as the ones we had at home. Tall palms, strange broad-leaved vines, huge ferns, trees with green pods like long beans dangling from them, bushes bursting with purple and pink flowers, long pointed leaves with serrated edges like the teeth of a saw. I leaned on the rail, looking down at the garden between the palm leaves; and something caught my eye which almost made me gasp.

Down on the smooth grass beneath one of the trees, I could

see a basket. Made of pale wickerwork, its tapering shape, starting narrow near the base and swelling out above the waist like a half-size human body, was instantly familiar.

"Nick," I said, staring at it, "Nick, come and look."

There was no one to be seen; the basket just sat there, silent and alone, like an object which had appeared in the shimmering garden out of a dream.

"That's the basket," I said.

"What are you talking about?" asked Nick.

"Damyata's basket," I said. "The one he had when he came to London. The one he kept his snake in."

Nick scoffed. "Don't be ridiculous. How can it be the same one? There must be millions of baskets like it."

But, although I didn't argue, I was sure I was right. I knew the basket the moment I'd seen it; I'd have recognised its shape anywhere. Nick didn't know it half so well as I did. I had *touched* it.

Our luggage wasn't expected until later in the day; and, when we'd washed, and changed into clean cotton clothes which had been prepared for our arrival, we left Lash in the big chair and went down to sample the tea upon whose provision the Professor had been so insistent. I wasn't sure I fancied hot tea in this weather, but, as we sat down and started sipping from the cups, we found it was surprisingly refreshing. Mystery and the other servants seemed to have disappeared, and we were on our own in the big book-lined room where the tea and fruit had been laid out on a long table covered with an impeccable white cloth.

At least, we *thought* we were alone.

On the far side of the room there were large glass doors leading into the garden, standing slightly ajar, with two enormous blue-patterned plant-pots either side of them; and, as I got up with my teacup in my hand to look out at the scene, in the glass pane of one of the open doors I noticed the reflection of something moving just inside the room. Down near the floor, I glimpsed a pair of hands, or possibly paws, scrabbling at the edge of one of the pots before disappearing behind it.

I jumped in surprise, and my tea sloshed out of the cup and onto the floor.

"Nick! There's something in the room!" I cried.

But, even as I spoke, I realised it wasn't some*thing* so much as some*one*. Ducking out from behind the pot, now, came a skinny brown girl-child, perhaps about nine or ten years of age, but tiny. Her hair was long and unkempt, and she watched us fixedly all the time as she moved. She was wearing nothing but a short apron or loin-cloth, made of what looked like dark brownish-red leaves. She made no noise, but didn't take her eyes off us as she darted sideways towards the table, took a piece of fruit, and popped it in her mouth.

Moments later, there was a brief echoing footfall from the hallway, and the Professor came bumbling in. The child's eyes darted to the door and, with a sudden phenomenally-acrobatic leap, she performed a handspring right over the table, past the Professor, and out into the hallway where she disappeared.

"Quite!" the Professor began, when he saw us, as though taking up a conversation broken off only moments earlier. "Jolly good. Well, I see you've, ah – jolly good."

"Who was that?" I asked him, astonished.

"What? What?" he shouted, as though he hadn't even noticed the half-naked creature practically somersaulting over his head as she left the room. "That? Oh, that was just Sarasvati."

"Sarah *who*?" asked Nick.

"Sarasvati," the Professor repeated, "she belongs to the fakir. Ah, that is, she's his daughter. Or so I believe. Undoubtedly."

"She belongs to the *what*?" I asked. I looked at Nick and he was trying not to laugh. The Professor must be beginning to think we were both completely stupid – or deaf, perhaps – but we really were feeling quite bewildered at the cascade of inexplicable phrases.

"Sorry, Professor," I said, "you might have to . . . we've only just arrived, and there's rather a lot to get used to."

"Undoubtedly," agreed the Professor, "not at all. Well! The fakir, you see, the fakir is a kind of mystic, sort of a holy kind of chappie, I believe. Well, you can see him out there now."

We stood up and went to the big glass doors, through which we could clearly see a man in a simple cotton garment like a wraparound shawl, pacing the garden barefoot, occasionally looking up, apparently talking to himself.

"He meditates, you know," the Professor was continuing, "spends a lot of time in a trance, sitting under that bo-tree over there. Mystic, you know, what's the word? Ah, an ascetic, that kind of thing. Denying himself the comforts of the flesh. Doesn't eat for months. Never washes or shaves. That kind of thing."

"And that girl is his daughter," I said, watching him.

"Ah, I suppose so," said the Professor. "Funny little thing, she is. Speaks English perfectly, would you believe, when she speaks at all. Seems to spend as much time with the animals as with people. Watches you, with those eyes of hers. Never misses a trick, don't you know. Sharp. Wily. Undoubtedly."

"Do they live here?" Nick asked.

"What? Well, yes, here and hereabouts. Part of the household, you might say. Don't know that I remember when they first came. They just seem to have been here all the time." He went over to the table to pour himself some tea. "You know, they were here first," he said. "The Indians, I mean. Some people seem to behave as though they have no right to be here at all. But this place is theirs, first and foremost, don't you know. At least, the way *I* see it. Make myself unpopular saying so." He coughed, almost apologetically, as though he thought someone might be listening.

"Does the elephant belong to you?" I asked.

"Oh – ah – you mean Punch?" said the Professor. "Well. Quite. I mean, yes. She's part of the family too. Quite the most, ah, venerable member, I should say. Punch, yes, indeed."

"Why's she called Punch?" asked Nick.

The Professor seemed to have to think about it – but then he laughed. "She was a baby," he said, "her brothers and sisters were working elephants, but they adopted her, don't you know, as a pet. The Indians went crazy over her. Like a person, they said. Too clever to work."

I wasn't sure I'd understood the answer.

"And Punch means . . . ?" I prompted him.

"Quite! Ah – Punch! Punch means five. *Paanch*, she's called, really. The fifth. She's the fifth in her family. Undoubtedly. A very special creature."

"How long have you lived here, Professor?" Nick asked.

"What? In this house?" The Professor slurped some tea while he worked it out. "Ah, forty-five, no, forty-eight years. This house was built for my father. Came out here to Calcutta when I was a boy. Only been back once. Hah! Life's here, you see. Can't imagine it now."

Sometimes it was hard to follow the Professor's abbreviated way of speaking. But my mind was working quickly.

"So – you knew Sir Septimus when he was out here, did you?" I asked, cautiously.

"Septimus, Harriet, Nicodemus, Hercules, Tarquin . . . knew the lot of them. The Cloys. And the Winters. *Liked* the Winters, don't you know. Jolly decent people. Such a shame about . . . Well, that's why I was so pleased to hear you were coming."

"And you knew our mother," I said quietly.

"Imogen?" said the Professor. "Yes, I did. I did indeed. Quite. Ah – I did indeed." His words slowed, and the mention of Imogen seemed to make him sink into deep reflection. We waited for him to elaborate: but it became clear once he'd been silent for half a minute that he wasn't going to, at least not unprompted.

There were a great many questions, I realised, which we were going to want to ask the Professor.

"Look, Mog," said Nick suddenly.

Outside in the garden, the fakir was crossing the lawn again: and this time he was carrying the basket we'd seen under the tree.

"So the basket belongs to *him*," I said.

"Has his snake inside it, I imagine," said the Professor. "Takes it with him all the time, don't you know. Deadly poisonous thing, it is, but it never bites him. Magnificent, heavy beast in there. But he's got some sort of power over it. The girl has too."

I caught Nick's eye.

"Where did he get it from?" I asked.

"Not sure I follow," said the Professor.

"I mean – have the snake and the basket always been his? Or did he – get them from someone else?"

The Professor blinked. "Don't know that I recall *when* he got them," he said. "I don't believe I remember a time when he didn't have it. Snakes can live a jolly long time, don't you know. Might have had it since it was hatched, for all I know."

Even now, I wasn't convinced I was mistaken. But as the Professor spoke, there was the slow squeak and clatter of a cart outside.

"Here come your things," he said.

Through the glass we could see a cart rolling up outside the house, drawn by a slow and stocky bullock with a big humped neck, and driven by an extraordinarily ugly-looking man. On the back of the cart was a big wooden chest; and its arrival provoked a flurry of activity in the courtyard. Mystery and a couple of other servants had bustled out of the house to deal with the delivery, and were speaking animatedly to the driver and gesticulating towards the chest.

"Why's Mystery called Mystery?" I asked, as we watched them.

"Beg pardon? Ah, well, quite. It's *Mistry*, don't you know. It means a kind of boss man, I suppose. At any rate, he's in charge of the other servants – lords it over them dreadfully, I should say. Loves to show them he's the boss, although he's a soft-hearted thing when it comes down to it. Wonderful, loyal chap, don't you know. Undoubtedly. Of course, he answers to Mrs Chakraborty like the rest of us."

"And who's she?"

"Ooh, the housekeeper," he said, in a tone of voice that hinted she needed to be treated with respect. "You'll meet her in no time, I've no doubt. But they know who you are. They've all had fair warning. You must ask for whatever you need."

He put his teacup down and gave us a beaming smile. "Well. I expect you'd like to go and unpack," he said. "The bearers will take your things upstairs. Why don't we meet again this evening, and you can tell me a little more about why you're here?"

*

"What do you think of him?" Nick asked me, upstairs, as we unfolded clothes from the heavy chest and looked for suitable places to put them away. The trunk had been stowed away on board the ship, and we hadn't opened it for months. After having worn the same clothes for so long, occasionally washing them out and putting them back on, finding all our things again was like a happy reunion.

"I rather like him," I said. "Don't you think he's just like an elephant?"

"Completely," agreed Nick. "Even the way he speaks – that kind of rumble he makes when he's trying to think of the words."

"Undoubtedly," I said, and Nick laughed.

"Were you watching him when he slurped his tea?" he said. "I expected him to dip his nose in it and suck it up."

"And he's got *tusks,*" I said. We both laughed again.

A puffed-up, pinky-white lizard watched us from high on the wall as we unpacked the trunk. I picked up a white linen dress that was lying on top of the pile of clothes in the chest: the most girlish piece of clothing I owned, which I'd found at Kniveacres but never worn. I supposed it must once have been Lady Cloy's: it certainly hadn't been bought for me. I held it up and looked at it. I'd brought it reluctantly, persuaded at the last minute to pack it, in case it was too hot to wear anything else.

"He knows a lot of things," I said quietly. "About Imogen."

"And about the Cloys, and our family," added Nick. "I'm sure he'll tell us if we ask him."

"I can't wait," I said. "He can tell us more than anyone's ever told us before. And yet, it scares me a bit. Do you know what I mean?"

Nick didn't reply directly, but I could tell he knew exactly what I meant.

"The first thing we need to ask him about is the diamond," he said. "That's why we're here, after all."

"I hope he can help," I said fervently.

"Melibeem said he would, didn't he? Said he's an antiquarian, and knows about local legends and that sort of thing, and there's no one more likely than him to know about the diamond, and what happened to it. And have you seen how many books there are in the house? Surely he can tell us *something* useful."

"Do you think the Captain's made it this far?" I wondered. "How would we know?"

"We'll have to go exploring and ask," said Nick. "Maybe tomorrow. We'll be able to find out. Someone like him can't arrive unnoticed."

"No," I said, "but, you know, neither can we."

There was a quiet rustle on the veranda outside. I started.

"A crow," said Nick.

"Does the Professor know what we've come for?" I wondered. "How much do you think Melibee's told him?"

"We'll find out, won't we?" Nick said. "He said he wanted to have a talk with us later."

I'd hung the white dress up in a cupboard, and now on top of the pile of clothes in the trunk was the little black diary with its ragged, torn spine. I'm not sure why we'd brought it with us, considering how little it told us: I'd just had the sense that it might be useful, or important. Moving some more clothes aside, now, I could see something else peeping out – something I'd completely forgotten we'd brought.

"Nick," I said, "look."

I pulled it out, and it made a tiny, high-pitched tinkling sound as I did so.

It was a jester's cap, a bit battered and dirty, made of multi-coloured cloth, with two little round brass bells sewn on the end of its cloth prongs.

"Remember this?" I said.

Again Nick didn't say anything. But another sudden noise on the veranda made me turn my head. There was a kind of scampering sound now, and a distinct moving shape in the bright sunshine out there.

"That's not a *crow*!" I exclaimed. I put the cap down and darted out to investigate. Something seemed to leap off the veranda as I moved.

Nick caught me up; and we were just in time to lean over the balcony and see the brown acrobatic form of Sarasvati, the monkey-girl, swinging herself off the lower branches of a climbing vine, and running across the lawn towards the far cluster of trees, with her head down, not looking back once.

CHAPTER 5
THE PROFESSOR'S STORY

Later, towards evening, it grew cooler, and the place seemed to come to life.

Mystery came to find us, and escorted us on a tour of the house. We hurried dutifully through the grand rooms, high-ceilinged and elaborately furnished with things brought from England, pictures and vases and books and ornaments. Far more interesting, though, were the kitchens and servants' quarters, with their bare floors and benches, little pictures of Indian gods, and cupboards and bottles full of exotic foods and spices: and Mystery became much more animated here, proudly bustling and ordering people around for our benefit. He introduced us to several more servants, with names like Dhobi and Bheesty and Chaprassy and Mussulchee, who hardly spoke English at all, but smiled a lot and seemed to make jokes about us to one another which they all found very funny. The thing I liked about them most was that they made a fuss of Lash, and immediately found some kitchen scraps to feed him, which he took and then licked their fingers clean for them, making them laugh.

After they'd been japing around for a few minutes, Mystery became stern, and barked something at them which obviously meant they should get on with their work. He held his arm out, to escort us away.

"Please to coming outside, Imogen and Dominic."

He was trying valiantly, and yet our names still didn't sound right the way he pronounced them.

"Call us Mog and Nick," I said. "It's what we prefer."

He seemed dubious, as though it might be overfamiliar; but he smiled with something like relief when we insisted.

"Is easier," he said. "Mog and Nick. Yes."

And now, as he showed us around the gardens, he used our names at every turn. "Mog and Nick, this is fishpond, with more than hundred *most* beautiful fish." And, "Mog and Nick, come and looking at rose garden. The Professor is most proud of his rose trees, Mog and Nick. Real English roses, just the tickety." And then: "Mog and Nick, come and meeting Punch."

I had never been close to an elephant before, and I wasn't sure how she was likely to behave as we approached her; but I was immediately spellbound by how gentle, and apparently understanding, such a huge creature could be. She was more docile than the calmest horse. She didn't shy away nervously, or make a sound, as we came up to her; nor did she so much as raise her head when we stroked and patted her trunk. Her skin was mud-brown, and almost as rough as stone, so that it felt a little like patting a small building. Her big eyes, far above our heads, looked down at us with the mildest curiosity, as though she had registered we were unfamiliar people, but wasn't the slightest bit troubled. I was making Lash keep his distance, because I was anxious at first that she might hurt him – and he did seem very wary of her long, mobile trunk – but she had plainly worked out in no time that he wasn't the kind of creature she was going to have to defend herself against.

Mystery was talking to her in a deep, musical voice; and after a few moments he summoned another servant, seemingly her keeper, and they both put out their arms and leaned against her huge flank as they had a conversation.

Mystery turned to us. "Would you like to riding her?" he asked. But, before we could answer, something dropped out of a tree behind us and, when we turned, came scampering past us. It was Sarasvati, the fakir's daughter; and with extraordinary agility she seemed almost to run up the side of the elephant, somehow finding sufficient footholds in the rough skin to make it all the way up onto Punch's back. She sat there, ten feet up, gazing down at us with her head on one side; and, despite the sudden unannounced presence of something on her back, Punch apparently remained unperturbed.

Mystery and the other servant stood back as Sarasvati leaned over and crooned something into Punch's ear; and then, with a lurch, the elephant moved off, taking the tiny girl out from under the shade of the palm trees and around the garden. She sat up straight, her feet tucked in behind the creature's great flat ears, chattering commands as they went, which Punch appeared to obey without hesitation.

"She's completely in control of it," murmured Nick.

We watched in admiration as they did a circuit of the garden, the giant docile beast and the tiny, agile child. As they came past us again, she shouted something down to the keeper, who shouted back rather crossly; and, with a screeched command from the girl, Punch stopped walking.

Sarasvati was suddenly standing right beside us on the grass, having slipped down from the creature's back with so little effort and fuss that we hadn't even noticed. I remembered the Professor mentioning that she spoke English.

"That was very good riding," I said to her.

She turned. "To show you," she said.

"When did you learn to ride her like that?" I asked.

She laughed, a short silvery sound. "Learn to walk. Learn to speak. Learn to ride elephant. Baby things. Long long time ago."

"You are Sarasvati, aren't you?" I said to her. "The Professor has told us about you."

"You are Mog and Nick, come from England yesterday," said Sarasvati. "But Professor has not told me one word about you." She looked at us, with a sly smile. "Perhaps you will tell me more, yourselves."

"Perhaps," I said.

Now that she wasn't hiding from us and we could see her properly, there was something quite beguiling about her. Although her features were pointed, like a monkey's, with hair which had certainly never been cut and probably never combed, she was impishly attractive. Her face wore an expression of faint amusement – of *mischief,* might be a better word – all the time. Her striking brown eyes were never still, darting this way and that, constantly alert to what was going on around her. She was so thin, she looked as though she had been assembled from a pile of brown sticks; but there was something in her eyes, and in the way she spoke, which suggested a wisdom far beyond her years.

"You going to ride Punch then?" she asked suddenly. "I tell her to be gentle with you." She darted off, and stood right in front of the elephant, speaking up into her face. The creature lifted her trunk, and its sensitive, animate tip sniffed and snuffled around the little girl's face and fingers.

"Get up," she called to us. "Punch doesn't mind. Mahout will help you."

I was quite excited at the idea of riding the elephant, but hadn't for the life of me been able to work out how we were going to get up there: so it was a relief when the keeper produced a long rope-ladder, and flung it right over the top of Punch, so that the opposite end of it dangled down her other flank. Mystery held the rope tight on the other side, and the keeper wordlessly signalled to us to climb up.

I looked at Nick.

"You first," he said. I grasped the ladder with both hands.

There was no saddle on Punch's back, just a rather dirty knitted blanket across her hairy shoulders, which, with Sarasvati shouting instructions from below, I clambered onto. Motioned by the keeper, Nick climbed up after me, and sat behind me; and now the keeper pulled the rope-ladder away.

Mystery called up to us. "You need to stretching out the feet," he said, "and tickling her behind the ears. That is how to control."

"Talk to her," piped up Sarasvati. "She knows commands, but you can just talk to her, say anything. Voice will reassure."

And, as I shifted my position so my legs reached down as far as they could, I found I could brush her great flat ears with my toes, and that squeezing my heels into her neck just behind them made her respond.

It took some getting used to: her pace was slow but she seemed to roll alarmingly, so it took a lot of effort to stay on her, with no harness of any kind. The keeper walked beside us, and Mystery watched us from under the tree where we started, occasionally showing his teeth in a smile or shouting "*Wery*-wery good!" For a time Sarasvati watched us too; but by the time we'd circled the garden once, she had disappeared.

"She's something, isn't she?" I said to Nick behind me.

He must have thought I meant the elephant, because he replied: "She's *completely* beautiful."

We were sitting up at the same level as the foliage of the trees, and monkeys which had been watching us from the safety of the branches scattered as we swayed towards them. I could see right over the garden wall, to the road outside, to the sun sinking between the houses on the other side of it, and even across to the ruined old fort in the distance, and the tops of the ships' masts that indicated where the river was. It was an extraordinary feeling.

When we'd been round a couple of times, the keeper led

Punch to the place we'd started from, and flung the ladder up to us. We scrambled down and I went to reassure Lash, who was looking as though he was quite sure we'd been abducted by this strange and enormous creature. I felt a bit dizzy, standing on the ground again.

We thanked Punch, and her keeper, for the ride. Beneath the broad-leaved bodhi tree we could see the fakir again, and the basket. There was a huge bare patch of ground nearby with a kind of mound in it, like a scab in the earth, and, as we walked past, my attention was caught by the ripple of movement. A line of ants, brownish-red in colour, was moving towards the mound, and as I knelt to look at them more closely I could see they were nearly all carrying something: pieces of leaves, other dead insects, or what looked like grains of rice and sugar.

"Look, Lash," I said, "we don't get ants like these at home, do we?"

They were huge, most of them an inch in length, so that I could make out each part of their segmented bodies quite distinctly, including the forked mouth-parts at the front of their heads. They were disappearing into various holes and cracks in the dirt, and others were emerging, their burdens lifted, dispersing to find more treasure. I tried to track down the end of the ant procession, but it stretched out of sight.

Nick had gone to watch the fakir. He was sitting cross-legged, in the shade of the tree, with his basket before him, humming quietly.

"Is your snake in there?" Nick asked him.

The fakir didn't reply. But, as he hummed, there was a small dry sound from inside the basket, and suddenly the lid began to move. Nick took a step backwards.

I went over to join him. The fakir's humming intensified, a repetitive keening sound, at a single constant pitch. As we watched, a small brassy-looking head appeared in the neck of the basket, sharply pointed at the front, with black eyes like tiny polished beads. It wavered, as though hanging on an invisible thread suspended from a branch high above. Out of the pointed head came a darting forked tongue, three or four times, each time so quickly it was hardly there before it was back inside. And now, as the snake hovered, its neck hunched and swelled, to form a hood with a curious curved white marking upon it, like a looping nose and two white eyes, a crude painted mask.

It rose, gently, and sank again. The fakir seemed to be controlling it with his low voice, holding it in thrall.

"How does he do that?" I whispered.

The cobra's head turned, slowly, from left to right and back again, its tiny black eyes unmoving, its tongue flicking repeatedly from its mouth, as though tasting the air for the scent of whatever prey might be nearby.

And then the fakir's humming died, and the snake hovered for a few more seconds, and then sank out of sight into the basket. The fakir seemed to emerge from a kind of trance. He reached forward to place the lid back on top of the basket; and then he seemed to see us for the first time. He showed a wide grin of atrociously grey, rotten teeth.

The shadows had grown long, and Mystery wanted us to go inside and get ready for dinner.

"Is the snake really dangerous?" Nick asked him as we walked in.

"Snake? Oh my, yes," said Mystery. "Wery-wery poisonous. Bite can killing a grown man, Master Nick. Much much pain, and person shaking, and sweating, and limbs going hard and stiff. Screaming pain and foaming mouth. *Wery* dangerous! Best to staying long long way off."

The path to the house took us back past the walled rose garden. The scent of the garden had changed with the coming of evening, and so had the sound of the bird-calls around us – which were no quieter, but seemed somehow less raucous than they had been during the daytime, and were being joined all the time by the rhythmic chirping of unseen insects. Silent flying creatures had started darting around our heads, coming down almost low enough to brush our hair with their wings before swooping back up into the trees: not birds, but bats, moving too quickly for us to see them properly in the dying light.

But now, through the bird and insect sounds, another strange noise met our ears.

"What's that?" asked Nick, turning his head to listen.

"I don't know," I said.

It was a human voice, but it wasn't speaking words – at least, nothing like any language I'd ever heard. It was more like a rapid, tripping rattle of rhythmic sounds, rising and falling slightly in tone as they were repeated.

"Dhara-ka-ta-ta-tang. Dhara-ka-ta-ta-tang."

"How strange," I said, "maybe it's a kind of song."

"Dha-ram-ta-ta-ta-tang, dha-jang-jang, ta-ta-ta-tam," went the voice.

"It sounds like a child," said Nick.

"Perhaps it's Sarasvati again," I said.

"Must be a kind of game," Nick surmised.

Mystery chivvied us inside. As we walked in beneath flower-strewn pergolas and high vine-covered walls, back towards the servants' quarters, we could hear the girl's voice more clearly than ever: we couldn't see her, but it sounded as though she were sitting on the wall almost directly above our heads. And the strange song rose into the air, with the myriad notes of the birds, and echoed out across the giant leaves and hot rooftops of the city.

"Dhara-ka-ta-ta-tang. Ta-tam-tam, dha-jang, dha-jang, ka-ta-ta-tam. Dhara-ka-tang. Dhara-dam."

After dinner, the Professor invited us to join him in his library, where the servants had laid out sweets and whisky. It was dark outside now, and the windows had to be closed to prevent moths the size of a grown man's hand from whirring into the room. To help the circulation of air, the big fans above our heads – or *pankahs* as we'd learned they were called – were moving to and fro constantly. Lash settled between my feet, and Majara the cheetah sat imperiously on a leather chair beside the Professor. Every now and again while he was speaking he'd place his hand gently on her head, and when he did so she closed her eyes in pleasure. The two animals regarded one another across the room, Majara lofty and unruffled, Lash with an expression of something like effrontery. But they showed no sign of aggression towards one another.

"Well! Funny sort of day," was the Professor's rather predictable opening comment. "Fact is, I get a letter from old Melibee telling me that Sir Septimus has been carried off – first I knew of it, sounds a funny sort of business, the way he tells it – and right at the end he says would it be all right if you two arrive in Calcutta, and he hopes so because you're more or less here already. Well, of course I couldn't be more, ah – delighted to see you. But I can't quite fathom – that is, I'm not sure I – well, maybe you'd better tell me what's brought you here, Imogen and Dominic."

Nick spoke first.

"We need your help, Professor," he said. "We've come to Calcutta to find something. It could be tremendously important. At least – important to the two of us."

With me adding the odd detail here and there, Nick retold the story of Sir Septimus's death, and the debts and troubles of the estate as revealed by the accountants. He told him about Charnock House, and the attempt to restore it, and how the rebuilding had had to be suspended because the money had run out. He told him about his encounter with the Captain, back in the Jolly Lighterman: the expedition to find the diamond, and the few details we'd been able to find out about it since. All the time, the Professor listened intently: sometimes leaning forward with particular interest, sometimes emitting a cough or splutter of astonishment, and nodding often.

"Well!" he rumbled, when we'd finished. "Quite! Ah – I can see why you felt the need to come. Undoubtedly."

"So what we really need to know, Professor," I said hopefully, "is where the diamond is now, or anything at all you can tell us about it."

"We've brought a map," Nick said, helpfully.

"Have you now?" said the Professor. "Well, that might be of considerable help."

"The only problem is," I said, "we don't know where it's a map *of.* It hasn't really got any place-names on it, or anything." I handed him the big, ornate sheet of paper we'd printed at Cramplock's shop, and which we'd carefully kept in the bottom of our trunk on the sea voyage. The Professor appeared to flap his ears slightly as he spread it out in front of him.

"Look," I said, running my finger across the paper, "all these lines must be roads. Don't you think? And here – see what it says. *The sole source of your fortune.*"

"*Seek the point to the right,*" added Nick, eagerly.

"Hmm," said the Professor, "as you say, most – ah – unconventional."

"Do you recognise it?" I asked anxiously.

The Professor squinted, looked bewildered, blew air from between his lips.

"We thought it might be a map of Calcutta," said Nick.

The Professor frowned. "Well, it's not that, Master Nick,

certainly not. Nor of any individual part of Calcutta I can immediately think of."

"Couldn't you find out where it's a map of?" asked Nick. "If it's somewhere near here, perhaps it might not be so hard?"

"You see, we *have* to stop the Captain finding it first," I added. "We're fairly sure he has a copy of this too."

"Does he now?" said the Professor, thinking hard. "I see."

"We were *so* hoping you could help us," I said. "Are there no other clues to where the diamond is? No secret papers? Or local tales?"

The Professor laughed, shortly. "Local tales, yes, there may be plenty of those," he said, "but written evidence, no, not a jot, as far as anyone knows. The diamond disappeared years ago. What you've already read, back in England, told you the main, ah – facts. As Melibee says, there isn't much left out of that account. I don't want to bore you."

"Really, Professor," I said eagerly, "you won't bore us. I'm sure. Please tell us what you can."

The Professor seemed surprised, as though it were the first time a young person had told him he wasn't boring.

"Well," he said, "if you're sure." We looked at him expectantly. "This diamond of yours," he continued, "the, ah – Blue Eye of Winter, as it's sometimes known, has a powerful legend attached to it. Undoubtedly, it's a Golconda stone, don't you know, from the same mines that produced all the greatest diamonds in the world. It's been talked of in Bengal legend since ancient times – far longer, I can tell you, than that book of yours allows. *Sasanka-ki-aankh* is what it used to be called, which is – ah – the 'eye of Sasanka', don't you know. Sasanka was one of the greatest of Bengal's rulers, way back in history. Whether it ever really belonged to Sasanka, all that time ago, no one can say; but it's been named after him, and it certainly belonged to the Bengal princes for hundreds of years. Every time there was a conquest, the new ruler would claim it as their greatest prize. They all guarded it jealously, some of them even tried to hide it, to stop it ever being lost. But by all accounts it was always being stolen, and taken abroad, and then stolen back. It must have changed hands countless times down the centuries. It's a most remarkable stone. Most, ah – extraordinarily beautiful, and valuable."

"What about the curse, Professor?" Nick asked.

"Ah, well. You know, a lot of stones like that have curses attached, maybe to make people change their minds about stealing them, and maybe just because the power they have over people is so great. They drive people to desperate, terrible deeds, which can make anyone with something so valuable in their possession seem cursed."

"Is that why the princes gave it to the British as a gift?" asked Nick. "To get rid of it?"

The Professor snorted. "I doubt it very much," he said. "The Nawabs wouldn't lightly give away something so valuable, that had been fought over for so many generations. I suspect the book you found wasn't telling the whole truth, and it was actually taken by force, or by some subterfuge. The British have a way of – ah – *encouraging* people here to give them gifts. If you take my meaning."

"So did the curse pass to the Winter family?" I asked.

"Hmm. You might say so," said the Professor. "And the Cloys had it even worse, if you believe the superstition. Certainly some jolly awful things happened after it was, ah – acquired. You know something about the history of your family, don't you?"

"Well, we—" began Nick.

"Not enough," I cut in. "*Do* tell us."

The Professor scratched his wrinkled head. "Quite," he said, uncertainly. "Well – where would you like me to start? You know, I *really* don't want to bore you. Maybe another time."

I wasn't going to let him stop now. "Professor," I said gently, "two years ago we both thought we were orphans. Neither of us had a *clue* about our family. Nobody's ever really explained it to us properly. Do you think you could?"

Again the Professor looked surprised; but he cleared his throat, and gathered his thoughts. "There might be details I've, ah – forgotten," he said, "but – well. I'll have a bash. Here goes."

He reached for the decanter on the little round table beside him, and poured himself another thumb of whisky.

"Your ancestors," he said, sighing, "in the middle of the last century – well, I suppose I mean your great-grandfather, and his younger brother – ah – I think that's it – they came here to work for the East India Company in their youth, and never left. You know, the Company has made a lot of men rich. It's made a lot of men rotten, too, and driven a lot of men mad. But your great-grandfather, particularly, built up quite a fortune. He had a big house built, out here, and raised a family, and when his estate passed to his son, John Winter, it included the diamond. John Winter looked after things well, and married, and in the Eighties, I suppose, or maybe the early Nineties, ah, he had a daughter. Called Imogen."

"Our mother," I said.

"Ah, quite," said the Professor. "Well – alongside the Winters there was another very powerful Calcutta family – the Cloys – whose ancestry went even further back, and whose wealth eclipsed the Winters', and pretty much everyone else's. There were seven Cloy brothers; Hubert was the eldest, but there were so many of them that, by the time the youngest was born, he was practically grown up. Well now. An aunt of your grandfather's, I believe, married one of the elder Cloy boys. Goodness, this is rather complicated, forgive me." He paused while he muttered to himself for a while, gathering his thoughts. "Quite. And a cousin of your grandfather's ended up marrying the youngest, Septimus. Well – that much you know."

"That was Harriet," I said, helpfully. "Lady Cloy, eventually."

"Undoubtedly," assented the Professor. "Ah – now then. Dash it all, I knew the Cloy family for years, I was one of their closest friends, but even I can see some of their conduct wasn't entirely – honest, don't you know. It might come as a shock to you two youngsters, but people tend not to come all this way just to help the Indians. They come to help themselves, in general, and make a pot of money they can sail home with while they've enough life left to enjoy it."

"That's not so much of a shock, Professor," observed Nick with a smile.

"Quite. Well, where was I? Ah, the diamond. Indeed! The Cloys' lawyers were jolly clever, you know, and they made sure that ownership of the Winter diamond passed to the Cloy family along with the marriage alliances. Well, the point is, they went about it a bit sneakily, you see. John Winter, your grandfather, don't you know, was an honourable sort of chap, and I don't know that he entirely understood what had been going on, until he realised that the Cloys had got their hands on more or less everything he possessed. Of course, he only produced a daughter, and there were the Cloys with all these male heirs, which made things even more difficult. Legally, you know. He was going to have one devil of a job wresting much back from them, even if he'd a mind to. Well, I imagine he thought it would make for an easier life if he was with them rather than against them, and he thought it might be a decent thing if he got his daughter married off to one of them too. This is Imogen, you know. And the chap he had his eye on was a nephew of Septimus, one of the two sons of Maximilian Cloy. But, well now – I don't know whether I should be saying this." He paused, and took another rather nervous gulp of whisky.

I leaned forward. "It won't be news to us, Professor," I said, "that unfortunate things happened in the family. Nick's right: we've already worked out that not everyone, er – behaved well."

"Well," the Professor said cautiously, "that might be a point to start from. Look here," he went on, "not to beat about the bush, some of the Cloys were pretty nasty people. I knew John Winter, and he was a jolly decent chap, but far too trusting. He let people run rings around him. He was always prepared to believe the best of others – and believe me, that's not a recipe for prosperity, especially out here. He was as misguided about the Cloys as anyone else. He should have kept his distance, but he was determined to ingratiate himself further. He brought Imogen into the close influence of the Cloys, right from her being a young thing. Ah – with disastrous consequences." He looked at us intently. "Your mother was betrothed to the nephew," he said, "and it was then discovered that Septimus had been – *wooing* her too."

"But he was married to Harriet," I said.

"Ah – quite. Undoubtedly, he was. And yet he still *wooed* your mother, and he *wooed* a number of other poor young creatures who were no doubt desperate to give him no encouragement. And of course it all became too horrible, and Lancelot, the nephew – the intended, as it were – ended up challenging Septimus to a duel, there on the bank by Tolly's Nullah." He waved an arm towards the window, in a vague direction, from which we assumed the place he meant wasn't very far away. He took a deep breath. "Well now. Septimus agreed to the challenge, and shot young Lancelot dead," he said.

Nick and I were staring at him.

"They tried to hush it up," the Professor continued, "but

there was too much talk, and the only course was to send Septimus home to England for good. Harriet went with him, of course, and his older brothers Hercules and Maximilian went too, to help arrange his affairs back at home. They had some influence in the government, don't you know, and they were jolly hopeful they could secure him a knighthood, that sort of thing, make sure he went back without too much, ah – dishonour. Well, John Winter was distraught, and when after that all the stories started to come out about Septimus, and about, ah, various other misdeeds down the years, he couldn't bear it and he died of shame, or so they said."

"And what did Imogen think?" I asked quietly.

"What what? Well, I was about to get to that." He seemed to search for the right words again. "In a way, ah – it was a blessing John Winter died when he did, and didn't live to see the scandal which ensued the following year, because that would certainly have carried the poor chap off. Imogen – ah – your mother . . ." He seemed to be sweating, and for the first time pulled out a large silk handkerchief with which to dab at his big forehead. "Young Imogen, having suddenly become free again, albeit under tragic circumstances, was seen by rather a number of young men as, ah – a fair catch. Moves were quickly afoot to rescue the situation by selecting another eligible and wealthy young fellow to be her, ah – suitor. But she was a jolly headstrong young woman. Knew her own mind, you might say. She was a *remarkable* girl, quite a – quite unique, I'd go so far as to say. There weren't many who could resist the Cloys, men *or* women, but by golly she was determined. Well, she pulled, as the phrase has it, the rug from under everyone's feet, by, ah – falling for an Indian."

"A man called Damyata," I said.

"A man very much called, as you say," the Professor went on, "ah – Damyata. Quite so. Well, the scandal of the shooting and the unwelcome attentions of Septimus was as nothing compared to the scandal attached to this. You'll notice, don't you know, that a great many Englishmen out here take Indian mistresses and wives. But for an English girl to fall in love with an Indian, and not only refuse to show remorse but to go about laying secret plans for him to become her *husband*, well, that's a different kettle of, ah – quite. I mean, that's, ah – just not done. At all."

"Not only that," I said, looking at Nick. "She discovered she was expecting twins."

"Well. You know the story," said the Professor, sitting back in his chair. "You two are the twins. You know it better than I do from that point onwards."

"And poor Imogen was sent home," I said, "and the twins were born before they got to London, and she fell terribly ill. And, knowing she was going to die, she wrote a letter to Harriet, begging her to look after us. But Sir Septimus came to London to collect us, and gave us away to orphanages instead, and then pretended to Harriet that we had died, like our mother."

The Professor chewed his top lip, rather grimly. "The Cloys defeated her in the end, for all her determination," he said. "Poor girl."

"So what happened to the diamond after all this?" Nick asked. "We heard that it had been lost after a family scandal. Was this it?"

The Professor stood up, and walked over to the other side of the room. At first I thought he was going to fetch a book, but it appeared he was just stretching his legs. He had a big patch of sweat in the middle of his back, from sitting in the leather chair in the hot evening: and now he stood under the swaying fans for a few minutes while he spoke.

"The truth is," he said, "it disappeared, and no one knows where it is to this day. It was found to be missing, almost by accident, not long after the business with Septimus and Lancelot. There was uproar. Septimus had only just left for England, and several people put two and two together and decided he must have taken it with him, without telling anyone. That's certainly possible. But then – what did he do with it?"

I looked at Nick.

"What about – Damyata taking it with him?" I asked cautiously. "Isn't that possible too?"

The Professor puffed out his cheeks. "Well," he said. "That was also widely believed, at the time. He seemed, ah – a convenient figure to blame. It's just that it's never turned up anywhere else, and he's never been seen again. So how can we know?"

I opened my mouth to say something, but Nick frowned at me.

"It's true, the most likely explanation is it was stolen," said the Professor. "By Damyata – who knows? By someone. But you know, there's another possibility. Someone in the family might have decided it was more trouble than it was worth, and disposed of it somehow. So many grisly things happened, during those years, that the family finally began to take the legend of the curse seriously."

"What sort of things?" Nick asked.

The Professor snorted. "Catastrophe upon catastrophe," he said. "Well, two of the brothers had died tragically, you know, long before the Imogen business ever happened. It must be nigh on sixty years since Sir Hubert died, when he was crushed by an elephant sitting on his tent. When I first came here the family had put that tragedy behind them, and there was plenty of money, and it all seemed to be going tolerably well. But then, you know, after a while, some jolly strange things began to happen again. His widow, Margaret, went missing one night and was found in a state of complete terror, cowering by the wall of a neighbour's house, howling like an ape. No one ever got any sense out of her as to what had happened, but she never recovered, and she died a few days later. Not long after that, the second of the seven brothers, Nicodemus, was working on an engineering project for the Company, down at Ballygunge, when he fell into a ditch. Nobody noticed in time, and they tipped a whole load of earth in on top of him, and he was buried alive. His widow was expecting a baby, but the poor child was born terribly malformed, and didn't survive more than a month."

"How awful," I said.

"I think it must have been around then that your mother came out to India," the Professor continued. "She was about ten years old, don't you know, when she first came here from England. Well, she was such a bright young thing, she cheered everyone up, and things seemed to get better again, for a time. But gradually the, ah – the skies darkened again, you might say. Business suddenly wasn't going so well, and there were all sorts of whisperings and gossip, especially about Septimus. Imogen, you know, had grown into a beautiful young woman by now. Then all that terrible business came up with poor young Lancelot getting shot, and Septimus being sent away. Then the diamond itself was lost, and poor John Winter died not long afterwards. Then there was the scandal of Imogen: and when Hercules and Maximilian were returning from England they were both drowned when their ship was lost on the voyage. And even that wasn't the end of it, because, bless my soul, Maximilian's other son, Galahad, was pulled to pieces by monkeys when he ventured into a cave on his own. The poor boy was just six years old."

I shuddered. "No wonder they thought they were cursed," I said.

"Undoubtedly," said the Professor. "Well, as you can see, what really happened to the diamond is still a mystery. I thought the curse had been laid to rest, but after hearing Melibee's account of what happened last year, I can't help wondering. Of course, now that Septimus is dead too, there's simply no one left who might know."

There was a significant silence. Until now, it had never

occurred to us that the awful events at Kniveacres last autumn, culminating in Sir Septimus's death, might have had anything to do with the diamond's curse.

Majara the cheetah had fallen asleep, keeled over on her side in the enormous chair next to the Professor, and was emitting a low, contented snoring sound. I suddenly found myself yawning. I felt quite light-headed: after the day's heat, and the excitement of our arrival, I was exhausted.

"It's all very exciting," I said, "but I'm afraid I'm going to have to go to bed."

"Well, well," said the Professor, "it's late. Undoubtedly. Ah – I have work to do tomorrow, but Mistry will show you the city. And please treat the place as your own. You seem to have settled in jolly quickly in any case."

"Thank you, Professor," said Nick, politely, as we took our leave. "You've been most helpful."

"And interesting," I added, reassuringly.

When we got back upstairs, we found about a hundred insects of varying sizes fluttering and dancing around the oil lamp I'd left burning in the room; and I realised with exasperation that the shutters were wide open to the darkness.

"I'm sure I . . ." I began. I went over and closed them.

When I turned back to face the room, I stood still.

"What's the matter?" asked Nick, seeing my expression.

"Something's wrong," I said slowly. "Someone's been in here."

He looked around. "Can't see anything missing," he said.

"Maybe one of the servants has been up, to get the beds ready, or fill up the water."

"No. Someone else," I said. "I can feel it." There was a tingling sensation down my back, similar to the way I'd felt at the top of the stairs, back in Charnock House in London a few months ago. I couldn't explain it. As I looked around the room, and my gaze ranged over the wall near the wash-stand, I noticed something I was almost certain I hadn't seen before.

There was a picture hanging on the wall, in an oval wooden frame, next to the mirror. I hadn't looked at the pictures in the room very closely before now; but I could have sworn the picture that hung there when we first arrived was smaller – and that it had been square, not oval at all. As I went closer to it, and saw what it depicted, I gasped.

This couldn't possibly have been here this afternoon. I would have noticed it instantly, if it had been.

"What is it?" asked Nick.

"Come and look," I said. "Who do you think this is?"

It was a painting of a young girl in a white dress, sitting in a green garden. With two baby cheetahs.

"Don't you think it must be Imogen?" I said, trembling. "It looks like the garden here. And that must be Majara, and the male cheetah who died. Who else would it be, Nick, in this garden, playing with them, all those years ago? It's a picture of our mother."

We both stared at it. If that's who it really was, it was the first time either of us had seen a likeness of her. There wasn't much detail in the face, but there was enough to see that she had been beautiful, and happy. She appeared to be about fifteen or sixteen. The way she was holding one of the cheetah cubs with both hands, just beneath its ears, reminded me of the way I always fondled Lash whenever I was sitting with him.

The longer I gazed at it, the more incredible it seemed, to be looking at a portrait of my mother for the first time in my life. I had dreamed about her, again and again, ever since I was a tiny child, without having a clue what she really looked like. And the portrait was sufficiently similar to the tranquil, reassuring figure of my dreams to make me quite convinced of whom I was looking at.

There was a lump in my throat.

"Is she the way you imagined her?" I asked, in a quiet voice.

"I suppose so," said Nick. "It's strange, isn't it – of course, we're not even sure it's her."

"It is, Nick," I said. "I know it is." I had never been more sure of anything. It wasn't just the Professor's story, ringing in my head, that convinced me: it was the way I *felt* when I looked at it. "You know, Nick, this wasn't here before," I said. "There was some other picture. A little square one, I think, but not this. I swear I'd have noticed it."

He shrugged. "Maybe the Professor had them changed around, to please us."

I went over to the chest containing our things.

"Something odd's happening, Nick," I said. "I just want to check." I lifted the lid and began hunting through quickly, lifting the layers of clothing we hadn't yet bothered unpacking.

All the clothes seemed to be there. The black cover of Miss Thynne's diary met my eye, where I'd left it. Further down, among the clothes, was an ornate box of dried fruit Melibee had given us for the voyage, which we'd put back in the trunk, the fruit long since eaten.

"It's all there," I said, relieved.

"Of course it is," said Nick. "Who would take our things? Any of the servants would know they'd be found out."

But I was looking around, on the bed, now. And lifting up the clothes in the chest again, to double-check.

"What have you lost?"

I looked up. "The jester's cap, Nick," I said. "It's gone."

"It can't have." He came over. "Didn't you take it out this afternoon?"

"Yes but I put it back. I know I did." I was rummaging among the clothes now, pulling them out one by one. "It's not here, Nick."

"It will be. It's just mixed up in all this mess you've made." He started folding the clothes, laying them systematically in a pile on the bed.

"It's *not* here, Nick," I protested. "I know what's happened. Sarasvati's taken it. She was out on the balcony, spying on us, when I got it out before, wasn't she? I bet she spotted it and fancied it for herself."

"I wouldn't be so sure," muttered Nick.

But I had dashed out onto the veranda already, to see if I could see her lurking in the darkness anywhere; or hear the giveaway sound of the little bells jingling on the cap.

I breathed in the hot air, full of exotic sweet scents wafting up towards the balcony from the broad leaves and petals of the plants in the garden. The Professor's story, and our mother's picture, filled my head. I felt very peculiar: as though, somehow, standing here in the dark, I was in the middle of everything that had happened then, not the events that were taking place now. As though I were not Mog, at all, but someone else.

"He's here," I said softly to myself.

I became aware of Nick, standing on the veranda by my side, looking out at the city. "What did you say?" he asked me.

"I don't know," I said. "I – I don't think I said anything, did I?"

But my head felt light, and the humid night air, the huge sky, the river and the distant swamps and jungles beyond, felt suddenly timeless: full of murmurs, full of invisible presences, of years ago.

CHAPTER 6
A VERY BAD PLACE

The next day we woke up itching.

"I've been bitten," I said to Lash as I sat up in bed. And, as I hunted around on my skin, I realised: "I've been bitten *everywhere*."

Lumps had appeared on my neck, my legs, the side of my face, and an especially angry one just in the crook of my elbow which was driving me to distraction as I got up and washed. We'd slept for a long time. I'd been vaguely aware of a flurry of activity in the house earlier, but had fallen asleep again, and now the sunlight outside the rattan shutters was bright and harsh, and the heat and humidity were fierce: so that, only a few minutes after I'd splashed myself with cool water at the wash-stand, I felt as though I needed to do so again. While I was inspecting my face in the mirror, I noticed Lash sniffing at something on the floor behind me.

"Leave it," I said to him suddenly. He was showing a great deal of interest in a kind of huge centipede, like a black scrubbing-brush, which was crawling along the skirting. "*Leave* it. It will bite you, you stupid dog. Or poison you. Come *here*."

I took another long look at the portrait of Imogen. The hazy light struck me again, the sense of heat the picture conveyed; it could have been painted yesterday, although I knew it must be more than twenty years ago. The indistinct features of her young face, the blur of her white dress. The elegant cheetahs on the grass in front of her. It seemed even more incredible, more dreamlike, than it had last night.

There was no sound from Nick's room next door; and I went to peep in, to see if he was still asleep. The room was bright with sunlight, and empty. The mosquito netting had been lifted clear of the bed, and a muslin curtain flapped idly at the veranda door, which had been opened in an attempt to get some air into the room.

I went out onto the veranda; and now I could see him, down in the Professor's walled rose garden, alone. He was standing on tiptoe beside an ornate plaster urn on a plinth, which was supposed to look elegant and impressive from ground level but which, I could see from above, was full of stagnant green rainwater and half-submerged rose petals. He was blowing on it, to make the petals stir.

I wasn't hungry, and it was almost certainly hours past breakfast-time; but the first place I went when we got downstairs was to the kitchen, to find water and food for Lash. The stone floor was wet, as though it had just been swilled down, and the place smelled strongly of the brackish, faintly-discoloured water that was brought regularly into the house in big pails. To get through the door into the kitchen I had to say "Excuse me" to a pair of boys, slightly younger than myself, who were standing fooling around in the doorway. One was rake-thin, the other much plumper: Mystery had mentioned them yesterday, and their names were something like Bulbul and Jumjum, though I had no idea which was which. Mussulchee, another of the servants I already knew, was there; and so was the housekeeper, Mrs Chakraborty, bustling from cupboard to cupboard, tidying up, with her long black hair tied severely in a bun behind her head, and barking instructions at Mussulchee. She was a drawn-looking, rather unsmiling woman, who made her displeasure clear when the other servants appeared to be enjoying themselves too much. She seemed especially brusque and cross this morning, as I approached her tentatively from behind.

She said something to me in Hindustani, with her back to me – believing, I suppose, that I was another of the servants. Then she realised who I was, and turned.

"Morning," I said. "Could I have something for the dog, please?"

"*Haa*," she said. "For dog, something." She knew quite a lot of English words, but her sentences sounded a little as though someone had thrown them up into the air and the words had landed in a random order. There were some scraps in a dish on the shelf, covered with a cloth: possibly set aside for Majara the cheetah; but she put them down quite happily for Lash, who began to wolf them down. Mrs Chakraborty turned back to her shelf of provisions. "Cupboards all today upside down isn't it," she said, crossly. "That girl is. Sarasvati is. Little thief, nothing else." She continued wrenching things around the kitchen from place to place. As she closed her hands around a big spice jar, she could suddenly tell something was wrong. A look of exasperation crossed her face; she took the lid off the jar, peered inside, and exclaimed loudly.

To my astonishment, she reached inside and pulled out a human arm.

Followed, seconds later, by Sarasvati climbing out, laughing. I blinked in disbelief. It was like a conjuring trick. The jar didn't look big enough for a baby to fit inside, let alone a child of ten. But the girl's joints were so supple, and her chest and hips so small, she could squeeze her way out of the narrow neck like a paper puppet that had come to life after being folded up inside.

"Sarasvati, wait a minute," I began, "don't run off, I want to—"

But Sarasvati was dodging a furious slap from Mrs Chakraborty, and had run out into the garden before I could get another word out.

"That child!" exclaimed the housekeeper. "So much *irritating* isn't it. Not like a person sometimes at all."

She had disappeared from view. Through the open door I could see a couple of peacocks strutting in the grass, their long blue tails dragging behind them. There were also several enormous creatures like storks which Mystery had told us were called adjutant-birds, stepping around on absurdly long legs.

And now I could see two other people, too, hanging around the kitchen door: people I hadn't seen before.

They were extremely strange. Although both were dressed like women, in rather plain sackcloth-coloured saris, a closer look suggested they were actually men. One was plump, barrel-chested, and very short, his growth clearly having been stunted, perhaps by some illness. His arms were too long, and his head too large, for the rest of his body. Apart from some long, wispy hairs around the back of his head, he was almost bald; he had large, sly-looking eyes and an ugly, flattened face, like a duck. The other was tall and thin, and was wearing lots of gold jewellery, but had hairy forearms and an unmistakeable beard, cut short and ragged. They were both chewing what looked like folded-up leaves, and sharing some joke which involved whispering to one another and then leering in at Mrs Chakraborty, who was doing her best to ignore them.

"Who are they?" I asked.

She peered out of the door contemptuously. "*Those* two," she said. "No-good people. I say bye-bye." And she leaned out of the open door and gave them a long angry mouthful of abuse. They pulled faces at her, and did a kind of dance around the corner into the courtyard, laughing.

Lash had finished his breakfast now, and, sniffing around after some scent on the ground, trotted out of the door into the heat.

"Thank you," I said to Mrs Chakraborty. Following Lash outside, I saw he'd spotted Nick, who had gone to see Punch, the elephant, under the broad shade of a tree. Lash took off towards him at a lollop. Sarasvati was there too.

"This is where you are," I said, joining them.

Sarasvati was eating something strange: it was green, and curved, and she split the skin to prise out a kind of milky-white core, like a bone.

"What's that?" I asked.

She laughed, like a bell tinkling. "*Kelaa*," she said. "A banana."

"I've never seen one of those," I said to Nick, "have you?"

"I think I saw some sailors eating them once when we stopped at Gibraltar," he said, dubiously, "but that time they were black, not green."

"What does it taste like?" I asked.

Sarasvati reached forward and handed me one. I turned it over in my hands.

"How do I . . . ?"

"You snap the end," she explained, "or cut it with your fingernail. That will do. Yes."

At first it was firm, then grew softer and pasty as I chewed it; it tasted quite sweet, but it made my teeth feel strange and furry. I gave the rest to Nick.

"I'd like to go back to the river today," Nick said between mouthfuls. "Would you take us?"

"Back to the river?" queried Sarasvati. "Are you sailing home again so soon?"

"No," said Nick, matter-of-factly, "I want to find out something. Look for someone."

"Without being seen?" asked the little girl, shrewdly. I couldn't stifle a quiet laugh of admiration.

"Ye-es," admitted Nick, "that would help."

"Then," said Sarasvati with a glint in her eye, "that is no problem."

Nick watched her fixedly as he chewed the last mouthful of banana, scanning her face for any sign of trickery. But she didn't sit still to be assessed. In an instant, she was upside-down.

"What am I?" she asked, and stood on her head, arching her back slightly with her feet perfectly together in mid-air, like a little brown comma. "A banana," she said, from ground level.

"Sarasvati, could you listen for a moment?" I said. "There's something I really need to ask you."

"And what am I now?" she grunted. Bending herself further over so that her feet touched the floor behind her head, she proceeded to take hold of her ankles with her hands, and form an almost perfect circle with her body. "A wheel," she said; and then, I swear, she rolled along the ground, like a wheel, several times around, until she reached the edge of the grass. Her silvery laughter sailed back towards us as she planted her feet on the ground and straightened up, ten yards away.

Nick and I exchanged glances. He was smiling. "She's very entertaining, isn't she?" he said.

"Yes," I muttered, "but I can see how it might wear thin."

"Don't be so grumpy." He called to her. "Sarasvati. Come back. Mog wants to ask you something."

"It's important," I said, as the little girl cartwheeled around us. "Can't you stand still for a minute?"

Eventually, she did.

"Something has gone missing from my room," I said to her. "You haven't been taking our things, have you?"

"What is missing?" She didn't deny it, at first.

"A cap. With bells on. A coloured cap."

She looked me in the eye.

"Funny thing to have," she said.

"It was a funny thing to take," I said. "Are you sure it wasn't you?"

"Never seen it. Is that why you want to go looking for someone?"

"Did you see anyone snooping around near our rooms, last night?" I persisted. "Who could have taken it?"

She shrugged. "Thieves. Monkeys. Spirits."

Something occurred to me. "Who are those two people who were at the kitchen door earlier? The little one, and the one with a beard?"

"You mean Nanak and Mohini. The eunuch and the man-woman. They mean no harm. Tell me where you want to go."

She had changed the subject, and was obviously not going to volunteer anything useful; but I was still convinced she knew more than she was letting on.

"Are you quite sure you can take us?" said Nick.

"That is no problem," said the little girl again.

"The thing is – how are we going to manage not being seen?" Nick wondered. "Should we go out in disguise?"

"Maybe we should cover up," I said. "I've got a shawl, up in the room, which would cover my head and face."

"Wear too many clothes, makes you look wealthy," was Sarasvati's sanguine advice. "Better be half naked. Wear rags. You have rags? Something old?"

We went upstairs and got dressed in the worst, shabbiest clothes we could find. But when she met us in the garden, Sarasvati twisted her face as though she could smell something.

"*That's* the best you can do? You still look grand. And English! Go back. I lend you something. Go on. I'll find."

Meekly, we did as we were told, and went back upstairs to wait for her in my room. A few minutes later she was there, on the veranda, knocking on the door-frame, with some clothes she'd found. They were awful: loose vests and leggings, torn, dirty and ancient. When we put them on, we looked for all the world as though we'd been sleeping on the streets of Calcutta all our lives.

Nick roared with laughter. "These are *great*," he said.

But I was wriggling with discomfort. "This vest thing," I said, "it's so huge, and where it's torn – the way it hangs, it doesn't cover me up at all."

Nick, of course, didn't understand what the problem was. "You're *meant* to look untidy," he said, impatiently, "that's the whole point." But in the bundle of dreadful clothes Sarasvati had brought up there was a kind of silk tunic, too, with a high collar, its buttons missing and its arms ragged; and I decided to put it on outside my filthy vest. It was hotter, and chafed maddeningly against my mosquito bites, but it revealed much less.

"Ready then?" said Sarasvati. "Now. Stay with me all the time."

We went down to the courtyard; but, instead of leaving by the big gates, we followed Sarasvati through the garden to an overgrown path, which led through a bright green, stagnant little ditch and up towards the road another way.

"No carriages," she said, "no palanquins. Too many people looking at them. Nobody sees you when you walk with the crowd. Come." And we scuttled across the road to where the ordinary people gathered and walked, as far as they could sensibly get from the imposing gates of the grand houses, for fear of being chided or chased away by soldiers or officious servants for making the road look untidy.

Sarasvati's advice had been perfect. In our ragged clothes we didn't stand out from the crowd at all, and we'd both become so tanned from spending so much time on deck on the voyage from England that we were almost as brown as Sarasvati herself. There was something reassuring about being inconspicuous: it felt just like the old days when we used to run around London, in just such rags as these, unseen, uncared for. In a very few minutes we forgot how uncomfortable the clothes were, and began to enjoy the adventure of disguise.

Even in the roasting, heavy air of the middle of the day, Calcutta was alive with activity. Throngs of people, and cattle, and chickens, and dogs, stood around the colourful market stalls, squeezing for shade under their awnings, and moving in a sluggish stream from street to street. People were selling beans, and tobacco, and salt fish, and pepper, and cloth, and tea, at the tops of their voices. Wallahs were running with buckets of water attached to poles across their backs. Here and there, groups of Company men or soldiers with white skin laughed and shouted in English or in broken, staccato Hindustani commands. Trees exploded with the sound of excited green pigeons as we passed; daring monkeys ran among the huts and stalls where they could, picking up fruit or other foodstuffs which careless people had dropped. Behind and above the hot tree-lined streets, behind railings and courtyards, stood whitewashed, flat-roofed buildings like the most elegant to be found in the west of London. Every few paces there was a different smell – alternately disgusting and delightful, depending on what we were walking past – and Lash was in ecstasy, straining to investigate every unfamiliar scent. Several times I had to call him to heel, especially when I saw him squaring up to groups of malnourished stray dogs, who seemed to mill about on every corner. At home, he'd long grown used to people being affectionately dismissive of his rather inelegant mongrel appearance; but here, where the street dogs were all but wild, he trotted about with all the airs and graces of a minor aristocrat.

Sarasvati proved an excellent guide. She knew the streets of Calcutta as instinctively as we had known the streets of London when we were her age. She knew when to hide, when to swagger, when to speak to people, in order to arouse the minimum suspicion on our behalf. Nick had been keeping his eyes open for people he thought he knew – one person in particular, obviously – but even once we drew near the river, and many of the noisy and ill-dressed people around us started to look as though they might be sailors, there was no face we recognised.

Until, from a wooden bridge crossing a muddy, swirling inlet from the river, we saw a figure on the walkway below, and Nick grabbed my arm.

"Don't stare," he said to me in a low voice, "but – that man down there. Have a quick look."

He was tall, heavy-set, weather-beaten, grim-faced. His right cheek bore a wide ridge of shiny scar tissue, stretching upward from the corner of his mouth almost to his ear, like a grotesque half-smile that was constantly at odds with the humourless expression in his eyes. He wore one silver earring, and was bare-headed – though he was carrying a dark-coloured hat whose wide brim he was using to fan himself – and his forehead and neck were visibly pimpled with sweat.

Nick waited until he had passed, and we had stepped over to the other side of the bridge, before he said any more.

"Did you get a look at him?"

"Yes," I said, "but I don't know him."

"He was in the Jolly Lighterman that night," Nick said. "He's one of Albacore's crew."

"Are you sure?"

"Sure as I can be. I think his name's something like Penagadder. I'm sure my— I'm sure I remember him from years ago."

It was the closest Nick had come for a long time to mentioning the bosun – whom he always used to refer to as "my pa", until we knew better.

So the *Lady Miranda* had arrived, it seemed. What might have happened, during the voyage, to any or all of those on board, was of course anyone's guess: but this man at least had made it to Calcutta, and there was every reason to suppose the Captain had too.

"Someone you know?" inquired Sarasvati. "Is that the man you came to look for?"

"Not precisely," said Nick. "Where's he going? Where does that path go?"

"Up towards Clive Street from the waterfront," she said. "Past warehouses, and lots of Very Bad Places. You want to follow him?"

It took Nick about two and a half seconds to make up his mind. "Yes," he said.

"Quick then," she said brightly. "He's gone ahead, but we can catch him. *Chalo*."

It was so hot that our filthy old clothes were sticking to us, and we couldn't muster the energy to run. Lash trotted with us, his tongue hanging out, but he was finding it hard work too. We followed Sarasvati, trying to cling to patches of shade between the buildings; but the sun was almost overhead, and they were few and far between. Fortunately the sailor wasn't moving fast either, and we kept glimpsing him, a comfortable distance ahead. We'd left the gleaming facades of the riverfront buildings behind, and were now in much narrower, shabbier streets, with ragged cloth or canvas awnings protruding from some of the house-fronts, and piles of rubble blocking the entrance to the narrow lanes between them. Children and dogs ran in and out of the buildings, but the grown-ups and old people were conserving their energy, sitting under the canopies fanning themselves, or sleeping, or drinking. Eyes watched us with idle curiosity as we passed. Some of the houses had painted signs above the dark doorways; and, here and there, chickens and goats scratched in the dirt by the walls.

"Wait," said Sarasvati, suddenly, holding out her arm to signal to us to stop.

Up ahead, we could clearly see the sailor leaning against a wall, looking at the ground, as though he were gasping for breath, or being sick. But then he stood up, took a quick look around, and slipped into a shabby house.

"What's that place?" I asked Sarasvati in a low voice.

"Very Bad Place," she said solemnly. "A very low house."

"It looks the same size as all the others to me," said Nick.

As we neared the house the sailor had entered, I gripped Nick's arm. Like most of the buildings here, the windows had no glass, only wide-spaced iron bars open to the air; and from one of the ground-floor rooms came the distinct sound of a man singing. It was a deep, weary, melancholy voice – and the tune was chillingly familiar.

"*O my lovely blue eye*
Blue eye that twinkle and shine
If it takes till the day I die
I shall make your blue eye mine."

There were other low murmurs from inside, now, and ironic laughter.

"There's a few of them in there," I hissed. "Maybe the Captain's with them."

We hovered near the open window, trying to catch snatches of conversation, but I was terrified that, at any moment, one of the sailors might poke his head out, and we'd be caught.

"I want to listen," said Nick in a low voice. "We have to find out what they're up to."

"It's not safe, Nick!" I whispered back. "We can't stay here."

But Sarasvati was looking around and, within a few seconds, she'd spotted a tall tree growing close by, whose branches almost brushed the wall of the house. Its trunk offered few footholds; but there was a high wall beside it, from which it would be easy to climb into the branches.

"Wait," she said again.

Exactly like a monkey, she had leaped up to the top of the wall in no time, and was negotiating her way through the branches to find a perch from which she could see straight down into the house.

She beckoned to us silently, from ten feet above our heads. I tied Lash to the trunk of the tree, and began to look for a foothold on the wall. It wasn't half as easy as she had made it look: but, with a bit of a leg up from Nick, I managed to scrabble up onto the top of the wall and join Sarasvati on the branch. We had an unimpeded view down through one of the windows, into a big, bare, dank room with walls painted in blue. We were no more than three or four feet from the open window, and I fervently hoped the bright green leaves of the tree were dense enough to shield us from view.

We couldn't see the whole room, but we could see enough of it to be sure that there were two or three people in there, smoking. Snatches of conversation drifted out of the dingy room.

"Not long now," said someone.

Another man groaned. "Ohh, my guts. This evil place has poisoned me, and no mistake."

"Pass the bottle," said the first. "The only thing what helps is to forget where we are."

I could even hear him spit. If we made the slightest sound, sitting here in the branches, I knew they'd be able to hear us quite clearly. Nick was looking for a way up onto the wall to join us, and I tried to point, in silence, to guide him. Lash had sat down thankfully in the shade of the tree to wait for us.

Something rustled in the branch above our heads and I almost jumped out of my skin. Looking up, I could see an enormous hornbill, eyeing us intently, with its head on one side.

"Aaaagh!" it said, shortly. My heart sank. The bird was so loud, it would be bound to attract the men's attention, and we'd be discovered. We had no choice but to sit here and pray it would stay quiet.

Almost as soon as Nick had made it onto the branch

beside us, we became aware of another sound – distant, at first, but approaching distinctly and deliberately along the road below us.

Click . . . click . . . click . . .

We didn't dare say a word.

The Captain pitched into view, moving slowly. He was dressed in the same heavy dark coat and hat he'd been wearing on that freezing night in London, and his lumbering gait in the unbearable heat made him look like a giant beetle, crawling along beside the buildings, swinging his crutches out to either side, with every alternate step, as he went. He paused by the door of the house, before turning laboriously and venturing inside.

I was trying to scratch my mosquito bites without making a noise or shaking the branch too much.

"Sit still," whispered Nick in my ear. I opened my mouth to make a retort, but as I did so, the clicking of the Captain's crutches echoed up from the window of the room, and we could see him stumping his way in. There was a long silence, as he stood in the doorway, panting.

"What news?" one of the other men grunted eventually.

"It's true," came the Captain's voice. Another long silence, with no response from the other men. "They *are* in Calcutta. I have reliable eyewitnesses. They have followed us, gentlemen, and with a piece of moderate luck they will walk straight into our web."

My flesh began to crawl. He was talking about us. I felt Nick's hand reach forward and grip my forearm, though

I wasn't sure whether it was a gesture of reassurance or an attempt to stop me scratching.

The men seemed unimpressed. As the conversation unfolded I got the distinct sense that the Captain had lost their respect, somewhere between London and here.

"Pray they'll do so quickly," said one, "and we can all get out of this devilish place. We've already been here as long as I can stand."

"Have you made any sense of the map?" came another voice – the man called Penagadder this time, I think.

"Aaaagh!" shouted the hornbill, suddenly, beside our ears – making the reply to the question inaudible.

"If you ask me," said one of them gruffly, "it's a hoax. The whole thing is a wild-goose chase."

"And if you ask *me*, sailor, you lack faith – and spirit – and any admirable human qualities, for that matter," barked the Captain, breathlessly. He stumped across the room, to stand before the man who had just spoken. He stuck out his left crutch at a sharp angle and leaned on it. "Mr Bartholomey," he sneered. "You been a Jeremiah all the way, aintcha? We all know what we've come looking for, and now we're here, the only way we're going to get it is if the few of us what's left are at least on the same side. But do you know what I've also heard while I've been out today? I've heard a whisper that you been letting your mouth run away with you in – shall we say, untrustworthy company."

There was a sudden gasp of alarm from somewhere in the room. I craned my neck to see what was happening. All

I could see was the top of Mr Bartholomey's head as he sat immediately beneath the window, and the bulky form of the Captain standing in front of him.

"After all that's happened, you ain't no wiser. That's a shame, Mr Bartholomey, a real shame," said the Captain. "But if you ain't with us now, after all this, my patience is too much for you to hope for in this climate."

"You don't frighten me," said the unfortunate man, sullenly.

"Well now," said the Captain, "that's a shame too. Maybe you ain't heard of the sailor whose head was sent home to his family, in a barrel of pickle?" There was a short, resonant silence. "In other circumstances," the Captain's voice went on, "I might let it go. I might let a warning suffice. But the stakes is high, Mr Bartholomey, and this is the very devil of a place. You must know I can't take the chance." He half turned, and began to heave himself towards the other side of the room, out of my sight. Sarasvati, a little further forward on the branch, still had a good view of him, and I could see her eyes following him as he clicked along the floor.

Someone started to cough violently, as though they were choking. "Gaaah! This filthy stuff!" And there was the sound of glass being smashed.

"Anyone else?" came the Captain's voice, now. "Either of you two want to side with Jeremiah?"

There was silence. The Captain was standing still again.

"Do your job, Mr Penagadder," he said, softly.

There was a flurry of movement in the room. A quick,

rough shout; a series of clatters as chairs were knocked over; a muffled scream.

"Aaaaagh!" shrieked the hornbill, in my ear. "Aaaaghh!"

It had happened quickly, but I'd seen enough to realise that Penagadder, the man we'd followed, had leaped forward and begun to grapple with the one in the chair called Bartholomey; and that the fight had lasted only seconds. Bartholomey now lay slumped on the floor beneath the window, beside his overturned chair, still clearly visible from where we sat. There was a rush of footsteps as the three other men made haste to leave the scene. And, as I stared down at the slumped sailor on the grubby floor of the room below us, I saw a spreading, crawling patch of dark blood growing and gathering rapidly around his body.

"Aaaaggh!" shouted the hornbill. "Aaaaggh! Aaaggh!"

We half climbed, half fell down the wall in our hurry to get away, and, pausing only to untie Lash, scuttled back along the road towards the river as quickly as we could. Rounding a corner, not looking where we were going, we bumped straight into some people coming the other way, and were about to apologise when we realised it was the strange pair from the Professor's – Nanak and Mohini, the eunuch and the man-woman, as Sarasvati had called them. Their mouths and tongues were bright red, and they were leaning heavily on one another's shoulders and laughing. When they recognised us, they looked plainly uncomfortable at being seen here; but they immediately covered their embarrassment with taunts and exaggerated finger-wagging gestures at us and at Sarasvati, who gave them a mouthful of abuse as we hurried on. When I glanced back, I could see them both still standing there, gazing after us, burbling with laughter.

We stopped when we got to a crowded corner, at the edge of the square with the gigantic open water tank in it. Nick and I were sweating so much I thought we were going to faint.

"Got to have a drink," I gasped.

Sarasvati beckoned a man over. "*O, bheesty,*" she called, "*pani denaa.*" Taking a hide pouch of water from him, she passed it to the two of us. It was warm, and in any other circumstances would probably have tasted disgusting; but we were in no mood to be picky. We downed it gratefully between us.

"Those bad men," she said to us, trying to follow what had been going on. "You know them?"

"They are after us," Nick explained. "They've come to Calcutta from England, looking for something. Something we're trying to find too."

I flashed Nick a glance. Surely he knew better than to say too much to Sarasvati!

"That is," I butted in, "they think we have something they want. We don't. But they are watching us. We have to be very careful."

She looked at us sideways. "They will kill you," she said.

"That's what we're afraid of," said Nick soberly.

"He killed that man in there. He will kill you. It was the one we followed. He had a knife."

"I know."

There was a large hairy pig standing beside us, minding its own business. Lash squared up to it and sniffed its snout – slightly too confrontationally, I thought. I yanked him away.

Sarasvati looked around. She had learned a lot about us, in a couple of short hours in the blazing heat.

"We'll go home," she said. "Long way round. Hiding. Follow me."

We stayed close to her as she took us through narrow lanes between buildings, past long stretches of high iron railings, across the backs of densely-planted gardens, through patches of trees. We were exhausted and thirsty again by the time we finally realised we'd arrived in the garden of the Professor's house.

As we came out of the shade of the trees towards the lawn, I could see two young girls, of about my age, both immaculately dressed in white. One of them had a parasol, and they were walking around the edge of the garden, talking with what looked like great excitement.

"Look, we've got visitors," I said. "I wonder who they are . . . ?"

"What do you mean?" Nick asked.

I turned back to the garden, and the girls had gone. I kept looking for them as we walked towards the house, thinking they might just have gone behind a tree; but they had simply vanished into thin air.

Stretched out on a low wall near the pathway to the

courtyard was the fakir, apparently asleep, his long untidy hair falling around him. Beside him, on the ground, stood the snake-basket.

"Who were those girls?" I asked Sarasvati.

She looked puzzled. "Girls?"

"Two girls, with a parasol, just there in the garden." I pointed.

"Nobody there."

"I know," I said, "they've disappeared, I just – I wondered . . ."

"Probably just spirits," said Sarasvati, simply.

"Sarasvati, we need to go and get changed," Nick explained. "If anyone sees us dressed like this, they'll be suspicious. Look – thank you for showing us the way today. I'm sorry it was a bit of a dangerous expedition."

The little girl's face showed no expression.

"I'm watching now," she said.

"Come on," I said to Nick, "let's go up the back stairs. We'll see you later—" I turned to speak to Sarasvati, but she had disappeared too.

We met nobody on the way upstairs, and we went into our rooms to get changed. Lash couldn't go another step: he flopped onto his side in the huge armchair with his legs sticking out and his tongue hanging out, and was asleep within half a minute of getting into the room. After I'd taken off the awful itchy clothes, I washed myself thankfully; and decided to stuff the clothes into a basinful of water, so that they might sit there and soak for an hour or two. I was just on my way through to Nick's room to fetch him, when I heard voices coming from inside.

"Worried *sick* we have been," someone was saying in a high-pitched voice. "I have alerted Professor sahib." It was Mystery.

I went in.

"Miss Mog," he said, "I cannot express relief enough. Wery-wery delighted you are safe. But where you have been? Whole household is searching for you. No trace! No message! In strange city! What were you thinking?" He was almost beside himself.

"We're very sorry, Mystery," said Nick contritely. "We've been with— we've been out on our own. We thought it would be all right."

"I was preparing to give you city tour," Mystery said. "I came to find you. Not a trace! Not here, not there! All over the place, everyone was searching."

"We haven't come to any harm," I said, "but we didn't think. We won't do it again."

"You must do as you wish," he said, staring at us. "But please to *telling* someone. Leave message. Anything might have happened. Calcutta is dangerous for strangers, easy to get lost, easy to go to wrong place. *Wery*-wery dangerous. Bad people everywhere. If something had befallen you, how I would know?"

"We didn't go far," Nick lied.

Mystery had got it off his chest, and he was calming down. "In any case," he said, "here you are, and it is all come right. But too late for city tour now. Is too hot."

"That's all right," Nick said, meekly, "we've already done some – exploring."

"Later, there is dinner invitation," Mystery said. "Professor sahib, and yourselves, are invited by Colonel Tweddle. At seven."

"He's right," I said, sitting on Nick's bed after he'd gone. "I suppose he's responsible for us. If anything happened to us, he'd be to blame."

"What a strange afternoon," said Nick, gazing out onto the veranda.

"They know we're here," I said, "and I expect they know where. 'I have reliable eyewitnesses,' the Captain said, do you remember? It makes me feel a bit sick."

"There are eyes watching us everywhere," Nick said.

"What do you think of Sarasvati?" I asked cautiously.

He stared at me. "You're surely not suggesting . . . ?" he began. "She's been brilliant. Surely you don't . . . ?"

"I'm not sure," I said. "I think you're too—"

"More likely to be those other two," he said, "the ones we met down on the waterside. Nanky and Hairy, or whatever they're called."

"Nanak and Mohini," I said.

"Yes, them. *They're* an untrustworthy pair, if anyone ever was. But look – the Captain's no nearer finding what he wants, now he's here, is he? All his crew have deserted him, or he's bumped them off, or something. There are only two or three of them left now, and their hearts are hardly in it, to judge from what we heard this afternoon."

"Well there's one less of them left, now," I said.

Nick was grimacing. "If *only* we can find out what that map's all about," he said, "we can still get there first. It's so frustrating, Mog! I just wish we could keep an eye on the Captain all the time, properly. Find out *everywhere* he goes, *everyone* he sees. We've *got* to know what he's up to."

"Maybe." I stood up. "It's too hot to think about it," I said. "I'm going to have a rest. What time did he say we'd been invited for dinner?"

"Seven, I think. I wasn't really listening."

"I expect he'll come back to get us."

I went back into my room feeling a bit dizzy. Perhaps it was the general effect of the heat, or maybe the water I'd drunk had been as bad as it tasted, and was starting to take effect. To be honest, I hadn't been feeling entirely well ever since we stepped ashore, and I'd barely been able to eat anything in the past couple of days.

There was a chair on the veranda, and I flopped into it. The house was still, everyone taking their rest in the afternoon heat, and I quickly slipped off to sleep. The calls of birds, and the rustling of the wind in the trees outside the window, drifted in and out of my dreams at intervals.

When I awoke, with a jolt, the sun had moved so that it was low and almost directly in my eyes. It felt a little bit cooler. High above, in the deep blue of the sky, a group of vultures was circling: so high up that, at first, I thought their tiny tattered shapes might be black specks blurring my eyes from gazing directly at the sun.

I rubbed my eyes, and looked around me. I couldn't tell how long I'd been asleep: but I was vaguely aware of voices and sounds of activity from the garden and the open windows of the rooms beneath. Sluggishly, I got up out of the chair and went inside. The clock on the mantelpiece said it was after half-past five. Lash was still asleep in the big chair in the bedroom, his flank rising and falling gently as he breathed. As I moved around the room, he made a sneezy sort of sound and reached up to brush at his muzzle with an idle paw; but he didn't open his eyes.

"You big lazybones," I teased him, in a gentle voice. He snuffled again.

The first thing I did was go over to the wash-stand to splash some water on my face and neck. The filthy clothes I'd put in the bowl earlier had made the water black. I squeezed them out, took the bowl and tipped it over the veranda onto the garden below; then went back in and poured some more water onto the clothes. They were still so far from being clean that I could see it would be black again within a minute or two.

As I moved away from the wash-stand, I glanced up at the oval portrait of our mother on the wall. What I saw almost made me cry out with surprise.

The portrait wasn't there any more. Instead, there was a slightly larger, square print of a city scene, with low buildings and boats on a river.

I stared. This was exactly what had happened yesterday. I couldn't possibly have imagined the picture of Imogen – Nick had seen it too, after all – so someone must have been in here, switching the pictures, while we were out – or while I had been sleeping this afternoon. But why?

As my sluggish brain, still not fully awake, struggled to make sense of it, I thought I heard something familiar, outside in the garden. I went back out onto the veranda to listen.

There it was, distant, but unmistakeable. Quite definitely Sarasvati's voice, I decided: coming from somewhere at the fringes of the garden, or even beyond.

"Dhara-ka-ta-ta-tang. Ka-tang-tang, dha-ra-dang. Dhara-ka-ta-ta-tang."

This much we'd heard before, last night at dusk, as we were going inside. But now, drifting on the scented air, came a response: another voice, deeper, richer, from further away. A man's voice, repeating the same staccato pattern of sounds, as though it were acknowledging, or replying to the child's call: like an exchange of secret messages in a strange rhythmic code.

"Dhara-dang, dha-ra-ta-ta-ta-tang, ta-tang. Dhara-ka-ta-ta-tang."

CHAPTER 7
FEEDING TIME

My brother, unmistakeable, his dark head bowed, his hands in his pockets, was walking out towards the lawn from the direction of the servants' quarters.

"Nick!" I called.

I thought he looked a bit uncomfortable when he squinted up at the veranda and saw me. He got up and came inside.

"What have you been up to?" I asked him, when he came into the room. Lash slid off the armchair and trotted over to see him. He didn't answer, at first. "Sorry," I said, "I went to sleep for ages. I've been feeling a bit strange, to be honest. You feeling all right?"

He nodded.

"I've got something to show you," I said. "Come here." I pointed at the picture which had taken the place of our mother's portrait. "What do you think of that?" I asked.

He went to stand in front of it. "Is it supposed to be a view of Calcutta?" he asked.

I stared at him. "I don't care what it's a *view* of," I said. "I don't mean what do you think of the *painting*? The point is, it's not our mother. The picture's been swapped again. Don't you *see*?"

"Is that the same one that was there to start with?"

"I can't be sure. But it's not the one that was there last night."

"Someone's playing games," said Nick, simply.

"I just heard Sarasvati again," I said, "making that strange sound. Tacka-tacka-tacka-tacka," I imitated it, badly. "And someone was answering her, from outside the wall. Another voice, a man's voice I think, doing the same noise. Like bird-calls, or something."

Nick came to sit on the bed. He ruffled Lash's ears as he spoke.

"I've seen Sarasvati this afternoon as well," he said. "I didn't hear her doing that. But . . ." He hesitated, as though he had something to tell me I wasn't going to like. "I was talking to her about the Captain."

"Nick," I said reproachfully, "what have you been telling her?"

"Just – nothing I shouldn't," he said, defensively. "But after we all sat in the tree this afternoon and watched . . . Well, she wanted to know who he is and what he's doing here. It seemed reasonable to tell her a bit more."

I was sceptical. "You've got a complete blind spot where she's concerned," I said. "I know she's funny and sweet, but we've no *idea* whether we can trust her."

He said nothing. I looked at him.

"There's something you're not telling me," I said.

"Well, while we were talking, those strange people appeared," he said. "Nanak, and – and –"

"Nanak and Mohini," I groaned. "And what did you tell *them*?"

"The little one started talking to Sarasvati," said Nick, "and it turns out he understands quite a lot of English. Doesn't seem to speak it much – but he knew we'd been talking about the Captain. He said he'd seen the Captain, several times, and had no idea we had any connection with him, but that when he saw us down on the waterside earlier, he realised that's who we must be looking for."

"Go on," I said.

"Well," said Nick, "he's offered to keep tabs on the Captain for us. He's down there in the rough parts of town all the time. It would be far less obvious, him spying on the Captain and reporting back, than us trying to run around watching him, in disguise."

"So you took up his offer," I said, drily. "How much did you pay him?"

"Mog, we need to know what the Captain's up to," Nick protested. "He's *desperate* to find the diamond. You know he'll stop at nothing, you saw what happened in that house. He's not just going to lie around in Calcutta waiting for the monsoon. And you didn't seem to mind when we got Water Jim to do the same thing for us back in London."

"I know," I said, "I'm just not sure that horrible little eunuch is the person to trust."

"Then who would you suggest? You don't think Sarasvati's trustworthy either. This is only our second day; Mog, we don't *know* anybody here."

"Maybe the Professor would have been able to suggest someone," I said. "Or Mystery. Look, I don't know, it might be fine, but I just don't think we can afford to take chances."

Nick was sullen. "Well. It's done," he said. "And in any case, he's already told me loads. He's been watching the Captain and his friends ever since they arrived. When I gave him money, he told me what he's found out so far. Do you want to hear it?"

I sighed. There was no point in pretending I wasn't interested.

"The Captain kept his destination a secret from the whole crew," he said, "until they were so close he could no longer hide it from them. They'd been waiting for their chance, and once they were on course for the mouth of the Hooghly there was a mutiny. They'd planned to murder the Captain and his few allies on board, chuck their bodies over the side somewhere down near Budge-Budge, then come and find the diamond using the map they knew the Captain had, and share the spoils between them. But they reckoned without Penagadder. He posed as a mutineer, and then when the uprising happened he turned on the rest of them and killed them all. Single-handed, by the sound of things. By the time they got into Calcutta ten days ago there were five of them left. The Captain, Penagadder, and those three in the room this afternoon. And now, as we know – and as the eunuch also knew by the time I spoke to him – there are just four."

I was impressed. "The eunuch told you all this?"

"With Sarasvati translating," he said.

"And he's found it all out just by eavesdropping?"

Nick shrugged. "Who knows how? But he's obviously no slouch at finding things out."

I went to the wash-stand and stared at my face in the mirror. "I feel really odd," I said. "I just know there was something wrong with that water this afternoon."

"Well, I feel all right," said Nick, stretching. "It's probably just the heat. Come on. It must be time to get ready for dinner."

People were arriving at the Colonel's in palanquins, like big oblong boxes carried by four servants, one at each corner. When they drew up at the front door, another servant came down the steps of the house to draw open the curtains, revealing the guest reclining inside, like some sort of Roman in an old painting. They swung their legs wearily out over the edge of the palanquin and held out an arm to be helped down, while the four poor servants at either corner struggled not to drop them.

"Not having any of that nonsense," snorted Professor Shugborough. "We'll go in the cart."

"It's like being in a coffin," Nick observed as he watched them.

"Might as well be," said the Professor cheerfully. "Been dead for years, some of these people. It's just that their hearts *will* keep beating. Good evening!" He beamed a greeting to some people entering the house ahead of us.

It was cooler, and there was an air of celebration – though I hadn't been able to find anyone who could tell us what the occasion was, or whether there even was one – but we still felt absurdly overdressed in the tropical air. A few hours ago we'd been running through the streets in the most dreadful old rags; now here we were in evening clothes, like lords and ladies. It had been a day of disguises.

With Nick's encouragement, I had put on the white dress I'd brought from home. It felt strange, partly because I had almost never worn a dress like it in my life, but also because it was someone else's, and old, and rather alarmingly starched, and my shape didn't quite fit it. But he had stared at me, and laughed – in admiration rather than amusement – and Mystery had gasped, and said I looked "*wery*-wery beautiful, just the tickety", and the Professor had said "Ah, quite!" and "undoubtedly" several times, so I had decided to give it a try.

When we got inside, the first thing I noticed was that the women were wearing the most enormous amount of jewellery. I couldn't help staring at the necklaces, the tiaras, the rings, most especially those of them which gleamed with diamonds. Of course, just because they were wearing diamonds, there was no reason why they should have a clue about the whereabouts of the Eye of Winter, or even have heard of it; but I *itched* to ask them, just in case.

Everywhere we looked in the Colonel's house, there were dead animals. It was impossible to escape from the sad, staring faces of antelopes and lions, ranged all around the hallway, as though they were poking their heads through the walls and we'd see the rest of their bodies standing on platforms in the adjoining rooms if we went around to look. On one wall, we were told, there used to be a rhinoceros's head, but it was so heavy it had eventually pulled the whole wall down, thus injuring more people than the rhino would have been able to manage by charging at them when it was alive. Wherever we walked, we trod on the backs of tigers, which had not long ago been stalking and licking their huge paws in the sharp jungle grass, but were now spread out flat and boneless across the floors, with their heads up, glaring at the guests.

We followed the other guests through into a cluttered, airless drawing room where drinks were being served. We could barely hear ourselves think, because of the noise of voices. There weren't more than about thirty people in the room, but they were making enough noise for a hundred with their laughter and chatter. Everyone was standing shoulder-to-shoulder, and sweat was running down people's faces and necks like raindrops on a window. Snatches of conversation met my ear as we pushed our way through, and most people seemed to be talking about the weather.

"Oh, quite unbearable," someone was saying. "And it's gone on for so *long* this year."

"If only the *cursed* monsoon would break," said another man, only the word he actually used was much stronger than "cursed".

"All very well for those who've gone off to the hills. Bet they don't give us poor slaves a second thought, stuck down here."

Most of the men were of a type: florid, forceful, bloated with self-confidence. Almost all of them had what I'd heard called "military bearing": standing upright, their stiff-bibbed chests pushed out, they spoke in loud voices and guffawed often, joshing the more timid guests, spilling other people's drinks as they swung their elbows. There were a few younger men among them, listening attentively to the comments and stories, laughing obsequiously at the right moments. An elderly man stood by a curtain and nursed a glass of whisky, watching a group of the others, looking rather pained and bitter.

The Professor leaned close.

"I'm so dreadfully sorry," he said, "I'm afraid you're going to find the conversation, ah – intolerably dull. So much petty gossip, about people you've never met. People here have two topics of conversation: one another, and themselves. I'm afraid it doesn't go much further than that."

But we soon found we ourselves were the subject of plenty of gossip.

"Why yes," cried the first person to whom we were introduced, a thin middle-aged woman with yellowing skin and terrible teeth. "The Winter twins, come from London. We've heard all about you."

"My dears," said another woman in long red gloves beside her, "such *dreadful* circumstances in which to be sent out. The death of your *poor* dear guardian must have been such a shock, and both of you still so *young*."

We moved through the crowd.

"Of course, they've lost everything," we overheard a bearded man saying, as he jabbed the lighted end of his cigar towards his companion. "The *entire* fortune, I've heard, is gone."

Faces peered at us, white and powdered and impertinently curious, as though we were exhibits. I began to feel dizzy again.

It was a relief when a gong sounded and servants waved us through to a much larger room, where a long table was set beneath softly-sparkling chandeliers. Nick and I were to sit together, with the Professor the other side of Nick. I found myself next to an elderly woman with a hook nose, dressed entirely in white, whose eyes looked in two different directions, and whose limbs shook very slightly, all the time. I learned she was called Lady Sheets. As she sat down beside me, she inspected me through a pair of spectacles on a stick. She seemed to have to strain to make her eyes as wide as possible, so that when she was staring at someone she looked like a big, fearsome sea-bird.

Saying nothing at first, she looked me up and down, almost from head to toe, until I felt really uncomfortable.

"Quite remarkable," were her first words. She looked around her for someone to talk to; but everyone else was engaged in conversation, and I appeared to be the only person left. "Really, truly extraordinary," she said, faintly, not to me but into the air in front of her.

"Yes, isn't it?" I said, brightly.

Servants were milling around the table, pouring wine into

everyone's glass, occasionally rearranging a napkin, making sure they missed no one out – while the guests ignored them completely. One man, directly opposite, lifted his newly-filled glass to his lips and tipped the entire contents into his mouth in one go. Tiny dribbles of red wine leaked from either corner of his mouth onto his shirt-front; but he slammed the empty glass down onto the table. And, silently, instantly, a servant reached forward with a bottle and filled the glass again.

Lady Sheets seemed to have gone into a trance, so I strained to catch the gist of other conversations going on around me.

"I simply told him," one man was braying, "the stuff wasn't up to scratch, and times are hard, and I sent him away with one fifth of what I promised him. One fifth, can you believe it? Of course, I pretended I never promised him anything of the kind. *That's* the way to treat them."

There was a ripple of applause, suddenly, and servants appeared carrying platters of food. Some laid down silver dishes of vegetables: tomatoes, spinach, and something they called ladies' fingers. And, in a large clear space on the tablecloth in front of me, they laid down a big oval plate bearing a roast peacock, trimmed with gigantic clams dug out of the Hooghly mud. There was another identical one further along the table. I realised I still wasn't the slightest bit hungry; in fact, as the rich, salty scent of the gravy reached my nostrils, I felt a sudden wave of nausea.

Once the initial excitement had subsided, and the servants had begun carving up the fowl and taking around the laden plates, the conversation struck up again.

"Were you at Jumbly's on Wednesday?" I overheard someone asking, over to my left. "No, wait – of course you were, I remember seeing you afterwards with that gorgeous little bit of – well, perhaps I shouldn't say."

I was about to dig my fork into my helping of meat when Lady Sheets suddenly seemed to judder into life again beside me, as though cranked up by some invisible hand. She lifted her lorgnette to her face again.

"Would you be so kind as to help me?" she asked, her gnarled old hand quivering towards the salt cellar. I reached out and passed it to her. She fumbled for it for a few seconds, and gave up. "Shake it for me," she said. "Not too much. That's it. Thank you so much." She didn't begin eating immediately, but peered at me again for a few seconds, first out of one eye, then, turning her head slightly, out of the other. "Really, quite extraordinary," she repeated to herself.

"I'm not sure that I—" I began, but my words were drowned in a burst of laughter from some men on the other side of the table, and I stopped.

"You should have seen it," one of them was guffawing. "Jenkins put out this hunk of meat, and the thing was so greedy it went straight for it. *Snap snap snap*, straight down its great gullet. Well, what it didn't know was that Jenkins had tied the meat to a dirty great stone! So there's this gormless adjutant-bird, with its belly full to bursting, and a string poking out of its bill tied round a stone, and the creature has no idea how to get away! Couldn't move!" And the group roared with laughter again, as the man mimed a tugging motion with his head, tears of laughter running down his own face.

Lady Sheets was having some difficulty picking up her knife.

"My dear," she said, leaning over towards me again, "I wonder if you could? Would you mind awfully?"

"With pleasure," I said, and reached over to lift the knife from the table and place it in her claw-like hand.

"No," she said, "I mean, cut it for me. Could you?"

Obligingly, I began to cut the slices of meat on her plate into a few bite-sized pieces. If she couldn't hold a knife, she should now be able at least to eat the ready-cut pieces with a fork. One of her staring eyes fixed me with a beam of what I took to be gratitude. The other was trained on the chandelier.

"And now . . ." she said. She gestured down at her fork, which she was having equal difficulty grasping with her other hand.

I picked up the fork and placed it gingerly between her fingers, waiting for her to close them around it.

"I'm terribly sorry," she said, "that's kind of you, but – I mean, feed me. Would you mind awfully?"

No one around me seemed to be treating this as anything out of the ordinary, so I assumed that Lady Sheets must have to be fed wherever she went. Leaving my own meal untouched on my plate, I proceeded to lean across and gather some of the meat onto her fork, and then lift it to her lips. She closed her mouth around it, chewed it a few times, and then threw back her head several times with an awkward movement, for all the world as though she were an albatross swallowing a cod.

Nick was leaning forward, on my other side, watching her in astonishment.

"Don't stare," I murmured out of the corner of my mouth.

Lady Sheets had disposed of the first mouthful and was gazing at me in the hope of another, her eye slightly watery now. I lifted a second forkful to her lips, and she repeated the exaggerated, bird-like swallowing performance.

And then, I swear, she squawked like a bird too. The meat seemed to be causing some slight trouble as it went down, and her throat emitted a short, involuntary croak as she fought to swallow it.

Nick had pushed himself as far back in his chair as he could, consumed by an attack of giggling, unable to watch her any longer. I could feel him quaking with suppressed laughter beside me, and I aimed a sharp sideways kick at his shin under the table.

I dutifully fed Lady Sheets another mouthful. When she'd shaken that down her throat, and clawed at the wineglass in front of her to signal that she wanted a drink to wash it down, she seemed sufficiently restored to begin a conversation. She turned to me, confidentially.

"My dear," she said, "has anyone ever told you . . . ? Oh, but you must know it – it's quite uncanny. You are the *image* of poor dear Imogen Winter."

A very strange sensation crept over me.

"She *was* my mother," I said quietly.

"I know, my dear, I know," she said, her lorgnette quivering in her palsied hand again, "but it doesn't always follow, you know. Let me tell you, when you walked into the dining room and I laid eyes on you, in that beautiful dress, well, my dear, it was as if we had all been spirited back fully twenty years. She wore her hair longer, of course, I suppose it was the fashion then, but in every other particular . . ." She gestured towards the wineglass again, and I lifted it and gave her another sip, like a priest. "My dear, when she was more or less the very same age as you, I would surmise, she came to a party in this very house. I recall it as though it were yesterday. I can see her, running around amusing some of the younger children, in a dress *so* much like that one it's – well, it's uncanny. *Quite* uncanny."

I gazed around, as I listened to her. The faces, the glow of the lamps, the plates of food, the reflections in the tall wineglasses, swam before my eyes. Everyone was engaged in their own noisy conversation, and no one else could possibly hear what Lady Sheets was telling me. The hubbub, the laughter, the clattering of knives and forks on porcelain, faded into a distant, throbbing murmur, and all I could hear was the measured, well-bred voice in my ear.

"She was a *wonderful* girl," the voice continued, "a really happy, lovely child. Everyone knew her, in those years. We were all desperately envious of her parents. The little children adored her and the young men were spellbound by her. It wouldn't be absurd to say she lit up Calcutta, my dear. She made it bearable to live here."

She turned towards the table, and clawed at the cutlery with her hand again. I fed her some more peacock, and then some vegetables, dripping with sauce. She swallowed them with the same jerky ritual as before, and again a little strangled squawk escaped from her throat as she forced them down.

"You really are too kind," she said to me, when she'd finished swallowing. "When you get old, my dear, like me, even simple things like eating are not so easy as they were. One's muscles – well, I mustn't bore you, you're still so young. You know, it was all too, too cruel, what happened to your mother."

"I know," I said: but my voice came out too quiet for her, or even for me, to hear.

"I could weep, I really could," she continued, "seeing you tonight. It brings it all back. My own dear daughter, Viola, was a few years older than Imogen, your mother, and we had such high hopes for her when she came from England, after her schooling was over. My dear husband, Sir Lumley, thought he could make her a secure future, out here. He adored her. We had all kinds of plans – and then, well, I don't know how to tell you. The Cloys." She pronounced the name as though it tasted disgusting on her lips. "Perhaps that's all I need to say."

She signalled to me that she wanted more wine. As I gave her another drink, servants started clearing the plates and removing the platters bearing the depleted remains of the peacocks – now little more than dispersed heaps of bone in shallow lakes of gravy, with a few clam-shells swimming in them.

I was feeling dizzier than ever. I gripped the side of my chair to steady myself. I wasn't sure whether I was here or not.

"That ungovernable, dissipated young ruffian, Septimus," Lady Sheets went on, "pursued our daughter, and did her the greatest imaginable dishonour, just as he dishonoured many others before and after her. Sullied her name, and ours. No one would take responsibility, or even apologise, for the young villain's atrocious conduct. Sir Lumley was so furious, it almost killed him, and he went after the Cloys in the courts. But, my dear, he was wasting his time and money. They were such bullies, to a man. They would stop at nothing to protect their wealth and reputation. Of course, his principal thought was to stop it from happening again, to anyone else. To protect others, you see." She was leaning closer and closer towards me as she spoke, and her eyes were very watery now. "But one can hardly calculate how many others there were. The boy was like a disease, carrying people off one by one. Our beloved Viola; then those lovely polite Welsh children, the Pugh girls – all three of them, some people were saying at the time, but there can be little doubt about the elder two at least. Did you know that one of them drowned herself? Couldn't bear the shame of it, you see. She was found floating in the river, face down, near the steps at Chandpal Ghaut. Eighteen years old."

She beckoned for another sip of wine. As I gave the glass to her lips again, she spilled some, and I used a napkin to wipe it from her chin and the base of the glass. She resumed her monologue. I really wasn't sure I wanted to hear any more, but I was feeling too weak to stop her.

"As for your dear mother Imogen – well, that little episode was enough to send her father to his grave, and in no time at all it led to that other business. And of course she was sent home, and then within months we heard the poor dear was dead. And there was the other young thing, her best friend, the governess's grandchild. Thynne."

Now that the table was clear of the previous course, more dishes were appearing: along with clean plates, clean napkins, more vegetables. The servants lifted the lids from the dishes to reveal water-buffalo steaks, braised in wine.

"I think you'll have to excuse me," I said, suddenly.

I was sure I was going to be sick. I pushed my chair back and squeezed my way between the servants who were milling attentively around the table. Finally finding a clear expanse of floor between me and the door, I ran from the room, and made for the quickest way out of the house into the night air.

The nearest doorway led down a short flight of steps into a yard at the back of the Colonel's house. I sat down on a low wall, taking deep breaths, relieved to be away from the noise, and the smell of the cooked meat, and the heartfelt but increasingly upsetting story Lady Sheets had been telling me.

But now I became aware of another sound, a combination of scratching and squelching, from just behind the wall where I was sitting. I peered into the darkness, and, as my eyes adjusted, I gradually realised that I was right beside the place where all the waste and effluent of the kitchens had been thrown out, waiting to be disposed of.

I could make out two or three low metal bins, completely

inadequate to cope with the remains of the foodstuffs used in the preparation of tonight's banquet. The heads, and feet, and innards of the beasts which had been used in the meat courses had overflowed onto the ground, and lay strewn everywhere, for several yards around. Stray dogs and jackals snuffled through the remains, their heads buried inside the carcases, tearing at the scraps of meat still hanging onto the bones. Rats dragged chunks of flesh and skin across the ground, sharpened their teeth on the bones, fought over raw limbs in the darkness. The ground was wet with blood and rank fluids leaking from the rubbish; and, as I stared at it, the whole revolting heap seemed to shimmer and shine, and I realised it was alive with cockroaches, which swarmed over every surface of the dead discarded animals and rotten foodstuffs, waving their greasy antennae as they trod over one another's backs in their thousands.

Only now did the stench hit me, as though a stirring of the tropical breeze had suddenly blown it in my direction; but it was so fetid it almost knocked me off the wall.

Nick was at my shoulder. He'd followed me out of the banqueting room.

"Are you all right?" he asked me.

I couldn't answer. I was being violently sick now, over the wall, adding to the general stinking mess.

The Professor appeared a few moments later, and I became aware of a fuss, and the shouting of instructions, as preparations were made for us to leave. I was helped up into a tonga-cart, and we drove the short distance home, the breeze in my hair, along with the fact that I'd emptied my stomach at last, making me feel a lot better.

Majara stretched, and came languidly to greet us as we strode into the hallway of the Professor's house. Mystery ran out of one of the side rooms to turn up the lamps and to take instructions.

"Miss Imogen's room," said the Professor, "is it clean? Is it cool? She must go upstairs and on no account be disturbed. She must have hot sweet tea. And pillows, fresh pillows. She is not well."

"I'm fine," I said.

"Overheated," the Professor said. "Overtired. Perfectly understandable. After two days in Calcutta, it hits everyone the same way. Place is little better than a swamp, after all. Ah, quite. We shouldn't have gone tonight. Parading you like that in front of those people, I'm ashamed of myself."

"I'm fine," I said, "I quite enjoyed it, until—"

"Hateful company," he said, "hateful arrangements. The Colonel's a harmless old sort, but most of those other people are parasites and witches. Shan't be going back in a hurry. Now then." He blew air out from under his moustaches again, like an elephant, partly to cool himself down and partly to express annoyance at the way the evening had gone. "Try and sleep," he said, "not that it's easy in this heat. Mistry will make sure you have everything you need."

Nick came up with me. When we got into my room, Lash woke up and showed great excitement at seeing us after being on his own for so long. Despite the Professor's insistence,

I didn't feel like going to bed straight away: I really did feel better than I had all day.

I couldn't resist checking whether, by any strange chance, the portrait of our mother had reappeared. It hadn't. The same bland view of boats met my eye.

"What a peculiar woman that was you were sitting next to," said Nick. "Fancy having to feed her like that."

"She's got something wrong with the muscles in her throat," I said. "She explained it. That's why she had to tip her head back like that all the time."

"She was getting very animated, while she was speaking to you," said Nick. "What was she telling you?"

I chewed my lip. "It was all rather horrid," I said. "It was about our mother and – about Sir Septimus. All the things he did when he lived here. And do you know what? She was just getting around to telling me about Miss Thynne, when I had to run outside."

"What about Miss Thynne?"

"Well, I imagine, more about what we already know," I said. "That Sir Septimus took a fancy to her, when she was young." I went over and unlocked the chest, and pulled out the battered old diary. "You know, it must all have been happening at around the time she was writing this," I said. "Perhaps the damage to the diary was deliberate. Do you remember Mr Cramplock telling us Sir Septimus burned down Charnock House? To destroy all the evidence of the bad things he'd done? Maybe he tore this book up, too, and threw it away, and didn't expect half of it to survive."

"Not that it's much use," said Nick. "We can hardly read a word of it."

I leafed briefly through the fragile pages again. One of the book's few legible passages met my eye.

> . . . bear the smell of that terrible place, let alone bear the gaze of all those eyes, and all that talk of spirits . . .

"That's a strange line, isn't it?" I said. "It reminds me of something Sarasvati said."

There was a knock on the door, and I put the diary back in the chest as one of the boy servants, whom Mystery called Jumjum, came in with a silver tray of tea. He placed it on a low table at the side of the room.

"Thank you, Jumjum," I said, as he retired quietly. The tea was steaming, and the smell, milky and sweet, drew me over to it. For the first time since we arrived, I found I had an appetite.

"Do you want some?" I asked Nick.

I didn't hear him answer. My attention was caught by a piece of paper, folded up neatly and tucked inside the sugar-bowl.

"What's this?" I wondered. I unfolded it carefully. "Nick," I said, "Nick, look here."

He read it, over my shoulder.

"Where did that come from?" he exclaimed.

"It was folded up inside the sugar-bowl," I said.

There were three lines of writing on the paper, in a scratchy, childish hand. My mind raced, as I read them again and again. At face value, they were comforting, thrilling: but it depended who had written them, and what their intentions were towards us. If only we could be sure!

DAMYATA WISHES MEET YOU.
BE AT BLACK PAGODA AT SUTANUTI
TOMORROW AT NIGHTFALL.

CHAPTER 8

THE BLACK PAGODA

Our hearts were in our mouths as we scampered through the streets in the low, golden sunlight of evening. I had been adamant about not telling Sarasvati, or trying to ask her for directions.

"I know where it is," I insisted.

"You do not," Nick challenged me. "How do you know?"

"Mystery pointed out the direction."

"*When* did he?"

We were just going to have to use our wits. I didn't want Sarasvati coming with us to meet Damyata, or even knowing about our appointment with him. This expedition was too personal to let her get involved, especially because I was still far from sure she could be trusted.

But we did take Lash. He was excited at being out among the noises and scents of the evening, and was straining at his lead to make us go faster; but I didn't dare let him run loose. The town was lively at this time of night: after the lethargy of the afternoon, everyone was paying visits and socialising, and carriages and palanquins were carrying people to and from one another's houses. Those who clearly thought themselves the height of Calcutta fashion trotted to and fro on horseback, observing the crowds, and making sure they themselves were seen and commented upon; and, hoping to catch the evening trade, Indian hawkers thronged the streets selling snacks, and sweets, and tea. There was evidently something on at the theatre, on the corner close to the street of colourful and strong-smelling market stalls which we'd learned was called the Lal Bazaar; and the crowd fanned out there from the front entrance for many yards, chattering excitedly. In the mass of people, up ahead of us, I thought I caught sight, momentarily, of a familiar gold-coloured sari. Sure enough, as we got closer, the tall awkward form of the bearded woman, Mohini, appeared; and, as a gap opened up in the crowd, there was the dwarfish eunuch, Nanak, standing next to her, as ever.

"Look!" exclaimed Nick. "It's them! Naki and Mincey, or whatever they're called."

"Nanak and Mohini," I said, helpfully.

"That's it," said Nick.

They hadn't seen us; but I wasn't keen to run into them. "We need to go that way," I said, dismayed. "I'm not walking past them."

"They wouldn't be going to the theatre," Nick said suspiciously. "I wonder what they're up to . . ."

"They're just hanging around," I said. "Isn't that what they do everywhere? Let's wait for a few minutes and see if they move away." As we lingered, trying to stay out of their sight,

I could see they were pestering the theatre-goers, trying to make conversation. At first people were tolerating them, pretending to be amused; but in the end they lost patience and just waved them away as if they were flies.

The next time I caught sight of Nanak he'd retreated to the fringes of the crowd, and he was deep in conversation again: only this time he was looking down, rather than up, as he had into the faces of the well-heeled theatre-goers. He seemed to be giving instructions and money to a ruffian child, who then ran off into the darkness of the Chitpur Road.

"Paying more of his spies," I said to Nick.

"Let's just hope he's paying them to find out something useful to us," said Nick.

After a few minutes, I could no longer see either of them. They'd evidently given up, and drifted off to bother someone else. We pressed on, northward, through the crowds, with Lash straining on his leash ahead of us, sniffing at scents and leading the way. And, quite soon, we found we were leaving behind the white palaces of the British part of the city, and entering streets lined almost entirely with small, ramshackle *cutcha* buildings, made of mud and timber, with roofs of straw. Most of them had no doors, only strips of cloth or sacking hanging at the doorways and windows. There were voices everywhere, and the soft lights of lanterns flickered in the low doorways, with people talking or cooking inside.

"Don't you think it's strange how quickly it gets dark?" I said. We'd noticed that, here, the transition from day to night – a process which took anything up to an hour on a summer's evening at home – seemed to be complete in about five minutes.

We were now in the part of town where, Mystery had insisted, British people didn't – and mustn't – go. And it was very obvious that, in the murmurs around us, there wasn't a word of English to be heard, and that, instead of the stiff evening coats and wide skirts of the people outside the theatre a few minutes ago, now everywhere we looked there were cloaks, and turbans, and saris, and white cloth *dhotis*. Men and ragged children stood outside the houses watching us as we scurried past in the darkness. The clothes Sarasvati had lent us yesterday weren't quite so itchy now that I'd washed them; but they were still far from comfortable. However much we might have prided ourselves on looking like Indians yesterday, we somehow felt a lot more conspicuous tonight, in the darkness, than we had in broad daylight. Whispers, low murmurs, and the growling of dogs, seemed to fill the air, and white eyes shone at us out of every doorway and shadow.

"Keep moving," Nick murmured, "don't stop anywhere." I kept Lash's lead pulled tight. There was something increasingly eerie about it all, and I was very glad we'd brought him with us.

As we got further and further up the road, nearer and nearer to the temple, I began to feel not just nervous, but really scared. It took me a little while to work out why; but then it hit me.

"Nick," I said, "have you noticed? It's gone quiet."

The Calcutta air was never quiet, never still: even when

there were no people shouting and chattering, there was always the squawking and shrieking of birds, and the hum and chirp of insects, surrounding you. But, gradually, it had all fallen weirdly silent: the murmurs of people in the houses, the cries of babies, the indeterminate distant howls and calls from the jungle fringing the city; even the cricket-calls in the foliage around us, had all died away.

"Do you think it's Damyata doing that?" I wondered in a whisper.

We were very close now. The dark pagoda-shaped tower of the temple stood out in silhouette against the blue-black of the night sky. We hesitated, by a wall on the other side of the road, watching.

"This is definitely the place," I said.

Lash gave a sudden short, low growl. And, as I followed his gaze, I saw a young woman in a white dress suddenly emerging from the bushes by the temple wall. Her dress shone strangely in the darkness, as though she were lit up from within. She looked anxiously around, stepped out of her shoes, and then disappeared quickly inside. I grasped Nick's arm.

"Did you see that?"

"What?"

"A woman in a white dress. Going in."

"Didn't see anything of the kind."

"Do you suppose it's time? How would we know?"

"The note just said nightfall, didn't it?" said Nick. "It probably means we're a bit late. He'll wait."

We ran across the road and up the low, broad steps of the

temple. The entrance was guarded by an ornate wooden screen, delicately carved with a lacework pattern of tiny holes which made it semi-transparent. All we could see through the screen was a soft, warm light. As we walked around the screen to enter the temple properly, the silence intensified.

There was no one to be seen; but the interior glowed with a hundred candles, flickering in clumps and lines everywhere we looked. There was a heavy, sweet scent, like coconut milk and flower petals. It took a while to establish that we were truly alone; but, as we paced around the marble floor, trying not to make a sound, it seemed clear that the temple was quite empty. We could see no trace of the woman in the white dress, or of anyone else. Many pairs of eyes followed us around, nevertheless: because everywhere there were statues and crude paintings of deities decorating the temple, most of them with thumb-sized smears of dye and rice pressed into their foreheads.

I stopped in front of a statue of a stumpy little elephant, sitting cross-legged, with its very human-looking arms held out in a gesture of peace or welcome, and its trunk curving down into its lap. It seemed to be made of pewter, or silver. Set in its forehead, where the other statues had a smudge of red dye, sat a tear-shaped ruby. I was transfixed. Reaching up, I slipped my fingers behind its trunk and tugged, gently.

"What are you doing?" Nick's whisper made me jump, in the charged silence.

"Nothing. I – I've seen this before – or something like it, at any rate."

There was a dull sound from somewhere in the shadows.

We both listened, intently. Was there someone else here?

There was no repetition of the thump; but now, as we stood in silence, I could hear something else. Someone was whispering.

It wasn't Nick, because I was looking into his face in the candlelight, and he wasn't moving his lips. I couldn't make out what the whisperer was saying, but whoever it was seemed to be extremely close by. The voice was almost in my ear.

And then there was another whispering voice, and then another. The heady, fragrant air was suddenly full of whispers, all of them sounding intimately close, yet still too indistinct to make out any words. My skin began to crawl. Cajoling, seductive whispers, from every direction now, combined in a hypnotic pattern of sound that acquired more and more layers. They were talking across one another, not in unison; each voice almost fighting to be heard above the others, and joined all the time by more, until there was so much whispering all around us it almost hurt our ears.

"What's going on?" I saw Nick saying; but his voice was drowned out. I pressed my hands over my ears. I wanted to tell him I'd heard this before, too. I wheeled around, looking for someone who might be responsible, seeing only statues, and paintings of gods, and flickering candles, and a profound darkness behind it all. I wanted to shout at Nick to help me, to tell me what it was; to allay my mounting terror with a rational explanation. Most of all, I wanted it to stop.

Although somehow the intensity of the whispering made it

hard to move, as though the voices were physically weighing me down, I fought my way back to the other side of the carved screen, and stood on the temple steps, gasping for breath in the hot night air. As soon as I emerged from the temple, the whispering died away. Nick and Lash joined me; and I reached down for Lash's muzzle to feel his reassuring lick filling my salty palm. There were still no people to be seen in the road outside, no bird-calls or insect sounds.

"What was *that*?" Nick asked. He sounded breathless; frightened.

"I've heard it before, Nick," I said. "It happened at Kniveacres, when I was on my own one night, just after Miss Thynne died. Do you remember when—?"

"Shh!"

Nick was holding up a hand. He'd heard something.

There it was again. Another thud, from back inside the temple behind us.

"We should go back in," I said.

"Can you bear to? What if the whispering starts again?"

"It must be Damyata," I said. "He's inside. I'm sure of it." I turned and looked at the glow from behind the screen again. "The voices have stopped. Are you coming?"

He still seemed reluctant.

"I can't help feeling it was some sort of warning," he said. "Maybe we should just go back."

"Come on, Nick," I wheedled. "We can't come all the way here and then just run away, before he's had a chance to speak to us." And, my curiosity about Damyata suppressing my fear, I gripped Lash's collar and went back inside, with Nick breathing heavily, a pace behind.

The whispers had died away completely. There still seemed to be no one inside; but as we stood among the statues there was another low thud, and this time a whole row of candles to our left flickered visibly, as though fanned by some unseen movement.

My heart was in my mouth. Damyata. Our father had kept his appointment. He had sought us out, defying the danger he faced in Calcutta, and we were going to see him again. For the second time in our lives, he was going to speak to us.

And now, staring into the darkness, I could see a human outline. A large, dark shape, standing still, as though it had quietly materialised there, too far out of the candlelight for a face or any features to be distinguishable.

I heard the sound of my own trembling voice, though I don't remember voluntarily speaking the word.

"Damyata?" I said.

But something was wrong. From the opposite side of the temple, the other side of Nick, there was another thump; and I suddenly realised there was another dark, silent shape standing there. And Lash had begun to bark.

Echoing on the marble floor, coming towards us, was another sound which made us freeze.

Click . . . click . . . click . . .

Loudly, fiercely now, Lash barked, straining on his collar. Panic mounted inside me, like sickness. The shapes to either side of us moved forward, and as their features emerged into the candlelight we could see the stony, knife-slashed face of Penagadder and, to the other side, another of the Captain's crew, equally menacing in the eerie light.

Click . . . click . . . click . . .

The Captain stopped. We could see him in silhouette, in the centre of the temple, just in front of the elephant idol. His three-cornered hat was screwed down onto his head, his huge frame supported like a tumbledown house by his wooden crutches leaning a long way out to either side. Lash was still barking and I was hanging onto him desperately, knowing that, if he broke free and lunged for one of the men, their knives would be out in an instant.

The candle flames were flickering crazily now, sending the sailors' shadows leaping up the temple walls. I was rooted to the spot with terror. I couldn't run; I couldn't cry out; I couldn't even look at Nick. We had walked into the simplest, most obvious trap imaginable. We were going to be killed, here, with not a soul around to witness it, and our bodies dumped in the Hooghly. And it was all my fault.

"Thank you for coming," came the Captain's voice, echoing strangely off the marble. "They told me you wouldn't. They told me you was both too clever to fall for it. But the Cap'n ain't often wrong, is he, men? The Captain ain't travelled thousands o' miles in a lifetime, to most every far-flung place your eye can make out on the globe, without getting to know human carrick'er." He shifted his bulk onto his good leg, adjusted the angle of his crutches, and then leaned on them again. "We both wants the same thing, it seems," he smiled, a gold tooth glinting in the candlelight. "And we wants it bad. Too bad to ignore an invitation, even one what sounds too good to be true. Sounds too good to be true, because it *ain't* true." He laughed, a short, wheezy sound. "Oh, no, the Captain ain't often wrong. And I fancy I ain't wrong when I say this, neither," he growled. "That diamond is mine. Rightfully yours, well, just maybe. But 'rightfully' ain't a word I ever 'ad too much use for. Ain't that so, men?"

Both of the others moved further forward, so that they were just a couple of steps away, to either side, towering over us. I was sweating, and my heart was thumping in my chest, so loudly I was sure all the others could hear it. There was no way, now, that we could get past the men to the carved screen and the temple entrance, even if we'd been quick enough to make a dash for it. We were trapped. Lash unleashed another volley of barking; but I wouldn't let him go. I could make out the details of the Captain's face in the candlelight now, and, as he looked down at Lash by my side, it was a picture of pure vicious loathing.

He spoke again, much more quietly.

"Do your job, Mr Penagadder."

This was it. A knife flashed in the candlelight and the huge man started to move forward. I remember opening my mouth to speak, as though I were about to try and strike some bargain with them, promise them an equal share in the diamond, or some such absurdity. Or perhaps all I was going to say was "goodbye, Nick".

But there was a sudden scuffle, a barely-audible squeak, a

gasp from Penagadder; and his arm was somehow wrenched back and the knife flung across the temple floor. It skittered over the marble, into the darkness, yards away. There was a grunt from the other sailor to our right, and he clutched his face, as though trying to wrench something away. Something had attacked them: it happened so quickly that we hadn't even had time to work out what, or who, it was. There came more squeaks; a ripple of noise like laughter; the sound of scurrying feet – or *paws*.

And now we could see them, emerging from the shadows, leaping down from the tops of the pillars and the decorated balconies of the temple, jumping onto the sailors and clinging to them. Monkeys. Twenty, thirty of them, forty even: more with every passing second, incredibly quick and agile. They bounded onto the temple floor, apparently from nowhere, leaped up and sat on the men's heads, scrabbled in their faces with their paws, blinding them; clung to their backs, bit the tips of their ears, tugged at their clothing, wrapped themselves around their legs and wouldn't let go.

"Gaaaah!" Penagadder struck out at them, trying to wrestle them off, shake himself so violently they'd fall to the ground. One or two of them did, but they were back on his coat in seconds, as though they'd simply bounced back up off the marble. Try as he might, he couldn't fling them off, and before long he was down, on the floor, wrestling with them, the one man set upon by perhaps twelve or fifteen monkeys at once.

The sound of the men's shouting was all but drowned out,

now, by the excited noise the monkeys were making. One of them had snatched off the Captain's hat and was racing around the temple with it, screeching. Another was pulling purposefully on one of his crutches, as though it had worked out they were the only thing propping the Captain up, and that knocking them out from underneath him could make him fall over. Sure enough, as more monkeys leaped onto him and the first crutch collapsed, he teetered for a few seconds, trying to get a purchase on the smooth marble floor with the brass tip of the other; but seconds later, with a bit more tugging from the monkeys, that too slipped from under him. And then he fell. Curiously slowly, he tipped forward, until gravity took over and he flung out his hands to break the fall. Amid the chaos, towards the back of the temple, I could see the crutches being waved in the air by the monkeys, passed from one to another of them amid chattering and shrieking, like trophies.

Not one of them so much as touched us.

In the confusion, it was easy to make our escape now. We fled into the darkness of the Chitpur Road. As we skidded down the temple steps I lost hold of Lash's lead; but he stayed as close to us as he possibly could, and was at my ankles all the way as we ran.

"Where is he?" Nick demanded as he marched into the servants' room, with me and Lash a yard or two behind him. It was the next morning, before breakfast. The laundry-man, Dhobi, was there, eating a kind of pancake; and the serving boys, Jumjum and Bulbul, were playing a game in a corner. They looked up as we came in. "Where's the eunuch?" Their faces were uncomprehending. "Nanak," said Nick. "Where?"

The servants exchanged a few words amongst themselves. As they were doing so, Mystery appeared.

"Mystery," said Nick, grimly, "where's Nanak?"

"I hope you are sleeping soundly, Master Nick and Miss Mog," Mystery said.

"Where's Nanak?" Nick repeated, impatiently; and at exactly the same time, only much more quietly, I said, "Very well, thank you, Mystery."

"Nanak," said Mystery, covered in confusion suddenly, "I don't know, Master Nick. That is – you wish me to calling him?"

"I want to speak to him," said Nick, with a face like thunder.

"Nick," I said cautiously, "go easy, we don't know it was—"

"I'm going to look for him," he interrupted me, and pushed through towards the little scullery-type space that led out into the yard.

With an apologetic shrug at Mystery, I hurried after him.

It was only a couple of hours since dawn, but already the heat was raging. Going outside was like walking too close to a furnace. Immediately outside the back door, the fakir was sitting on the ground, cross-legged, with his back to the wall of the house. Nick stopped when he saw him.

"Nanak?" he demanded.

The fakir moved slowly, as though he were waking up: like a lizard who hadn't yet quite absorbed enough of the sun's warmth to have the energy to move. He turned his head to look up at Nick standing above him.

"*Achha*," he said, eventually. He lifted an emaciated arm and pointed shakily in the direction of the outhouses that backed onto the rose garden. Nick marched off, purposefully.

"Nick," I called after him. He didn't show any sign of having heard me. "*Nick*," I implored.

He didn't stop. Lash and I scurried after him. He'd already reached the outhouses and was pushing the door open roughly. "Nanak," he was shouting, "are you in here?" The longer it took him to find the eunuch, the more furious he was getting. I had hardly ever seen him like this: normally Nick was one of the most placid people I knew.

We'd got back to the Professor's late last night and gone straight up to hide in our rooms, still in shock, and terrified that the Captain's men might at any moment escape from the monkeys and come after us. Nick had been cursing the eunuch all the way back. He was convinced he was the one who'd betrayed us. I thought his fury might have died down by this morning; but the first thing he'd heard when he woke up was the eunuch laughing, down in the garden beneath his balcony. He'd leaped out of bed and gone after him straight away, pausing only to pull on some clothes.

Mystery was running after us now, calling: "Miss Mog! Master Nick!"

But Nick had found Nanak. In one of the outhouses was

a kind of workshop, or den, which was evidently where the eunuch slept, sometimes or always. There were a couple of low wooden beds in there, each with a coarse, grubby blanket draped over it. The morning sunshine was lancing into the den through the gaps in a slatted blind, and revealing Nanak sitting calmly on one of the beds, grinning all over his bloated face. His legs were swinging over the edge, too short to reach the floor. As Nick marched in, there was the sound of clattering metal. I stood in the doorway and could see Nick kicking over some tin dishes, and a hookah, which sat on a carpet in the middle of the room. The room smelled rancid and airless. Dust flew up in glittering clouds in the rays of sunlight.

Lash gave an anxious bark. He wasn't used to Nick in this mood, either. Nick had gone over to the bed and had the eunuch by the throat, now. The muscles in his upper arms were tense, and he seemed suddenly to have grown. Nanak was leaning back, abject and fearful. I thought Nick was going to pick him up and slam him against the wall, or something; but, in fact, once he had hold of him, he didn't hurt him. He pressed his face close to the eunuch's frog-like features and spoke through gritted teeth.

"It *was* you, wasn't it?" he snarled. "Don't pretend you don't understand. You know what I'm talking about. You almost had us killed, you lying, double-crossing toad. I paid you money to give *us* information. Not to betray us! How dare you use Damyata's name to trick us? You sneaky, evil, cheating little – *rat*!" He seemed to struggle to find enough insults, but he was quite enjoying it. The eunuch was making a sort of high-pitched strangled whine, and begging for mercy in his own language. He had a voice like a duck. Over Nick's shoulder I could see his wretched, sly little face, and was suddenly filled with loathing for him. Nick was right. He was greedy, cowardly, deceitful.

"If you breathe another *word* about us, or where we are, or what we do, or where we go," Nick said to the eunuch, "your life won't be worth living. Do you understand? Not to *anyone*."

"Master Nick," said Mystery, breathlessly, from the doorway behind us. "If something wrong perhaps I can being of some assistance."

Nick let go of the eunuch and he flopped onto the bed, limply, like an oversized puppet. He sat there and whimpered, his broad green eyes regarding us with an expression somewhere between hatred and calculation.

Nick stood up.

"I just had to have a word with Nanak," he said, quietly, turning back to face Mystery and me. There was a light film of sweat on his temples and upper lip, picked up by the shafts of sunlight coming through the blind. The air was charged with tension and subtle violence. For that brief minute Nick had seemed like someone else entirely: an adult, forceful and frightening; not my slight, sensitive, rational, cautious brother.

"Nanak does not speaking English," Mystery called after Nick as he stalked out. "Master Nick, you have something to tell, perhaps I can translating."

Nick didn't reply.

"Do you think he did understand you?" I asked, hurrying to keep up with him.

"He knows perfectly well what he's done," Nick said – and then gave a small chuckle of relief. "I scared him. He got the message. You could see that, couldn't you?"

"Not like you to be scary," I said.

"Perhaps I just choose not to be," he replied, loftily.

"Forgive me," said Mystery, catching up with us, "but what is your quarrel with him?"

We stopped by the corner near the entrance to the rose garden. "It would take too long to explain," I said.

"He has not done what I asked him," said Nick. "He has done the opposite. He betrayed our trust."

"Not to be trusted," tutted Mystery, nodding his head sideways. "*Wery*-wery untrustworthy fellow. You were not wise to relying on him, Master Nick. Most unreliable person in whole of Calcutta."

I shot Nick a significant glance, which he pretended to ignore.

"Master Nick, forgive me, but did I overhear you mentioning the name – Damyata?" Mystery asked. Nick cursed, under his breath, just about loud enough for me to hear. "It is simply that – that name is not customarily mentioned in this house," explained Mystery, quietly. "It is long long time since I heard it at all."

"But you know who he is," Nick said, without looking at him.

"Everyone knows who he is," said Mystery. "But his name

is forbidden. It brings wery-wery painful memories for British people, even now. Professor sahib is not so strict, but in many houses servants can be instantly dismissed for uttering it."

Nick was thinking hard, his brow damp and furrowed. He still wasn't looking at Mystery.

"He's our father, Mystery," he said. "You know the story. Everyone knows who we are."

"I am saying be careful, Master Nick," said Mystery. "It is not I who wish the name to remain unspoken."

"He's here, isn't he?" Nick said. "He is somewhere near."

Now he lifted his head and looked into Mystery's face. The servant's expression betrayed alarm.

"He is not safe in Calcutta," he said. "Many are here who wish him harm."

"But he's still alive," Nick said, "and he knows we are here."

"Alive, Master Nick," said Mystery, "alive, yes, wery much. He is eternal. He will always be alive. But his magic is formidable. You cannot pursuing him."

"But he's already—" I blurted, and Nick turned to me with the briefest, most urgent of hisses to keep quiet.

Mystery looked around him, and evidently decided it was time to change the subject. "Please to coming inside, in any case," said Mystery. "Breakfast is served. Professor sahib is there. And there is something else for you."

He went ahead of us, through the arch in the wall, towards the house.

"He knows a great deal more than he dare say," said Nick, in a low voice, as we watched him go.

We had made a vow not to mention the encounter in the temple. The Professor would be furious to hear we'd ventured that far on our own – and I was embarrassed at how transparent the trap had been, and how easily we'd fallen for it. Anyone to whom we told the story would think us fools. Now I was afraid that Nick's rage against the eunuch would arouse too much suspicion. Nick just shrugged. But, as we began to walk after Mystery towards the house, we found our path suddenly blocked by the fakir, who staggered out into the centre of the archway.

His eyes were misty and unseeing; but he had a kind of ecstatic smile on his face. He showed his dreadful teeth at us, and, suddenly nervous, I reached for Nick's forearm.

"Damyata," the fakir hissed. He'd obviously been listening all along. He intoned some words in his own language, which we had no way of following, and then grinned, as though he expected us to take comfort from what he said, or find it amusing.

"Come on," said Nick quietly.

But the fakir stood there, still blocking our path. He leaned towards us, and held up both of his hands; and this time, in a confidential whisper, he spoke in English. "Children of Damyata," he said – and grinned again. "Spirit master," he hissed. "Lord of the diamond! *Godofmischief!*"

We left the fakir standing there nodding after us as we went inside. A feeling of tremendous excitement was swelling inside me. It felt as though we had started something: as though our presence had suddenly caused a whisper, a single repeated name, to be uttered in Calcutta, and to spread, for the first time in years. The thrilled, uplifted face of the fakir was like that of someone who had been liberated.

The forbidden name of Damyata was taking hold.

Chapter 9

AN UNEXPECTED GIFT

I took Lash into the kitchen to get him something to eat; and then we joined the Professor in the breakfast room, where the table was laid with huge plates of fruit pieces, and honey, and curd, and goats' milk.

"Ah – quite!" he greeted us. He gestured towards the table. "Will you have tea? And this watermelon is good. Or the mangoes."

"Professor," said Nick as we sat down and helped ourselves, "I don't suppose you've had another look at that map? Or managed to find out anything about it?"

The Professor made a kind of embarrassed rumbling sound, and his ears twitched.

"Rrrhmmm, not exactly," he said. "Can't say I've, ah – had much success with it yet. May have a chance to find out some more today, don't you know."

Majara appeared from under the breakfast table and rubbed herself around our legs as we ate. I reached down to scratch her head in greeting, and took the opportunity to scratch at my own leg as I did so. I was peppered with angry pink insect bites, many of which had acquired a little dome of pus at the top. I'd already brought the top off some of them by scratching, with painful results.

"I just don't think we can afford to waste any time," said Nick. "The days are going by, and we've still no idea where the diamond might be."

"Quite," mumbled the Professor again.

I suddenly felt a bit sorry for him, confronted with Nick's impatient mood this morning. "Mystery said there was something for us," I said brightly, changing the subject.

The Professor swallowed. "Yes," he said. "Undoubtedly. Over there."

He'd been opening his correspondence; and, intriguingly, there were also some cards and letters for us. Since the banquet at Colonel Tweddle's, people in Calcutta were evidently beginning to know we were here, and had started inviting us to things. We were graciously invited to an afternoon party at Garden Reach, by a Mrs Cardew-Botheringay, who considered that we might provide most excellent companionship for her delightful children, Philomel and Mirabella. Another card suggested we might like to join a tiger-shoot this coming weekend. I was about to pooh-pooh the idea when it suddenly occurred to me that Nick might want to go. I passed him the card. He reached down beside his chair and stroked the top of Majara's head. "So that someone can have another rug," he said dismissively, to my relief. "I don't think so."

"I must admit," I muttered, "after last night, I think

the fewer people who know we're in Calcutta the better."

"What what?" said the Professor.

"If you don't think it too rude of us," I said, "I don't think we ought to be seen much at the moment, Professor. We've— that is, we're worried that the Captain knows we're here, and means us harm. We need to keep a low profile."

"Well now," said the Professor. "You're right. You must be careful." He picked up a small brown-paper parcel, and handed it to me. "Did you see this? This has come for you, too."

There was a little inscribed card with it. It was from Lady Sheets.

For Miss Imogen Winter, it read, in a neat hand, *with fond thanks.*

"I bet she didn't write that herself," I said, "she'd never be able to hold the pen." Curious, I tore the brown wrapping open.

"What is it?" Nick asked.

"It's a book of some sort," I said, intrigued. "Look, it's got a binding just like—" I stopped. Taking the book out of the wrapper altogether, I could see it was in fact just half a book. Torn in two down the spine, exactly like Miss Thynne's journal which was, even now, sitting in our trunk upstairs.

I turned it over. The leather cover was not the front of the book, but the back. I held it the right way up, with the pages uppermost. It was all handwritten – and the hand, I realised with mounting excitement, was exactly the same as in the journal upstairs.

There was absolutely no mistaking what it was. And,

furthermore, it was in much better condition. I flicked through the pages to check: and, apart from its being only half a book, it was almost as good as new. The ink had faded a bit, with the years, but there was no water damage to speak of, and far fewer stains of mould obliterating the writing. Words leaped off the first page.

> ... my excitement and I'm sure I shall blurt it out one day. I don't even know whether it's safe to write down ...

"Nick," I said with mounting excitement, "Nick, this is *it*."

It was the other half of Miss Thynne's diary. And it was completely legible, from the first page to the last.

Nick's fingers were visibly trembling as he came over to take the book from me. He stared at the first page for a few seconds, before exclaiming, "It's here!"

He was right. After all these tantalising months – when we'd had barely more than a single sentence which stopped in mid-stream and told us virtually nothing – here it was. The rest of the diary entry in which Justina revealed where the diamond had gone. It was dated 3rd July 1814.

> Damyata is meanwhile nowhere to be found, and I have heard at least one suspicious person linking him with the diamond's disappearance. We will never betray him, of course. He promised he would come back. I do not know whether Sasanka's

palace is well fortified against those who would take back the diamond; but all the local legends have it as the diamond's place of rightful origin, and surely it will not be long before they think of looking there. Our hearts are with him as he conceals it, and himself.

"I can't believe it," said Nick quietly. "This is it, isn't it? This is what we've needed to know, all this time."

We read the paragraph to the Professor.

"Sasanka's palace," he said, intrigued.

"Where is it, Professor?" I asked, eagerly. "Is it far away?"

"Ahem – I'm very much afraid that might not be as easy a question to answer as you think," he said. "It's a most *terribly* long time ago. The Nawabs of Bengal have built many palaces over the years, and most of them were ransacked by successive, ah – conquerors and plunderers. Nearly all of them have fallen down. Dear me, there must be three or four sets of old ruins which at least have a claim to be the site of Sasanka's palace."

"Oh, *surely* we can find it," I said. A sudden thought occurred to me. "What about our map?" I said excitedly. "It *must* be a map of one of the ruined palaces. Can't we just find out which one has a layout that matches?"

The Professor exhaled, and as he did so he made an accidental sound a bit like a trumpet. He lifted a large handkerchief and used it to dab at his brow. "I really don't want to see you disappointed, after such a long voyage," he said. "I'm worried that you seem to think it's frightfully easy, and I'm not so sure. But –" His frown softened as he looked up at us; and he smiled, and spoke with a more reassuring tone. "I'll, ah – have a try, don't you know, by all means. Don't expect miracles. And don't forget, this was written fifteen years ago. It may be of no help at all in determining where the diamond is now. But I'll see what I can find."

I looked at Nick. His eyes were shining. Even though we'd never heard of Sasanka's palace until a few minutes ago, we were already constructing it in our heads: its two grand, elongated wings, its long corridors, one in particular with doors branching into seven rooms.

I leafed through the diary, my eye returning again and again to the crucial words on the first page. "Damyata is nowhere to be found," I quoted. "He promised he will come back."

"There's not much doubt it was him who took the diamond," said Nick. "No wonder he daren't ever show his face in Calcutta."

"Lord of the diamond, the fakir called him," I remembered.

The Professor pricked up his ears. "The fakir?" he said. "Did you say the fakir had, ah – spoken about Damyata?"

I went red. I suddenly realised I might be getting other people into trouble. "Just – in passing, this morning," I mumbled. "It's just that, since we arrived, his name seems to have been mentioned a few times, here and there."

"Has anyone here *ever* seen him," Nick asked, "since the scandal over our mother?"

The Professor had been about to leave the room, but now he came back to the table. "He disappeared," he said. "Into thin air. You know, the Cloy brothers were minded to have him caught and put to death, when the scandal emerged. To hear them rage, at the time, you might have thought they were going to, ah – slaughter every native in Bengal. Something stopped them, I don't know what, from causing absolute mayhem. But Damyata never showed his face again, and for years his name wasn't even allowed to be uttered."

"That's what Mystery said," I murmured to Nick.

"This might sound like a strange question, Professor," said Nick solemnly, "but who *was* he?"

"Hmm. Quite." Professor Shugborough stared out of the window for a moment, as though working out how to put it. "It depends whom you ask," he said, after a while. "Some people would have it that he was a fiend. A demon, or incubus, come from hell to ruin the Cloys and drive the British out of India. Now, if you ask an Indian, he'll tell you a different story. They have Damyata down as a hero around here, even a sort of god, with the gift of eternal life. Someone who's waiting, biding his time, before liberating them. There are plenty of myths, you know, a lot of superstitions the Indians have. And, well, however plainly absurd it might be, that's what some people say."

I remembered the excitement in the fakir's face – and Mystery's furtive whisper: "*He is eternal. He will always be alive.*"

"So what do *you* think, Professor?" I asked.

The Professor seemed flummoxed. He blew a lot of air out from behind his tusk-like moustaches, and it made him seem so elephant-like it was all I could do to stop myself laughing.

"Ah – well, bah – ah – that is, I really couldn't say," he said. "There were theories at the time that he was the rogue son of a prince, or a travelling magician. But you know, there is someone who I think can explain it better for you. I should – ah, let you meet him. Yes. Yes, what a good idea." He went over to the desk, and began to write something down.

"So where did he come from?" I persisted.

"Well," said the Professor, "that's just it. He appeared from nowhere, and disappeared into nowhere again afterwards. But he had quite a hold over poor Imogen, you know. She was determined, and quite sure she knew her own mind, and she kept telling everyone in no uncertain terms that they were ridiculous to suggest she'd been entranced, or hypnotised, or any such thing. But it was obvious she was under – well, if you want to put it that way, under some kind of spell."

"So how did she meet him?" I wondered.

"Indeed," said the Professor, "the family were rather keen to know that, too. But you know, she was on a jolly loose rein while she was here. She'd always been a carefree kind of soul, and spent a lot of time running around. Who knew where she went, or whom she met? Especially after poor John Winter died, the family were too busy to care much. They came to regret it, of course."

As he spoke, I was leafing through the diary again. Phrases leaped off the pages as I turned them, all in Justina's elegant, meticulous handwriting. We were going to be able to learn so much by reading this, I realised.

Septimus says no one would believe either of us in any case, and it is his word against ours. Perhaps none of his brothers will believe any ill of him, but he makes a grave mistake if he underestimates the number of people in Calcutta who would willingly see him brought down.

"What I don't understand," said Nick, "is what Lady Sheets was doing with this. Did you mention it to her the other night? That we had half of the diary, I mean?"

"No," I said. "She talked about our mother, that was all. And she did mention Justina. But how she came to have this diary, I've no idea."

"But she knows what's in it, doesn't she?" said Nick. "She knows fine well it can help us. That's why she's sent it."

Lady Sheets suddenly seemed an unexpectedly intriguing figure.

"Professor," I said, "Lady Sheets told me quite a lot about Justina, the other evening, and about our mother, and her own daughter, Viola. They were all friends, weren't they? Do you remember them?"

"Viola was older," said the Professor, frowning. "But certainly your mother and Justina were, ah – inseparable. When your mother's, um – predicament was revealed, and it caused such scandal and heartache, and she was sent home, Justina was heartbroken."

"Lady Sheets called her 'the governess's grandchild',"

I recalled. "But she was a governess herself. She was *our* governess. Was her grandmother a governess too?"

"Her grandmother," said the Professor, slowly, thinking hard. "Now then, it's, ah – all such a long time ago. Undoubtedly. But she *was* a governess, don't you know. Of course she was!" It was coming back to him. "She was Septimus's governess, when he was a boy. Penelope Thynne. She had the most dreadful time with him, and I'm afraid many people laid the blame for his, ah – misconduct, at least partly at her door. They say he used to be wretched, don't you know, torturing animals, stealing from other children, even when he was tiny. As for his conduct towards the natives and servants, well – goodness me, he took his cue from his brothers, of course, but he seemed to have an ingenious cruelty all his own."

"Ungovernable, she called him," I said, the bizzarre dinner-table conversation with Lady Sheets flooding back into my head.

"That would be about right," agreed the Professor. "And I seem to think," he went on, "that he was close to Penelope Thynne's daughter – Justina's mother – for a time. There was a hope that they might marry. Instead, of course, he married Harriet Winter, your grandfather's cousin, and eventually, years later, it was the next generation he, ah – took a shine to, you might say. That is, Justina, and your mother."

I was finding it all rather hard to follow. "I've heard so many names since we got here," I said, "of people who lived decades ago, that – well, I mean, they're interesting, but – it's hard to remember who was who."

"I can see that," said the Professor. "Undoubtedly. I get confused myself, don't you know, half the time. Would it help if I drew you a family tree?"

"It might," I said, doubtfully.

"Well, I will," he said. "I'll do that this morning, if I have time. And I'll start making some investigations into where this mention of Sasanka's palace might take us."

We were both excited as we chased Lash upstairs. For the first time since we'd arrived, we felt as though we were making progress, and were well and truly on the trail of the diamond. The first thing we did when we got to my room was to take out the battered, washed-out old chunk of Justina's diary which we'd brought with us, and put it together with the new section. They fitted together perfectly, the torn edges of the cover matching one another all the way down the spine: but the contrast in their condition was even more obvious when they were placed side by side.

"I'm going to read this all the way through," I said. "We might not have found the best bits yet."

"Even so, we must surely be a step or two ahead of the Captain now," said Nick, triumphantly.

"Here," I said, my eye lingering on another passage I'd found at random. "What do you think this means?"

He even accused her of shaming her poor late mother's memory. Plainly, he has never heard the truth about her mother, but that is another secret I have sworn to keep.

Nick shrugged. "Maybe we can ask the Professor later," he said. "Seems there were a lot of people in the family with secrets, of one kind or another."

I found a strong piece of twine and tied the two halves together. No sooner had I finished doing so than there was a tentative knock, and Mystery's face peered around the door.

"Master Nick, Miss Mog, may I coming in?" he asked.

He looked slightly uncomfortable. His attitude to us – particularly to Nick – seemed to have changed, just this morning, since he'd witnessed the outburst in the eunuch's den. He suddenly seemed less bossy.

"Nanak is offering apology," he said.

"That little creep," said Nick crossly. "Apologise is the *least* he needs to do."

"He says," continued Mystery, "he wishes to offer you information, in spirit of friendship. Would you like to meeting him?"

We put the diary away in the trunk, and followed Mystery down the stairs and through to the kitchen, where the servants were cleaning up after breakfast. Lash came with us, and started a low, consistent growling when he spotted Nanak, hovering by the back door. I had to bend down to shut him up with a stern word into his face.

The eunuch's expression curled into a toothy cringe when he saw us: perhaps it was intended to be a smile, but we didn't smile back. Mystery exchanged a few words with him.

"He says he is making amends," he told us. "He is sorry about deceitful behaviour. There is something he has found out which he wishes you to know."

"Tell him we've paid him for information, and he has done nothing but trick us," said Nick. "How do we know this is not just more trickery?"

Mystery spoke to him again, briefly, and the eunuch answered in his reedy, duck-like voice, looking at us sullenly out of the corners of his eyes.

"He says you can choose to believing him, or not," said Mystery. "But it concerns the Captain."

I looked at Nick. We didn't have much choice.

"What does he have to say?" I asked.

The little eunuch spoke, and Mystery translated as he went. "The Captain is about to leave Calcutta in search of the diamond," he said. "He believes he knows where it is, and he will set sail upriver, in a small Indian boat, tomorrow. He makes his preparations today at an inn for sailors behind Custom House wharf."

"Which inn?" demanded Nick.

"It has no name," said Mystery, translating. "There is a sign outside which saying 'Wery Pleasant Time'. Nanak will show you the way, if you wish."

"We can find it," Nick sneered. "How does he know all this?"

"*Sahaparaadhi*," said Nanak.

"Boy-spies," said Mystery.

"Does he know any more than this?" asked Nick.

Nanak shook his head, without being asked.

"Apparently not," said Mystery.

I gazed at the eunuch, trying to read his expression. His eyes were shifty, but that was the way they looked all the time. He shrugged his shoulders and made a brief noise like a quack, as if to say: Take it or leave it.

I caught Nick's eye, and gave him a small barely-perceptible nod.

"Go away," said Nick to the dwarf.

"Sounds like we're off to the docks again, then," I said in a low voice as we went back inside. "Mystery will try and stop us. He'll say it's too dangerous."

"I wonder how long Nanak's known about this," muttered Nick, furiously. "He obviously wasn't going to breathe a word about it, until we scared him into telling us."

Nick stopped, in the big cool hallway, at the bottom of the stairs. Majara was lolling, imperiously, in her basket, and Lash paced around her, nervously, at a distance, his paws making skittering sounds on the tiles. Mystery caught us up.

"Master Nick," he said, breathlessly.

"Mystery," Nick interrupted him, "we need you to keep a secret. It's very important. Mog and I have something *very* important to do this morning. We must follow the Captain. We'll be careful. We'll be all right. Please don't tell anyone where we are. You *must* promise."

He could see we were in deadly earnest.

"Wery good, Master Nick," he said meekly.

There was a whole cluster of inns, and gambling-houses, and other unsavoury establishments, down near the water in the old part of the city. We'd passed some of them the other day, when we'd followed Mr Penagadder up into the bazaar: ramshackle wooden hovels, many of them painted in garish colours, pressed close together, some of them with upper rooms jutting out above street level, or over the foul orange-brown ditches that spilled from the city into the river. But many of them had been built on top of the foundations of older, more substantial buildings: so that, although the rooms above were little more than reeking wooden boxes, they had stone cellars.

And, when we spotted a scratchily-painted sign, just as Nanak had told us, advertising a *Very Pleasant Time*, it was down a set of steps into one of these cellars that we crept, desperate at all costs to avoid being seen. At the bottom of the steps we were faced with a heavy door across the cellar entrance: but a concerted push made it yield, with a scraping sound.

Poking our heads inside, we were assaulted by a powerful stench, a combination of intense damp and the searing ammonia smell of animal droppings.

"*Gaaah!* . . . I don't know if I can stand it in there," I said, holding my nose.

But I followed Nick in, as he stepped gradually further and

further into the dark, stinking space. The door had swung back into a closed position behind us; and, after the bright sunlight outside, it was a minute or two before our eyes adjusted to the darkness. As things became more distinct, we found we were in a tiny cellar, about three paces square. It seemed to be empty: but the walls and floor were wet, and the corners were just too dark to see into.

"You've heard stories about the Black Hole of Calcutta, haven't you?" I said, as we peered around. "Maybe this was it."

"Shh!" whispered Nick. "Over here. Look."

He was peering upwards: and, as I joined him, I could just about make out the shape of a square lattice of metal in the ceiling. In fact, as I stared up into the hot darkness, I could see there were two, a few feet apart. They looked like the kind of windows or hatches you'd find in a medieval prison cell. One of them had a couple of bars missing, and so the gaps between them were wider; though they were still only a matter of inches across, and impossible to get through. Pale shafts of sunlight from the room above were filtering through the grilles, and hitting the mouldering stone wall above our heads, making a large but faint crisscross pattern. I tried to work out how high up they were. If I'd stood on Nick's shoulders, I guessed, I'd just about have been able to grasp the bars. The grilles appeared to be glistening wet, and something was dripping from them, sporadically, falling into the space in which we stood. Perhaps they were there to allow fluid to drain from the floor of the inn into the cellar below. Or perhaps the cellar had once been a kind of dungeon.

Whatever the case, the latticed openings allowed voices in the room above to float down, unimpeded, to our hiding place. And, as we listened, a hollow and familiar sound from the flagstones above dispelled any lingering doubts that the eunuch's information might have been suspect.

Click . . . click . . . click . . .

The Captain was up there, sure enough. The clicking sound moved around above our heads. He was stumping around the room, first in one direction, then the other. For a long time there were no voices, no other noises. We couldn't tell if there was anyone else up there with him, or not. We waited, listening, in the fetid darkness, for what seemed like an age . . .

And then, suddenly, there was an outburst. Even down here, it made me jump.

"The devil rot this place!" the Captain's voice shouted. "Another day of waiting! Another day of sweating and scratching in this stinking inn. I shall be driven mad, Mr Penagadder, and that will be an unpleasant experience for all."

"Cloke has given his assurance," came Penagadder's gravelly murmur.

"Aye, this bargee, Cloke as you call 'im," the Captain fumed. "He'd better turn out to be more trustworthy than the old crew, Mr Penagadder, or you will be busy on the voyage and we will be navigating by our wits."

"All he has to do is get us there," said Penagadder.

"Quite right, Mr Penagadder, and when we 'ave the stone in our 'ands, then his reward will be a nice big stone around 'is neck."

Penagadder said nothing in reply, and the Captain fell silent for a while. There was the occasional echoing *click* on the stone floor as he moved briefly, or shifted his weight on his crutches in agitation.

"I can't sit here a moment longer," he growled at length. "I'll see you later. Chances are I'll be out for the rest o' the day."

"What will ye do?" asked Penagadder.

"Who can say?" snarled the Captain. "All I know is, I've 'ad it with lying low, Mr Penagadder. If I'm seen abroad, so be it. We 'ave our information. At dawn we will be afloat, and not a minute too soon. Meantime – I might go and strangle a eunuch." Despite the menace with which he uttered the last phrase, I couldn't stifle a wry smile, down in our dark hiding place.

"Would ye recognise Mr Cloke's boat?" Penagadder asked him. "Only I might be aboard when ye come."

"I'll know it," said the Captain, stumping towards the door. "Peacocks and pelicans on the prow. How long will you be here?"

"No time at all," growled Penagadder sourly. "Waiting here's intolerable, even with your companionship. If you're going out, so shall I."

"It's indifferent to me, where you go," said the Captain, "but make it somewhere apart from where I am. We shall be getting enough of one another's – *companionship*, these next few days."

There was the sound of scuffling as they got up to leave.

Their figures cast a shadow down into our hiding place, and one of them made the grille above our heads ring with the tread of his boot, as they made for the door.

Click . . . click . . . click . . .

The Captain seemed to pause by the door. He let Penagadder through, and then, before following him into the stifling humidity of outside, he rumbled the lines of a familiar tune, as though in anticipation of a prize that would soon be his.

"*O my lovely blue eye,*
Blue eye that twinkle and shine,
If it takes till the day I die
I shall make your blue eye mine."

And, half chuckling, half coughing, the Captain's footfall receded until we could hear it no longer.

Click . . . click . . . click . . .

They'd gone. I'd hardly dared breathe while they were talking upstairs, which had certainly helped when it came to not inhaling the noxious stench down here – but now we both gasped in relief.

"It's just what Nanak said," I whispered. "First thing tomorrow morning."

"Somehow, we have to follow him," said Nick. "In fact, we have to get there first."

"But he hasn't said where he's going," I whispered back.

"I know." Nick was fanning his face with his hand. "It's so hot down here," he said, "I'm sweating like a pig. I can't think straight. Come on, let's get out."

He made for the cellar door. I followed him, and waited while he opened it. It was taking him a long time.

"*Come* on," I said impatiently, "get it open. I need fresh air."

"Mog, I can't." He wrenched at it.

"Don't muck about. It must open. We got in here all right, didn't we?"

"Mog, I'm telling you, it won't budge."

He moved aside while I had a go: but it was no use. However hard I tugged at it, bracing my foot against the wall, nothing happened except that my sweaty hands slipped repeatedly away from the iron handle. We tried combining our strength and both pulling it at once, my hands tight around the handle and Nick's hands clasped around mine: but to no avail.

"Please don't say we're trapped in here," I said, starting to panic.

"It's all right," said Nick, "if we really can't get out, we'll just have to shout up through the grilles. Someone's bound to hear us. Just pray it's not Penagadder or anyone still hanging around." He went to look up through the grilles again. "I can't hear anyone up there," he said, "but maybe we'd better wait a few minutes before we shout for help – and give them time to get a long way off. We don't want them coming back and finding us down here."

And then, without warning, as he stood looking upward, there was a clatter: and someone lifted the grille from above, swinging it open on a hinge.

I started, and reached out instinctively for Nick's arm.

Did someone already know we were here? Had they heard us? Who was it? I stood rigid, incapable of deciding whether to call out to them, or not. His face close to mine, Nick put his finger to his lips to warn me to say nothing.

The clattering continued from above us; but still no face appeared at the hole. Instead, a big, bulky shape was heaved into the gap, squeezed with some effort down through the square hatch, and started to descend towards us, suspended by a rope. Perhaps someone was lowering some goods down into the cellar to be stored?

As it sank, getting nearer and nearer our heads, I began to make out what it was. It was a large basket. A strange dread crept over me, as it swayed and hovered on its rope. Hearts in mouths, we stood aside, as it came lower and lower, to let it swing its way down into the dark space between us: and now I knew I recognised it. It was *the* basket – the fakir's basket.

"No," I said in a loud whisper, "surely not!"

As the basket sank to the floor and rested there, the rope was dropped after it into the cellar, where it hit the ground with a damp smack. And then, immediately, the iron grille above our heads was heaved back into place, with a deep, resonant grind and clunk.

We were trapped in here, with the snake-basket.

"This can't be happening," I said, in a panic, not caring about whispering now. "It's the snake! We've been tricked again, Nick! It was all a trap!"

Nick had run across the cellar and was tugging at the door

again, in case a renewed effort would make it budge; but it was as hopeless as ever.

"I can't – get it – open," he growled.

Meanwhile, there was a distinct dry, slithering noise from within the basket – and then the lid toppled off. Whatever was inside was making its way out. And there was absolutely nowhere to go.

CHAPTER 10

SURPRISES

"Get back," said Nick, pulling me back against the closed door, as far from the basket as we could get.

"This is your fault," I said, panic-stricken. "*You* brought us here. And why couldn't you be more careful about leaving the door open?"

"Someone locked the door on purpose," he retorted. "It wasn't an accident."

"We're trapped in here with that *thing*!" I said through clenched teeth. "There's no way out, Nick. We're going to die!"

The scraping sounds continued from inside the basket; and I waited, terrified, expecting at any moment to see the small, shiny head of the cobra rising up above the neck, its tongue tasting the air to gauge the direction of its prey.

And, a moment later, something did emerge from the basket.

But it clearly wasn't a snake. It was something much bigger: something with a dark hairy head. I cried out in surprise.

"There's a monkey in there, Nick!"

The basket toppled over, and the creature squeezed its way out, like a big gangly bird hatching out of its egg-case, as we watched in alarm from the dark corner of the cellar.

"Who you calling monkey?" came a familiar voice.

It was Sarasvati. I could see her now, as she wriggled free of the basket and stood up.

"Don't worry," she said, in a whisper. "Keep quiet. It's only me. No snake!"

She looked up at the shaft of sunlight coming through the grille above our heads, and ducked out of the way, tutting. As she did so, there was the sound of laughter from the room above.

"Quiet," she whispered again. "They will go away."

"Who is it?" I hissed.

"You-know-who," she said. "Nanak and Mohini. They think the snake was in the basket. But it was me." A thought occurred to her. "*Don't* be quiet," she said. "Scream. Cry out. One of you."

The relief of seeing the child's familiar face, instead of a deadly snake, was making me want to laugh out loud. To release the tension, I did as she said. I screamed, as though the snake really were crawling towards me.

There was more sniggering from up above, and the sound of feet running away. They were too cowardly to wait around to hear the consequences of their deadly trick.

"I don't believe it," said Nick. "Of all the nasty, sneaky things . . . !"

"They thought it would teach you a lesson," Sarasvati said solemnly. "I heard them planning. So I crawled into the basket instead."

"They were trying to kill us," I said.

"I don't think so," she said. "It was a prank. They are just too stupid to think what might happen."

"We need to get out of here," said Nick.

Sarasvati looked around the tiny cellar, briefly. It took her a couple of seconds to work out how she was going to get out. "Help me up there," she said.

Standing on Nick's shoulders, she took a kind of flying leap up to the broken grille, and dangled there, by her hands, from the remaining bars. There was no way Nick or I could possibly have squeezed through the gap between them; but she swung her legs up like the most agile of monkeys, and began somehow to fold her limbs so that they fitted through. I watched her, open-mouthed. Within seconds, she had wriggled through the gap and was peering down at us from the room above, her hair hanging down around her impish face.

"No one up here," she whispered. "You could climb up – but no. I'll come down and open the door!" She disappeared.

"Did you see that?" I said to Nick. "First she squeezes herself into that snake-basket. Then she crawls through that grille like – like someone made of string. She's *extraordinary*."

"Thank goodness she found out what those two were up to," said Nick.

"I really thought that was it, when the snake-basket appeared," I said. "I'm sorry, Nick. I was terrified."

There was a squeak as the bolt was unfastened on the heavy cellar door, and a tall, blindingly-bright streak of light opened up and flooded the wet little room with sunshine.

"This door is *heavy*!" panted Sarasvati as we emerged. "You would never have got it open. Those *bad* people!"

Shielding our eyes from the daylight, we made our way back up the discoloured, mossy stairs to the street. The first thing we did was take a good look around, in case there was any sign of the Captain, or Penagadder, or anyone else we didn't want to bump into. But the coast seemed to be clear.

"I don't know how we can thank you," said Nick to Sarasvati. "If that had really been the snake, we might have been in real danger."

"No need to thank me," she said.

"Did they carry you all the way from the Professor's house, in that basket?" I asked her.

She laughed, in her tiny, tinkling way. "Yes. A bumpy ride! But they didn't guess it was me, and they were too afraid to look inside."

"And what happened to the snake?" Nick asked.

Sarasvati looked up at us, bashfully.

"I played a trick of my own," she confessed. "I hid it in the eunuch's bed. A special surprise. For him to find later."

We stopped, close to a corner where the dingy little street met a much wider thoroughfare leading to the dockside. She looked around, nervous of being overheard, and lowered her voice.

"Is it true you are the children of Damyata?" she asked,

solemnly. "That is what some are saying. I didn't know. But all of a sudden I am hearing his name everywhere."

"It is true," I said.

"Then," she said, "you are protected. Others will protect you. He will protect you."

"We thought he had come to Calcutta to find us," I said. "But we haven't – seen him yet."

"Damyata is in danger in Calcutta," she said. "Even his name makes people angry. They think he is dead, or gone away. He must stay hidden."

"Do you know him?" I asked her, intrigued.

"I know him in here," she said, touching her breastbone. And that was all she said, before giving a sudden gasp, and darting back down the street towards the inn we'd just come from.

"Sarasvati, wait!" Nick called. "Where are you going?"

"To bring the basket," she called. "I forgot it. Go home! I will see you there."

Nick was thinking hard about something, and hardly said a word as we made our way back through the energy-sapping heat to the Professor's. I kept glancing at him, trying hard to read his expression; and I'd have pestered him to make him reveal what he was thinking about, if it hadn't been too hot to walk and speak at the same time. When we got back, I fully expected him to go straight round to the outhouses and confront the eunuch again. But instead he came and sat with me inside, in the garden room with the glass doors, under the cool breeze of the *pankahs*. Bulbul, the plumper of the boy-servants, peered around the door, saw us, and disappeared again. A few seconds later, Mystery came in.

"Miss Mog, Master Nick," he said, his eyes lighting up. "Professor sahib has been looking for you. It is long past lunchtime. You will have something to drink?"

I had sweated so much this morning I felt as though I was dying of thirst: I had genuinely thought, at one point on our walk home, that I was going to collapse. We told Mystery, in as restrained a way as we could manage, that yes, we'd love a drink.

"Just the tickety!" he enthused; and retreated again.

"He didn't say anything about these clothes," I said to Nick, "but he *must* have noticed. We look a fright. Look, I've got stains all over me, from the walls of that horrible cellar. We've got to go up and get changed before we see the Professor."

Bulbul came back in, with a tray and two tall glasses full of the juice of mangoes. Nick downed his in one go, and exhaled in relief as he put his glass down. I tried to drink mine more slowly, not wanting it to be finished. I felt overwhelmingly tired: the effort of the morning's adventure, and the heat, had suddenly made me want to lie down and sleep. I knew if I went upstairs to change now, I wouldn't come down again until at least the evening.

"It's no good, I *have* to go to sleep," I said. "Can you apologise for me, if you see the Professor? And if he's got something to tell us about the map, I'll find out later."

Nick nodded, wordlessly. He didn't look very pleased.

"What?" I challenged him. "I'm *exhausted*, Nick."

He looked at me.

"It's fine," he said, "you go and sleep. I'll be fine. I've – I've got an idea," he said. "I might go out again. Don't worry, I'll be all right. You go up and sleep."

The bedroom was cool and shady. Lash was still asleep in the big chair, exactly where I'd left him before we went out this morning; and I sat down to make a fuss of him for a few minutes. Then I got up and went over to the wash-stand, splashed some water on my face and neck, dried off, and climbed thankfully onto the big bed and pulled the mosquito net down around myself.

No sooner had I done so, however, than there was the most appalling shrieking sound from outside.

I got up and went out onto the veranda. It was the eunuch, hopping in terror along the path which skirted the house, screaming and flapping his too-long arms. At first, with a frown, I thought it must have been Nick who had scared him: but then I remembered what Sarasvati had said.

Of course! He must have come back from the inn and discovered the snake – curled up in his nasty little bed, where she had hidden it.

The screeching continued, as I went back inside to lie down; and I fell asleep on the crisp sheets in no time, with a broad smile on my face.

Lash woke me up by licking my face. He'd pushed his head underneath the mosquito netting, trying to get me to wake up, and when I opened my eyes I found myself nose to nose with him, his chin resting on the sheet as he gazed hopefully at me.

"Ohhh, how long have I slept?" I asked him, sitting up. "Are you hungry?"

I'd slept for less than three hours, as it turned out: but I felt a great deal better. Nick wasn't in his room, and, indeed, was nowhere to be seen as we hunted for him in the house and garden. But we did find the Professor, who beckoned from the open windows of the garden room as we walked past.

"Imogen!" he bumbled. "The very – ah, undoubtedly! Look, I've been doing a bit of work on this family tree I promised you. Why don't you come in? Isn't Dominic with you?"

"He's – around somewhere," I said, uncertainly, as Lash sniffed around under the table looking for remnants of the last meal that had been served in here.

"Quite. Well, well. You know you were finding it a bit, ah – confusing, all the family history, and who was who, and that sort of thing. Well now, I made this very sketchy genealogy – can't say I've put everyone in, mark you, but I think it's got most of what you might need to know."

He led me over to the writing-desk, which was open, with various pencils and a bottle of ink arranged around a large sheet of paper. He pulled the chair aside, so we both had room to stand there and see what he'd done.

"Well now," he said, "these are the lines of the Winter family – your own, starting here at the top with the first John Winter, your – ah – great-great-grandfather, I do believe. Then it comes down to your great-grandfather, and your grandfather, John Winter the younger, and then his daughter, Imogen, your mother. And these two branches here, no need to explain those – those are yourself and Dominic. So it comes down to the present day. See? So far, so good. Now: on the opposite side, here, this is where I've laid out the Cloy family. Old Barnabas Cloy here, at the very top, and then his son, Lancelot, the first of the family to make his fortune in India, don't you know. And then, down here, his seven sons – off this broad line here, don't you see. Hubert, then Nicodemus, then Augustus, then the twins, Hercules and Maximilian, then Tarquin, and finally Septimus – whom you know all about. Ah, quite! And then, down here . . ."

I stared at the tree the Professor had drawn, with its scratchy vertical and horizontal lines indicating parentage, kinship and marriage. He was moving the tip of a pencil back and forth along the lines, occasionally jabbing it at a carefully-written name somewhere on the page, as he talked about the person in question. But I'd stopped listening to what he was saying. I was too astonished, too transfixed by the drawing in front of me, to pay much attention to his rambling explanation.

I had seen this before.

The lines and branches cascading down the two halves of the page; the pattern of points and connections; most obviously, the long horizontal line with seven spurs coming down from it, which represented the seven children of Sir Lancelot Cloy. It was so obvious, now that I was looking at it laid out in front of me like this. Why on *earth* hadn't I realised it earlier?

It was almost identical to the map we had printed off in Cramplock's old shop, and brought with us all these thousands of miles, expecting that it would show us a route to the treasure we sought. The map we'd given to the Professor, in the vain hope that he might be able to match it with the layout of any towns, or palaces, in the vicinity of Calcutta.

It wasn't a map we'd printed at all. It was a family tree. *Our* family tree – with the names removed, presumably to throw others off the scent. How stupid we'd been!

"As for this line here, don't you see," he was saying, "this is where the two families' histories join up, because—"

"Professor," I interrupted him.

"This is Harriet, your grandfather's cousin," he continued, undeterred, "and this—"

"Thank you, Professor," I tried again, "thank you *so* much, Professor, I—"

"*This*," he ploughed on, wielding the pencil, "is the line that indicates her marriage to Sir Septimus, don't you know, thus *linking*—"

"Professor!" I persisted.

At last, he petered out, in mid-stream, puffing slightly.

"Thank you very much for this, Professor," I said. "You really don't need to go on. I've realised something – terribly important."

"Well, well," he said, scratching his head.

"Does this look at all familiar, now that you've drawn it?" I asked him.

He gazed at it, unsure what I meant.

"Have you still got the map we gave you?" I asked him.

"Ah – yes, I believe so, in this very desk," he said, rather confused.

And, as he unfolded the map, and laid the two drawings side by side, the similarity was so undeniable I gave a whoop of excitement. We'd been so fixated on this being a map of somewhere, that we'd failed to recognise how completely like a family tree it was, with its branching, descending pattern. And we'd wasted *such* a long time before working it out!

"Well – bless my soul," the Professor murmured. "What a clever old thing you are, Imogen, undoubtedly. Yes, yes. Bless my soul."

"Which means," I said, pulling the map towards me, "that the points on this map, which we've always thought are meant to be places, are actually people."

"Ah – quite! You must be right," said the Professor, shaking his head in amazement. "*Here is love, and wisdom, and eternity*," he read. "That's written underneath this bifurcating line here, which, ah – means it must refer to the two of you. You and Dominic."

"But this is the important one," I said. "*Seek the point to the right, for this is the sole source of your fortune*. What does that mean?"

The Professor pored over the two pages, comparing them. "Hmm," he said. "There is no point to the right. That is – the two don't quite match, at this point." I leaned over to look. "See here," he said, "on the family tree I've drawn. This is your mother, Imogen – and that's her father, John Winter, on the line above – and that's her mother, Sophia, next to him. What this drawing shows –" he reached for the printed design we'd brought from London "– is a futher spur on the other side of Imogen's mother. What might that mean? A brother or sister of hers? I never knew of such a person. I would have sworn Sophia was always said to be an only child, as Imogen herself was."

"I can't work it out," I said. The longer I stared at it, the less I was able to concentrate on the closely-packed rows of half-familiar names, and I was rapidly losing track of the logic of it. But our attention was distracted from the papers for a moment, in any case, when Lash pricked up his ears and suddenly gave a *woof*. Moments later there was the sound of footsteps in the hallway outside; and, as Lash trotted out of the room to greet the visitor, I heard Nick's voice.

"Nick!" I called. "In here!"

He looked a bit rueful as he came in. I think he'd been hoping he could sneak upstairs without being noticed. But I was too excited to worry about where he'd been. I showed him the two pieces of paper, the family tree and our map. He was instantly fascinated, and full of admiration for our detective work.

"How could we not have realised it was a family tree?" he exclaimed.

"It's obvious, isn't it, when you know?" I said. "But it's because we *wanted* it to be a map. We couldn't see beyond our first silly assumption."

"So what's all this about?" he wondered, looking from one design to the other. "*Seek the point to the right . . .*?"

"Ah – quite. We're still far from sure about that," admitted the Professor.

"A family member, who's the source of our fortune?" queried Nick. "Who, then?"

"I don't know," I said, " but I tell you what. I bet the Captain hasn't worked out what this really is. I bet he still thinks it's a map of somewhere. And wherever he's going, he probably still thinks it can help him when he gets there."

Nick looked at the Professor, and seemed a bit uncomfortable again.

"Professor," he said, "Mog and I might go up and change, if that's all right with you. I guess it won't be too long before dinner?"

"Goodness me, yes," said the Professor, consulting the clock. "And we have guests for dinner this evening too, did anyone tell you? Well, we shall pursue this, ah – another time. Undoubtedly!"

"You're in a rush," I said to Nick in a low voice as we got to the top of the stairs. "And where have you been all afternoon?"

"Shh!" he replied. Only when he'd closed the door of his room behind us did he say another word. It seemed to take him a little while to decide how to start. A sudden, uneasy kind of dread crept over me.

"Mog, I told you I'd had an idea," he said. "It was down in that cellar, listening to the Captain. I've been wondering how on *earth* we're going to find out where the diamond is, and stop him getting it first. And now that he's setting sail, and he seems to think he's tracked it down, well – that puts him a step ahead of us, as far as I can see." He was watching my face intently, gauging my reaction.

"Maybe," I said, cautiously.

"He's leaving Calcutta tomorrow morning, at dawn," Nick continued. "Now, we may have found out that his map isn't quite what he thinks it is – but as far as I can see, we don't stand a chance of finding out where he's going, in time to stop him, or get there ourselves. Do we?"

I said nothing.

"Are we any nearer knowing where the diamond really is?" he asked. "Well, are we?"

"Damyata will help us, one way or another," I said quietly, "I feel sure of it."

"Damyata hasn't been much help so far," said Nick.

He got up and walked around the room, peering briefly out onto the veranda as he went, to make sure we weren't being spied on.

"No, I've had an idea," he said. "You're probably not going to like it, but it's the only thing I can think of. Because we haven't got much time. We haven't got any time at all, in fact."

"What's happened?" I asked. "What have you done?"

He paced around the room a bit more; then stopped, and took a deep breath.

"I've been to see that man they call Mr Cloke," he said.

"I've volunteered to go as part of his crew. In disguise. First thing in the morning."

At first I thought he was joking. I couldn't believe what he was telling me.

"You've done *what*?" I squeaked. He started to explain again, but I interrupted him. "So let me get this right," I said, "you've arranged to crew the ship the Captain has hired to take him upriver, tomorrow."

"Exactly."

"You've volunteered to spend goodness-knows-how-many days on board the same tiny boat as the Captain? And Penagadder? Just so as not to let them out of your sight?"

"Mmm."

"And you think they won't realise who you are?" I shrieked.

"They'll have no idea," he said. "Mr Cloke didn't. He thought I was just a sailor-lad from the city."

"Mr Cloke hasn't been trying to murder you!" I said. "Think about it. The Captain turns up and finds a boy on board, completely unexpectedly. He's the same age and build as one of the kids the Captain's just spent the past week trying to get rid of. You think he won't put two and two together? He might not have got a proper look at you in the black pagoda the other night, but he heard your *voice*, Nick. He'll recognise you at once!"

"He won't," said Nick, "and I'll tell you why not. One, he won't care about some kid Cloke brings on board. He's too busy worrying about getting his hands on the diamond. Two, he only thinks of us as two twins, not one. Three, he'll never dream that either of us would dare go anywhere near him. It would just be too unlikely to be true. I'll just be Cloke's boy. He won't associate me with me, at all."

It was so fantastic, I laughed, open-mouthed.

"You'll *never* get away with it, Nick," I said, "and what's more, you'll get yourself killed. You can't possibly be serious."

But he was. I could see from his face that he'd made up his mind.

He'd been down to the docks, this afternoon while I was asleep, and hunted down the boat with painted pelicans and peacocks on the prow, just as the Captain had said. At first, Mr Cloke wasn't aboard, and he'd skulked around among the boats for an hour or so, waiting. Eventually Mr Cloke had appeared: a tall, taciturn Indian sailor with a cotton shawl drawn around his face against the heat. Nick had introduced himself, using some bogus name, saying he'd learned the boat was setting off upriver, and could he join it. I didn't doubt that he'd done a convincing job of pretending to be a sailor-lad. That was more or less what he had been, for the first twelve years of his life. He knew, without even having to think about it, the names of every rope and every sail, every job that had to be done on board, and the real names and nicknames of every part of a ship. He knew the names of enough well-known East Indiamen on the Calcutta route to pretend he'd been aboard any number of them. He could talk about water, and weather, and currents. If you asked him which point of the compass the wind was coming from, he could always tell you.

But, by the sound of things, he'd also been incredibly lucky. Mr Cloke had agreed to let him join the crew, even though in truth he almost certainly didn't need an extra hand, given that his two passengers joining the boat next morning were also professional sailors.

"He's stringing you along, this Mr Cloke," I said. "You'll get there in the morning, and they'll already have gone, without you."

"Which is why I'm going aboard tonight," he said.

"You really are serious about this, aren't you?" I said.

He just nodded.

"I can't *possibly* let you sail off to heaven-knows-where with those two," I said. "At least let me come with you."

"That's the whole point, Mog," he said. "If two of us show up, they'll realise who we are straight away. Besides, it's too dangerous. You *have* to stay here. I'll be all right."

"And what am I supposed to do till you get back? Spend every minute worrying that you've been thrown overboard with a rock tied round you? How would I know if you were in trouble, or help you? What on earth are you going to do when you get there, to stop them getting the diamond? Assuming they ever find it, of course. What if this Cloke fellow's leading them on a wild-goose chase? What if he turns out to be a villain too?" The more I ranted at him, the more dreadful the possibilities which opened up, and the more inevitable they all seemed.

"Keep your voice down, Mog," said Nick quietly, looking nervously towards the veranda.

My eyes almost popped out of my head. I was too frustrated to say any more, except to emit a high-pitched growl, and clasp my hands together in a kind of mime of strangulation. I left him, clicked my fingers for Lash to follow me, and went into my own room, slamming the door.

I was determined Nick wasn't going to go; and yet I could tell he wasn't going to let me stop him. I had to do something. My mind was working furiously as I changed for dinner, throwing on some clothes which looked half respectable. I really couldn't have cared less about the guests the Professor had invited, or what impression I made on them. When I heard the dinner gong, I didn't go and call for Nick. I checked my reflection briefly, and winced at the sight of an angry and painful insect bite on my cheek; I bent to speak into Lash's face as he lay in the big chair, telling him to stay and be quiet; and went downstairs on my own.

"Ah! Imogen," said the Professor, who was serving drinks to his guests as I entered the dining room. "Come and meet Mr and Mrs Weem, long-standing, ah – friends of mine here in Calcutta. And Dr Shastri."

I shook hands politely with the guests. Mr Weem was a Scot, about the same age as the Professor; quietly spoken, with a concave face, as though he'd walked into a solid object at some point in his life and his features had been knocked back into his skull. His wife was short, and heavily built, and never stopped smiling. Dr Shastri was standing over by the sideboard with his back to me, as the Professor fixed his drink. When he heard me speaking to the others he turned to greet me, glass of water in hand; and I don't think I can have made a very good job of concealing my surprise when I saw him, because he looked at me slightly quizzically when I met his eye. He was much younger than I had expected a guest of the Professor's to be: in his early twenties, perhaps, a clean-shaven, very handsome Indian with soft brown eyes. I should have returned his greeting, said something friendly and funny; but for some reason I found myself unable to think of anything at all sensible to say, and I just nodded at him, dumbly, feeling my face getting hot. I expect he just thought I was shy.

"Isn't Dominic with you?" the Professor was asking.

"I expect he'll be down in a minute," I said, distracted.

I made polite conversation with the Weems for a few minutes, responding to Mrs Weem's good-natured questions about my impressions of Calcutta. They meant no harm, I knew, but I was finding it impossible to concentrate on what I was saying, or to give coherent answers, really. My eyes kept wandering around the room, waiting for Nick to come in, wondering what he'd been doing, wondering what on earth I was going to say to him that might change his mind; and, if I couldn't, how I might possibly make sure he was safe on his ridiculous, lethal expedition. The Weems must have thought me very rude, or, at best, a little lacking in social graces.

At last Nick came in, followed by Mystery, who nodded to the Professor; and then the servants started to appear, bringing dishes of food into the room as we sat down at the table. It was impossible, now, in company, to say any more to Nick about his plan. I caught his eye a few times across the table, and he sort of smiled, though his eyes were defiant and his lips tight.

I suppose I should have realised he was actually very scared. I didn't. I just thought he was being stubborn.

Amid the clattering of china, and the bustle of the servants as they served the food, the Professor explained his acquaintance with the three guests, and what they each did here in Calcutta. I'm afraid I didn't pay too much attention: something to do with their having been drawn against one another at bridge one evening, a long time ago. Everyone seemed very nice; but I felt as though it was only my body that was here, smiling emptily, while my real self was somewhere else, wandering round the house in an agony of fear and indecision.

I only started to pay proper attention to the conversation when I heard the name Damyata.

It was the Professor who had uttered it. He was explaining to his guests who Nick and I were: the circumstances of our birth, what had happened to us when we reached London, our separate upbringing, and our recent discovery of our past – just as we had told it to him. I could see the dawning of understanding on Mr Weem's face, as he made the connection between his memory of the Imogen Winter scandal and our being here. Dr Shastri, who had sat in interested silence for much of the meal so far, was watching me with his gentle brown eyes; and despite myself, when I caught his eye, I couldn't hold it, but found myself looking away again, shyly.

"Forgive me, Professor," I said, to cover my sudden

embarrassment, "but I thought polite society in Calcutta didn't like to utter the name."

The Professor snorted. "Polite society," he repeated. "Bah – there are plenty of people in Calcutta who won't, you are quite right. But one of the reasons these people are my friends, don't you know, is because they have no such grudge."

"We remember your mother well," offered Mrs Weem, smiling. "Such a lovely, kind girl."

"Did you know Damyata, too?" Nick asked.

Their eyes turned to look at him.

"N-no," said Mr Weem slowly, "I'm afraid not. We – that is, I believe not many people ever actually *met* him."

"You might find the Doctor did," said the Professor. "Is that right, Doctor?"

Doctor Shastri wiped the corner of his mouth briefly on his napkin. "You will realise that I was only a boy," he said, in a soft, cultured voice, "but at the time your mother knew Damyata, I knew him slightly, too, yes."

"We – still don't know very much about him," I said, cagily.

"Indeed," nodded the Doctor, "you are not alone. He has a reputation as an – enigma. And he was a mysterious figure even then. We local boys knew him as – well, we would describe him as *jadoogar*. A magician. He used to perform tricks for us. He was a musician also. He would adopt disguises, to fool us. He was a master of illusions. He could charm snakes, and tame monkeys, and make people believe all kinds of things that could not be. Startling power, he had."

We listened, transfixed. All of this matched what we knew of Damyata.

The Doctor's eyes twinkled slightly. "And he had obviously enchanted your mother," he said. "She used to come and watch him doing his silly tricks for us. And then, after a time, they would walk off, together."

"Where did he come from?" I asked him.

He shrugged. "No one knew, I think," he said. "But no one questioned. It seemed – what do you say? – an irrelevance. He just *was*." He broke into a laugh when he saw our intent expressions, as we struggled to understand. "Let me put it more simply," he said. "He had a very powerful presence. Something indefinable – extremely affecting, about him. You might say, something *supernatural*. Not fixed to a place, or even a time. But he was kind, and good."

"You say *was*," said Nick. "But you know that he is still alive."

There was a silence, which went on for just long enough to make me start to think Nick must have said something terrible. Then the Doctor spoke.

"I believe he is," he said, with a small bow of the head.

"*Eternal*," I said, remembering Mystery's words.

Dr Shastri gazed at me as though I had read his mind. His eyes held mine. There was excitement in them, but also a deep calm – as though, for the first time, he had found someone who really understood.

"Eternal," he repeated, incredibly quietly.

I tore my eyes away from his; and looked around the table at the others.

"And you have come – to look for him?" asked Mrs Weem, intrigued.

"Well – in a way, yes," I said. "We thought we might be able to find out where he is."

"If anyone knew that," put in Mr Weem, "I imagine he would have been hunted down. I well recall the fury that accompanied his disappearance, especially because I seem to remember he was linked to the loss of a precious heirloom."

I tried to catch Nick's eye, but he was looking resolutely at his food. The Professor, to my relief, didn't mention our quest for the diamond; and the conversation drifted on to topics of far less interest to the two of us. I kept watching Nick, and thinking about the Captain, and Mr Cloke, and the river. I knew what I was going to do. I hadn't discussed it with anyone, and I didn't remember making a decision; but suddenly it seemed obvious.

We finished eating, and the servants came to clear away the plates; and the guests remained around the table, talking, for a while. I sat on my hands, trying desperately not to fidget. An adventure was about to begin. Part of me couldn't wait; and another part of me was dreading it. The thing I was most worried about was that Nick would notice my restlessness, and guess what I was thinking.

At last, the guests took their leave. We stood in the hallway with the Professor, to bid them goodnight. Mystery was outside on the gravel, shouting at the drivers as carriages pulled up. The Doctor went out onto the threshold, and looked up at the sky.

"Rain is coming at last," he said.

"Thank you so much for letting us meet Imogen and Dominic," said Mrs Weem, beaming at the Professor, and then at us. "Such charming children, and they bring back so many memories of their mother. What a pleasure to have them in Calcutta."

Dr Shastri placed the palms of his hands together, and bowed his head.

"Damyata will look after you," he said quietly. It almost sounded like a standard blessing, the kind of thing people said to one another in order to be polite. But I was certain he spoke the truth. In fact, as I watched him walk out into the hot night air, down the steps of the house towards the waiting carriage, unaware of my gazing so intently after him, I had rarely been so certain of anything, in my whole life.

CHAPTER 11
THE HOOGHLY RIVER

Nick slid over the bars of the balcony and dropped quietly to the dry ground below. He looked around him, several times, as he ran through the garden. He was carrying a tiny little bundle of clothes, the size of a newborn baby. I watched him, from the darkness of my own veranda.

"I'll be fine," he had assured me, minutes earlier.

"Don't do anything silly," I said. "It doesn't matter if you don't find the diamond. Don't take risks. Just come back safe."

His eyes said: I wish you were coming with me. But all he actually said was: "I promise."

"Are you sure you're all right?"

"I feel a bit dizzy," he admitted. "Probably just nervous. Wish me luck." He gave me a brief, tight hug, and melted off into the night.

Another pair of eyes watched him too, as he went: the alert brown eyes of Sarasvati, perched high in the branches of a tree, like a silent marmoset. I knew she was there because I'd been out to have a whispered conversation with her, unbeknown to Nick, after the household had gone to bed. I had explained Nick's plan, described Mr Cloke and the boat. I'd told her I was going to follow him, and stow away on board, to make sure he was all right, and help him if he needed to be helped. She had listened solemnly, in the dark. She'd agreed to look after Lash, and to talk to Mystery, and stop him exploding.

"You will not be alone," she said, cryptically.

When he'd gone, I went back into my room and got changed, as quickly and quietly as I could in the dark, so that my clothes were identical to his. It was important that we should be indistinguishable. Ever since we'd met, we'd been mistaken for one another: surely it wouldn't be difficult.

I spent a long time kneeling next to Lash, whispering to him: telling him how my plan was going to work, mostly to reassure myself. I told him to behave and look after Sarasvati, and we'd be back in no time.

And then, I was gone too. Like Nick, I had no intention of going down the stairs, past Majara and the slumped servant who always guarded the hallway at night. I clambered over the veranda and dangled, kicking my legs in the air for a few seconds, before letting myself fall the few feet onto the path that fringed the house. Nick would be a long way ahead by now: but I wanted to keep my distance, to avoid any possibility of his seeing me. I would hide, and bide my time.

I wondered if Sarasvati was still watching, from the branches above my head, as I left the garden. But, sure enough, long before I was out of earshot, the furtive signals began.

"Dhara-ka-ta-ta-tang," came her voice. "Dha-jang, ta-ta-tang, ta-ta-ta-tang." For the first time, I found it not disconcerting, but reassuring. And the signals were taken up by other voices, as I moved through the dark city. Secret echoes, passing back and forth, ahead of me and behind me, from trees and walls and rooftops: signs that someone was alert, watching out for us both.

"Dha-jang, dha-jang, dhara-ka-ta-ta-ta-ta-tang, ta-ta-ta-tang."

I had to have my wits about me, down near the waterside. It was the middle of the night, but there were still lights in some of the inns and warehouses, close to where we had overheard the Captain from the cellar yesterday; guards and night-watchmen, some dressed in military uniform, were patrolling the docks; and murmured voices or the sudden sound of laughter occasionally burst from a nearby open window as I crept past. It was still almost unbearably hot, and sticky, and the river smelled dreadful. I could feel the mosquitoes feasting on my neck and legs.

The timbers of the boats creaked as they jostled, moored close together, row upon row, down at the water's edge. Some of the smaller ones had lights in the little canvas shelters on their decks, and there were lamps on the bigger ships anchored further out in the river, too. Many-coloured reflections flickered across the surface of the water. Here and there, the silhouette of a sailor would show up, standing on a deck or stepping from boat to boat with a clatter. But there was no sign of Nick. He knew exactly where he was going, but I didn't stand a chance of picking out Mr Cloke's boat in the dark: I would have to hide, and wait for dawn. I prayed I'd be able to find it in time.

I was going to have to do a lot of hiding, in the next day or two. I found a warehouse doorway, deep and dark enough for me to stay hidden until morning; but, as I sidled into it, I bumped into someone who groaned and snapped at me in Hindustani. A few yards further on there was another entrance, this time with no one else using it: and I sat down in the dark, against the wall. I missed Lash, and for a moment I wished I'd decided to bring him with me; but then I thought about where we were going, and told myself once again that it would have been impossible.

I gritted my teeth. "Don't go to sleep," I whispered. "*Mustn't* go to sleep."

But I must have done: because a horribly familiar sound invaded my dream, and then I was suddenly aware that it was no longer a dream. Startled, I opened my eyes. It was no longer dark. Peering tentatively out from the doorway, I could see the masts of boats, and the movements of merchants and dock-hands already busy loading goods in the pinkish light of dawn. The swooping whistles and shrill squawks of birds filled the riverside trees. And someone with an unmistakeable gait was coming past the warehouse.

Click . . . click . . . click . . .

I shrank back into the shadows. Now that it was getting light, anyone who so much as glanced into the doorway where

I was crouching would be able to see me. Perhaps, if I didn't move, I'd look like a bundle of rags.

The Captain stumped past me. He was alone. As I watched his receding back from my hiding place, I realised he was probably the widest human being I had ever seen: with his gigantic build, and his crutches leaning out further still to either side, he was nearly as broad as a house. There was hardly room on the dock for anyone else to pass him.

He didn't turn his head. As he stumped out of sight, I crawled out of my hiding place and followed him, staying close against the warehouse wall. He walked about another forty or fifty yards, surveying the boats as he went; then he planted himself against an enormous bollard right on the edge of the dock, and roared at a sailor in a boat below him.

"Hoy, get me a plank, there! I'm comin' aboard!"

Now I could see it, second out from the dock in a rank of barges: a long, shallow-bottomed vessel with a single mast, its hull painted completely blue, with an ornate border of colourful bird-designs around the prow to bring good fortune – just as we'd heard the Captain say. And, with a sudden tingle of excitement, I noticed Nick. He came up through a hatch from below deck, glanced briefly at the Captain, and went to the stern to coil a rope. As I watched him, I began to realise he might have been right all along. He just looked like any other sailor, with his ragged linen breeches and bare feet. He was doing absolutely the right thing: not trying to hide, simply getting on with tasks on board, in order not to draw attention to himself. If he was already busy on board when the

Captain arrived, why should anyone even give him a second glance?

My heart was in my mouth as I watched the Captain negotiating the plank down into the nearest boat, and then clambering, crutches outstretched, over into the next. It took him a long time. Nobody on Cloke's boat helped him, until he was very nearly aboard; at which point a tall, wiry, almost naked figure appeared, with a white scarf covering most of his head, and reached out an arm to guide the gigantic man onto the deck.

There was a low exchange of conversation which I couldn't hear. The tall man must be Mr Cloke.

At the other end of the boat, Nick stood up. It was already hot, and he was wearing no shirt as he worked to prepare the barge for departure. He wasn't as tall, but his body was almost exactly the same colour and build as Cloke's. I clenched my fists in silent jubilation. I'd been terrified the Captain would take one look at him and give a furious roar of recognition. But Nick was completely convincing. He was Cloke's boy. No one would have questioned it.

Now, of course, I began to realise how inadequate my own disguise was going to seem. I'd been careful to match my clothes to Nick's: but I knew I couldn't move around the deck with anything like his air of confidence or familiarity. And I *so* wished he hadn't stripped to the waist.

Yet, in order to get on board, I was going to have to wait until he wasn't there, and then somehow pretend to be him. How on earth was I going to carry it off?

The air this morning felt heavier and stickier than ever. The Hooghly was wide and sluggish, a muddy grey-brown, like the water in which a giant child's paintbrush had been rinsed. A few little punts and dinghies were moving, but the traffic had yet to get going properly this morning. In an hour, the water would be seething with movement, vessels of every size veering past one another, jostling for passage, the boatmen shouting at one another. Even though it was only just dawn, the waterside was getting busier by the minute: there was something magical about the way it was coming to life, all around me. Bullock-carts were arriving, now, laden with boxes and sacks to be loaded onto boats; and the carters were piling the boxes up on the dockside, talking and shouting. The air was full of the sweet and pungent smells of the spices they were delivering. Birds were swooping in – great black crows, as well as smaller, alert, exotically-coloured ones – to pick up fallen grains and seeds and general refuse. A couple of rather mangy little monkeys ran along the dock, peering into bags, rifling through the bundles with their agile fingers, and every now and again gazing up at the passing people with imploring faces, like tiny beggars.

To have any chance of sneaking aboard Cloke's boat, I was going to have to make it over to the wharf's edge, where I could keep an eye on the comings and goings. But that meant crossing at least twenty or thirty yards of open ground, with nowhere much to hide when I got there. I was just going to have to brazen it out.

Time to practise being a sailor-lad, I told myself. I waited for two or three minutes, until there were a few more people on the dockside, and then I slid out from behind the wall and strolled, looking as purposeful as I could, over to where a stack of tea-chests was piled so high that they formed a kind of wall, almost dividing the dock in two. No one challenged me. I hovered, pretending to be inspecting the piles, as though working out whether they were securely stacked. When the coast seemed clear, I ducked into a little gap, like an alleyway between the rows of tea-chests, from which I had a clear view of the deck of Cloke's boat, the to-ings and fro-ings on the dock, and the whole river beyond.

The Captain had sat down on deck, and was scanning the dockside and the nearby buildings, with his hand shading his eyes against the rising sun. Although it was Mr Cloke's boat, it seemed the Captain was assuming command, and he had begun barking instructions at Cloke who was standing a few yards away, securing a sail. Nick came over and said something in a low voice to Mr Cloke; then he looked around, and stepped carefully over one of the Captain's crutches on his way off the barge. In a couple of leaps, he crossed the next boat, and jumped ashore.

He didn't look in my direction. I watched him walk – seeming slightly worried, I thought – over to a low wooden hut adjoining the waterside buildings, which couldn't have been anything other than a privy.

My heart was in my mouth. This was it. It was now or never. But, as I squeezed my way out of my hiding place, the first thing I saw when I stood up was a familiar, heavy-set and purposeful figure with a string bag over one shoulder, striding towards me along the dockside.

Mr Penagadder.

I froze, and he stared at me for about half a second, before jumping down onto the barges and making his way over to snarl a greeting at the Captain and Mr Cloke.

I followed him. Perhaps the distraction caused by Penagadder's arrival would mean they took no notice of me. Mr Cloke had turned away, and gone to gather in the mooring-ropes. Trying to be nonchalant, I tottered across the boards, and climbed onto the deck, a few feet away from the Captain and Penagadder, as they stood grimacing and gazing around the barge with what looked like scorn.

"Not very robust is she?" the Captain was saying. "Monsoon's coming. I can *smell* it this morning."

I didn't look at them. Instead, I made straight for the nearest hatch, and slipped below deck.

"Who's that?" I heard Penagadder snarl, as I descended.

"The bargee's lad," said the Captain. "We can get going now. And not a minute too soon. When you're ready there, Mr Cloke!" he shouted, and banged on the side of the barge.

In the shadowy space below deck, I stood biting my lip in horror. It hadn't occurred to me, of course, that, in mistaking me for Nick, they might end up leaving Nick behind. But there was nothing I could do.

"*Achha, achha,*" came the deep voice of Mr Cloke. "Two minutes. Ready to go in two minutes, Captain. Someone that side to untie her, please."

Nobody moved, for a moment.

"You 'eard 'im," said the Captain gruffly.

And, as Penagadder grudgingly went over to loosen the ropes, and the Captain turned around to watch him, I realised I was going to have to brazen it out. We were going to set sail without Nick, and they would be relying on me to do whatever he would have done.

I tried to steady my nerves with deep breaths, out of sight down here in the hold; but the air was roasting and fetid, and I was rapidly beginning to feel dizzy. Maybe that was the answer! Maybe I had to pretend to be Nick, but suddenly be too ill to help.

I sank down to sit on the heavy keelson, thinking rapidly. But then, as the boards above my head thumped from the impact of bare feet preparing the boat for departure, I distinctly heard the Captain say: "Oh, there you are. I thought you'd gone below."

And, ignoring the Captain but responding to a shouted instruction from Mr Cloke, there was the unmistakeable sound of Nick's raised voice in reply.

I could have fainted with relief. He'd made it back on board, somehow – and now, if they weren't going to work out there were two of us, I had to find somewhere to hide.

There was a lot of clutter down here in the long, narrow space below deck – ropes, rolled sails, tackle, blankets, barrels – but there were no cabins, or cupboards, or crannies, into which I could squeeze and not be seen. The best I could do was crawl under a couple of big tarpaulins, which had been rolled up together and shoved right up into the bows. I could see absolutely nothing; but I was surrounded by the sounds of the hull knocking and grinding against the barges moored either side of us, as we floated clear of them and out into open water. I prayed I was properly hidden, and that no one would decide to come down and yank the tarpaulins out for use.

It was even hotter, crammed into this little space, and not at all comfortable. I realised quite soon that I had forgotten to bring something to drink, and what a stupid mistake that had been. I could hear murmurs of conversation from the deck above, but I couldn't really make out much of what was being said. The voice I heard most of was the Captain's; and every now and then there'd be a characteristic *click* . . . *click* . . . *click* . . . as he stumped around the deck. Penagadder was largely silent, and Mr Cloke only spoke in reply to the occasional question from the Captain, in his deep, quiet voice. It was clear, nevertheless, that Nick was getting away with it: incredibly, no one seemed to have worked out who he was, there had been no awkward questions, and no shouting.

And, as far as I knew, no one had a clue I was down here either.

I didn't dare move. I couldn't breathe if my head was under the tarpaulins, so I half sat against the curve of the bows, in a position where I could pull them back over my head in a hurry if anyone came down the ladder. Thankfully, hardly anyone did, for hours. The sun was high in the sky, and the boat glided calmly up the wide river in the merciless heat; but I could see nothing of the paddy fields and dense palms we were passing on either bank as we left the noisy docks and the rooftops of the city far behind.

The Captain began to sing, to while away the journey. No one else joined in. I couldn't catch all the words of the songs, though I suspected some of them were highly improper. More than once, he broke into the familiar melody we'd first heard on that freezing night back in London that had started the whole adventure.

"*O my lovely blue eye,*
Blue eye that twinkle and shine
If it takes till the day I die
I shall make your blue eye mine."

Occasionally someone came down the steps into the hold, and I'd sit rigid under the tarpaulins, praying they'd quickly find what they were looking for and go back up on deck.

But then, in what must have been the early afternoon, to judge from how long we seemed to have been underway, I became aware of an increased level of conversation on deck. I think I had probably gone to sleep for a while, and the voices had woken me up. My mouth was atrociously dry, my lips cracked and painful, and my head ached. What wouldn't I give for a drink! For a few insane seconds, I was almost convinced it would be worth giving myself up, and going up on deck, just to get some water. I began to rehearse what I might say.

"Hello! I know I'm not supposed to be here, but – ha! ha! Could I just get a drink, do you think?" That was a possibility.

"Goodness, I must have gone to sleep in the hold. Where

are we? What day is it? Would any of you have some water you could spare me?" That might work too.

But I was brought to my senses by the sound of anxious voices coming close to the hatch. I lifted my head, and listened. Something was happening on deck. The singing had stopped, and someone had started issuing commands. Had something gone wrong?

Moments later, there was the sound of footsteps on the ladder, and I hastily covered myself up again. It was Nick who had come down: his voice called up through the hatch, just a few feet from my ear.

"There's a big tarpaulin down here."

I froze.

A clunking sound on the boards above suggested the Captain was stumping over to the hatch. It went dark as he bent to peer in and his bulk shut out the daylight.

"Ay, whatever ye can find," the Captain said, "The rains are comin', lad, any minute, and we need something up here to keep things dry."

And, in no time, Nick was kneeling just inches from my head, fumbling around with the edges of the big tarpaulin, trying to lift it out. I tried to inch backwards, without being seen, further into the dark, narrow bow. But, as Nick pulled the tarpaulin aside, he uncovered my leg. Then the other.

I had to do something. He would shout for the others, any second now, to say he'd found a stowaway. He had no idea who I was: all he could see was a pair of legs scrabbling to hide themselves. It was a miracle he hadn't cried out in alarm.

"Nick!" I whispered, flinging the tarpaulins off and sitting up. "It's me! Hush! Don't say a word!"

He was utterly astonished: dumbstruck, in fact. He stared at me for what seemed like several seconds, as he struggled to convince himself it was really me.

But then he did speak – in a furious whisper.

"What the *blazes* do you think you're doing here?" he wanted to know. "How did you get aboard?"

"I took a risk," I whispered back, "I wanted to come too, Nick. I needed to know you were all right."

"I am – I *was*, until now," he retorted, "but not for much longer! It was all going brilliantly. But how am I going to hide you, on this tiny boat, you silly girl?"

"Something up?" came the Captain's voice, booming down the hatch.

"Nothing," called Nick, "just muttering to myself while I'm heaving this here tarpaulin." He gave a passable imitation of someone grunting and cursing as he pulled something heavy – to make the Captain go away.

Then he started again.

"You *idiot*," he hissed, "you'll give the whole game away. I could *throttle* you!"

"Nick, I need a drink," I said. "I've been down here for hours. Can you get me some water?"

He looked up at the hatch. "It's about to rain," he said. "Can't you feel it in the air? There'll be more water than we know what to do with in a few minutes."

I gathered up the smaller of the tarpaulins and shoved it at him. "Take this up with you," I said, "leave me the big one. Tell them you couldn't get it up the ladder. I promise I won't do anything silly."

"It's a bit too late for that, Mog," muttered Nick. He stood up, and folded the tarpaulin a couple of times until it was the right size to fit through the hatch. Then he started up the ladder with it.

"Stay hidden," he whispered, glaring at me. "I'll come down when I can."

There was a lot of activity on deck for the next few minutes, as the four of them worked to make everything secure and to cope with the rising wind. I could feel the altered motion of the boat, down here below the waterline. There was a faint, slow popping sound, which I didn't at first recognise, until it gradually built up to more of a rapid pattering, then, within minutes, a continuous drumming. It was the sound of rain.

"Batten down that hatch!" shouted the Captain.

"Wait!" called Nick.

And he slipped quickly into the space, slithering down the ladder towards me, and pulling the hatch down after him. It went completely dark.

"Nick!" I called out. "I'm still here."

"I've brought you a drink," he said from the darkness. "But I have to take the other tarpaulin up to them. We're going to have to find something else to hide you."

I got up out of my hiding place. I could hardly see anything with the hatch closed; but I crawled over to where I thought the ladder was; and I soon found my hands making contact with his bare shoulders and hair, in the dark.

"I can't stay down here for long," he said. "It's started to rain, and they'll miss me if I'm not helping. Here you are."

I fumbled for the water flask he held out for me, and drank gratefully from the neck. The water wasn't cold, but to me it was like the first fresh mountain meltwater of spring. I swallowed it, and gasped with relief. The sound of the rain on the deck was so loud, now, that we could probably have talked at a perfectly normal volume without running the risk of being heard. But, just to be safe, I kept my voice to a whisper, and Nick had to lean close and ask me to repeat myself.

"I said, how much further do we have to go?" I asked.

"I don't know," Nick replied. "But earlier on, the Captain was talking about tomorrow. I think it's more than a day's journey."

"You're *soaking*," I exclaimed.

"I know," he said, "it's teeming down out there now."

"People have been saying they're desperate for it to rain, ever since we arrived," I said. "Now they're getting their wish."

"I'm going to get that tarpaulin and go back up," he said.

"You're shivering," I said. "And you're not *wearing* anything. Come and get dry, over here. They won't miss you for a minute or two. Three great big sailors, surely they can manage." When I'd come down I'd noticed a big piece of soft cloth or towel hanging on a nail near the ladder; my fingers found it in the dark and I passed it to him. "Dry off on this," I said. "I don't know how clean it is, but . . ."

He took it with him, rubbing it around his head and neck as he crawled into the bows to pull the tarpaulin out. But, before he'd had a chance to get back, there was a sudden clatter, and the hatch burst open above my head, sending a shower of drips down into the hold.

"What's that boy *doing* down there?" came the Captain's voice; and, as he thrust his soaking head down into the hole, I found myself face to face with him. What could he possibly think, except that I was Nick? He leered at me, showing a row of nasty brown teeth. The forward point of his three-cornered hat formed a spout, which poured all the rainwater that had gathered in the brim in a thin stream onto my forehead.

"Up ye come," the Captain grinned. "I dare say we'd all like to hide down there, where it's dry. But there's work to be done." And, before I had time to move or speak, he'd reached down and taken hold of my collar.

I was forced to climb up the ladder, and join the others on deck. The sky was an extraordinary colour, the low cloud picking up and dispersing the orange light of the still-roasting sun. We seemed to be steering close to the riverbank, as I was aware of a dense wall of encroaching trees not far away, unless they were an illusion caused by the fury of mist and rain. The Captain and the others were no more than lumbering grey figures in the downpour; the deck was running with water, and the river ahead of the boat was barely visible. We had to shout to make ourselves heard above the noise.

"We has to keep going," the Captain bawled at the rest

of us. "The river will soon be in spate, and then it will be well-nigh impossible to carry on. We has to make it as far upriver as we can."

Mr Cloke came over. He was holding a large waterproof cape over his head. "No, Captain," he pleaded, "we must moor up. We cannot *see*."

I'd never seen rain like this in my life. Having been completely dry when I came up from below, I was now drenched through to the skin, after less than a minute. Water was descending in sheets from my hair down into my eyes and down my neck. Plenty of people had told us about torrential monsoon rain, these last few days; but nothing had prepared me for this.

"I knows what I'm doing," the Captain snarled. "We ain't close enough yet." He turned his head to look at me, standing there stiffly in my soaked clothes, and then threw me the end of a rope. Startled, I caught it.

"Lad!" he shouted. "Don't stand there like a statue. Make me a bowlin'. I need to make sure this sheet don't slip. You tie me a good strong bowlin'. And quick about it!"

He stood over me while I stared at the rope-end in despair. It would have come as second nature to Nick, of course: but I had absolutely no idea what to do. He might just as well have asked me to turn it into rhubarb.

"You 'eard me, lad," he said. "A good strong bowlin'. I'm waitin'."

And I knew, from the ironic tone of his voice, that he knew. He knew I wasn't Nick. He had worked out who I really was.

And he had probably known fine well I'd been aboard, ever since we set sail this morning. I felt sick. I folded the rope into a loop, and curled the free end back through it a couple of times, pathetically. It fell apart.

"Well now," he said, "seems the lad don't know how. Who ever 'eard of a boatman what didn't know how to tie a bowlin'? Can this be the same lad what got us all this way? Mebbe he bumped his head, down below, and forgot everything he ever knew about how to sail a boat."

I became aware of the dark, towering figure of Penagadder, standing with folded arms behind him. They were going to kill me.

"'Course, it may just be that it's not the same lad," said the Captain. "Which must mean we've two of 'em on board. You got *two* lads sailing with you, Mr Cloke? More or less the same to look at, 'cept one of 'em's got a big red bite under his eye, and the other ain't?"

Mr Cloke had come to stand close by now, too. I cowered, tight-lipped, beneath the Captain's threatening bulk. I could think of nothing to say or do that could get me out of this. What an idiot I had been! Nick was absolutely right: if I hadn't insisted on coming aboard too, he would have got away with it. It had been sheer madness to assume I might stow away without being spotted – and now I was going to get us both killed.

"Mebbe we should find out," the Captain was grinning. "We could go and 'ave a look in the hold, and if there turns out to be another of 'em down there, we'll know what we're dealin' with. *Two* stowaways means twice as much food for the crocodiles. Eh, Mr Penagadder?"

Penagadder turned, unsmiling, and went over to the hatch. He was in the hold for about six or seven seconds, and then he was back up on deck, hauling Nick out into the torrential rain. He flung Nick across the deck; he slipped, and staggered, and finally steadied himself by holding on to me. We stood, side by side, rain pouring down our faces.

The Captain stood in front of us, his crutches widely splayed to give him stability on the slippery deck. He surveyed us both from beneath his big black hat.

"Snap!" he said. And he burst out laughing. "Snap! Snap! Snap!" he shouted; and threw back his head, and roared his laughter up into the cascading rain. "We got 'em, Mr Penagadder! We didn't even 'ave to put up a fight. The Winter twins. They *walked* aboard, first one, then the other, thinking we wouldn't even notice! What more could we ask for? And now we're going to get the diamond, and they're both going to the bottom of the Hooghly, never to get in the way again. What an 'appy day, Mr Penagadder! What blessings the rains bring, in this part of the world!"

He roared with laughter again; but no one joined in. Mr Cloke lifted his cape above his head, and spoke.

"I cannot allow this, Captain," he said. "These are innocent children. Before you lay hands on them you will have to throw me overboard first. And then there will be no one to guide you."

The Captain's face darkened.

"Your duplicity has condemned these children, and yourself," he said. "I am paying for this trip, yet, behind my back, you give passage to my enemies."

"Their claims are rightful, Captain," said Mr Cloke, "and yours are criminal."

I was astonished and thrilled to find Mr Cloke defending us, but even more so to hear him say this. How on earth did *he* know?

"I will take my chance, without you or the brats, Mr Cloke," snarled the Captain. "We have come this far, and I has no intention of lettin' you nor anyone else stand in the way now. We can fend for ourselves."

"You are making a mistake, Captain," said Cloke. "These waters are treacherous. Without a guide, you will founder."

The Captain stared at him with utter loathing, as though he were a cockroach that had dared to crawl across his shoe.

"I fancy your mistake is the greater," he sneered. "Do your job, Mr Penagadder."

Penagadder stepped forward. Cloke was a tall man, but he was nevertheless a full six inches shorter than the murderous sailor. I grabbed hold of Nick's hand instinctively. If we were going to have to make a dive for it, I had no intention of letting him out of my sight again.

For a tense few seconds, the two men stared at one another, as the rain teemed around them. Then, Penagadder turned his head to look at the Captain.

"I ain't so sure my job is what you wants it to be, on this occasion, Cap'n Albacore," he said, slowly.

The Captain's expression changed.

"We come a long way, you're right about that," continued Penagadder. "And ain't I been biding my time, waitin' for the moment when the stone is well-nigh in our grasp? Well, looks like this is as close as you's goin' to get, Cap'n. I ain't sharin' that diamond with nobody. You got so near, and yet so far."

For the first time, I saw Penagadder smile. It was as though the long scar in his face split apart and opened up: a broad, sinister grin, lasting only a split-second. Then his face became thunderously violent and he lunged towards the Captain.

There was a sudden almighty bang and a crunch, and the deck was thrown into confusion. The boat gave a sideways lurch, and Penagadder missed his target, lunging past the Captain, and skidding instead towards the edge of the deck and crashing against the low bulwark. It took me a few seconds to work out what was happening; but Cloke was shouting instructions above the noise of the rain, and I realised we'd hit something. In all the drama, no one had been steering the barge. We had ploughed into a rock or a protruding tree-trunk close to the eastern bank, and we were holed.

The barge was spinning, now, taken by the rapid waters of the flooded river, the sheets loose and flailing, the bows rapidly filling with muddy water. The Captain, by some distance the least agile person on board, was standing knee-deep in water, roaring. Cloke had leaped up onto the rigging to get a better view of what was happening. Penagadder had disappeared. There was another sickening crunch, and the boat began to tip over. We had hit something else.

"Jump!" I screamed at Nick.

My hand still tight around his, I pulled him with me, and we went under. I could see nothing, and my nose and eyes were immediately choked with sand and grit being churned up by the water. Desperately, I fought to get back up to the surface and breathe. Behind us we could still hear the Captain shouting as the rain continued to teem; the river bubbled in fury around us; and we lurched along, utterly helpless, at the mercy of the swollen current.

Chapter 12
THE RUINED PALACE

We went under and came up again several times, travelling downstream fast. We didn't look back; I tried to claw at overhanging branches to slow us down, but I missed them altogether, or they slid from my grasp, as we were carried along.

After what can only have been about a minute, but seemed like half a lifetime, an eddy swept us in a wide arc towards the bank. When we were just a few feet from the mud and tree-roots of the bank, I tried digging my heels into the river bed beneath us; and, to our relief, we found ourselves standing up in the swirling water.

Only now did I let go of Nick's hand. I scrambled out onto dry land, and looked back to see if he was following. He was gasping, on his knees in the water; and I went back to haul him up onto the bank before another current could sweep in and take him away.

"Sorry," he panted, "I swallowed about a barrelful of water out there. Thank you."

"Don't thank me," I said, "it was all my fault."

We found some solid ground, and he flopped onto his back. The riverside was so densely wooded that patches of clear ground were few and far between.

"They knew who we were from the beginning," Nick groaned. "I really thought I'd fooled them."

"You might have done, if I hadn't come aboard," I said. "You were absolutely right. It was only when they knew there were two of us, I think, that they got suspicious. I'm so sorry, Nick. I completely messed it up."

"It wasn't your fault. I should have known they were too clever. It was a ridiculous idea to begin with and I wish I'd listened to you." He heaved himself up onto his elbows and looked out at the fast-flowing water. "I guess that's it," he said. "We're not going to make it to Sasanka's palace now, are we? We blew it, Mog."

There was a kind of constant hissing sound all around us, as thousands of raindrops burst on the broad leaves of the trees high above us. We could hear birds rustling and whooping in the branches, and the distant howls of unidentified wild animals. It was beginning to dawn on me how much of a catastrophe had befallen us. Not only had we not reached the palace, we were now stranded on the edge of a jungle, many miles from the city – with crocodiles, snakes, tigers, and any number of other lethal creatures, lurking just a few yards away, for all we knew.

We waited until we'd got our breath back. We were soaking, and the rain was still coming down with an intensity which almost defied belief, bloating the river and forming a kind of opaque curtain of water between us and the opposite bank. I couldn't help remembering the Captain, standing guffawing "Snap! Snap! Snap!" into the falling rain. Every rustle, every unexpected sound in the undergrowth was making me jump out of my skin.

"Nick, we can't just sit here," I said. "We'll get ourselves eaten. We have to move."

"Where to?" He looked around. All we could see was the swollen brown river on one side, and the wet jungle on the other.

"I don't know," I said, biting my lip, "but anything's better than sitting here waiting for the crocodiles. Look! Do you see any boats out there? In this weather, we might sit here for days waiting for someone to come past. And there's too much mist and rain for anyone to spot us from out on the water anyway."

The dense canopy above us was at least providing some shelter from the torrent. There was no sign of human habitation anywhere in sight; but perhaps, if we walked a little way, we might find a village, or a road? We started trying to pick a route among the trees; but we soon found it was slow progress. Even though it was wet, it was extremely hot, and stepping over the huge tree-roots and around the swampy holes of the jungle floor was hard work. I'd thought about calling out, to attract attention, in case there were any people anywhere near: but then I'd remembered the Captain and Penagadder. I hadn't seen what had happened to them after the boat sank, but it was quite possible that they had made it ashore too, and were even now making their own way among the trees, close enough to hear me if I shouted out.

A sudden snort and thrashing of the undergrowth made us both cry out; and as we fell back against the broad trunk of a tree we could see a huge wild boar, with three or four piglets, running away into the forest.

My heart was pounding. "I thought we'd had it, then," I said. "I'm a nervous wreck, sorry."

"Mog, have you *any* idea where we're going?" Nick asked in a slightly tense voice, as I set off again.

"I – don't know," I admitted.

I stopped, and turned. He was five yards behind, looking at me with a pained face. I felt suddenly furious: he wasn't helping us at all. "*You* think of something, then!" I said. "If you think you can lead us out of here, you go first. I'll follow on behind, in admiration."

I sat down defiantly on a huge, damp tree-root. Something was playing havoc with my ankle; I lifted my left foot onto the other knee to inspect it, and was horrified to find a pointed, purple little leech, about the size of a spike on a hairbrush, squirming around with one end clamped to my flesh. Revolted, I grasped it between finger and thumb and tried to pull it off. It wouldn't budge.

"Nick!" I wailed.

He came over and, after we'd both tried again to prise it off to no avail, he found a sharp stick.

"Careful!" I said. "Ouch!"

A sharp jab had separated leech and skin, but seemed to have brought quite a lot of my ankle off with it, to judge from the big smudge of blood which was left behind, and the sharp sting of the wound.

"They're *horrible*," I shuddered.

"They'll be everywhere, in this wet undergrowth," said Nick soberly. He looked up, trying to decide which way to go. "We have to get our bearings," he said. "I'm scared it's going to get dark."

Then, almost as soon as he'd said it, we both noticed that the jungle seemed to open out into a steamy clearing a few yards ahead. Helping one another now, we stumbled forward; and, emerging between feathery bamboo plants and huge ferns, we quickly found we were standing on the side of a wide, muddy track.

There was no one to be seen; but surely this track must lead us back to civilisation? And it would be a great deal easier to walk on than the tangled undergrowth of the jungle.

"Nick, look!" I said, excited. "A kind of road! Come on!"

I peered into the distance, to our right. The track, a brick-red stripe slicing the greenery apart, disappeared into mist and rain; and there were big puddles at intervals which were still sloshing and rippling with the falling rainwater. But the surface was mostly firm, and had been patched up with big flat stones here and there, as though it were in regular use.

"This is almost a proper road," I cried, hopefully. "Look, it's been shored up with these stones. There must be people coming along here regularly. Maybe it will take us back to Calcutta!"

"Mog, it's miles," said Nick. "We came a long way in the boat, you know. And it won't be light for much longer."

"We won't have to walk all the way back. I'm sure we'll meet someone who can help us, before long," I said, pretending to be cheerful. "Or maybe we'll come to a village." But I was casting surreptitious, anxious glances up at the sky. Nick was right, it must have been almost evening. The last thing we needed was to be stranded out here after dark.

We set off, along the edge of the muddy road, in what I was fairly certain was a southward direction, trying to avoid the puddles which were rapidly appearing in the uneven ground. And, before we'd been walking for many minutes, there was a sploshing, crunching sound from up ahead, and something emerged gently out of the mist. Something quite huge, swaying slowly from side to side.

At first I'd thought it was a bullock-cart, piled high with grass or something to the height of a small house. But, as it came closer, I realised it was an elephant.

I gasped, and clutched Nick's arm.

The elephant had someone sitting on top. And both elephant and rider were suddenly familiar.

"Nick!" I squeaked, hardly able to get the words out. "It's – look who – Nick, it's Sarasvati. And Punch!"

I couldn't believe my eyes. We ran, splodging through the puddles, to meet them. I hugged Punch's flank, and she curled her trunk around to nuzzle the side of my face with its tip.

"We came after you," Sarasvati said, from up on Punch's shoulders. "Just in case. And here you are! What happened to the boat?"

I explained about being found out, and the Captain trying to have us killed; and Mr Cloke stepping in, and the accident. Sarasvati's brown eyes grew wider and wider as the story unfolded.

"Such danger you have been in!" she cried. "And now, the two of you walking alone in the jungle. What about all the wild animals? I could have come too late!"

"Sarasvati, it's *such* a relief to see you!" said Nick.

"Let us get you both up here," Sarasvati said. She hadn't brought stirrups; but she held down an arm to guide me while Nick gave me a leg up from below, and in no time I was sitting up there behind Sarasvati. She took one of the blankets that were draped over Punch's back, and shook it out before arranging it over my shoulders. "Try to stay dry," she said.

Nick tried a couple of times to climb Punch's flank, reaching up for my hand; but he found he couldn't do it without climbing up onto a fallen tree-trunk he noticed by the side of the road, which provided a perfect platform. He swung himself up onto Punch's back behind the two of us, and we were off, swaying, holding on to one another, getting used to the elephant's motion.

"Aren't you going to turn her around?" I asked Sarasvati.

"You want to go back?" she asked, surprised. "Without the diamond?"

At first I was too astonished to reply. Plainly, she was intending to take us to Sasanka's palace.

"But – isn't it too far?" I asked.

"You want the Captain to get it instead?" she said.

I laughed out loud. "No, I don't think we do!" I said.

So we rode north, on the muddy red road, for the remainder of the daylight hours. Sarasvati had brought provisions with her, in a canvas bag around her neck; and she handed us a water bottle to sip from, and passed us dates and dried apricots to munch as we went. Here and there the jungle thinned out, and we found we were surrounded by flat, swampy land where the river had spread out, or, in some places, by cultivated paddy fields. The rain subsided, a little, and whenever we were among trees the overhanging branches kept us dry as we went.

As the light was beginning to fail, we came to a tiny settlement of huts made of wood and straw, with hump-backed cattle meandering around amongst them; and Sarasvati guided Punch off the road. "Too dark to go any further," she said. "We'll rest. Then not far to go tomorrow."

"You mean we're nearly there?"

She said nothing, but looked at me with the amused twinkle of someone enjoying her ability to amaze her friends.

She slipped off Punch's back and went to find someone in the little village to speak to. A farmer, in a cotton *dhoti*, came out of a hut, and Sarasvati engaged him in conversation with a lot of arm-waving. She was making him laugh. His face creased up several times, and he opened his mouth to reveal a single tooth.

"He says we can shelter here," she said when she came back. "He can give us food and a fire. And we will be dry. We can start again at dawn. It's not even an hour to the ruins from here."

We set up a kind of camp, in one of the huts, with blankets from Punch's back, and a crackling, steaming fire onto which we kept loading damp, moss-encrusted sticks. The farmer's wife brought us cooked rice and dhal. We had certainly fallen on our feet, I reflected as we ate it in the firelight, after the disaster on the boat this afternoon. Every time I thought about what had happened today, I burned with shame at my own stupidity. I kept apologising to Nick and he kept telling me not to be silly; but I felt sure he mustn't quite be thinking straight, in all the excitement, and that, once we got back to Calcutta, he'd realise how imbecilic I'd been, and be rightly furious.

I was slightly ashamed, too, at having to rely for our survival on someone so much younger than we were. I watched her as she ran around the clearing, gathering wood to stoke the fire, and soothed Punch with soft cooing noises as she stood quietly near the hut in the dark. And it struck me again how impossible it was to believe Sarasvati was just a child: she had a calmness about her, an air of wisdom, that seemed older than time.

We sat by the fire, the heat of the flames drying off our clothes in the dark.

"What do you think happened to the Captain?" I asked Nick.

"I'd almost forgotten the Captain," he said. "We didn't really see what happened to any of them, did we? We weren't that far from the bank. Chances are they made it onto dry land. But maybe they throttled one another, or maybe they were eaten by crocodiles. Who knows?"

I shuddered. "I expect we've left them miles behind, at any rate," I said. "Unless there was a handy passing elephant to pick them up, too."

"The Captain was certainly determined to get the diamond," Nick reflected. "Cloke wanted to find somewhere to wait until the rain subsided. But he wasn't going to let Cloke slow him down. He kept talking about the map. Gloating about it, all the way up the river. He's convinced he's got it all worked out. Thinks he's found clues to points of the compass, and everything."

"Little does he know it's not a map at all," I said. "I really hope we get there first, Nick. I've no idea what we'll find, tomorrow. But I *so* hope we don't find the Captain."

"Dhara-ka-ta-tang, da-tang-ta-taa, dhara-dang."

I woke, in the grey light, to hear the familiar sound of Sarasvati, somewhere over among the trees, signalling, calling. Who could possibly hear her, this far from the city?

It wasn't raining. The jungle was waking up, and the whoops and whistles of birds and monkeys were starting to fill the trees for miles around. Nick was still fast asleep, beside me on the blanket in our little hut; and, when I crawled out, I could see Punch, tearing leaves and branches off the nearby trees with her trunk, and munching them with what looked like a smile.

When Sarasvati saw me standing at the door of the hut, she came scuttling over, almost on all-fours, looking this way and that.

"Not far to go," she said. "We should make a start. Come on. Help me."

A sudden thrill ran through me. Could this really be the last leg of our long journey? Were we about to find what we'd come all this way for? I helped her load the blankets onto Punch's back, waking Nick gently in order to pull the last one out from underneath him. The animals were prowling around among the huts, but there was no sign that the old farmer or his wife had yet woken.

"Who were you calling to?" I asked Sarasvati, as she sat on Punch's shoulders and caught the blankets I flung up to her.

"Just making sure of everything," she said, evasively. "Are we ready?"

The sky was pink, the sunrise diffused by the mist and the blanket of cloud which threatened another day of monsoon rain. We left the little homestead behind, as quietly as we could. Everything was glistening with water; all along the road and in the grassy clearings, as we swayed by, there were pools left by yesterday's downpour. The lull in the rain had brought traffic onto the red road again, and we passed a couple of rumbling cattle-drawn carts which were already out in the dawn light, their drivers looking amused to see three young people atop an elephant, swaying by.

We didn't spend long on the red road this morning, though. After a mile or two, Sarasvati steered Punch over to one side and began breaking a route through the damp jungle.

"Very close, now," she said.

High up on Punch's back, we found ourselves eye to eye with families of monkeys and large, indignant-looking birds, as we crashed through the trees; and, stretched out along a long branch, parts of it hanging off in coils like a fat vine or ivy-stem, a dark and languid snake.

"Listen!" said Sarasvati suddenly.

Amid the bird-calls and rustles of the jungle foliage, we could just make out a peculiar, rhythmic sound. It wasn't quite a human voice; but it wasn't made by an animal or bird, either.

"It sounds like a – *drum*," I said, straining to hear it.

"That's what it is," said Sarasvati.

And, the more we listened, the more familiar its pattern became. *Dha-ra-ka-ta-ta-tang, ta-ta-ta-tang,* it seemed to say. *Dhara-dang, dha-jang-jang, dhara-dang.*

"Dhara-dang," echoed Sarasvati now, responding, lifting her head high. "Dhara-ka-ta-ta-taa, ta-taa, ta-tang."

"I don't believe it," I said, "all this time you've been imitating a drum?"

"Or," she said, "the drum imitates the voice."

"And you understand it?"

"Of course. It means words." She listened again, and the drum clattered on the warm, wet air.

"Dha-jang, dha-jang-jangg," she called in reply. "Dhara-dang, ta-ta-ta, ta-ta-ta, ta-ta-ta-tang."

"What are you telling them?" I asked her.

"That we're coming," she replied.

And, as Punch took us through a particularly dense patch of trees, with creepers clinging to them and dragging against us as we passed, the ruins began to appear.

Bathed, suddenly, in the fiery light of dawn, were the towering walls and archways of a huge, once-magnificent building, or complex of buildings. It was like stumbling on the palace in the fairy tale, around which a hundred years' worth of forest had grown. Vines and thorns had wormed their way into the stonework, and wrenched open great cracks. Storks and monkeys had colonised the tops of the walls and towers; spiky nests poked out from every cranny; the eyes of wild cats flashed in the crumbling windows. The sounds of the jungle birds bounced off the ancient marble, sounding like the ethereal cries and laughter of another age. Statues and carved figures gazed at us from the walls as we approached: row upon row of serene, silent animals, gods with many arms, contorted half-human shapes, comical gargoyle faces, unclothed female figures. The whole place seemed to shimmer, as the sun rose: like a dream city, an hallucination.

"Sasanka's palace," I said, hardly able to believe it. "This is *it*, Nick."

"Journey's end," said Sarasvati, with a touch of drama.

Digging her toes behind Punch's ears, she made her stop in front of a big tumbledown arch which seemed to lead through to the grandest buildings at the very core of the palace.

"We'll stay here," she said. "The two of you go. He is waiting for you."

I slipped down off Punch's back, and reached up to help Nick.

"Be careful," said Sarasvati. "If I see any danger, I will signal. Listen for the talking drum."

We left them, and ventured in. Our shadows followed us, high on the walls; and our hearts were in our mouths. Monkeys ran here and there, chattering, disturbed and excited by our movements; and we had the sense of being watched by other eyes, too, as we walked in wonder among the dripping ruins.

Passing under another arch, we found ourselves inside the palace itself, under a high ceiling, looking down a long passageway in which the magnificence of the ancient marble mosaics and decorations was still visible among the invading plant-life. Around us there was the scuttling sound of claws, like dogs running along the floor, as alarmed animals dispersed into the ruined rooms on either side; but we couldn't see what they were. And up ahead now, in a shaft of light at the far end of the passage, we could see a human figure.

It was Mr Cloke. He must have made it this far, somehow, after the boat capsized. He lingered for a few seconds in the bright light, looking down the passageway, in our direction, and then melted off into the shadows to the right.

"Did you see who it was?" I asked in a whisper. "Don't say he's come hunting for the diamond too. I thought he was on our side!"

"Everyone's after it," Nick whispered back, disappointed. "I hoped at least we'd have got here first."

"This had better not mean the Captain and Penagadder are here too."

"Perhaps they've killed each other by now. They certainly looked as though they wanted to."

We picked our way along the passageway, the remains of grand and ornate rooms appearing through tumbledown doorways on either side. In one room to our left, a fallen chandelier sat in the middle of the floor, smashed and leaning like a great wrecked ship. Huge windows high in the palace walls, now no more than gaping holes invaded by ivy, flooded the rooms with the red sunshine of morning, picking out golden statues, tiles and borders of gold leaf and green malachite in the walls, impossibly-intricate painted designs and patterns in the ceilings and floors. Once upon a time, it was obvious, this had been the most breathtakingly grand and ornate palace imaginable.

We reached the point where we'd seen Mr Cloke standing, and looked around us. To our right, now, there seemed to be a kind of cloistered garden or courtyard. We followed the direction in which we'd seen him go.

"There were seven rooms off that passageway," Nick observed, absently.

The garden was completely overgrown; but once upon a time it must have been the cool centrepiece of the palace, surrounded by high shady walls, with an ornate fountain and pool in the centre which was now a green, stinking ruin. In one corner of the courtyard there was a kind of giant thistle growing out of the stone wall, with spiny leaves which were longer than I was from head to toe. Huge dragonflies whirred around the enormous leaves and the weed-clogged water in the fountain. There was no sign of Mr Cloke, or anyone else. We kept going, through the garden, and in through another ornate doorway whose wooden door had long since rotted and crumbled away.

We were standing at the head of another passageway, with a black-and-white chequerboard pattern of tiles on the floor all along its length, and more openings on either side. I was trying to keep a mental picture of the route we'd taken so far, afraid that, if we didn't concentrate, we might never find our way back through the warren of magnificent rooms.

Nick peered through a doorway to the right, and went in. A couple of enormous birds rose into the air and flapped out of a big window as he entered.

"See what you can find. I'm just going to have a look in here," I said, quietly.

I could see a brightly-lit room up ahead, casting an orange glow out into the corridor; and when I got there I peered around the doorway very cautiously, in case there was anyone inside.

I couldn't believe my eyes. I walked slowly in, gazing around me. I was in a kind of gallery, with pictures and statues ranged along the walls, and tall cases of books. It wasn't like the rest of the palace at all: this room wasn't a ruin, it was richly decorated in red and gold, perfectly preserved, and somehow *alive*, as it would have been in the heyday of the princes who lived here. In the middle of the room there were neat plants, in pots and urns; and drapes, and velvet-covered couches, and carpets, and sumptuous cushions, and low tables. I was gripped by the most peculiar sensation, as though I'd suddenly been transported into another world, as though everything else in the ruined palace had melted away, leaving me here, amid all this beauty and colour.

I ventured into the middle of the room, my heart beating fast. Sunlight was lancing down through big skylights. On a table, I found a big, magnificent book, made of sheets of parchment sewn together, decorated with gold leaf and dyes of every colour, and bearing dense blocks of tiny lettering, like some ancient sacred text. I couldn't understand any of it, of course; but I had the sense that it must have been put here just for me. I picked it up and took it with me. I walked, now, the length of the gallery, looking at the portraits of princes and the statues of gods and animals. A sculpture of the Lord Shiva, just like one we had in the library back at Kniveacres Hall, standing on one leg, with two sets of arms spread out in a kind of dance. Another plump, seated elephant, with raised hands. A calm-faced goddess festooned with bracelets. A jester, with a two-pronged cap.

A prickling sensation ran right down my spine.

"He is here," I murmured.

Nick had to see this. I clutched the parchment book close, and went back out into the passageway. Instantly, I was among ruins again: walls green and slimy with algae, ceilings collapsed and gaping, feathery weeds growing up high between the chequered floor-tiles. And Nick, emerging from another doorway.

"Nick! I've got something to show you," I said, excitedly.

"So have I." He came closer, and noticed the big parchment book under my arm. "Is that it? What is it?"

"It's a kind of book. But that's not all – come and look. Come on."

"No, you come in here first."

I followed him into another of the ruined chambers, this one especially bare and dilapidated, with one wall almost completely collapsed, and little to see except a filthy flagstone floor and a long, solid marble chest against one wall.

"It looks like a tomb," I said.

"That's what I thought. But I couldn't resist having a peep inside."

"You're braver than I am, then," I said, pulling a face.

We went over to it. The lid was cracked in a couple of places, and one of the cracks had opened into quite a wide fissure, right across the middle. Nick took hold of one edge of the lid, and pulled.

"Look," he grunted, "you can move . . . this . . . aside, like this, and . . . guess what?"

I watched, nervously. If this really was a kind of tomb, I wasn't at all sure I wanted to find out what was inside. But he'd soon heaved the lid apart, sliding one half away from the other with a slow scraping sound, and opening up a gap of about eighteen inches: just large enough to afford a decent view inside. What had he found in there? Some kind of treasure? Or something gruesome?

I hovered, trying to peer in while at the same time keeping my distance. The light was poor, but all I could make out were some pale objects, like little white balls, in clusters.

There seemed to be lots of them in there. Hundreds, possibly.

"What do you think they are?" I asked.

He looked up at me. "I think they're eggs," he said.

I peered in again, in slightly revolted fascination.

"What – *kind* of eggs?" I wondered.

But I didn't wonder for long. Disturbed by the noise of the lid moving, or possibly by the light invading the interior of the tomb, the surface of one of the eggs nearest the top was beginning to bulge.

As we watched, it buckled inward, as though melting in enormous heat. Something sharp then immediately began making a small, clean slit in the shell from the inside: working quickly, opening up a two-inch gash in no time. As we watched, fluid began to bubble slowly out of the slit.

I moved further back, in alarm. Now that the slit was opening up, I could see something moving inside. I could have sworn it was an eye, peeping out.

And then, almost too quick to be sure it was there, a little tongue darted out and back in again.

"Did you see that?"

There it was again. Tasting the air: to see if it was safe to emerge.

"It's a snake, Nick," I said. "They're snake-eggs!"

Others had begun to move now, swelling slightly, and shifting, as the creatures began carving their way out.

"There are hundreds of them, Nick," I said, "I'm not hanging around here to watch them. Come on."

"Maybe I should try and close the lid again," Nick said, grasping the marble with his fingers.

"Nick, you'll get bitten," I said. "Leave it! Let's just *go*."

He heaved with all his bodyweight at the lid, which slid with a sharp grinding sound – and the loose half bumped up against the other again, the crack almost completely closed, so the eggs were hidden from view.

"Right, now come on!" I urged him.

Out in the passageway again, we listened carefully, in case our voices, or the sound we'd made moving the heavy marble lid, had brought anyone to investigate. Satisfied that all was quiet, I beckoned to Nick, and we went back towards the room with the jester statue, where I'd found the parchment book.

"What was it you wanted to show me?" Nick whispered, as we got to the doorway.

I looked around, confused. This wasn't right. Had we turned the wrong way when we came out of the room with the snake-eggs? All I could see, where the lavish red-draped gallery had been a few minutes ago, was another decayed, greenish-grey, overgrown part of the palace ruins.

"Someone's playing tricks," I said. "When you saw me, a few minutes ago, I was standing right here, wasn't I?"

"Yes," said Nick, uncomprehending.

"Well – it wasn't like this. I'd just come out of a room with statues and pictures. It was all furnished. I brought *this.*" I lifted the parchment book, its cover still gleaming with ornate gold-leaf illustration.

"So what's happened?"

"I – don't know, Nick. I could swear it was right here."

"Perhaps it was a trick of the light."

I snorted. "It was a pretty elaborate trick then. There were books and *couches*. There was a Lord Shiva and a jester."

I walked, slowly, into the ruined room. This was definitely where it had been. And, as I looked around, I realised this was the same room: it was just that it had fallen into ruins, as though not just years, but *centuries,* had passed since I was last here. Amid the fallen stones, and thorns, and bat-dung, there were moss-engulfed pillars which had once borne statues, at the same points in the room where I'd seen them intact just a few minutes ago.

I went over to a stone shelf on the wall, where there had been a whole stack of books like the one I was holding under my arm, hand-ornamented. Now, as I ran my hand along the shelf, I found nothing but some flaky old remnants of paper which crumbled to dust under my touch.

"This can't be happening," I wailed. "I've just been here. I saw the jester, Nick."

But Nick was staring ahead of him.

He'd seen Mr Cloke.

Standing over at the far end of the ruined gallery was the bargeman, in his cape, watching us.

"Why did you come?" Nick asked, warily. "Is anyone else with you?"

"I came to meet the two of you," came Cloke's deep, quiet voice.

And, suddenly, as he lifted the cape off his head, I knew who he was; who he'd been, all along. I gasped.

"Was it you – all the time?" I said.

Damyata took a few steps forward.

"I had to look after you," he said.

How could we have failed to recognise him before? His voice was the same; his distinctive nose, his jet-black eyebrows, his piercing dark eyes, were all the same as the man we knew to be our father. As he stood in the sunlight I could see that, the cape aside, he'd changed out of his bargeman's clothes. He was dressed in a silk tunic, and on his head he wore a kind of turban, with something glinting brightly above his forehead. He must have come straight here, to wait for us.

"You knew we would come," I said.

"I made sure you would come," he replied. From behind him, he produced a little *tabla* drum, which he tucked into the crook of his arm; and with the quick fingers of the other hand he tapped out a brief rhythm. *Dhara-dhara-dam, dha-jang, dha-jang.*

Suddenly, it all made sense. Sarasvati had been talking to him from the moment we arrived. He'd been hiding in Calcutta, or somewhere on the edge of the city, waiting for the moment when he could talk to us, unseen; and she had been serving him, guiding and protecting us. He had willed us to come here. He had made it happen. When Nick came asking for a chance to travel on the boat with him, of *course* he had said yes. And he knew he would be taking us both: because the only person to whom I had breathed a word of what I was planning was Sarasvati.

"How did you do that, with the statues, and this room?" I asked him. "Complete one minute, in ruins the next. You did it before, a long time ago, in London. What do you do?"

He smiled. "It may not be me," he said, "it may be you, Mog. You are especially sensitive to the past. You see things from the past, people from the past, places as they used to be – at times of great importance. You can see things which others cannot. All it requires is the right conditions."

He must have seen I was struggling to understand what he was telling me, because he laughed, gently.

"In a garden in London," he elaborated, "you are momentarily transported into another, in Calcutta. In an empty house, you experience it as it used to be, when there was life and passion there. But it is in your mind, in your *soul.* The very fabric of your being remembers the moment, passed from generation to generation. It is a very special gift, but it can cause confusion, even fear. Do not fear it, Mog."

"Is this really the end of our quest?" Nick asked, from behind me.

"You have undertaken quite a journey," said Damyata. "You are most remarkable children. I believe even I underestimated you. But you know, I have said to you before that you are more special than you will ever know. You are your mother's children, and my children."

"Don't leave us this time," I said.

He put the drum down, and walked a few more paces towards us. He held out his arms, and we both went to him, slowly. He put an arm around each of us, and hugged us to him.

He was real. I had never touched him before. Part of me had never quite believed he existed outside our imagination. A handsome, shadowy visitor we had seen again and again, fleetingly: who had left us notes, followed us, scared us sometimes, and terrified our enemies so much that he had left them dead. To his enemies, a demon; to his supporters, a kind of deity. To us, a voice, a presence, a memory. No more. Now he was real, and physical.

A father. I buried my face in the silk of his jacket and tried to hide my wet eyes. I had never, until this moment, really understood the word. Our *father*.

CHAPTER 13

THE BLUE EYE OF WINTER

Damyata cleared the moss from a marble bench, and sat down with us. The light was fading, and he frowned up at the gaping windows in the ruined wall. From outside, in the distance, there came the unmistakeable rumble of thunder. "Rain is coming again," he said. He looked grave. "The Captain cannot be far away," he said. "He survived the accident on the river. I have seen him, in the forest. He will not give up."

"Maybe a tiger will eat him, before he gets here," said Nick.

Our father smiled. "That, we cannot count on," he said. "Alas, I have no control over tigers."

"You can control monkeys," said Nick.

Damyata didn't respond. He appeared to be listening, intently, to the sounds in the palace and in the jungles beyond.

"Better that you are not here when the Captain comes," he said.

"Come *with* us," I said.

He reached out and put his fingertip on my cheek, as though to brush away the last traces of a tear.

"Come with you, to where?" he asked, gently. "To Calcutta? Where neither you nor I belong? Where I am held responsible for so much, as a violator, and a thief? Or to England, where I am only known as a murderer?"

"You're our *father*," I protested.

He sighed, and held his hands out in front of him. We took one each.

"You have had so much misfortune in your lives," he said, "compared to what could have been. It was not how I wanted it. But the darkness is about to end, and years of light and happiness can be yours at last." He reached up to the folded silk scarf he wore on his head, and took down the ornament that was mounted upon it. It was a jewel, the size and rough shape of one of the eggs we had just seen in the marble chest.

He held it in his palm. The daylight picked up its thousands of pure flat surfaces and it seemed to shine and ripple as he turned it. There was a faint, slightly chilly blueness to the light that bounced off it.

"Know what this is?" he asked.

"The Blue Eye of Winter," said Nick.

"*Sasanka-ki-aankh,*" he said. "I speak its name with weariness. I cannot tell you how much trouble this has caused." He closed his fingers around it again. "You must listen very carefully," he said. "I know you have come a long way to find this. I know you have been denied your birthright, and cheated, and left with nothing; and I know you believed this would be your fortune. Many have believed so. Many have laid claim to it, inherited it, stolen it. Many more have coveted it. It has done none of them any good at all. It is a false thing. It has not been their fortune. It has been the cause of misery, and disaster. From Bengal princes to Mughal conquerors to British colonists, all who have possessed it have found alike. Misery, and disaster."

We watched his face intently as he spoke, his eyes holding ours.

"I have looked after it," he said, "because it is yours. You can take it. You *must* take it. It must not pass into anyone else's hands, to cause more suffering and misfortune. And if it is not to cause you misfortune, and all who come after you," he said, "you must lose it where it can never again be found."

He held it out.

I hesitated. Nick reached out and cupped his palm beneath it.

"Before I give it to you," Damyata said, "you must promise me. Take it away from Calcutta with you, and cast it into bottomless water. Its curse has destroyed hundreds, including your dear mother. It must never again be allowed to tempt the greedy, nor betray its rightful owners. Drown it. Cast it clean away. The world will be a better place, and only then will you be happy." He looked at Nick, and then at me. "You must promise," he said again.

"We promise," said Nick quietly.

I nodded. "Promise," I said.

He let it fall into Nick's palm.

"You know," I said slowly, "that we know about the family tree. The one you left for us, in London."

He was watching us.

"The Captain still thinks it's a map," I said, "and so did we, for a long time. But now we know what it really is."

"Then . . . ?" he said.

"What we don't know is," I continued, "why the point to the right represents the sole source of our fortune. What point? Can you tell us?"

"I thought you might have worked it out," he said. "Your mother told me something important, a long time ago. And she told a good friend of hers, whom you also knew."

"Miss Thynne!" I said, suddenly remembering the diary. "Did she – write about it in her diary? There *was* something about Imogen's mother, and a secret she had sworn to keep! But we haven't had a chance to read it all."

"I do not know whether she wrote it down, or if so, where," said Damyata. "But there are people who know who are still alive."

He broke off and looked up, now, alarmed.

"Listen," he whispered.

Amid the sounds of the birds shrieking on the palace walls, there was another sound, distinctive and chilling, echoing towards us from somewhere inside the ruins. And getting closer by the second.

Click . . . click . . . click . . .

"Run," said Damyata. "Save yourselves. I must deal with

the Captain. I will follow if I can. Find Sarasvati, and she will take you home. And do not forget what I told you about the diamond – where it can never again be found, by anyone. Do you understand?"

As he spoke, I felt drops of water hitting my face and arms, coming through the holes in the palace roof. It had started to rain again.

"You have all the clues you need," he said, standing up. "Run, now. Save yourselves!"

Click . . . click . . . click . . .

By the sound of things, the Captain was almost certainly in the passageway outside. Nick started for the door. I was about to follow him; then I turned back, and flung myself at Damyata with a desperate hug.

"I will never forget you," he said, his hand on my head. "I have never forgotten you in all these years, and now I know you will find your fortune. It is all I ask." He looked down at my face, with his profound brown eyes. "You have the book to remember me by. Now go!" he whispered. "Go!" he called softly to Nick. "I will not forget you."

Blindly, my eyes full of tears, I blundered after Nick, holding tight to the parchment book. The rain was starting to fall heavily through the broken ruins, and some of the marble floors were already slippery. It was suddenly thunderously dark.

As we got out into the passageway, we stopped dead. Our way out was blocked – by the enormous figure of the Captain, standing just a few yards away, with his back to us. He was looking down at something he was holding in his hands; but, at any moment, he'd be bound to turn and see us. We couldn't possibly escape the way we'd come.

"In here," said Nick, shoving me in through the nearest doorway on the other side of the corridor.

It was only when we'd been in there, our backs pressed against the slimy old wall, for half a minute or so, that I realised where we actually were. This was the room with the snake-eggs.

But the wall had almost completely fallen in around the window – and would provide an easy escape route from the palace, without our having to encounter the Captain.

Click . . . click . . . click . . .

He had stopped again, outside in the chequered passage, just short of the doorway. We could hear his heavy breathing and his low muttering.

"Seek the point to the right," he grunted, beyond the doorway, "for this is the source of your fortune. Seek the point to the – right."

Nick clutched my arm.

"He's got the map," he whispered in my ear, "and he's following it. He'll come in here, won't he?"

"He might not," I whispered back.

"But he will! Think about it. He thinks the line on the right of the map is this passageway. The point on the extreme right is this room."

"I'm getting out of here," I said.

"Wait," he said. "One second."

He went over to the marble tomb.

"No, Nick," I whispered.

"Let's leave him a surprise he won't forget," he said, determinedly.

"*No*, Nick!" I hissed. "Let's just get out. You'll get bitten. You're mad!"

But he had already grasped the edges of the heavy tomb lid, as he did before, and heaved the two halves apart, by just a few inches.

It was enough. In the grey light, the bodies of snakes spilled out of the crevice. The eggs must have been hatching away in there like a chain reaction, while we'd been talking to Damyata. The marble lid was suddenly teeming with foot-long baby cobras.

"Who's there?" called the Captain. He had heard the sound of the lid being moved. *Click . . . click . . .* He was on his way in.

I was already on the ruined wall, ready to jump out into the undergrowth beyond. "Leave it, Nick," I said, "come on!"

He lingered by the tomb a split-second too long.

"Come *on*!" I hissed at him.

But he had been bitten. Doubled up, his hand in his armpit, he followed me over the wall and out into the pouring rain. At first I didn't realise: I just ran, trying to protect the ornate decorated book inside my shirt, looking back to make sure he was coming. But when I saw his face, and the way he was holding his arm, I stopped.

"What's the matter?"

He could hardly speak, for gasping. There were tears in his eyes as well as rainwater running down his face.

"One of them got me," he said. "I was too slow. I didn't let go of the lid in time."

"It *bit* you?" I exclaimed. "Show me!"

Gingerly, he proffered his hand. It was already red and starting to swell. There were two neat little punctures, with tiny little beads of blood growing in them, on the fleshy base of his thumb.

The rain was coming down like a waterfall, as bad as yesterday now. I grabbed his hand and put it to my lips, trying to suck the wounds. I'd heard that's what you did. If I could just draw out the poison in time, before it took effect . . . I spat onto the sodden ground, and tried again. I had no idea whether I was doing any good.

"I feel sick," he groaned. "I think I need to sit down."

"By this wall here then, come on. But be quiet. The Captain's still in there."

We were just yards from the broken-down wall we'd just climbed through to escape, and we could clearly hear the Captain's crutches echoing on the stone flags inside.

And now, the drum sound resonated among the ruins again. *Dhara-ka-ta-ta-ta-ta, dhara-jang, dhara-jang.*

"Who's there?" the Captain was barking.

Nick, his face contorted in agony, tipped his head back against the palace wall. His whole arm was going stiff.

"Don't cry out," I whispered to him. "Try to stay quiet." Despairing, I tried to hold his hand out into the falling rain, thinking the cool water would, at least, be good for it.

Now, there was more than one person in the room behind us. Their words were picked up and magnified, clear as crystal, by the marble floors and walls.

"We meet again," came Damyata's distinctive, deep voice. "Who was that man who brought you upriver, Captain?"

"Well, I'll be damned," said the Captain. "You? The lord of the diamond." He began to laugh, sarcastically. "People has plenty to say about you," he sneered, "and I reckoned I might make your acquaintance one day. Little did I know I already had. Mr *Cloke*!"

"You won't find the diamond here," said Damyata. "It has gone, where it can never do harm to another human being again."

"You lie," growled the Captain. Then he must have seen the look on Damyata's face. "Am I too late?" he said. "Those brats have got it, ain't they?"

There was some grunting, as though a struggle had ensued.

"Either you tells me where they've gone," the Captain said, menacingly, "or you pays for it. Mr *Cloke*."

"You can guess where they've gone," replied Damyata. "But you won't be going after them, Captain. This is as far as you go. Your tomb is here. See?"

Nick had started shivering. He was clutching his hand under his armpit again, and his teeth were clenched. From within came the sound of crashing. The two men were fighting. The Captain wasn't agile, but he was huge and powerful, and he could swing a crutch with deadly force. I didn't dare climb up to peer back into the room, but I could imagine the scene, the Captain trying to pin Damyata against the wall and beat him senseless, Damyata trying to outmanoeuvre his enemy and force him into the tomb of snakes.

An almighty crash told us the lid of the tomb had been heaved right off.

"I can't bear this," I said, desperately. "We have to get out of here, Nick. Can you move? Do you think you can come with me?"

His arm clutched to his chest, his face grim with pain, he nodded, and I helped him to his feet. As we went, there was an angry roar from the room on the other side of the wall, and then the most bloodcurdling noise of someone shouting in agony.

I couldn't be sure, because we were further away now, and the noise of the rain was drowning it out: but it sounded as though more than one person was screaming. And it went on for a long time.

I couldn't bear to think about it. We left the awful noise behind, staggering through the ruins, around the outside of the palace, back towards the gateway to the cluster of buildings: past the temple with its rows of intricate sculptured figures standing ten or twelve high – and the arch where Sarasvati and Punch waited, anxiously.

"What has happened?" asked Sarasvati. "There was a signal, long time ago. But I thought you would never come!"

"It's Nick," I said. "Help – we must get help for him. He's been bitten by a snake."

Her face fell. "Let me look." Nick showed her his hand, much more swollen now than it had been at first. "You feel all right?" He shook his head. "No. Not good. We have to get him up on Punch," she said. "Help me."

Together, somehow, we heaved him up, and he slumped on Punch's back, in the rain. Sarasvati climbed up and started arranging blankets over him.

"Quick!" she urged me.

Punch started to move, and we tried to wedge Nick between us, Sarasvati in front and me behind, so that he wouldn't fall off as Punch rolled along. He was beginning to lose consciousness. We struck out through the jungle, heading back towards the red road; but we'd only been underway for a few minutes when Sarasvati changed her mind.

"It's no good," she shouted, "we have to get him under cover, somewhere he can rest. He needs sleep, and warmth. Look. There's something over there."

She guided Punch through the mud towards the river, a few hundred yards away through the trees. Her sharp eyes had spotted a houseboat – old and dilapidated – pulled halfway up onto the bank.

There was no one to be seen. Evidently the houseboat had been abandoned: perhaps it was damaged, and would no longer float. We broke in, without difficulty, through the wooden doors at the stern. It was dark and musty-smelling, but blissfully dry inside.

Sarasvati found a little dustpan, and spent two minutes bent double, peering into corners. With deft movements she scooped up two agile yellow-brown scorpions, and flung them out of the cabin into the jungle mud. At length, she stood up.

"All safe now," she said, seriously.

I settled Nick on a low, cushioned bench-seat inside the boat, while Sarasvati went out to fetch blankets from Punch's back. The rain drummed noisily on the wooden roof.

"I wonder who this belongs to," I said to myself. It seemed clear that, once upon a time, it had been quite grand. There were traces of decorative paint on the outside which hadn't quite been weathered off; and inside, although it was shabby, there were the remnants of ornate fittings and expensive upholstery which suggested it might once have belonged to a maharaja or a high-ranking British official. There were even a few useful objects still here, as though it had been used quite recently: a couple of oil lamps, some boat-hooks, rolled-up quilts smelling of mothballs, and a firm, bolster-style pillow. There was even some food in one of the cupboards: some biscuits and a jar of fruit preserve, both long rancid and covered in mould. I took them out onto the afterdeck and flung them into the river. And I pulled the parchment book out from under my shirt, now, and laid it on a bench to dry out.

"You must stay with him," Sarasvati said, coming back inside with the blankets. She looked like a half-drowned little vole. "I'll take Punch, and go for help. The Professor will know what to do. A doctor must come."

"I've found these," I said, "I don't think we need the blankets."

We tucked the quilts around Nick, and laid his head on the pillow I'd found, until he looked quite comfortable. Sarasvati had brought in a small pile of pale, brittle leaves, which she must have been gathering outside just now.

"Medicine," she said. "Just wait."

She produced a pewter cup from the canvas bag she carried around her neck, and took it outside to catch the rain in it. A minute or two later she came in, tore up a few of the leaves, and placed them in the cup of rainwater.

"Soak them," she said. "Best to warm them, if you can. Then make him drink it. Sip at a time. And don't take the leaves out."

"What is it?" I asked her.

"For fever," she said. "It will make him relaxed, and cooler. So he sleeps better, at least." She helped me give him a dose: I held his head up while she tipped a few drops into his mouth.

"Sarasvati, I don't know what we'd do without you," I told her. "When this is all over—" I suddenly realised there was something we'd forgotten to tell her. "Look," I said. "We found what we wanted, in the palace. Damyata has given us this."

I reached under Nick's quilt. Safely hidden in his breeches pocket was the diamond.

Holding it for the first time, I turned it over in my hands. It was heavy and gorgeous. Its blue tinge was fainter, in here, but still visible. Sarasvati was watching it, spellbound, her brown eyes wide.

"It's cursed," I said. "It brings nothing but bad luck."

"Riches," she said solemnly, "and bad luck, are the same thing. But Damyata will look after you."

I bit my lip, not sure what to tell her. "Perhaps," I said.

She stood up. "I will be quick," she said. She reached into her bag again, and found the last few dried apricots and some nuts. "Not much," she said, "but eat these. Don't move! I will come, with help."

And she was gone, closing the door behind her with a rattle. I watched, through the window, as the elephant's backside swayed off into the jungle. The rain battered on the houseboat roof, and down on the couch my brother was still shivering, stiffly, under the blanket; his face deathly pale.

I realised I was trembling. It had been the most extraordinary morning. The excitement of finding the palace, meeting Damyata, and getting the diamond; and then the arrival of the Captain, and the shock of the bite, and that terrible fight in the room with the snakes. There hadn't been time for it all to sink in; but it was beginning to, now.

"Be quick, Sarasvati," I murmured, terrified. "*Please* be quick."

I tried to work out how long it would take Sarasvati to get help. I'd never seen Punch move especially fast, and it was a long way back to Calcutta. Then she, and whoever came with her, had to get back here. We had no chance, I decided, of seeing anyone until tomorrow. I prayed it would be soon enough.

I was still dripping, and I took the wettest of my clothes off and wrapped myself in another of the quilts. There seemed to be nothing I could do, except keep talking quietly to Nick to reassure him help was on its way. I lay down beside him, to wait.

And I fell asleep, to the sound of the rain hammering on the houseboat. The sky outside was dark with clouds, and the intensity of the rain showed no sign of letting up. So much water was falling out of the sky that, if it kept up for many days, I felt sure the whole jungle, and the palace ruins, and probably Calcutta itself, would be submerged under the flood.

In my dreams we were floating, travelling down the river on Punch's back. The water was getting deeper and deeper, and Punch was having to work harder to stay afloat. She had to hold her trunk higher and higher out of the water as we went, and I was terrified that our weight would cause her to drown. More and more people were swimming up to us, and trying to climb onto Punch's back. I was trying to shout at them that we were overloaded, there was no more room; but they took no notice, and continued to try to haul themselves onto Punch, weighing her further down. She trumpeted in terror, sinking under the rising water, as I tried in desperation to kick all the people away.

I sat up with a jolt. Thank goodness, it had been a dream. The rain was still tipping down outside, and Nick was asleep beside me – looking calmer now. I reached out a hand towards his forehead: I was suddenly gripped by sick terror that I might find it completely cold. Tentatively, my fingers made contact, and I exhaled with relief to find his face warm, and his whole body shifting in unconscious annoyance at my touch.

But now, as I listened and concentrated, I became aware that something was different from before. It felt as though we *were* moving.

I went to the window and peered out, having to rub hard at the glass to get rid of the condensation and several years of grime and lichen. But there could be no mistake. Through the little patch of clear glass I could now see the trees of the riverbank moving rapidly past us. And, beneath my feet, I could definitely feel the boat rocking.

I went to the stern and pushed open the cabin doors. We were in the middle of the river, being swept along at several knots by the current. The river-waters must have risen so high they had lifted the houseboat off the bank, while we'd been asleep inside, and carried it off. Sweeping downstream with the flood-waters, we were moving many times faster than we had in Mr Cloke's boat: but we were veering and turning in the current like a piece of old flotsam, and the mooring-rope was trailing behind us in the water, uselessly.

It was only a matter of time before we hit something, at speed.

I went in and tried to shake Nick awake, but he was limp, quite unable to respond. If the boat started to sink, I'd have to drag him out, and hope I could manage to pull him ashore. I felt a rising sense of panic. I had to try and stay calm.

Fortunately, there were almost no other boats on the river:

although we passed many little fishing dinghies and other vessels tied up, or hauled up onto the mud, wherever there was a settlement; and in several places I saw people watching us from the bank as we sped by. It was pointless shouting to them for help: there was nothing for it but to wait and hope that, somehow, by some accident or miracle, we might come to a halt.

And, at a point where the river came out of a long eastward bend, we did. We had drifted dangerously close to the western bank, and then been swept back out into the middle; but now the current took us and turned us around several times, all the time getting closer to the eastern bank as we spun through the mist and rain.

There was a massive jolt and a grinding sound as the bottom of the boat hit the mud. Nick and I were both flung across the width of the cabin and bounced off the cushioned seats on the other side. The cupboard doors flew open and everything fell out on top of us with a great clatter: ropes, boat-hooks, lamps, the lot. The stern end of the boat swung around until it, too, hit the bank; and we were grounded, facing upstream.

I scrambled to my feet and dived out onto the afterdeck to see where we were. But apart from the rain, there was very little to see. It was impossible to tell how far downstream we'd come, except that we must have covered about ten miles even since I woke up. We were sitting on a mud bank, with shallow brown water all around us, with the edge of the forest a few yards away, and no sign of civilisation or people.

I could hear Nick groaning. I went back inside and crouched next to him, excited at hearing his voice, even though he was nowhere near fully conscious.

"Nick, we've had an accident," I said, "we've run aground. Can you hear me? I'm going to try and moor the boat so we won't move again. I won't be long. Then I might be able to see if there's someone who can help."

He groaned again. Gathering up my still-damp shirt, and pulling it on, I went back out into the rain and leaned over the side, looking for the mooring-rope. When I'd found it, I slid into the water and sploshed across with it to the line of trees, where I made it fast to a sturdy trunk. With luck, even if the current swept us off the bank again, it would hold us. I leaped back on board and went to make sure the other end was securely fastened to the boat.

And I turned around again, hearing a splashing sound in the water behind me. At first the rain was in my eyes and I had to blink a couple of times to be sure of what I was seeing. But I could feel my blood curdle, as it sank in.

A crocodile had launched itself out into the water from between the trees, just seconds after I'd been wading across there. It must have smelled me, or been disturbed by my movement. It was floating, now, in the calmest part of the water just behind the houseboat, its dark, rough back breaching the surface. It was huge.

And there was another, slithering out from the trees to join it. And another, waddling across the mud on splayed legs and sploshing belly-first into the water to my right.

Then I counted a fourth . . . and a fifth. The houseboat was surrounded by them.

I began to wail, quietly. It had been a relief when we'd run aground, and at last stopped hurtling downstream, out of control. Now, suddenly, I desperately wished I could cast us loose again and get out of here. To anywhere. I began to calculate whether they'd be able to lift themselves onto the afterdeck: and, if they did, what I'd do. I looked around. I could jump onto the cabin roof, and fend them off with a boat-hook. But how would I get Nick up there, in the state he was in?

And, just as I was standing there panicking, I noticed a little boat appearing out of the mist upstream, with the blurry shape of a man standing up in it, sheltering his eyes from the rain, looking at us. He was making straight for us. My heart leaped. Someone must have seen us racing helplessly past, and was coming to rescue us.

I had no idea whether he would speak English, but I leaned over the rail and shouted at him: "Help! Help us! We've run aground! We need help!"

In the pouring rain, he came alongside, his little boat wobbling, hard to control in the fast-moving flood-water.

"Here!" I shouted. "Can you help us? There are crocodiles! All around, crocodiles! We are trapped! Please help!"

Saying nothing, the man tied up alongside. Through the pouring rain I couldn't see his face, and I still wasn't sure he'd understood what I'd said; but at least he'd stopped to help us. It was *such* a relief.

"Thank goodness," I gabbled, as he stood up and stepped

aboard near the bow. "Please help us. They're *everywhere*. You see, we—"

I stopped abruptly. The shock was like being hit in the stomach.

The man clambering back along the side of the houseboat towards me was Penagadder.

He dropped onto the afterdeck beside me, and smiled. Even though he didn't say a word, the expression on his face said: You didn't think I'd give up that easily, did you? And it was true. It had been ridiculous to hope that he might just have disappeared, after the accident on the boat, never to return.

"Which one are you?" he asked.

I swallowed hard.

"We're both the same," I said defiantly. I was absolutely petrified, but I was determined not to show it. He smiled again.

"Where's the diamond?"

"I haven't got it."

His eyes looked past me, through the open doors into the cabin. "The other one's got it, then. Is he in there?"

I didn't reply.

"I said, is he in there?"

And, without warning, he slammed his fist so hard into me that he took all the wind out of my body, and pushed me against the cabin.

"I'll just 'ave to throw you overboard so's I can get in and 'ave a look, then," he snarled. And he picked me up, still winded, and literally dangled me, by my collar, over the side.

"Nooo!" I screeched. I could see the long brown heads of at least two crocodiles within a few feet of the boat.

"Well then," said the sailor, yanking me back onto the deck, "are you going to tell me where the diamond is?"

"It's inside," I sobbed, terrified.

"Now. Let's be clear. I could cut pieces off o' both of you, one by one, to throw to the crocs," he said, quietly, standing over me. "An ear, first. Then a couple o' fingers. Just to give 'em a taste for ya. Get 'em all excited." He dug in his pocket and found the remains of something he'd evidently been eating earlier, and flung it to the crocodiles below. There was a frenzy of movement, and four of them darted for the morsel, snapping and fighting to get at it, making the water froth.

He smiled. "Or," he continued, "you could give me the diamond. Which is it to be?" And, like a conjuror, he gave a brief flick of his wrist and a knife seemed to appear in his hand from nowhere, with a six-inch, double-edged blade. He moved it rapidly backwards and forwards once. *Swish-swish.* He meant what he said. And, I had no doubt at all, he'd enjoy it.

"It's in his pocket," I said, nodding towards the cabin. "Please just take it. Don't hurt him. He's ill."

He ducked, and went inside. I closed my eyes, blinking back tears. When was this all going to end? While he fumbled over by Nick's slumped form, I reached for the boat-hook I'd brought out onto the afterdeck.

He came out, after a matter of seconds. He'd found it. His

face was triumphant. He clutched it in his fist, and brought his fist to his lips, as though to kiss it. His eyes shone.

"*O my lovely blue eye*," he sang, quietly. "*Blue eye that twinkle and shine . . .*"

I couldn't bear it. He was gloating.

"You've got what you want," I said. "Please leave us alone."

"What's the matter with him?" he asked, gesturing back at Nick.

"A snake bit him," I said, my lip trembling.

He made a face of mock-sympathy. Then he stared at me, steely-eyed. "It's no more'n you deserve," he said. "You caused us all too much trouble." He saw the boat-hook in my hand, and frowned. "I 'ope you wasn't thinking of using that as a weapon," he said.

"I brought it out in case I needed to fend off a crocodile," I said. "Please, leave us alone now."

He stood still on the afterdeck. The rain fell around us; and there was a splashing sound as two of the crocodiles jostled in the water again. Their hunger had been aroused, and they were alert and jumpy. I could see their long shapes out of the corner of my eye, floating there, waiting for something else to happen.

"Thing is," said Penagadder, "I don't know as I can trust you to keep quiet. Why don't I just cut both o' your throats anyway, afore I go? Save others any more trouble you might be minded to cause, in future? And then them crocs could have their fill, too. Why don't I do that?"

"Just go," I pleaded with him. "Your boat's there. Go. Take

the diamond. Just leave us alone." For the life of me, I had no idea how we were going to get off this houseboat and find help for Nick; but at the moment it seemed more important to get rid of Penagadder.

"I ain't so sure I can do that," he said.

"Oh, I think you can," said Nick.

I gave him the briefest of glances, not daring to take my eyes off Penagadder for a second. But I felt a rush of joy as he emerged from the cabin, right beside me, holding a boat-hook out in front of him.

I grasped my own boat-hook with both hands and, for a few seconds, we feinted at him from both sides, jabbing with the hooks at points either side of his face, making him flinch and step backwards.

But we couldn't afford to play games for long. In a moment, he'd gather his senses and would just wrench both poles out of our hands. Nick's next jab stopped just short of his face. His eyes flickered in momentary alarm.

Something had ripped his face apart once before. You could see him reliving it, for a split-second.

"Again," said Nick quietly.

I thrust my boat-hook at him, now, up towards his face; no sooner had he flinched from that than Nick moved forward again, jabbing with his. He couldn't cope with the relentlessness of both of us, threatening him one after another, the jabs coming just half-seconds apart, from different directions. Instinctively, he took another step back, blinking as the sharp hooks missed his face by fractions of an inch. And it was a step too far. He caught one of his feet in a cleat at the edge of the afterdeck, and over he went.

The diamond flew out of his hand and sailed through the rain as he flung out his arms to try and save himself. There was a splash as he hit the water, and an even bigger one as the crocodiles lurched forward *en masse*, to fight over him. Somewhere in the middle of the foaming chaos, the diamond plopped, and instantly sank, into the muddy river. I turned away, terrified, unable to look; all I'd glimpsed was the first sight of the orange-brown water turning bright red.

I hugged Nick, as terror and relief shivered through me at the same time.

"You're better!" I exclaimed.

"I'm not too bad," he said. "I feel a bit weak."

"That was a pretty brave performance for someone feeling a bit weak."

"I think it must have worked. You must have sucked the poison out."

"I thought you were going to die."

In the rain, further downstream, where the erosion of the riverbank had created a kind of muddy cliff, I thought I could hear a dog barking. I climbed up and peered over the cabin roof. There *was* a dog, up there on the bank, and it was running closer and closer, barking all the time.

"Lash?" I said, incredulously.

Nick turned, astonished. It was Lash, all right: leaping about on the fringes of the trees, well aware of who we were, and frantic with excitement.

"The crocodiles!" gasped Nick. "Lash, stay back!"

But now, on the crest of the bank above us, some human figures appeared too; and, before we could work out who they were, we were ducking back inside the cabin to avoid the gunfire.

Shot after shot hit the churning, bloody water near the boat. I pressed my hands over my ears, not daring to put my head outside the cabin. Nick had pressed his eye to the nearest window, and was just able to identify the people through the film of rain.

"It's the Professor," he said, "and Dr Shastri!"

After a few minutes of shooting, the crocodiles had either been killed, or dispersed. One of their corpses bumped, lengthways on, against the stones along the nearest point of the bank. Others had got away, and their backs were receding in the rapid current, like broad, flat logs.

Of Mr Penagadder, there was no trace, except streaks of bright blood running away in the swirls and eddies at the edge of the great river. And no trace of the Blue Eye of Winter either. Perhaps it was inside a crocodile; or perhaps it was lodged somewhere in the river-bed, buried comprehensively by the thrashing reptilian tails churning up the mud. Either way, it seemed certain it would never again be found, by anyone.

The Professor waded across to the boat and carried us to the bank, one at a time. Lash couldn't contain himself. He was soaking wet, but I hugged his neck, and buried my face in his clammy fur, and held him tighter than I ever had in my life.

"That was some convincing shooting, Professor," said Nick, sitting on the broad root of a tree in the shelter of an overhanging branch.

"Ah, quite. Well, there is *some* virtue in keeping one's eye in, don't you know. Undoubtedly."

"Here," said the Doctor, stepping forward and draping a coat around my shoulders. "Put this on, goodness me. Stay dry."

"How on earth did you know where we were?" I asked them. "Sarasvati has hardly had time to get back to Calcutta yet, has she?"

"The Professor became worried about you," explained the Doctor. "When he found that both of you were gone, and then Sarasvati and Punch went after you, he questioned the household and found out where you were headed. He summoned me, and we have come, with horses." I looked up at him, hardly able to believe what was happening. "We had no idea how far you would have got," he said. "We have just been keeping our eyes open, from the road, and asking people if they have seen you. And, when we noticed the grounded houseboat in the distance, and heard shouting, we came straight away."

"You must take a look at Nick's hand," I said. "He was bitten by a cobra."

The Doctor gasped. "When?"

"This morning," said Nick. He held out his hand.

"He's been unconscious for most of the day," I explained, "and it swelled up much more than that, at first. I tried to suck the poison out just after he'd done it. But he was *so* ill. I thought he was going to die."

The Doctor felt Nick's head. "You did the right thing," he said, impressed. "*Very* much the right thing. I have something I can give you, back in Calcutta, to stop the swelling. But the fever is improved. Very good. Very lucky."

"It was just a baby snake," I said. "Maybe that's why."

"You are too modest, Mog," said the Doctor. "Without you he may not be alive. You have been very sensible, and very brave." I knew that my behaviour had actually been utterly brainless and terror-stricken, for the whole of the past two days: but I felt myself blushing bright red at his praise.

"So where is Sarasvati?" the Professor asked.

"She's coming back to Calcutta, with Punch," I said. "She thinks we are still by the palace ruins. She's coming as fast as she can, to get help. She will be surprised."

"Who told you where we had gone?" Nick asked.

"Nanak," said the Professor. "I had guessed the palace ruins might be the first place to try. But he said you had gone with a boatman."

"We've got a lot to tell you, Professor," said Nick.

I suddenly remembered something.

"The book!" I said. "It's still on the houseboat – Professor, can I rescue something from the boat before we go back?"

He made me stay with Lash on the bank, and he waded back out to the boat, returning with the parchment book. He seemed instantly excited, and was taking the greatest of pains to keep it dry. When we got back to the road, where they had left the horses, it took him fully three or four minutes to plan the seating arrangements so that the book wouldn't get damaged.

"So it's all right for us all to get soaked," Nick teased him, "so long as the book is safe."

"You will dry out in no time," said the Professor. "If the ink on this magnificent document gets washed off, or, ah, smudged, you know – it will be as good as worthless. In any case, the rain is stopping."

Nick rode with the Professor, and I sat up behind the Doctor, while Lash ran alongside. The rain did stop, for the rest of the day; and the journey took us under an hour, mostly at a trot. By the time we'd run aground, it turned out, we had been hardly any distance from Calcutta at all.

Chapter 14
LADY SHEETS'S STORY

Dr Shastri insisted on attending Nick at the Professor's for another couple of days, and I was glad to have him there. At last, Nick's swollen hand subsided, and his muscle function returned to normal. Sarasvati was especially relieved at his recovery. She and Punch had arrived home, drenched and agitated, soon after us. Her mouth fell open when we greeted her: especially when Nick strolled out into the garden. She spent a lot of time, over the next few days, fetching and carrying for him: as though she were making up for having failed to make it back to Calcutta in time to raise the alarm, as she had promised.

Professor Shugborough arranged us a passage home, in a week's time. We told him the whole story, of the Captain, and "Mr Cloke", and Damyata; the ruined palace, and the drowning of the diamond. He promised he'd get the beautiful gold-leaf book translated.

"*To remember me by*, Damyata said," I recalled. "I would love to know what's in it, Professor."

"Such adventure, you had," Sarasvati sighed, admiringly.

"We'd have been in real trouble, if it hadn't been for you," Nick said. "Thank goodness you came after us. When the boat sank and we were stranded in the jungle, I thought we'd had it. Until you and Punch rescued us."

"But is it true about Damyata?" she asked in a quiet voice. "Did he and the Captain both fall into the chest of snakes?"

I tried to soften the blow, but it was hard to contain my own grief. Quite how close and loyal to Damyata Sarasvati was, we had only just begun to realise. "I didn't see," I said, "so I can't be sure what happened. Perhaps Damyata survived."

"Damyata can never die," she said, with a child's naïve certainty. "It cannot be."

"Perhaps," I said again, gently, blinking back tears. I would have given almost anything for her to be right: for her confidence – her supernatural faith, almost – to be justified.

There was something, the Professor said, we must be sure to do before we left Calcutta: and that was to pay a visit to Lady Sheets. She had specifically requested our attendance upon her. So, one afternoon during our last week, Mystery delivered us at the door of her big, square, white house, in a tonga-cart, to take tea with her. Brilliant green ivy and clematis crawled up the walls and, in places, disappeared in through the open windows. Storks stood, like plaster sculptures, at each corner of the roof.

A turbaned servant showed us upstairs. The house was furnished in a style which, at home, would probably have been fashionable a hundred years ago. Lady Sheets was sitting up in bed, surrounded by carved teak screens and peacock-feather fans. Dressed in a billowing silk nightgown, with several pillows propped up behind her, she resembled an enormous swan. She lifted her glasses to her eyes when we were shown in, and croaked in welcome.

"Come and sit down," she said. "Meerut will bring tea, presently."

We settled ourselves on a low Ottoman-style couch beside the bed, and smiled nervously at her.

"There, now," she said. "Forgive me for receiving you in this manner, but I am not well, and rising and dressing are, I fear, beyond my failing powers. But I do find it so refreshing to have the company of young people. And so much must have been happening to both of you since you arrived in Calcutta. Tell me about your adventures."

Nick looked at me. "Well," he said, "I hardly know where to start. We have had some really – unique experiences since we got here. Neither Mog nor I had been—"

"That girl, that fakir's girl," she interrupted him. "What's she called? Sarasvati? Is that it? Yes? She's your half-sister. Didn't anyone tell you that?"

Nick stared at her, and my mouth dropped open.

"She's our . . . *How* is she?" I asked, incredulous.

"She's Damyata's child, just like you," said Lady Sheets. "A few years younger. Not the fakir's daughter at all. A local girl, a servant, had her, and Damyata was the father – but she fell too ill and couldn't care for her, I seem to remember. The

Professor adopted her, and he likes to tell people that silly story because she spends a lot of time with the fakir. But fakirs don't have children, you know. They're ascetic, everybody knows that. No pleasures of the flesh."

"I see," I said.

"Anyway," she said, "now you know. I'm most surprised no one told you. You were saying?"

Nick gave a short laugh. Almost anything we told her now was likely to seem a bit lame, compared with that extraordinary revelation out of nowhere. We were neither of us quite sure whether to believe her, or not.

"We took a trip up the river," Nick ventured. "Quite an experience! With a local boatman. The jungles, north of the city, are something, aren't they? We've seen crocodiles, and—"

"He was wonderful," she interrupted again. "*Wonderful.* A wonderful, irresistible man."

"Er – who was?" I asked.

She stared at me through her glasses. "Damyata," she said, as though I were stupid. "Wonderful. Like a source of energy. Life-giving. You could meet a million men and find no one like him. No wonder she couldn't bear to be without him. She radiated happiness, my dears."

"Who did?" I asked, with a nervous glance at Nick.

"Oh do try and keep up," she said. "Your mother, Imogen. The tragedy of it."

"We – met Damyata," Nick said, slowly, "the other day."

He said it at exactly the moment the servant came in again,

with a trolley. The servant was too well-trained to say anything, but he looked at Nick with alert, curious eyes as he went about arranging the tea things on the little round bedside table. Nick stayed silent, nervous of revealing any more for the rest of the time the servant was in the room; but Lady Sheets had no such qualms.

"Oh, plenty of people say he's alive, and not far away," she said. "The servants talk about him all the time. They whisper, you know, believing they're keeping some great secret." She leaned forward, slightly. "But my Hindustani vocabulary is more extensive than anyone thinks," she confided. "Tea?"

I was watching her nervously, as the servant poured the tea and placed pieces of cake on the plates. Would he help her with the eating and drinking routine, or would it be up to me again? But she set my mind at rest.

"Forgive me, my dears," she said, "if I don't join you. My digestive system . . . I shall be content to keep you company, while you eat." I almost sighed with relief. "I shall listen, while you talk to me," she said. "It is such a pleasure to have young and interesting company. Such a rarity."

"Well," Nick said, swallowing a mouthful of cake. "I think I was telling you about our trip up the Hooghly, to—"

"Now listen here," she said, cutting in again, "this inheritance of yours. That ruffian, Septimus. The hardships he put you to, and then be blowed if he didn't fritter away the entire family fortune so there's not a penny left. The little beast. I could boil him in oil." She said this with real feeling, and her face was so indignant I had to lift my teacup quickly to my lips to hide a broad smile. "Damyata was everything that he wasn't," she said scornfully. "He was insane with jealousy. There's no wonder he didn't want Damyata's children in his house, haunting him. But the way he treated you just piled tragedy upon tragedy."

I put my cup down on the table. "Your Ladyship," I said, "it took us a long time to find out the story of what happened to our mother, and to us, when we were tiny. We've had to piece it together from what a great many different people have said. Now that I've been here and seen where she grew up, and heard the stories, I think I understand a lot more about what she was like, and why she did what she did."

Lady Sheets had fallen quiet, now, and was listening intently.

"Good," she said, sincerely. "I'm glad, my dear."

"It was kind of you to send us the diary," I said. "I've been reading it, a little at a time, but I'm afraid I haven't finished it yet."

"I merely thought it would be of more use to you than it is to me," she said.

"Of course, I don't understand all of it," I went on. "I don't recognise all of the names she mentions, and she often talks about keeping secrets, without saying what the secrets are."

"Very wise of her," observed Lady Sheets.

"She does say something about – the truth about Imogen's mother," I said.

"And?" Lady Sheets was looking at me through half-closed eyes.

"Well – that's about all," I said. "I haven't been able to find out what it means."

"I shall tell you," she said. She lifted her glasses, on their stalk, to look at us again. "You have heard enough people telling you that your mother was a great beauty," she said, "me included, I don't doubt. Heaven knows what details I bored you with at dinner at the Colonel's that night, you poor thing. Well, Imogen was not the first Winter to be conspicuously beautiful. Her mother, Sophia, was greatly admired. And I hope it will not embarrass you to hear that she had several male suitors, in addition to your grandfather John Winter. In truth . . ." She paused, briefly, perhaps working out how to phrase things delicately. "Her marriage did not prevent her from receiving the attentions of others. It has long since ceased to cause me pain. It was all before he met and married me, after all. My late husband, Sir Lumley, when he was a young and handsome man, was very close indeed to your grandmother, when she was a young and lovely woman – albeit a married one. And the consequence was that your mother, Imogen, was not John Winter's daughter. She was Lumley's."

I wrestled, mentally, with the links on the family tree.

"It was a family scandal, if you like, a full twenty years before your mother's misfortune," she said. "But a great deal easier to keep quiet. A *great* deal easier."

Things were starting to fall into place. This was what Damyata had been talking about, too.

"So Imogen herself knew," I said.

"Imogen knew, because her mother told her," said Lady

Sheets. "It was hushed up quite successfully, and I wouldn't be surprised if there's no one alive in Calcutta today, apart from myself, who knows. I am sure many people *suspected*."

"Damyata knew," I said.

"Who knows what your mother chose to tell Damyata?" said Lady Sheets, wistfully. "Every secret and every piece of silly babble she had ever heard, I don't doubt. But, some would tell you, Damyata was all-seeing and all-knowing, in any case."

"But you kept your husband's secret," I said.

"My dears, I am getting terribly old," she said, "and I have lived well on my dear husband's fortune, since he passed away. I can't take the rest of it with me, and my poor dear Viola did not survive to see her own inheritance. With that in mind I have made a decision, which I shall communicate to my lawyers." She leaned forward, and began to cough. She didn't stop coughing, for a long time, and her body convulsed. I started to become alarmed. I got to my feet to help her. Surely she wasn't going to die before she had told us what she'd decided? I had just made it over to the bedside when she seemed to recover; her eyes watering, she sat back on the pile of pillows.

"I'm so sorry," she said, "you see, I am really not well. Forgive me." She coughed again, briefly, and continued. "As I was saying, I have no heirs to whom I can leave my estate. Sir Lumley left nothing in his will to his illegitimate children. But it is within my power to leave something to them, when I go." She peered through her glasses at us. "Heaven knows, I never had any intention of doing so," she said. "However, I have taken a shine to the two of you, my dears. It was most intriguing to have the chance to meet you, after all these years, and I have been enchanted to find that you are kind, honest children. One becomes so used to people being self-serving and deceitful, here in Calcutta, that one has almost forgotten human nature can have any goodness in it. Well, I should like to think that my dear husband's blood has at least a part to play. Be that as it may, I intend to reward goodness, and do what little I can to make your hitherto quite *dreadful* lives into something worthwhile."

"Our lives haven't been—" began Nick, but I punched him discreetly, and he stopped.

"When I go," she said, staring at us, "you will be my sole legatees."

Nick beamed at her.

"What does that mean?" he asked me, out of the corner of his mouth.

"It means," I whispered back – then I caught Lady Sheets's eye again. "Forgive me, your Ladyship," I said aloud, "if I understand you properly, that means – you intend to leave your money to us?"

"Quite so. By the terms of the will I am drawing up now, the estate will pass to the illegitimate line of Sir Lumley, after my death. Unless, of course, you have another source of income, of which I am not aware, and can afford to decline it. In which case, I dare say, I can find some charitable foundation which—"

"We have no income, that we know of," Nick assured her

hastily. "We were advised that Sir Septimus's entire estate was swallowed up in debts."

"We were left penniless," I added.

"So I was led to believe." She fanned herself, watching our faces. "I have assured the Professor that I will pay for your passage home," she said. "My lawyers will doubtless be corresponding with yours in due course. I do hope it goes some way to making up for your misfortune. And it will give me satisfaction," she added, "to know that Septimus, who caused so much distress to my poor daughter, as well as to you and your mother, has been prevented from ruining your lives entirely."

"Thank you, your Ladyship," I said, humbly.

"Thank you, your Ladyship," said Nick.

"I don't want thanks," she said. "If it enables you to do some good in your lives, that is as much as I wish for. Well, now. When do you sail?"

"Friday," I said.

"Take my blessings with you," she said. "We will never meet again, I am sure. I wish you the safest of voyages. Meerut will show you out."

The servant returned, and stood by the open door.

"Goodbye, my dears," she said. "Your being in Calcutta has made my last summer *most* memorable. I shall not forget you."

The first thing we did when we got home was find the family tree the Professor had drawn, and the version we'd brought with us from London.

"Here's John Winter," I said, running my finger up the line of Winters, from our mother's name. "And here's Sophia, her mother, next to him."

"So when it says, *Seek the point to the right*," said Nick, slowly, "that means whoever's at the other end of this little horizontal line leading from Sophia."

"Which is – Sir Lumley Sheets," I said. "Do you see? He *and* John Winter are both linked to her, one as a husband and the other as a lover."

"Yes. That makes sense. And look," said Nick, pointing at Damyata's design. "The line to Imogen comes down from the *other* axis. Not from the two points that stand for Sophia and John, but from Sophia and Sir Lumley."

"It's so obvious, now that we know," I said.

"So Lady Sheets is our sort-of grandmother," said Nick.

"Well," I said, "not quite. It's a bit complicated, but – she's our real grandfather's wife."

"And Sarasvati is our father's daughter," said Nick. "Do you think that can really be true?"

"I don't see why she would make it up," I said. "And it would explain why she was so upset when she heard about – what happened." I gazed at the family tree for a long time. After all the stories we'd heard, I felt as though I half knew some of these long-dead people: and, having spent time in the place where their lives unfolded, I felt as though we might walk outside and meet any of them, at any moment. "Can you believe this is *our* family?" I asked Nick. "It's too strange, isn't it, that all this happened to our ancestors? And yet we've been walking around in the same gardens as them, riding around the same city streets. At times I've had this weird sensation, as though I've slipped back twenty years, and I *am* my mother. It's like we've – invaded someone else's life."

"I suppose," said Nick, "hard though it is to believe, we were *meant* to be here, really. It's only by accident, or by a cruel turn of events, that we grew up in London and became the people we are."

As the day of our departure approached, Sarasvati became listless. She seemed to stop breaking into spontaneous cart-wheels on the lawn, or playing tricks on the servants. Even Mrs Chakraborty remarked on it, regretfully.

"That child, out-of-sorts is. Not any-more *naughty*, isn't it? Something wrong."

"It is not like him," Sarasvati said, as we whiled away our last long afternoon of monsoon rain under the shelter of the trees with her and Punch. "For a few days, I knew he would be silent. Too far away. Waiting. But then he should make contact. I wanted to reassure him that you are safe. But I cannot reach him."

"It's strange," Nick said, "having a father you can't be with. We feel it too. But you have said yourself, he can never really die. You know him in here." He touched her momentarily on her breastbone, where she had placed her own hand, after rescuing us from the dungeon.

"Come home with us," I said.

She stared. "To London? All that way on the sea?"

"You're part of our family," I said. "We have never met anyone closer to us in kinship than you are."

"There *is* no one," said Nick.

"You can live with us. Meet our friends."

"But I live here," she said, simply. "And what about my friends?"

"After all this," I said, "it seems too unbearable to leave you behind. Nick and I discovered we were brother and sister two years ago, and we have not been apart for one day since. How can we find out you are our sister, and then leave you here and sail halfway around the world?"

"You don't take an elephant to London," she said, fondling Punch's trunk, "or a tiger, or an eagle. They would not know how to live. They belong here, and I belong here."

I nodded.

"But we will not forget each other," she said. "Will we?"

Mystery was in his element, presiding over the bustle in the household on the morning we were due to leave. Wicker chests and containers of provisions and gifts had stood in the hallway for two days, gradually filling up. Jumjum and Bulbul were chivvied to bring our trunk down from the bedroom. All the servants were put through an inspection, in a military fashion, to make sure they were presentable; and they were all made to line up, to say farewell, one by one.

Dr Shastri came early, to see us off, and brought gifts of a gilt flask for Nick, a handcrafted leather collar for Lash, and some delicate, exquisitely-crafted gold jewellery for me.

"I can't accept this," I said, blushing again. I had never worn such things in my life. Dr Shastri was the first person who had ever so much as hinted that I ought to.

"I will write," he promised. "Keep you informed of Calcutta news. You will find you miss our gossip, so many thousands of miles away."

"Then I shall write back," I said to him. He took my hand. "This has been such an adventure," I said, turning the jewellery over and over in my hands. "I can't believe it's nearly over. Now that the time has come I – I'm not so sure I want to leave."

I looked up, and his deep, benign eyes were gazing down into my face. "Perhaps it is time for a period involving fewer adventures," he said, reassuringly. "If so much had happened to me in so few years, I should need a rest now."

There were more gifts from the household, including a little statue of the elephant-god, with a dark red stone, shaped like a teardrop, set in its forehead. "With Ganesh in your house you will never want for prosperity," explained Mystery. "Wery-wery lucky. Just the tickety!"

He ran outside, to shout loud and unnecessary instructions to the drivers.

"Professor, we'll never get all these things home," I laughed. "Tell them to stop."

"I'm afraid I've something else to give you," said the Professor, rather bashfully handing us a flattish, oval-shaped parcel wrapped up in brown paper. "I want you to have this."

"Are we allowed to open it?" I asked.

"Ah, quite! Please," he said.

I unfastened the string and slid the paper off.

It was the portrait of our mother, in the sun, with the two cheetahs.

"I thought it would be more appropriate in your house than mine," the Professor explained. "I, ah – had it taken down days ago, actually. With the intention of giving it to you, don't you know. Then it occurred to me you might have thought it rather, ah – odd, that it had disappeared."

"Thank you, Professor," I said. "We will treasure it."

Mystery returned, most officiously, from the forecourt. "Miss Mog, Master Nick," he said, "time to departing. Please checking one last time that you are not forgetting anything in your rooms, and then come down again. All ready to go. Embarking wery-wery soon."

We went up and checked the bedrooms, as he had asked us to. They looked sparse and sad, bereft of our things; the beds standing in the middle of the rooms, bare and white. I wondered how long it would be before anyone next slept in them, and who it would be.

"Where's Sarasvati?" asked Nick.

"I don't know," I said, "she wasn't with the others, was she? She'll be off somewhere, playing her games."

But, as we took our last look at the view from the veranda, of the white buildings, and the trees, and the masts of the ships on the river down which we'd be sailing so soon, we could hear her. She must have been sitting somewhere, on a wall, or in a tree; and she was signalling in her familiar way. There was something plaintive about the sound this time, I thought. The phrases seemed to end on a rising tone, as though they were asking a question.

"Dha-dang, dha-ta-ta-ta-tang, dhara-dang? Dhara-ka-ta-ta-tang, ta-tang, ta-ta-ta-tang?"

The voice stopped, as though she were listening, wishing, hoping. Nick and I stood listening to the silence. I felt sudden tears prickling in my eyes.

And then, from somewhere far away, on the wind, came the pattering sound of a drum, in reply.

Dhara-ka-ta-ta-taa, ta-taa, dha-jang, dha-jang-jang, dhara-dang. Dhara-ka-ta-ta-tang, ta-ta-tang, ta-tang.

Our carriage rolled out onto the long, tree-lined road towards the docks. We cast a last glance back at the Professor's house: and, scampering out of the gate after us, running to catch up with the tonga, was Sarasvati. Her wild black hair was flailing behind her like a mane, and she was laughing.

EPILOGUE

Charnock House
8th January, 1830

My dear Dr Shastri,

It is now almost a full year since we first heard mention of the Blue Eye of Winter, and when I think of the adventures we have had since that foggy day, it makes my head spin. Already it is months, not weeks, since we returned home, and it shames me that this is only the second time I have written. We seem so busy, the time has flown by. As you know, we had the news of poor Lady Sheets's death as soon as we returned to London, and we have seen such flocks of lawyers since then, I have lost count of them. Nick pays them more attention than I do, and our servant, Melibee, and my old employer, Mr Cramplock, have both been helping. But the consequence is, all of Sir Septimus's years of debts appear to have been honoured. Kniveacres has been sold, the creditors have been paid, and we are now living at Charnock House, which has been completely restored. What is more, it was all ready in time for Christmas, and we had a house full of guests. I cannot tell you how much fun it was.

We toasted Lady Sheets, principally, for I do not know what we would have done without her generosity. But we also thought of all the friends we are so happy and proud to have made in India, including yourself, and the Professor.

You must thank the Professor most sincerely once again, for sending the translation of the parchment book. How wonderful to hear that it turned out to be so ancient and valuable. I shudder to think how we treated it, carrying it back from the ruined palace of Sasanka, and what would have happened if it had been damaged by rain, or if I had dropped it in the river, or something. The spirit of Damyata must have been protecting it! It is astonishing to read his name mentioned in a book written so many centuries ago. I was becoming aware, the more time we spent in Calcutta, of how much his name was revered, and what sort of a legend had grown up around him. But I believed it had all happened since he fell in love with our mother, and then disappeared. I did not understand that Damyata has been a name associated with magic and strange events, that has brought excitement to all the good people and terror to the wicked, almost since time began.

And yet I know how real he was, and how much our mother loved him, and how much effort he has taken to ensure our well-being; and also what a thoroughly good person he was. I would not have understood any of this, completely, without coming to Calcutta.

Sarasvati told us that Damyata would always protect us. Now that I read what the book says about the children of Damyata,

I understand why she has so much faith. Do you know that we are supposed to be unlike any other people alive: blessed with wisdom and the ability to bestow happiness on others? It also says that we will enjoy endless good fortune, so long as we use our gifts well. For my own part, I am far from sure about the wisdom; but, since we returned to London and, most importantly, since we cast away the diamond, I cannot deny that good fortune has been ours. Damyata's memory is with us always, and his energy and presence seem to fill our house, and our heads.

Sarasvati is not short of wisdom, of course, and there can be no doubt that she makes everyone around her happy. We wished she could have come home with us, but both of us understand why people wish to remain in the place where they feel they belong, where they have grown up and where they know everyone. I must admit that I simply cannot picture her in London in this current winter weather. She belongs in the warm sun, with the sounds and trees and animals of India. I hope you will give her all our love.

Our house is now full of things we brought from Calcutta, which provide so many memories. Our mother's portrait has pride of place in the main drawing room. The elephant statue stands on a plinth at the top of the stairs. And the diary written by Justina Thynne, which you will remember I told you Lady Sheets gave us, is kept safely in the library. It tells the whole story of our mother's love affair, during that summer of 1814, and the ordeal she went through when it was discovered. It is a very strange sensation, reading about events that happened to our mother before we were born, recorded by her best friend. It is humbling to know that we were the consequence of it all.

You know that Justina Thynne went to great trouble to protect us, here in England, when we went to live with Sir Septimus. She lost her life trying to ensure our safety. We did not have time to get to know her well, but now I feel I know her so much better, after reading her words, and I like her more than ever. She was so angry at the injustice, for all those years, and she would have been so happy to see how things have come right in the end. Mr Cramplock has suggested that the contents might be published one day. I cannot see that anyone else would be interested enough to read them, but they are precious to us.

I think about everyone in Calcutta often, but I hope you will not misinterpret me if I confess I think about you especially often. Your last letter was so entertaining, I read it again and again almost until I knew it by heart! It is so exciting to read that your travels are to bring you to London. You will be most welcome to stay here with us now that we have a large place again, with many spare rooms. It is the least we can do to repay the kindness you showed us, especially your caring for Nick when he was bitten.

I could spill stories onto paper for much longer, but, as we are soon to see you in person, I will close, otherwise I will have no news to pass on when you arrive. I cannot wait to hear of all that has happened to our friends, and I hope we can extend hospitality even half as warm as that we received when we came to Calcutta.

I remain your humble and respectful friend,

Imogen Winter

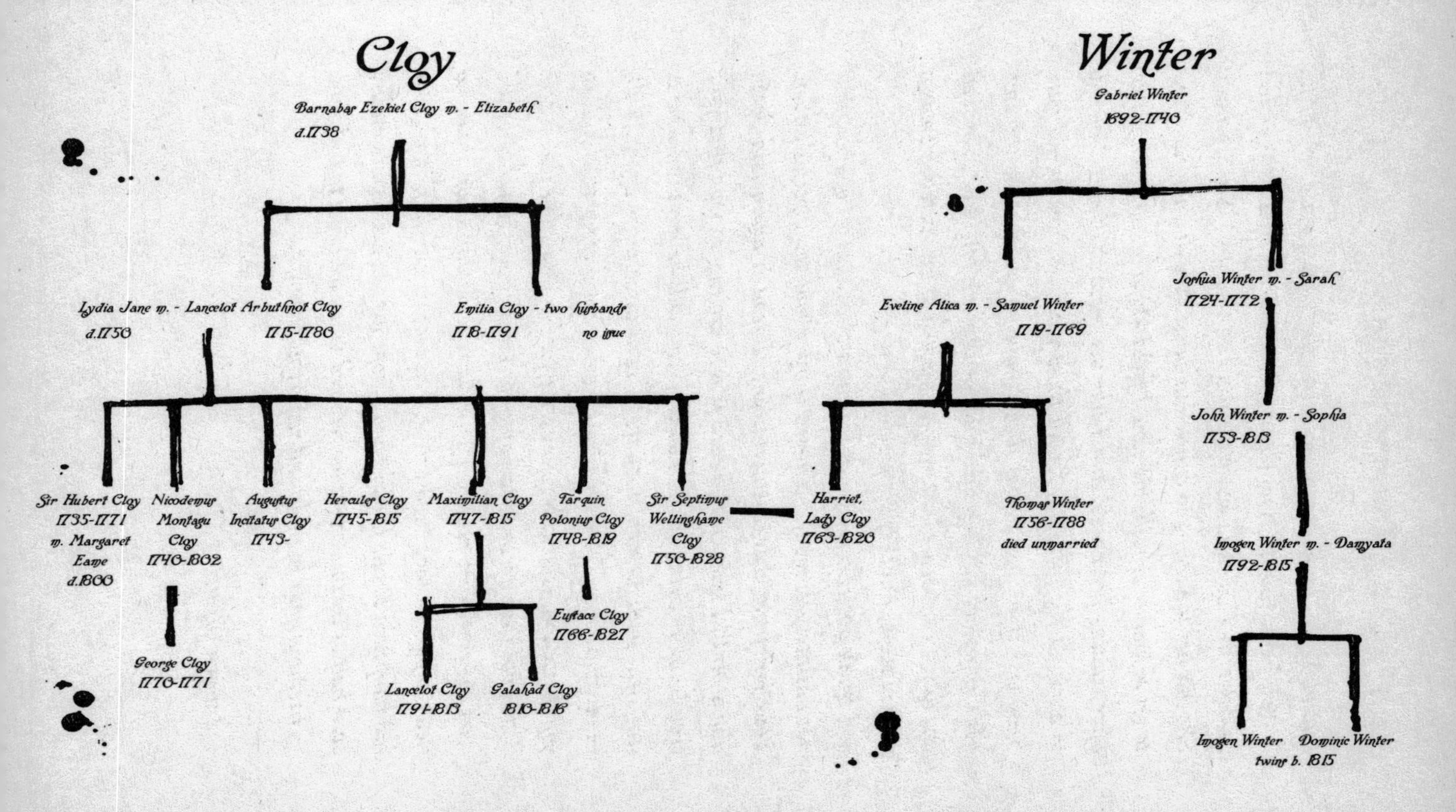
Cloy
Barnabas Ezekiel Cloy m. - Elizabeth
d.1738
Lydia Jane m. - Lancelot Arbuthnot Cloy
d.1750
1715-1780
Emilia Cloy - two husbands
1718-1791
no issue
Sir Hubert Cloy
1735-1771
m. Margaret
Eame
d.1800
Nicodemus
Montagu
Cloy
1740-1802
Augustus
Incitatus Cloy
1743-
Hercules Cloy
1745-1815
Maximilian Cloy
1747-1815
Tarquin
Polonius Cloy
1748-1819
Sir Septimus
Wellinghame
Cloy
1750-1828
George Cloy
1770-1771
Lancelot Cloy
1791-1813
Galahad Cloy
1810-1816
Eustace Cloy
1766-1827
Winter
Gabriel Winter
1692-1740
Eveline Alica m. - Samuel Winter
1719-1769
Joshua Winter m. - Sarah
1724-1772
John Winter m. - Sophia
1753-1813
Harriet,
Lady Cloy
1763-1820
Thomas Winter
1756-1788
died unmarried
Imogen Winter m. - Damyata
1792-1815
Imogen Winter
Dominic Winter
twins b. 1815

THE PRINTER'S DEVIL
Paul Bajoria

"this impressive debut is the story of Mog... a winning protagonist..." *The Sunday Times*, Children's Book of the Week

Convicts, murderers and the shady inhabitants of the London underworld are part of daily life for 12-year-old printer's devil, Mog Winter - after all, Mog prints their WANTED posters... But a face to face encounter with a real crook - a prison escapee - leads to Mog becoming enmeshed in an ingenious theft, a series of mistaken identities and a murder hunt... all connected to a recently docked ship from the Indian subcontinent, and Mog's own mysterious past.

ISBN: 9780689872860

THE GOD OF MISCHIEF
Paul Bajoria

"a richly written Gothic thriller... an atmospheric tale designed to send a shiver down young spines." *TES*

Sent to live with their nearest living relative, Sir Septimus Cloy, Mog and Nick find themselves spending a lot of time on their own, exploring. Two elderly manservants, Melibee and Bonefinger, guard Cloy and his house like malevolent ravens and, when strange things begin to happen - a falling gargoyle just missing them in the churchyard, a flagstone collapsing beneath their feet - the twins start having the same dream. Is Damyata at large again? Can the twins discover the truth behind the house and its family secrets, before their own lives become endangered?

ISBN: 9781416901136